Also by William Heffernan

Broderick

CAGING
THE RAVEN

A NOVEL BY
William Heffernan

Wyndham Books

NEW YORK

DEC 1 1981

Copyright © 1981 by William Heffernan
All rights reserved
including the right of reproduction
in whole or in part in any form
Published by Wyndham Books
A Simon & Schuster Division of Gulf & Western Corporation
Simon & Schuster Building
Rockefeller Center
1230 Avenue of the Americas
New York, New York 10020
WYNDHAM and colophon are trademarks of Simon & Schuster
Designed by Stanley S. Drate
Manufactured in the United States of America
1 2 3 4 5 6 7 8 9 10
Library of Congress Cataloging in Publication Data
Heffernan, William, date.
    Caging the raven.

    I. Title.
PS3558.E4143C3   813'.54   81-879
                                     AACR2
ISBN 0-671-61056-2

ACKNOWLEDGMENTS

Special thanks to Stewart Dickson and Haygood Redfern who provided their help and expertise during the weeks of research in the Florida Everglades; to Jack Agueros and the staff of El Museo del Barrio, New York, who offered insights and introductions to the Puerto Rican independence movement; to past and present members of both the FBI and FALN who, though requesting anonymity for different reasons, offered honest answers to honest questions; to the New York City Police Department Intelligence Division; and, again, to Gloria Loomis and Larry Freundlich, for their continued faith, support, and advice.

*This book is for Ildiko,
friend and lover,
a small token for
unselfish support.*

We will kill all the birds.
All. All, said the ravens in the dusk.

And in the silence of the night I heard
some in the garden killing my birds.
And I knew
that now there would be in my mornings
no songs,
and I felt
sadness lay hold on my spirit.

All. All the birds, they said.
And I felt
beating around me
dark wings
and glaring at me between them
a raven's yellow eye . . .

FROM "All the birds,"
Dane Zajc

Part One

1

Palm Beach, Florida   October, 1978

The water was green and flat close in to shore and it moved against the beach almost without sound, typical of the autumn ocean in Florida. One hundred yards out where the water became blue again a school of dolphins played ecstatic early morning games, jumping and screeching like young children, often coming within a few yards of the small fishing boats that already dotted the shoreline. Beyond the games, almost unnoticed, a lone gull fought the repeated assaults of the sea's greatest robber, struggling in its slow methodical way against the diving, circling, silent intimidations of the frigate bird's unquestionable superiority. From the high dunes that overlooked the private beach, Edmund Norris stared out at the spectacle, one hand shielding his eyes from the rising orange sun. He was dressed as usual in a suit and tie, not yielding to the casualness demanded by the surrounding palm trees, and there was a slight stoop to his shoulders that seemed to suggest a man who had earned his living carrying heavy, physical burdens. Standing there now his eyes appeared fixed on the dolphins, but actually stared beyond them, through them, taking no pleasure from their childlike games. Instead, he watched the black frigate bird turn, soar, then dive again, reasserting its claim as the fastest of seabirds, its long, split tail spread into a premature sign of victory.

From the wide, grassy area that rose up behind the dunes, a bulky, square-shaped man approached, then stopped several paces away. He, too, wore a suit and tie, but the suit was badly fitted and the bulge of the heavy 357 magnum he wore on his right hip could be seen through the fabric.

"Excuse me, Mr. President." The agent's voice was soft, intended

13

not to startle. "Everyone back at the house was a little concerned that you slipped away from us again."

Norris glanced over his shoulder, then back to the sea to the frigate bird. His face was set in the perennial frown that seemed, in recent years, to have become his normal expression, the line of his mouth dropping down, following the fall of his slightly sagging jowls, returning to the once familiar smile now only when cameras were present.

"Everyone has to slip away once in a while, Frank." Norris's voice was flat, almost toneless, sounding more resigned than annoyed.

The agent looked down at his inappropriate wing-tipped shoes. "I didn't mean to be critical, sir. It's just . . ."

Norris cut him off. "Yes, yes. I know, Frank. You all wet your pants if I take a walk without you."

The gull had moved closer to the shore and the frigate bird dove again, this time forcing its victim to drop the mullet it had fought to keep. Like a slender black streak the frigate bird continued down, catching the small fish before it struck the water, then leveling off, tossed it into the air again, recapturing it head first this time so it could be swallowed in the manner preferred. Norris nodded his approval, then turned and strode past the agent, almost as though he were marching, and started back toward the house. The agent moved quickly to his side, speaking a brief, whispered message into his walkie-talkie to let the others know Norris had been found.

"I'm sorry if I upset you, sir." The agent walked briskly, keeping abreast of Norris. "It's just that we're not supposed to lose sight of you. We're supposed to protect you."

"From what?" Norris snorted. "Nobody wants to do me any harm, Frank. Certainly not physically."

Norris marched on silently across the wide rear lawn that sloped down from the house to the dunes. The house was a sprawling single-story structure, more common to California than to Palm Beach, where elevated views of the ocean were considered desirable. But the recurring gout he suffered had made Norris choose a house without stairs, and the rise of the land on which it stood provided an adequate view of the ocean, if not the beach itself. He had found the house years before and had been able to use it as a vacation White House because of its isolation. It was located on the divided portion of North Ocean Boulevard in Palm Beach, a mile and a half north of the old landmark Paramount Theater, and the four acres on which it sat were surrounded by an eight-foot cement wall that extended down to the sea. Outside the wall a tight row of Spanish bayonets had been planted, their sharp, slender leaves rising three feet above the ground, making the wall inaccessible to intruders. Along the interior of the wall a thick hedge of sea grape eased the sense of isolation and added a note of beauty when its dark fruit ripened. But it offered protection too; it was the only vegetation that could grow dense and strong so close to the salt of the ocean.

The house itself was an unusual design, shaped like two "Ls" one sitting atop the other, the base of the lower "L" serving as a suite of offices, with large double French doors opening from the main office on to a private garden. Although the interior was square the office had reminded Norris of the presidential suite at the White House, and it had pleased him when he purchased it that he would leave the presidency and retire to a setting reminiscent of his days in power.

As Norris approached the house, three other agents watched discreetly, then turned away to avoid embarrassing the former president, assured now that no foul-up had occurred that would bring the wrath of government down on their heads. Norris entered the office through one set of French doors and walked directly to a waiting silver service that had been placed on a side table. He poured a cup of rich, French-roast coffee and stood there sipping it thoughtfully, making sure it had been brewed to his liking. The office was paneled in dark, polished wood, another contrast to the prevailing tastes of the area, but one he found quiet and comforting. He looked about it now, pleased with what he saw. It was dark, restful. He preferred working in dim light, keeping his mind from the distractions of objects about him and often, in the evening, he would work with only the desk lamp lighted, leaving the remainder of the room veiled in shadow. Slowly he walked to the center of the office, his black shoes sinking into the deep, sea-blue carpet and sipped at his coffee again. The coffee was in an oversized mug that bore the presidential seal, part of a set that had been given to him by a business friend almost two years after he left office. He looked at the mug and thought about that two-year period, a lapse of time his friend had no doubt considered a suitable period of mourning. He smiled weakly at the foolishness of the thought and recalled how he had often wanted to tell him so. But the friend had provided yet another service. The nature of his many businesses demanded a certain secrecy and various countermeasures against industrial espionage, and members of his friend's security staff now visited Norris's office at irregular weekly intervals to sweep the room and telephones electronically for listening devices. He had been certain from the beginning it was an unnecessary precaution; he doubted that those who now controlled the government would resort to blatant eavesdropping. The embarrassment of discovery would far outweigh any intelligence it might produce. But he had learned early in his political career that one must consider the highly improbable as possible, so the precaution had been taken. But Norris also knew that the Secret Service agents assigned to him inadvertently provided adequate intelligence data about him, information that was easily gleaned from their required weekly reports. Lists of visitors and their duration of stay, along with records of telephone contacts, when obtainable, guaranteed others a certain insight into his activities. He shook his head at the thought, at the annoying sense of helplessness it produced. Protection was always a double-edged sword for the person being protected, which was why the government expended so much effort monitoring the people who provided that protection. There could be no better informant, he knew, than a man sworn to safeguard the life of another.

Norris stepped back and rested his buttocks against the edge of his desk, taking the weight off his legs. His right foot had begun to give off a mild, dull pain, and he cautioned himself to elevate the leg for an hour or two to avoid serious discomfort later in the evening. The visage of old age, he told himself. "A sixty-six year old eunuch crying to himself about lost glory and worrying about his aches and pains," he said aloud.

He walked behind the desk and looked into the mirror that hung on the wall behind his leather swivel chair. The hair was still good and fairly dark for a man his age, he decided. It had begun receding in his early thirties, but had suddenly stopped, and the gray had come late avoiding the necessity of touch-ups that so many of his peers had relied upon, especially during the sixties when youth had become the most admired political asset.

"Aging pretty boys," he said to himself, turning his head slightly to reflect more profile.

He had never been greatly concerned about his attractiveness or his physical proficiency; there had never been a reason for it. No. He had always relied upon intelligence and guile. But his confidence in those assets had produced the same error that handsome or athletic men fall victim to, the arrogance of assured success that inevitably leads to failure.

It was a good thought, he decided, a reasonable explanation, and he slid into his chair and repeated it into his dictating machine, while propping up his foot on a hassock beneath the desk.

"Explanations," he said aloud. He leaned back in the chair and allowed his eyes to wander absentmindedly over the photographs and mementos that lined the walls and the tops of tables. At one time he had thought about removing them, of hiding them away, but had decided against it. After all, it was a near-history of his years in public service, detailing moments of triumph, times when his decisions had produced change and advantage, when legislation had altered the course of the nation, given it firmer root in its historical traditions, the very thing he hoped history would one day judge him by. All it lacked was a visual commentary on his *difficulties* and that was not needed. It was something he carried with him, something that never left his thoughts. *Explanations.* The word ran through his mind again. The American people were a gullible lot. They expected their leaders to be pure and forthright, a concept that people of other nations laughed at, found beyond belief. He smiled to himself, recalling now without pain the confusion his *problem* had produced among other world leaders, how difficult it had been for them to understand. They, like he, knew the realities; they understood, they accepted the fact that there had been few Boy Scouts in the Oval Office.

He formed a steeple with his fingers and held them in front of his eyes. But the others who served before him would have handled the problem far better than he had. And that was precisely where he had failed. Being too inept to handle it well. He folded his hands and placed them on the desk in front of him like a small boy on the first day of school. But there was still hope. His gray eyes dropped to the stack of photocopied statistics on his desk and the large file cards he had used to make notes from them. He picked up the cards. This would be part of it, a new approach dealing with his major strength. His writings since leaving office certainly had not produced the results he had hoped for. They had been viewed as self-serving, unfairly, he thought, but that was certainly moot now. He had written from seclusion and that had been a mistake. Now he was cautiously reestablishing himself in the public eye and, even more important, among former political allies. It was where he belonged, not playing the role of a recluse. And in time he could again be a force, enough so that his proper place in history would be assured, he was certain of that, perhaps even by the next presidential convention, if his plans materialized fully. But if not, certainly by 1984. He smiled at the thought.

"No doubt George Orwell would have something to say about that," he said aloud.

Norris shook his head. The habit of talking to himself had been increasing lately and it jarred against the feelings of self-confidence he had gradually begun to reimpose upon himself. He picked up his telephone and buzzed his secretary's office and was mildly surprised when it was answered by the agent on duty there.

"Has Mary arrived yet?" Norris asked.

"No, sir. It's only eight o'clock. She's expected at nine."

Norris was silent for a moment. "I'll be in the aviary if there are any calls. Advise her of that when she arrives." He replaced the receiver without waiting for a response, then walked to the side table and poured a second cup of coffee. He felt tense, uneasy; the feeling had been with him since he awakened and the walk along the dunes had failed to help. He knew it would intensify if he did not find some release.

He opened a side door and entered the bird room. The only illumination came from the solitary light attached to a mounted magnifying glass on the worktable. The light was shielded to concentrate the beam, and it spread a dim glow throughout the remainder of the room that seemed to darken the mahogany paneling and cast strangely ominous shadows on the color prints of birds that lined the walls. The anhinga wing he had been studying late into the previous evening was still pinned to the worktable, and the green-black iridescence of the lower surface feathers seemed to shimmer under the light, almost as though the detached wing continued to move with a life of its own. He approached the table and peered down into the glass. The upper portion of the wing was a mottled silver-gray throughout the major converts of the primary and secondary feathers and along the scapulars. He picked up a probe and gently separated a row of secondary feathers. Tonight he would dissect the wing and study the lack of preening glands that forced the creature to perch and spread its wings to dry in the sun after each foray into the water. Nodding to himself he replaced the probe and walked quickly across the room to a second door that opened directly into the aviary. Outside, the morning heat had already begun to settle in the large, wire-enclosed area, and the movement of the tropical plants that filled the twenty- by forty-foot enclosure told him that the wind was coming from the west, from deep within the Everglades, and if it remained so he knew it would soon be oppressively hot.

Quietly, carefully, he seated himself in one of four director's chairs scattered about a small patio area and propped his foot on a small, canvas-covered stool. The noise of the birds seemed to fill the enclosure, almost as though the wire walls and twenty-foot high, domed-shaped roof were made of a solid material. Directly in front of him, in the center of the aviary, a Louisiana heron assumed its camouflage position in a patch of high grass next to the shallow man-made pool. Startled by Norris's arrival, the heron stood motionless, its bill pointing straight up so its long, slender, blue-gray body seemed to blend into the grass. Nearby, a less timid snowy egret strutted along the edge of the pool on spindly black legs, seeking one of the fresh minnows the groundskeeper placed there each day, while a glossy ibis used its long, curved beak to preen its shimmering chestnut and green plumage like some matinee idol preparing to receive his public.

Easing back in his chair Norris's eyes roamed the aviary, locking on various species—orchard oriole, limpkin, oystercatcher, royal tern, chuckwills-widow—his mind instinctively, almost compulsively, clicking off the characteristics of each, noting size, weight, range, nesting habits, then continuing on, searching out his favorite, the raven he had named Lyndon, the scallywag of the aviary. Moving slowly, so as not to frighten the birds closest to him, he raised the back of one hand to his lips and sucked against the skin, the act known as pishing, which produced a high sucking sound that for some inexplicable reason aroused the curiosity of birds and drew them close. Almost immediately, Lyndon's deep, guttural croak sounded in response, a wooden, wonking noise coming from the upper branches of an aracaria tree that occupied the southeast corner of the aviary. Norris pished again and the four-foot span of purple-black wing leaped from the upper branches and glided gracefully to the ground only four feet from where he sat.

As it touched the ground the raven began strutting about, moving in quick, jerky motions, its eyes darting with the mysterious sense of intelligence that had caused the species to be held in awe for centuries. Like most ravens in captivity, Norris had noted, Lyndon exhibited a sense of gravity that bordered on the preternatural, an attitude that was delicately mixed with an almost cavalier spirit of mischief, and the greater his misdeeds within the aviary, the greater his sense of absolute innocence.

Norris watched the strutting bird and smiled to himself as his mind compulsively clicked into gear. *Corvus corax. The largest of the crows; the most intelligent of birds. Twenty-five inches in length. Ranging from Alaska and Greenland through wilderness areas south to Nicaragua. The first bird mentioned in the Bible. Forbidden as food to the Israelites; considered a bird of augury by the Romans but later, throughout Europe, held responsible for plague, pestilence and famine, accused of shaking contagion from its sable wing. Shot and poisoned by shepherds. The most persecuted of birds.* Norris's jaw tightened as he held the thought, watching the magnificent black bird continue to strut about the small patio. He had watched ravens often in the wild, almost from the beginning, three years now, since ornithology had become his avocation, his remedy for personal pain, watching them as they raided colonies of seabirds, consuming the eggs and the young, then later soaring on rising currents of air, offering spectacular displays of aerial acrobatics, assured that God himself had forgiven them.

"What have you been up to today, Lyndon?" Norris spoke in a practiced whisper, a gentle, soothing sound that was little more than a gust of air. "You appear particularly innocent and that can only mean one thing."

The raven continued to move about the patio, its head jerking quickly, its eyes looking everywhere but toward the sound of Norris's voice. A few feet away the marsh birds stood motionless in the pool, listening to the jarring whisper, closely watching the prancing black menace with a caution gained from both instinct and experience.

The four-foot black wings moved violently, lifting the raven up and away, back toward the towering aracaria; the marsh birds scattered in fear toward the tall grass. Norris's head snapped around, his eyes fixed angrily on the intercom on the wall of the house. It buzzed again. He stood and moved quickly to the source of the disturbance. The mild, dull pain he had noticed earlier in his right foot was gone now; even the short rest had helped. He pressed the speaker button. His voice was crisp, annoyed.

His secretary's voice was equally crisp, businesslike, as she knew he preferred.

"There's a telephone call for you, Mr. President. General Hall."

Norris looked at his watch. Nine-ten. More than an hour had passed in what seemed like ten minutes, surely no more than twenty.

"Is he calling on the private line?"

"Yes, sir. As usual."

"I'll take the call in the bird room. Please see that I'm not interrupted."

The telephone was on a small table placed at the right arm of an oversized leather chair. Norris eased himself into the well-worn leather and propped his foot on a round sofa table, the toe of his shoe almost brushing the pale gray breast of a mounted peregrine falcon. The lone light of the worktable flashed against the bird's lifeless glass eye, making it seem as though the predator was watching, waiting, perhaps for some command to move. Norris picked up the receiver.

"Hello, Alec. I've been expecting your call. How is everything at the Pentagon?"

"The same nonsense. If the administration continues on this way...," he paused, then continued. "Well you know what the situation is, there's no point in repeating it. We're being chopped all to hell. All those geniuses can think about now is this Begin-Sadat thing, and keeping the Jews in New York happy."

Norris waited, letting his silence play into the telephone, play against the frustrations of his former senior aide.

"I've been thinking about our previous conversation," Hall continued. "Do you consider this telephone safe, Ed?"

"It was purged yesterday."

"Purged? Was there something wrong?" There was a note of concern almost approaching fear in Hall's voice. So typical of the military, Norris thought.

"No. Nothing at all. I just prefer the word." Norris smiled to himself.

"Well, I'm prepared to make the move you suggest ..." He paused again. "Right after Thanksgiving would be best for me, I think. I have several speeches scheduled out in the hinterlands this month and next, which should give me the opportunity to shake up the hicks and lay an adequate foundation, in addition to what I've done already." He paused again as if trying to decide how to continue. "Look, Ed, there is one thing. I still question using Soviet military expansion and its threat to our oil supplies as the cornerstone. I wonder if the voting public isn't too in love with détente to accept that kind of cause-and-effect reasoning, especially from a member of the military who is openly laying a foundation to seek the presidency. I know they're not all that bright, but I'm worried that they're still wary of the man on horseback."

Norris laughed softly into the telephone. "You're suffering from prepresidential jitters, Alec." His voice was soft and steady, similar, only louder, to the tone he had used with the raven. "Our first job, Alec, is to raise the proper premise, create a believable concern, if you will. Then once a majority of small town rednecks have accepted that concern as viable they will begin to move in precisely the direction selected for them. In short, they'll become our base of support and they'll respond favorably to the person who made them aware of the problem. Then others will follow. And they won't even consider what that person is. They'll be convinced it's just another case of the government hiding the truth from them."

"I wonder, Ed. I really wonder."

Norris waited, almost as though he were timing his words.

"Alec, have you ever studied the feeding habits of the brown pelican?"

Hall chuckled into the telephone. "Is this to be another of your ornithological lessons, Ed?"

Norris stiffened. "It is. If I had my way the subject would be required reading in every law school, political science department and military academy in the country. Do you want to hear the analogy, Alec?" Norris's voice had taken on a hard edge.

"Of course, Ed. Of course."

Norris nodded to himself, "Normally, Alec, the brown pelican feeds by diving down on his prey. But there are times when the pelican finds that the school of fish he is after are too deep to reach by diving. At those times he hovers over the water and beats his wings furiously. Those fearful sounds, you see, are magnified by the water and they throw the school into a panic and drive them toward the shore—toward the shallow water, Alec—to where they can be plucked up at will." Norris hesitated, savoring his own analogy. "Think back to your history, Alec. What I'm proposing worked for

Eisenhower in '52 and again for Kennedy in '60. It's merely a variation of a theme that has proven successful throughout American political history, whether it was played for the hicks in Iowa or the pseudointellectual Jewboys in New York. We ... excuse me, Alec. *You* will not be taking anything away from the people, or even appearing as if you are. You will be exposing a problem they were unaware of and offering a solution. You will not be denouncing détente, or anything else that appeals to the public. Détente, of course, will continue as they believe it should. What you'll be doing is pointing out the administration's failure to *challenge*—and that's a key word here—challenge the Soviet activities in the Third World."

Norris paused to let his words sink in. He knew that Hall, like most military men, thought slowly, evaluating each idea as though it involved the complex advancement of many troops.

"Consider the points in our favor," Norris continued. "We have the Soviet dominance in Afghanistan since the coup last April, their expanding influence in the Middle East, and their air and naval bases along the east coast of Africa, all of which give them the potential of choking off the oil lifeline leading from the Persian Gulf to the West, a situation this administration has *allowed*—again a key word—allowed the Soviets to develop. Now we add to that the escalating problems in Iran. The voting public is already frightened by the growing oil situation, and justifiably so. And the Jews are afraid we're going to abandon Israel over it. Now everybody is suddenly confronted with the fact that the problem is even more complex than they assumed. It's not just our inability to deal with the Arabs. It is suddenly a twofold problem involving both the Arabs and a new threat, the Russians. And all of it, they find, is linked to the administration's weakness and ineptitude. In short, we combine foreign and domestic fears and channel them right back into the teeth of the White House."

"I agree fully with the premise," Hall said. "I suppose my real concern is whether or not a soon-to-be retired Army general is the person to execute it."

"You're referring, of course, to the lingering sentiments toward the military."

"Precisely. And I'm sure the administration won't waste any time alluding to my background, when I finally resign and announce for the presidency."

Norris laughed softly again. "But we're going to make your military background an ambiguous asset. First of all, Alec, the voters know—and will be told again—that you previously worked in the White House in an administrative, not a military, capacity, and as such worked toward a solution of the Vietnam question, among others. This places you in more of a maverick's role for the antimilitarists, and it's a role we can build on. Secondly, we are talking about a problem that cries out for military expertise to achieve a satisfactory resolution. You have it. And finally, we will not be taking a hard line position or even hinting at an abandonment of détente. We'll be supporting it. But we'll be insisting that we cannot continue the present irresponsible course and ignore blatant Soviet activities in the Middle East, especially when it threatens our survival by endangering our energy supply."

Hall grunted agreement into the telephone, forcing Norris to smile again to himself.

"And remember we are also speaking of a double threat. The threat to our oil supplies and also the possibility that other Western nations now allied with us could be forced closer to Moscow if *their* energy resources were threatened. And that could leave us isolated and increase the danger of war. It's an approach that appeals to all the major fears of our time and the broadest number of people, right-wing hicks in the country, Jews in the city, WASP bankers, everybody. And it will be a very difficult one for the administration to ignore, or even treat lightly, especially since it will be coming at the beginning of winter when the fear of adequate oil supplies will be on everyone's mind. So basically, Alec, you'll have our friend, President William Lee Jordan, by the short hairs."

Hall laughed loudly. "There's nothing I'd like more, Ed. I'd love to make that sanctimonious little bastard squirm."

Norris slapped his left hand against the arm of the chair. "You will, Alec. You will. Just don't overrate the gullibility of the voting public. They want simple answers. In the meantime I've taken the liberty of calling in some debts at CIA, and I'm presently putting together some updated figures on the Soviet military-industrial complex and its aid picture among the various Third World nations. I know the same figures are available at the Pentagon, but I thought it might cause undue comment if you tried to ferret them out yourself."

"Should we plan to meet then?"

"I don't think so—I think we'd better keep things going by telephone."

"You're the boss, Ed."

"Then we'll talk again soon, Alec."

"Righto."

Norris slid the receiver back into its cradle. Hall's final words ran over and over in his head. No, not quite yet, he thought. But you can be led. Just like all the other bastards I've always had to lead to get what I wanted. And somehow they never even realize they're being led. He snorted to himself. And all of them think they can be president. He leaned his head back against the chair. His face had grown solemn again, but he knew now that things were finally moving in the direction he had hoped for. He looked across at the lifeless glaring eyes of the falcon. Again, in the dim, muted light from the worktable, it seemed as though the bird was preparing to move.

2

Washington, D.C.   October 1978

John Walter Henry seemed relaxed, completely at ease, as he sat at a small corner table in the expansive dining room, his back toward the rich, wood-paneled wall. He sat rigidly upright in his chair and it gave him an almost military bearing; it emphasized his long, slender body and sharp Anglo-Saxon features and all of it combined to make him seem younger than he was. Even his well-tailored suit marked him as someone who belonged amid the elegance of the high ceilings and tapestry-covered walls. Since his return to Washington six months ago the dining room at the Hay-Adams House had become a lunchtime sanctuary. It allowed him to feel he was still part of the government, still a ranking member of the FBI, even though he knew it was now little more than a mental game he played with himself. The captain and waiters still treated him with a certain deference, but not as much as they had at first, he thought. Perhaps they, too, had noticed how other members of the Bureau had begun to avoid the restaurant once he had become a regular fixture. Washington was, after all, a place of few secrets, especially those that involved an individual loss of power. He was still an assistant director of the Bureau, but one without authority or responsibilities and even the waiters would be aware of that by now. Just the former head of the New York office who had directed black-bag burglaries against terrorists and who had been recalled to Washington and hidden away in a small isolated office to sit and wait for some action to be taken against him.

The waiter served his third martini, and as he sipped it he could feel a dull warmth begin to move through his body. He looked about the room and noticed, without any real concern, that he was the only

26

person seated alone. Some distance away two members of Congress, whom he knew only by reputation, spoke quietly to each other, but only through habit, he thought. The Hay-Adams was not a place where serious government business was discussed. It was more like an elegant club that produced a sense of self-importance to buoy the egos of government officials. Two tables to his right, three State Department aides with whom he had dealt in the past enjoyed some private joke. They had ignored him when they entered, and it had amused more than offended him. He was an embarrassment to them now, to everyone who knew him, because he refused to go away, to simply accept his generous pension and remove the problem.

Twenty-nine years and it came down to that. No wife, no family, just the job—the only one he had ever had since graduating from law school. And now at fifty-three the job was divorcing him. But at least it would be a contested divorce. He smiled at the idea and sipped at his drink again. If he had been a different kind of man, he could have remained there all afternoon dulling his brain with gin. His absence back at FBI headquarters would be noted but he would surely not be missed. And if he did that long enough, it would provide the opportunity for a forced medical retirement. He smiled to himself again. But if he had been that kind of man, he would have already given them what they wanted.

He looked across the restaurant, then squinted his eyes to assure himself he was not seeing things. Grant Desverne moved quickly toward his table, still demonstrating the jaunty stride that had marked him as a fresh young kid when he had joined the Bureau twenty years ago. As he came closer now, Henry could see that the same familiar boyish grin was spread across his face.

"Mind if I join you, chief?" Desverne dropped into the chair without waiting for a reply.

"You sure you want to? I'm supposed to be wearing a quarantine sign."

Desverne's grin widened. "I've already got the disease. We caught it together, remember?" He was much shorter than Henry and slightly overweight and what was left of his brown hair was going fast.

Henry grabbed his hand. It was the first display of warmth he had received or given in weeks, and he could feel the eyes of others nearby as they watched the display of affection, wondering no doubt who the fool was who had made the impolitic gesture.

"What the hell are you doing in Washington?" Henry asked. His eyes narrowed quickly. "Any problems?"

"Apparently not. It was the first thing I thought, too, when I got the orders, but it seems to be nothing more than one of our bullshit restraining deals. They're shipping me to Quantico tomorrow for ten days. I guess I'm being rehabilitated. The word around now is that only the bosses are going to take the weight. Apparently it's been decided the front-line troops were just following orders. Sounds like Nuremburg, doesn't it?" Desverne smiled again, but weakly this time.

It had been ten months now since Henry had seen him. They had gotten drunk together when Desverne's orders had come, banishing him to the Omaha office, and they had drunkenly joked about the burglaries he would soon have to commit there once Cesar Chavez began organizing farm workers in the midwest.

"I hear things are pretty bad for you, Pat."

Henry had not heard his nickname used in months. It had been given to him by Hoover early in his career as an affectionate comment about his overriding sense of duty.

"It's not that bad. The pricks who are running the show now are just trying to make believe I don't exist, hoping I'll take the hint and disappear. There was some verbal support at first, but that didn't last long."

Desverne shook his head. "Can a guy get a drink around here?" he said, turning and motioning to the waiter. Henry still looked good, still in control, he thought. Still slender and fit, more like a well-conditioned forty-year-old. "I see you're still dyeing your hair," he added, trying to lighten the conversation. "Where are you living?"

"I took an apartment in Georgetown. A short-term lease."

"You think it's that bad?" Desverne's eyes had become softer, more honest.

"It's just a question of time, Dez. They're just trying to figure out a way of doing it without admitting to anything. It's not for my sake. I'll have thirty years in next January and after that they'll use the pension to force it if I don't do the right thing."

"Right thing, shit," Desverne grunted. "We did the right thing all along, exactly what they wanted and what had to be done to keep the fucking country from blowing up in their faces. The old man must be spinning in his grave right now."

"Don't even talk about it that way. Not to anyone. You can already count on finishing out your career in Omaha. It could be worse. There's always Boise, you know." They grinned at each other, like errant school boys for a moment. "How'd you find me?" Henry asked.

"Your assistant. And a very beautiful one I might add. She almost fell off her chair when I asked."

"She doesn't get too many requests to see me. All I do now is make up personnel charts that get forwarded to wastepaper baskets in other offices. She hasn't answered the phone in three days and that last call was from my lawyer."

They laughed, insincerely, Desverne thought. "You sound like you're going to pack it in. Give the fucks what they want." There was a sound of resignation in Desverne's voice, but his eyes seemed hard, almost defiant.

"Not right away. I'll play the string out. But the end result is pretty inevitable unless I get lucky." He smiled across the table. Dez's concern made him feel warm, pleased with the friendship. "You know, it's hard to let go of the only thing you've ever done. And I'll be damned if I'll ever admit that they were right and we were wrong. How about you? You'll hang on in Omaha?"

"I guess. Shit, Pat. I don't know what else to do. Nobody's hiring retired burglars these days." He laughed, shaking his head at the sad truth of his humor. "I suppose I'll put in as many more years as I can take and hope things quiet down enough so I can tie in with some security outfit. With the kids and all, I sure as hell couldn't live on my pension right now. Maybe I'll write a book about it all. Confessions of a cat burglar or something like that."

Henry smiled at the thought. "I wish it was that simple, Dez. But that would only hurt the Bureau. And it's not the Bureau, it's the people who are running it now. The organization has just gone off the track ever since Norris got his ass in a sling. But it'll turn around in time. Not soon enough for us, but sooner or later, when the country stops going crazy with this self-destructive kick it's on. Then they'll be saying how we were right and how the crazies almost destroyed the country."

Desverne looked at him across the rim of his glass. He was still a true believer, he thought. He would always be one, would always have the same fierce loyalty that had driven him up the FBI's bureaucratic ladder. He found himself wondering what kind of life

Henry must have now. Like Hoover he had always lived for the job and now it didn't exist any longer, not in any real sense. At least *he* had a wife and kids back in Omaha, something to fall back on, to retreat to. Henry had nothing. His wife had been killed in an automobile accident five years after he joined the Bureau and since then only the job had mattered. Desverne looked at him more closely, now. Henry did look older, he just hadn't seen it at first. But the jaw was still square and firm, the hair trimmed short, the back straight against the chair. Even the suit was well tailored and neatly pressed. The picture of what a senior government agent was supposed to look like, what he himself had never quite been able to manage.

"I wish there was something I could do, Pat." Desverne polished off his Scotch and turned to catch the waiter's eye.

"You already have, Dez. Just by coming here. Listen, if you have nothing to do tonight, I found this little Italian place not far from my apartment. I'd like to buy you dinner. You still like Dago food as much as you used to, I suppose."

"There's nothing I'd like better. But only if you let me buy the wine."

Henry winked at him. "You're on," he said. "We can sit around and tell each other how good we were and how we all got screwed because Norris made mistakes." There was a sudden sense of strength now and he realized it was the first time he had felt anything even close to that in months. It was like the old days in New York, when everything seemed to have a purpose that drew men together. Back when things worked for him.

~~~~~

It was past midnight when he settled back in the worn easy chair that had come with the apartment and stared without listening at the inaneness of a late-night talk show. But he felt pleased with himself. The liquor and the Italian food had done their work and he felt pleasantly dulled as he sat there reminiscing about the first pleasant evening he had spent since his return to Washington. It had taken a great deal of courage on Dez's part to make more than a courtesy visit to his office, and it was something he would not forget. Others who had worked for him in New York had found excuses to avoid him completely, and he had learned early on not to extend social invitations that would be discreetly refused. But he couldn't blame them, and it was coming to an end anyway. He had played it out as far as he could, out of a sense of loyalty to both himself and the Bureau, and now the point of the fight, on both grounds, had become moot. But God. The idea of it all really grated. Deep down he was concerned about the Bureau itself, and with good reason, he thought. This whole idea that the government lacked the right to protect itself was maddening, more than maddening. It was insane. He could handle the problem of being a scapegoat, although that bothered him as well. But it would have been easier if he at least knew that everything he had devoted himself to for the past thirty years was not going down the tubes as well. Sure, Norris and Hoover had had their faults. But the Bureau and the government had come first, and anyone who had tried to harm either had been devoured. People who felt that way, as he did, he could truly care about. The bastards who were there now were survivors, and if their survival required the castration of the Bureau, and the government along with it, they were only too willing to let that happen.

He reached out and turned off the television set, then stood and walked to the window. Below him lay the river, and along the path that ran beside it a young man and woman strolled arm in arm. Students, he thought. And probably in full agreement with the course that was now being followed by their government. He watched them until they disappeared under a row of trees that obscured the path. He remained at the window watching, even after they were gone, then smiled to himself. They might even be right, he thought. At this point it really made little difference. He turned and walked to the kitchen and poured some malt Scotch into a glass, then leaned against the counter and thought about his wife. They, too, had often walked that way and talked of how they thought the world should be. It was strange even thinking of her. Mary. Mary who had been gone for so long now. All his thoughts centered around the worn photograph that was still in his wallet, the last one he had of her. She too would be fifty-three now, but in that photograph, taken only months before she died, she was thirty and he could only think of her that way.

He walked into the bathroom and stripped off his shirt and slacks, uncharacteristically letting them fall in a heap on the floor. He turned on the shower and adjusted the water until it was as hot as he thought he could stand it. In the full-length mirror attached to the back of the door, he looked over his body. It was still firm and reasonably muscular. The years of careful exercise had kept him at a trim one hundred and seventy pounds and according to his doctor his health could not be better. So what the hell do you do for the next twenty years? he wondered. You pack it in this December and get out by mid-January. But what do you *do* after that? Practice law? Christ that would really be a joke after all these years. Join some absurd security firm as so many other agents had? Wonderful.

He climbed into the shower and let the hot water beat against the back of his head. He had always thought he would work until the mandatory age and then simply go fishing, sit on some beach somewhere and occasionally show up at retired agents' luncheons and swap lies with the other old farts. At least there would be some dignity in it, some respect, deserved or not. The way it was now there was nothing. They had left him nothing but surrender, and they had done it in such a way that the idea seemed almost appealing. Just to get away from the humiliation. But when it's all over, what the hell do you do then? He did not know the answer and the fact of it frightened him more than anything else.

3

New York City   November 1978

Carlos Rivera sat at a battered wooden desk in the makeshift office that occupied one corner of the large open kitchen. His legs were wrapped awkwardly around his chair and as he sat there, hunched over his notebook, it made him seem smaller then he was, almost like a teenaged boy struggling with his homework.

From a distant sleeping area the staccato voice of Jose Feliciano erupted from the stereo; it told him that his second in command, Juan Hernandez, was now stumbling about, trying to recover from a late evening in the Spanish bars of the East Village. He wished, now more than ever, that he could influence Juan's taste in music, perhaps one day even convert him to the recordings of pianist Jesus Maria Sanroma. He shook his head. It would be easier to convince him to become celibate.

"Heah, Juan. Turn down the music, man," he shouted, trying to overcome the din.

The volume intensified for several seconds in defiance of the request, then was lowered so it was only slightly softer than before. He drew a deep breath and smiled at Juan's display of machismo, then closed the notebook and leaned back in his chair, waiting.

He had blond hair and blue eyes and to the average person he did not look Puerto Rican and it was something that had often worked in his favor. The pure Spanish blood, not uncommon to the island of his birth, was something other Puerto Ricans recognized, a part of the broad racial differences among their people, but it was one few Anglos understood and it allowed him to move about as two separate men. To those who knew him in New York's *barrio* he was Carlos Rivera, the well-spoken young nationalist who talked endless-

33

ly of the need for independence; to the Anglos he dealt with he was simply Carl Rivers, a bright, twenty-eight-year-old free-lance photographer, who lived in a Soho studio with an assortment of friends and whose work had appeared in such prestigious publications as *National Geographic*. Few among either group would have guessed that the man they knew was also the terrorist leader that the tabloids referred to as El Tiburón, the Shark, the man whose name appeared on the communiques of *Ejército Mundo de Revolución*, the World Army of Revolution, which had been involved in more than a dozen bombings and which the newspapers had so typically nicknamed WAR.

Sitting there now he ran a hand through his moderately long hair and thought about the complexities his various identities presented. At the moment he was El Tiburón, working in the office he and his fellow revolutionaries referred to as *Comando Central*. It was nine o'clock and already he had spent two hours writing in the heavy, three-ring notebook that contained both the philosophy and history of WAR's fight against imperialism, a book, he believed, that would one day be read by Puerto Rican children in the same way that Yankee children studied Thomas Paine. But the writing had not gone well this morning, and as he looked about the loft he shook his head at the contradictions that surrounded him. Beyond the office lay the trappings of a photographer's studio with a few added items. There, behind a screen, was WAR's mimeograph machine and covered boxes of weapons and explosives that could rival the arsenal of any small police department. Certainly unlike the studio of the revered James Vander Zee, he thought. But Vander Zee was from another era of struggle, from a different age of oppression. He reopened the notebook and looked down at the partially filled page. He could not argue against the premise written there. It was time for WAR to change, to begin to take more dramatic action, but his ability to explain the need for that change had failed him this morning, and if he could not explain it to himself, how could be possibly hope to make the others understand, no matter how deep their commitment.

On the desk next to the notebook there was a volume of poems by Clemente Soto Valdez, the poet warrior who had led Puerto Rico's underground army in the 1930s. The previous evening he had read several of the poems he knew so well, and it had struck him for the first time in his life that he might no longer be part of it, a part of the mood of his native soil. He might have gone beyond it, or simply lost it in the way people do who reach beyond that for which they have been fighting. The thought, the fear of it, had still been with him when he awoke that morning, but he had rejected it, even though he knew it might be true.

The thought evaporated as Juan stumbled into the work area and moved unsteadily toward the open kitchen where a freshly brewed pot of rich Cafe Bustelo sat on the battered old stove. He watched him with a little sympathy, noting that his normally hard brown eyes were glazed with pain. He was barefoot and naked to the waist and the jeans he wore looked as though he had collapsed in them the night before.

Juan poured coffee and moved awkwardly to a stool at the makeshift breakfast bar and sat heavily, cupping one hand over his eyes.

"I don't know how you can stand that music with a hangover," Carlos said.

"Heah man, I'm just tryin' to make sure I'm alive." Juan's voice was hoarse and weak and the cup seemed to tremble in his hand as he sipped at the coffee.

"Another good night?" Carlos was grinning at him now.

"Beautiful, man. Beautiful. You shoulda been there. There was pussy everyplace." He rubbed his fingers in his curly black hair, then raised both arms into the air and stretched. The movement seemed to bring some life back into his body and he looked across at Carlos for the first time. "How long you been up, man?"

"Since seven. I'm trying to work out some of the things we talked about the other day. I could use your help."

Juan pulled his shoulders back and dug a knuckle into the corner of his eye, twisting it as though he were trying to screw it into the socket. "Right now?" he said.

"If you're up to it." He stared at Juan for a long moment, before deciding to go on. "I'm going to leave for Florida tomorrow to see Wally Rogers, to see if what we talked about can really be done."

"Shit. I've been thinking about it, man. You really think he's the right person to grab? I mean he got his ass dumped. You think anybody's gonna give a shit if we take *him*? He was just a sweaty lying little faggot, man."

Carlos watched him, studying the doubt in his friend's face. He was questioning the only part of the plan he was truly sure of, the only facet he was certain would work. If Edmund Norris could be kidnapped and held for ransom, it would throw the government into confusion, produce a period of inaction that would be needed to give the plan a reasonable chance of success. And it was the very controversial nature of the man, he believed, that might force the government to give in to the demands.

"He's the only one," he said. "I think they'd sacrifice anyone else, make a martyr out of them. But they wouldn't want that hypocritical bastard to become a martyr, and they wouldn't want it said that they let him die because of what he was. Besides, he's an ex-president and the man in the White House now knows that he's going to be an ex-president someday too. I don't think he'll establish that kind of precedent."

"And you think they'll really give us something?"

"If we don't box them in. If we make the demands reasonable enough. Make sure we ask for things they can do. Remember we'll *have* him and the world will be watching them . . ." A feeling of uneasiness spread through him. "And they'll be watching us, too," he added.

"Yeah, sure. But what if they just send in the fucking Marines? Look what the cops in Philadelphia did to that MOVE outfit last August."

Carlos stared into Juan's face. "You afraid of not living to be an old man?"

He watched the glaze leave Juan's eyes, the sudden harshness set in as a touch of red appeared in his sallow complexion. It had been an unfair remark, unwarranted, unnecessary. He was playing off his friend's machismo; that sense of masculine pride so important to his race. He went on quickly.

"They have to find us first and that's one of the things I've got to make sure of in Florida. That they can't find us."

"And if they do?" Juan shaped his fingers into a gun and made a popping sound with his mouth. "They blow us up like the Fourth of July. I think we should just off that pussy, man. We don't know shit about kidnapping. Our training hasn't been in that area. All those years in Cuba and Chile and Nicaragua they taught us how to fight like the guerrillas we're supposed to be. And it's got nothin' to do with dyin', man."

Juan would not let go of the insult, could not. He motioned with his head at the quotation taped to the wall behind the desk, the words of one of the century's greatest revolutionaries, General Augusto Sandino, the man who drove the U.S. Marines out of Nicaragua in 1933.

"I live by those words too, Carlos," Juan said. He snapped the words out like a challenge.

Carlos spun around in his chair and read the words aloud. "Everyone dies sooner or later. All that is important is how one dies." He turned back to Juan and grinned at him. "I know you do, man. I'm just helping you remember."

"I don't need any help." Juan's words were still crisp, but he had turned his attention back to his coffee and his eyes had softened.

Carlos stood and walked toward him, moving on the balls of his feet with the ease of a dancer or finely conditioned athlete. He was wearing jeans and a western-styled denim shirt that fit close to his body, accenting its lean hardness. He had smooth, clean features and his blue eyes had a dramatic quality that could make him appear fierce or gentle, unlike Juan, whose dark brooding features always made him seem on the verge of rage.

He stood next to Juan and placed a hand on his shoulder. They had gone through much together and for years they had lived like brothers. "I wasn't fooling before," he said, keeping his voice soft. "I really do need your help. The others have to be convinced. They have to understand that this is why we broke with FALN, because the bombings and the communiqués aren't enough anymore. Christ, Juan, look back on it all. We've been pissing in the wind for the past five years and nothing has changed. Those fools in FALN will continue to do it, but we have a chance to turn it all around. And we can take the leadership away from them in the eyes of our people. But we are going to need the others to make it work."

Juan looked up at him and grinned. "They'll do whatever we say. If Richie objects, we'll just tell him he's acting like an Anglo pussy and he'll shit his pants. As far as the ladies go, man, you just smile at them with your prettyboy face and I'll show them my big prick and they'll go anywhere we want."

Carlos walked back to his desk, laughing. He was amused, not only by the display of machismo but at the total accuracy of Juan's crude assessment of the others. Richard McGovern would indeed react to any reference to his Anglo blood. He had left the Weathermen and come to FALN and then to WAR for the simple reason that he regretted having been born white. It was the one thing he would change if he could, the thing that made him feel he would never truly be an equal in the revolution. And the women, that, too, was accurate. Richard's wife, Carol, and Norma Epstein could be manipulated sexually, although it was something he tried to avoid. Sex had become their declaration of freedom and they used it to emphasize that freedom and could therefore be used themselves through it. He sat in the chair and looked across the room at Juan's still-grinning face.

"I'll let you handle the ladies," he said, knowing it would please him. "I thought we'd have a meeting tonight and discuss the idea, not as an absolute, but as something we'd like them to think about while I'm away."

"How long you going to be gone?"

"Four days in Florida, maybe five. Then I want to go home for a day or two. I want to visit my father's grave in Lares, breathe the mountain air."

"You want to remind yourself that you're a Rican, eh?"

Carlos bristled inwardly, but fought not to show it. "Something like that." He studied Juan, wondering if he realized how close he had come to his own thoughts of the night before, of earlier that morning. He doubted it. He was simply repaying him for his own previous slight, and as Juan sat there, grinning now, Carlos looked at the uneven row of badly formed teeth that so clearly defined the difference between their upbringings. Perhaps that was part of it as well. His father had been a well-known painter whose work was highly regarded by the island's intelligensia, and he had been raised in an atmosphere where art and learning were as vital as honor and commitment to his people, a soft comfortable life by the standards of others. It was a far cry from Juan's world of the San Juan *barrio*, of the mean streets of the poor, where survival meant something far different. But the revolution was a blending of those worlds; it needed both, was nurtured by each in its own way. And, too, it was understandable for those who had lived with nothing to wonder about those who had lived with much, even to suspect them at times.

"Aside from keeping the ladies in line what do you want me to do? By the way, where are the others?"

"They're out, doing other jobs. You think you're up to going outside in the bright sunlight?"

"I'll wear shades. What do you want?"

Carlos thought for a moment as if mentally timing his moves.

"Our friend at the Cuban Mission," he said finally. "I'd like you to meet him this afternoon. I looked over our finances last night and we have about fifteen thousand. I'm not sure yet, but it might not be enough to do this thing right. We'll need ten more to be safe. He'll probably chisel us down to five, but we'll take what we can get. I just want you to tell him we're broke. I don't want him to know what it's for. He might tip off those bastards in FALN and I don't want them getting their political noses in it. I don't trust them. I'll call him and set it up. I thought you could meet in the park, across from *El Museo*, if that's okay."

Normally Carlos dealt with the Cuban himself and he could see the pleasure in Juan's eyes at being asked to do this alone. The level of involvement would commit him to the plan, and though he had told Juan otherwise, he was more concerned about his commitment than that of the others. The others, he knew, would follow if pressure were applied.

By midafternoon he was again working at his desk, the words pouring into the notebook, arranging his thoughts in the way that worked best for him by putting them on paper. It was a process of girding himself for the fears and uncertainty that lay ahead, the self-doubts that were sure to come. Days, he thought. Probably weeks. Perhaps even longer. The escape to safety once the plan succeeded, *if it succeeded*, would be difficult, but possible. The kidnapping itself, that was a different matter. If failure became inevitable during the operation, they would kill Norris, it would be the only alternative. Killing was something he was trained to do, something he had been taught to do efficiently with an assortment of weapons. Yet, despite years in the mountains of Chile and Nicaragua, killing was something that had never been forced on him and he knew he would rather avoid it. Political killing was not the way of the Puerto Rican, not part of his history. Even the bombings were planned to avoid killing, if possible.

Carlos thought of his involvement in the FALN bombing at Fraunces Tavern and of the deaths that had resulted from the simple blunder of a poorly trained commando. Still, it had not been intended. The detonator was to have been set for midnight, when the famous lower Manhattan restaurant would be closed and empty. Instead it had gone off at noon and people had died. The planned symbolic destruction of the historic site where Washington had said farewell to his troops had turned into a bloodbath that had served no purpose. He had felt shame then, both for himself and the cause, and the feeling returned as he thought of it now.

And if you kill Norris, will you feel shame also? he wondered. Yes, he thought, he would. But the step was necessary. Violence was now necessary, even if it meant the taking of lives. People, not only his people, but all people were being swallowed up by powerful governments, by even more powerful multinational corporations. The time of concern for the disadvantaged had passed. Poverty and suffering were now to be accepted as part of the natural order. Even those who led the socialist nations had been corrupted. And the few who resisted that corruption were trampled under foot. He thought of 1973, of Salvatore Allende and of Norris and of the CIA assassins. It had been the time for violence then, but they had chosen another course. Now it was more than time. The threat of statehood for Puerto Rico was growing. The promises of the revolution for other oppressed nations were not being fulfilled. Even the Blacks had all but abandoned the struggle and had moved into the establishment like poor relations finally invited to Christmas dinner, happy to be there, convinced they had finally been accepted when, in fact, they were only tolerated.

Hispanics, he knew, would follow that course as well; many on the island already did, led to it by newly wealthy countrymen who had sold their nation and its people for the money and position offered by the corporations. As Carl Rivers he had seen those who controlled the wealth and power, and as Carlos Rivera he had witnessed the success of their corruption. And he knew his people needed a leader to change that. A Ché to lead the people of Puerto Rico, someone other faltering revolutionary groups could look to, join and support, both from without and within. In his mind he knew he wanted to be that leader and the egoism of it disturbed him, made him wonder if his commitment was tainted by personal ambition. But no one else had stepped forward. No. It would not be Carlos Rivera who would lead. It would be El Tiburón. *He,* too, had waited, hoping for someone to follow. But it had not happened. Perhaps it was up to *him* to take the first step now, even if just to encourage someone better prepared than *he.* Perhaps it was WAR's small group of committed men and women who could create the spark through one dramatic act that would unite the many diverse and floundering groups. Or perhaps they, like so many others were also doomed to fail. But failure did not frighten *him.* The only true failure, *he* knew, was the failure to struggle. Success was an accident of fate. He put his pen to his notebook again and began to write.

First one must be a man vitally concerned with all problems of social struggle, never allowing himself to withdraw from life, but rather sustaining himself by providing for the needs of others, always living as a conscience of his culture.

He must be a man performing his biological function of producing growth and change, much like a tree produces flowers and fruits, never mourning their loss each year, knowing in his heart that the next season the blossoms shall come again, bearing anew.

Carlos put his face in his hands. He was suddenly very tired and wished he had time to sleep. But there was too much to do.

No. Carlos Rivera had no more to do. His job was now finished. That had been the cause of his misunderstanding, the reason for personal doubts. From this moment Carl Rivers would disappear and Carlos Rivera would retreat into suspended animation, waiting there for a day when the struggle was over. From this moment El Tiburón would act, using all his training and skill for the work that had to be done. And El Tiburón could kill if it became necessary, and he would do so without hesitation. He could feel renewed excitement building within him and his body felt strong and alive. Tonight, with the others, El Tiburón would set the plan in motion and it would be only *he* who would exist until the final conclusion was reached. It would even be *he* who would visit the grave of the gentle painter in Lares, the revolutionary fruit paying homage to the tree that bore him.

~~~~~

They were gathered in a circle on the floor in the loft's main studio and were praising Norma Epstein for the black bean soup she had prepared for dinner and joking with each other. El Tiburón sat quietly, watching the others. Behind him hung a painting by Jorge Soto Sanchez depicting the heads of four women, their faces distorted in pain and suffering, the birds of the air, the sea, the sun imbedded in their images, the torture of the island homeland itself. Beneath the painting a quotation by the artist had been printed on a separate sheet of paper. "We swallow, consume everything, and then spit it out again transformed." Carlos Rivera sat there transformed. El Tiburón sat rigidly upright, waiting patiently for quiet to descend. He had been silent throughout most of the dinner, while the others had been gregarious. Juan's meeting had been a success; $7,500 dollars had been assured, more than he had anticipated, and the success of his first singular dealing with the Cuban had lifted Juan's spirits and the transformation could be seen now, transmitted through his penis, as he flirted with Norma Epstein, laying plans for the evening.

El Tiburón watched as Norma giggled in response. She was not an extraordinarily attractive woman, but she was blatantly sexual, pleasingly so, like one of Gauguin's South Sea women. She was wearing an oversized man's shirt but her unencumbered breasts filled it and pressed against the material when she laughed or moved. Norma was an oddity to him, a Jewess who hated Israel and all those who supported it. Religious upbringing and ethnic pressures had challenged political philosophy and had failed. It was something he doubted could ever be the case in his own feelings toward his homeland or its people. La Raza no longer played a part in Norma's life, it only confused her.

Beside her, Richard McGovern sat, his feet folded like a yogi mystic, his bushy Afro-styled hair and wispy beard set off by simple steel-rimmed glasses, making him look like some albino African scholar. His face was intense and his eyes darted from one person to the next, impatiently waiting for the foolishness to end. The meeting that was about to take place was all-important to him. Richard was a *meeting person*, his life seemed to revolve about those events, his life between meetings just a passing of time. He would have made a splendid corporate executive, El Tiburón thought.

Carol McGovern, his wife, sat beside him, seeming loose and easy, almost aloof to the playfulness of the group, but still taking part in it. Her long blond hair hung down along her cheeks, reaching to the top of her breasts. She had finely defined facial features, of Scandinavian origin, he had often thought, and she had a lean, agile body, like that of a modestly developed teenager. It, too, was a contradiction. Her look of innocence and her commitment to violence was second only to Juan's. And there was also a false sense of cruelty about her that mingled with self-fear, and he had accepted the cruelty with difficulty, attributing it to her need for a defense and the knowledge that she had never been truly tested. She, like Richard and Norma, had devoted years to the Weathermen faction of SDS and like him and Juan, had trained in Cuba with the Venceremos Brigade, although the training of Anglos there had not been as extensive. But later, they, too, had become disillusioned by the absence of positive action within the struggle and had eagerly come to WAR, intrigued with its promise of escalation, something more in keeping with what was being waged by their peers in Italy, Germany, and Palestine. Now, two years had passed and little of what WAR had promised had materialized. It, too, had become content with selective bombings, followed by written demands that all knew would never be met.

Carol McGovern looked across at him and smiled. She stood quickly and moved next to him, changing her formal position in the circle. It was a signal, he knew, stating simply that she planned to sleep in his bed that night, a choice she was free to make in their communal existence.

Across the circle Juan noted the change and smiled. Sexual games amused him and he enjoyed them equally whether he was a party to them or not. His only concern about this game was Richard's benign acquiescence. It would have been different if he sent her to another man's bed with the understanding she was going out of respect to his wishes. But the choice was always hers, and it had always been a weakness in Richard that amused him, but one that also created a basic distrust about the man himself.

"Well, now that we're all in our proper places, we should get started." Juan glanced at Richard, then looked away, realizing this remark had not been understood.

El Tiburón folded his arms across his chest.

"We are meeting tonight to discuss new plans for the struggle," he began. He paused, looking at each member of the group in turn to emphasize the importance of what he was about to say. He was sitting rigidly, his back ramrod straight, his voice a dull flat monotone.

"Tomorrow morning I will be leaving to set an important operation in motion and I will be gone slightly more than two weeks. During that time each of you must decide whether or not you wish to participate. If you do not, you must be replaced, because all of you will be needed."

The group was suddenly silent. Even their bodies had stopped moving. Only Juan smiled; he watched his friend with amused interest, studying the technique he had chosen to manipulate the others. Agreement or banishment. Very pretty, he thought.

"*Ejército Mundo de Revolución* was formed two years ago in the belief that the struggle here in the United States had become a lifeless shadow of the worldwide movement. We were convinced that the courageous actions being taken daily in Europe and the Middle East had to be emulated if the corporate bosses and their puppets in government were ever to respond to our cries for justice. Now two years have passed and *Guerra*, or WAR, as the newspaper lackies have renamed us, has done nothing but imitate the petty frightened actions of the Weathermen and FALN. The heroes of the Red Brigade would laugh in our faces. The selfless courage of Black Septembrists would make us look like small children playing at revolution. Today, even our friends in Northern Ireland no longer maintain communication and we cannot blame them."

El Tiburón folded his hands and lowered his eyes almost as if he were about to pray. "To some degree it has been necessary. We have had to solidify Third World contacts of support. But we have waited too long. Crimes are committed daily without adequate response. The people for whom we struggle *see* our inaction and in their hearts they know we are failing them. It is now time to change that, change it with one bold stroke that will signal an end to our passiveness. And this first act must not only be powerful in itself, it must also be symbolic. It must rival the Jews' capture of Eichmann, something that in itself will stimulate the imagination of the world and make our enemies tremble at what is yet to come." He paused and opened a manila folder that lay before him, extracting four mimeographed sheets of paper, each containing an identical list of names and addresses. He waited while each member of the group silently read the names of ten leaders of government and business.

"At some time within the next month, on one specific date, at the same hour, bombs will explode in either the homes, offices, or automobiles of each of these individuals. Maximum destruction will be the intent, but the death of the targets will not be the goal. The devices will be set and placed by others, and when they explode, we shall be fifteen hundred miles away, preparing to take our primary step. The bombings will be a diversion and the communiqués sent will make everyone believe we are here in New York. The following morning, just as the newspapers are screaming about our atrocities, we shall attack and we shall kidnap Edmund Norris from his home in Palm Beach."

Next to him, he could feel the startled movement of Carol McGovern's body. Across the circle Norma Epstein's mouth had become a small circle and her eyes seemed to have dilated.

Richard McGovern's voice was an excited whisper and his face was alive with the thought of what he had heard. He repeated the words, "holy shit," over and over.

"Now you understand why you must decide whether or not you will be a part of the primary plan. There will be lesser work to do here, things that I intend to assign to our less active supporters. These things can, however, be left to those of you who choose not to go. The dangers are obvious, and there is no need to discuss the consequences of failure."

"I don't have to think." Richard McGovern's voice seemed to break as he spoke. "We'll be taking the man who planned Allende's murder. It will be the most powerful political act of this century. Like killing Hitler." His eyes seemed to glaze over as he spoke.

"How will we know that we can take him so soon after the explosions?" Norma's voice seemed hesitant, but he knew it was only because her mind required precise detail.

Richard began to object to her question, but El Tiburón raised his hand, stopping him. "I've been assured it can be done. An old comrade has been watching him and it seems his life has begun to follow certain daily patterns that will be an advantage to us. My trip, in part, will be to verify that fact and our surveillance will continue up to the final moment. The bombings will also take place less than ten hours before the attack to minimize the remote possibility that the government might increase his protection. You will notice, however, that those we're going to attack are actively involved today. I think the government will concentrate any increased protection on the same kind of person. And interest in us should be centered in New York and other major cities where we've operated before. Florida has not been one of our areas, and I think it will be overlooked." He waited, looking Norma in the eye. "I am not minimizing the risks. A month from now we may all be dead. But we shall have tried and that alone will be a victory. It will be the spark that will shake others from their complacency." He smiled at her. "But I intend to succeed."

Carol McGovern slipped her arm into his and squeezed against him. "I'll be with you," she said. She looked across at Norma. "You'll be there too, won't you?"

Norma smiled. "Haven't you heard. Jews love Florida in the winter. Besides, I want to see if that sexless pig can get it up."

They began to laugh, destroying the tension.

"Heah. I didn't know you were Jewish," Juan said.

Their laughter intensified.

"There will be things to do while I'm gone," El Tiburón said. "Quiet surveillance will have to be made of the people on the list to fix the best locations for the explosives." He nodded toward Juan. "Juan will be in charge of that. It's something we have all done before, but this time we must be even more cautious. The stakes are much higher now."

Carol McGovern squeezed his arm again. Across the circle Juan whispered something in Norma's ear, causing her to laugh again.

"Shit," Richard McGovern said, repeating the word over and over, his face radiating his excitement.

4

National Airlines flight 93 climbed away from LaGuardia Airport at 8:45 A.M. headed nonstop for West Palm Beach. From his window seat in the first-class section El Tiburón watched the ground fall away. Briefly, the cluster of buildings that comprised Riker's Island prison slid past and he thought of the many Puerto Ricans who sat within its bleak modern buildings. Most of them had come to New York believing the lies they had heard at home, stories of the friends who had returned showing photographs of their automobiles, wearing the new clothes not available to those left behind, never speaking of the crowded tenements and welfare lines that were the true reality. But soon they would hear that others were fighting back, exacting a price for the betrayal, and perhaps it would ease the burden. He felt a sense of guilt sitting in the spacious comfort of the first-class cabin. But he had been taught long ago to dress well and move about with an affectation of affluence to reduce the risk of detection. It was the American way. One need not fear those with money. A man became respectfully conservative when he had something to conserve; it was only the poor who could not be trusted. And he did not appear poor. From his well-tailored, tan suit to his glove-soft Gucci loafers, he bore the mark of privilege. Even the leather camera case, stowed beneath the forward seat, marked him as someone accustomed to finer things. He smiled to himself, wondering if Ché had traveled to his death in Bolivia that way. He doubted it. The struggle was not as sophisticated then, but still it was an amusing thought.

He looked toward the forward part of the cabin where a slender, blue-eyed stewardess was beginning her ritualistic pantomime of the aircraft's safety devices, while the unseen voice of another accompanied the minor morality play. What to do in case this particular 727 decides to kill everyone on board, he thought. Next to him a middle-aged man watched the performance intently, studying the young woman's more interesting equipment. Mixing travel with pleasure. He looked out the window again. There was a tightening in his stomach, the anticipation of what was to come. The plane had leveled off and beneath him now thick mountainous clouds spread out with an ethereal beauty that was both soothing and awesome.

If the plane crashed now Norris would be saved; the plan would be aborted probably never to be revived. He smiled at the thought. Fate played such a large part in things. He believed that. Perhaps it was his Puerto Rican upbringing, his early life in the mountains, something that even his extensive education had not removed, much in the same way that many well-educated religious cling to their belief in a pure, simplistic creation even after studying the scientific evidence of evolution. Zango, the voodoo styled spiritualism of the mountains. He smiled again at the thought. Perhaps he would go to the old woman of his town who practiced it and obtain a talisman from her after he visited his father's grave. Something to ward off evil fate and assure success. He laughed quietly at himself. Juan would understand what he meant, any fellow Puerto Rican would. A simple act of fate could decide so many things. If Lee Harvey Oswald had fallen and broken an ankle on the way to the Texas Book Depository, John Kennedy would probably be sitting down to breakfast at this moment. Now, one tragic mistake on WAR's part, one unforeseeable change in Norris's routine and everything would collapse. All you can do is plan well and hope that fate smiles, he told himself.

"Headed for a little sunshine?" The man seated next to him smiled from a well-tanned face.

"Business. Mixed with a little pleasure, I hope," El Tiburón said.

"Charles Michaels," said the other, introducing himself. "I have a little condo on the Intercoastal that I sneak away to whenever things slow up at the shop. Have a little Buick dealership in Queens and things start to ease up in late October after the initial rush for the new models." He shook his head sadly. "People are mostly buying the small cars now when they buy at all. It's a damned shame what those Arabs have done to us over here." He emphasized the "A" in Arab.

"Certainly is. I never thought I'd see it happen." He resisted the impulse to smile and looked out the window again, hoping to thwart further conversation.

"What line you in, if you don't mind me asking?" Michaels said, obviously not caring if he was intruding.

"Photography. I'll be taking some wildlife photographs in the Everglades."

"Jesus, that's a god-awful place. Ever been there before?"

El Tiburón shook his head.

"Nothing but bugs and snakes and alligators. You know there isn't a bit of fresh water in the whole state that doesn't have alligators in it. And the damned fools down there go swimming in that water." He shook his head. "Me, I'll stick to the ocean. Great fishing down there. You oughtta try to get some in if you can. Best in the world."

"I'm afraid I may be too busy." *I'll be preparing to kidnap your former President,* he added to himself.

"That's too bad. Best in the world. No question about it. What's your name, friend?"

El Tiburón smiled, thinking how much he would enjoy telling this fool what his name was. *Yes, that's right, the chap you read about in your newspaper. I even blew up a General Motors office once. Probably fucked up the delivery of your cars.*

"Carl Rawlings," he said. *Always keep the same initials.* They had taught him that from the beginning. *The same first name too, if possible.*

"Well, Carl, you'll love it there," he said, the instant familiarity of the car salesman coming through. "The Palm Beach area's the prettiest spot in the country. Expensive, but worth it, if you know what I mean. Where you going to stay?"

"I really don't know. A friend is making arrangements for me." He thought immediately of Wally Rogers, the big, innocent-looking country boy whom he had first met years ago, almost a lifetime ago in Cuba.

The stewardess interrupted their conversation with offers of food and drink and now fully occupied Michaels' attention. He was a fat, leering man, El Tiburón noticed, and now, talking to her, beads of perspiration had begun to form on his domed forehead.

El Tiburón resisted the stewardess' consecutive offers of breakfast, coffee, and champagne, finally agreeing to a bloody mary just to rid himself of her insufferable maternalism. His stomach did not want food. The tightness did not concern him, but he did not want to do anything to intensify it. He was still worried about FALN. Worried they would find out about the plan and try to abort it to maintain their dominance with the people.

Michaels turned and grinned at him when the stewardess departed. "Great-looking babes they have on these airlines, eh?"

El Tiburón smiled wanly and looked back out the window. It would be a very long flight, he decided.

~~~~~

It was exactly nine o'clock when Henry arrived at the door of his basement office in FBI headquarters. It was raining in Washington, and he was grateful they had at least left him his parking privileges in the subbasement garage. As he walked into the small outer office, his assistant looked up at him. Her name was Mary, his wife's name. And there was even a faint physical resemblance, he thought. Right now she seemed embarrassed, concerned.

"Mr. Henry. The associate director called and asked if you would go up to his office as soon as you arrived."

The slight hint of a blush on Mary Roche's cheeks seemed very appealing, he realized. Almost provocative in an odd sort of way. She was a striking woman, tall and supple with beautifully shaped legs and round breasts that always seemed ready to burst through the tight-fitting blouses she favored. Her hair was a sandy blond, shoulder length and soft, like his wife's had been; there was the same upturned nose and chiseled cheekbones.

And she was young, twenty-five he guessed, far too young to be posted with an assistant director and he knew the fact that she had been, under the current circumstances, had probably concerned and unnerved her.

He smiled at her. Put the poor thing's mind at ease, he thought. "Call him and tell him I'm on my way," he said.

He walked into his sparsely furnished office and placed his briefcase on the long table behind his desk. Feelings of desire had crept into his mind as he spoke with his assistant, this other Mary; he purged himself of the thought and looked about the cramped little room. Even the traditional FBI seal and American flag, necessary to any senior official's office, were missing, not to mention the absence of a window. It was like a burial vault, he thought now. And intended to be like one. The associate director. Malcolm Welch. He considered the purpose of the summons. It would certainly not be a social visit. He and Welch had entered the Bureau together and had been competitors almost from the start. They had both worked as junior assistants under Hoover and, as such, had vied for his favor. No, there would be no help from that quarter. Only a sense of victory and defeat. But if they were going to exert more pressure, they should be smart enough to know that it should come from another source. He would resist Welch at all costs.

The elevator opened on to the seventh floor executive offices and Henry moved smartly down the deep-carpeted hall, passing the offices of other assistant directors who had not been banished to the basement, keeping a spring in his step for the benefit of anyone watching. Welch's office was directly down from the director's suite, which marked the end of the hallway with two oversized wooden doors, the office never occupied by Hoover, even though the building bore his name. But it was a different building, a different FBI, and only a handful now remained who fought to return it to what it once had been. When he entered Welch's office a middle-aged secretary offered a friendly smile."

"Good morning Mr. Henry. Mr. Welch is on the telephone, but he'll be with you shortly."

Henry glanced at the console on her desk and noted that none of the buttons were lighted. Welch could be on a private line not hooked in to the console, but he doubted it. It was more likely *sit and wait time*, the opening move in the petty power game he expected. But he could sit and wait, all day if need be, and then still greet the silly sonofabitch with a smile that would infuriate him. He had decided months ago that he would not let them get to him; they could harass and humiliate him as much as they pleased and he would simply ignore it. The thought of it amused him now. It was something he had learned from Martin Luther King. No matter how much they had harassed and persecuted him, he had simply smiled, said something pleasant to the agent involved, and then gone about his business as though nothing had occurred. It had nearly driven Hoover crazy.

The buzzer on the intercom dismissed his thoughts and he watched as the secretary answered it, then smiled and motioned him toward the inner office. Inside he found Welch seated behind his oversized desk, fumbling with a handful of papers.

"Grab a chair, Walt," he said without looking up. "I'll be with you in a minute."

Henry glanced about the room, then took a chair farthest away from the desk. He knew Welch was nearsighted and hated to wear his glasses. It would force him either to sacrifice his vanity or squint to see the expression on his face. He looked about the office again, studying it more closely. It was the first time he had been invited into Welch's seat of power since his return to Washington. He had seen Welch twice each week when Henry had appeared, uninvited, at the eleven A.M. conference each Tuesday and the Thursday breakfast meetings in the executive dining room. His presence had seemed to disturb the others, but he had enjoyed the fact that no one had dared suggest he not come. Of course, there had been hints. The meeting was a requirement for all assistant directors and above who were assigned to headquarters, and each week unnecessary written reminders were sent to the fourteen men involved. The fifteenth reminder, his, was never sent, and he had simply ignored the *oversight* and gone anyway.

He studied Welch now, fiddling with his sheaf of papers. The office suited him, he thought. It was large and impressive as Welch himself would like to be thought of, nearly five times as large as Henry's office, and that was another comparison Welch would find to his liking. But Welch was neither large nor impressive. He was a relatively short square-shaped man with the kind of body that always looked poorly in even the best of suits. His once blond hair was almost gray now and next to his pale skin it gave him a pasty look. Henry noticed that Welch still wore his FBI ring. He had surrendered his own twenty-five years ago, placing it in his wife's casket in a parting emotional gesture that made little sense to him now. But he had never replaced it either.

Henry took a pipe from his pocket and had just finished lighting it when Welch finally looked up from his desk. His eyes immediately narrowed as he tried to focus on Henry in the distance.

"Why are you sitting way the hell back there, Walt?"

Henry ignored him, noting his continued refusal to use the nickname, Pat. They had both been working as junior assistants to the director when Hoover had so named him and it had grated on Welch's nerves then and Henry was sure it still did.

"This is some office you have here, Malcolm." He paused and

looked at it more closely, noting the fine, red carpeting, the leather chairs and sofa, and, of course, the traditional seal and standing flag. "I never did like big offices myself," he added, drawing on his pipe as he spoke. "Always felt lost in them."

Welch squinted at him again, trying to catch his expression, then gave up and sat back in his high-backed chair.

"Yes. Well, I'd like to have time to discuss offices and such, but it's a very heavy morning." His voice was brusque, intentionally officious. It almost made Henry laugh out loud.

"You know you're quite a problem to us right now, Walt."

Henry brushed a piece of lint off the knee of his gray pin-striped suit. "I'm sorry to hear that, Malcolm. Believe me, I wish I could resolve it."

Welch sat forward again, squinting. "You can, you know, by simply retiring. Your pension would be a little over thirty-two thousand a year, probably closer to thirty-five if you took accumulated leave until your thirty years are up next January. I think we could arrange that."

Henry puffed on his pipe. So the pressure was beginning with the pension. And even a veiled threat that he might lose three thousand a year if he failed to act. What a venal bastard, he thought.

"I have been thinking about it, Malcolm. But I hate the idea of going out under a cloud. It's not only because of how it would affect me, but I'm honestly concerned about how it would affect the Bureau and the other people facing the same kind of problem."

Welch's pasty face reddened. "How the hell do you think it affects the Bureau with you sitting *here* under that damned cloud?" he snapped. "You and the others insist you did nothing wrong. And at the same time you refuse to cooperate with the investigation into all that black-bag bullshit. Christ, we want to help you, but you won't help us. And so we have to sit here and wait to see if more indictments come down against active, high-ranking members of the Bureau. There have already been three. How do you think it's going to make us look if it happens again?"

Henry watched him sink back in his chair, then slowly tapped the ash from his pipe into a free-standing ashtray next to his chair. He had no doubt a tape was quietly turning in Welch's bottom drawer, and he had no intention of saying anything that could be construed as a refusal to cooperate with an official investigation. If they wanted to get him on that, they would have to trump it up without his help.

"Malcolm, I've told everyone the same thing, from Mark Slocum in the attorney general's office, right down to those here who've questioned me about it. I'll answer any questions I can. I don't have a damned thing to hide. But I can't answer questions honestly and accurately unless I can review the reports I filed and any written orders I received at the time of the incidents in question."

"Why the hell do you have to read reports to be honest?" Welch snapped. "You know the Norris era is over in this office."

Henry smiled at him. "For Christ's sake, Malcolm. Some of these things happened five, six, seven years ago. How the hell can anybody expect me to remember what was said and by whom; what was done and by whom, let alone dates and details of actions taken. I'll bet you can't remember who the hell you had lunch with a month ago without consulting your appointment diary. So how can you expect me to sign affidavits about things that happened in hundreds of different actions against a dozen different groups. If I even tried I couldn't help laying myself open to a perjury charge. And that certainly wouldn't help the Bureau, or me."

"We can't make those files available. There are too many questions of national security involved." Welch spun his chair to the side and stared at the distant wall, offering a double-chinned profile to Henry.

"Malcolm, let's not bullshit each other. I wrote half those damned reports and countersigned the rest, as well as the orders. And I am still working for the FBI, aren't I?"

"For the time being." He snapped the words out, but there was no sharpness in his voice. "If we made them available to you and subsequently you became involved in litigation against the Bureau, they could show up in court and that would make them public. You have retained an attorney, you know."

"Did I *have* any choice?" He clenched his teeth, holding his anger in. He hated Welch, but he knew showing that hatred would be foolish. "Malcolm you know damned well where my orders came from, and you know these reports will bear that out. You want me to take the heat so the Bureau won't have to explain its justification in ordering those actions." There goes your fucking tape, Henry thought. You wouldn't dare erase that part of it.

"I know no such thing." Welch spun around in his chair again and tried to glare at Henry, but it became impossible because of his need to squint. He realized it and gave up. "I'm not going to discuss that any further, there's no point. You understand the Bureau's position and I don't have the power to change it." He paused. "And I wouldn't if I could."

Henry laughed. "That may be the first sincere thing you've said to me today, Malcolm."

Welch folded his butcher's hands in front of him and stuck his lower lip out. "The attorney general would like you to have lunch with him today to discuss this matter. He suggests one o'clock at the Capitol Restaurant. That's a block behind the Rayburn Building."

"I know the place." Henry's voice registered his surprise. The secondhand invitation so overwhelmed him that it overshadowed Welch's attempt to sucker him in to some admission before passing the message on. He caught himself. "I'm just a little surprised he wants to meet in a public restaurant."

"So am I," Welch snapped. "You'll be there I take it."

"With bells on."

"I'll have my secretary inform him. Thank you for coming in."

Henry stood, smiling at the abrupt dismissal, and as he went through the door he realized the entire matter had Welch confused and concerned as well. No, more than concerned. He was afraid now that some deal might be made that would be beyond the Bureau's ability to control. Could it be, my dear Malcolm, that you've only scotched the snake? But if so, there would be a price for him as well. They'll offer to kiss you before they fuck you, he told himself. He walked down the hall toward the elevator and watched as another assistant director started out of his office, then turned back inside after seeing him. That's right, he thought. Never ride the elevator with a leper.

By twelve-fifty it had stopped raining, but the sky was still dark and ominous and promised that more would come. The taxi moved slowly in heavy traffic along Pennsylvania Avenue and seemed to gain on the distant Capitol inches at a time. Henry glanced at his watch. He had no desire to keep the attorney general waiting and the probability that he would was making him nervous. That would be even worse. Nervousness was an indication of guilt. Every investigator knew that, was taught that and believed it, whether it was true or not. He noticed the cab driver looking at a young woman signaling from the curb.

"I'm in a hurry. If you don't stop for anyone else there's a five-dollar tip in it for you," Henry said.

The driver glanced at him in the rear-view mirror and shrugged his shoulders as he passed the woman by. With the average cab ride costing one dollar eighty cents in Washington, the legal additional fare was well worth passing up.

Add bribery to the charges, Henry thought.

It was two minutes past one when he climbed out of the cab, seven dollars poorer, and started up the long path that led back to the nearly hidden restaurant. Despite its physical location it would be far from secluded for either the attorney general or himself. The restaurant was a favorite of congressional staff members, as well as lower ranking members of Justice, HEW, and a half dozen other departments, the core of the grapevine for official gossip. There would also be the probability of an odd reporter or two, although most satisfied themselves at the Press Club bar in the National Press Building. But still, the mere probability of it was more than a little curious.

He stepped through the main door onto an elevated area that looked down on the main dining room; there was a stairway to the right that curved upward to a balcony above the dining room that held an office and restrooms. He descended the three short steps into the dining room as the maitre d' approached.

"I was to meet Attorney General Baldwin," Henry said.

"You must be Mr. Henry. The attorney general's office telephoned and said he would be a few minutes late. May I show you to the table?" The small, tuxedoed man had raised his voice when mentioning the *attorney general*, making sure nearby customers heard. His restaurant was not frequented daily by cabinet members and Henry doubted if the maitre d' could remember the last time he had served lunch to one. It was an event for him.

He followed the smaller man to the table and asked him to have the waiter bring a martini while he waited. He was feeling slightly numb. Even a telephone call to explain he would be late. That was a bit more consideration than even Baldwin's southern upbringing demanded, he decided. And the fact of a public meeting, that made no sense at all. He had met with Baldwin several times in the past, but always in his office and always with Slocum present. He had been cordial then, even friendly, but there had been no question about what was wanted, and he had always known what to expect when summoned. The White House wanted a resolution of the problem. The president had promised to clean up the intelligence community, rid it of those who had abused their power, and there was no way it could be ignored. As Welch said, the Norris era was over, even if it had been a game played by many administrations, over the years. Already charges had been filed against two of the Bureau's retired senior officials and a former director, and additional evidence was needed against them. And there were others, himself included, who sat waiting for similar action, and at times now it seemed to come so close he felt he could almost hear the whisper of the axe.

It was one-fifteen when Earl Baldwin walked through the main dining room, drawing the attention of everyone present. It was a typical Washington reaction, an attention to power, not to the man, but to the power the man represented, and as he watched him approach Henry wondered what effect that produced on someone so obviously not accustomed to it. Baldwin had the plodding gait of a farm boy. He was only slightly above average height and his clothes were baggy and rumpled, defying any guess at his physical condition. He had a soft, but weathered, face and the only hint of intelligence seemed to come from the old-fashioned spectacles he wore. It was a face that would seem equally at home peering out from behind the wheel of a tractor or the cluttered desk of an obscure academician. When he reached the table he smiled with his lips, keeping his teeth hidden, and extended his hand. Henry noticed the fingers were heavily coated with nicotine, and his detective's mind told him immediately that Baldwin was right-handed.

"Sorry I'm late, Walt. Every time I think the barn door's shut and bolted the telephone rings and I find out it's not. Hope you weren't inconvenienced any." Baldwin's voice was a soft monotone, a conspirator's voice, and the emphasis he placed on certain words was not shown by any change in inflection, but rather by the tilt of his head, or set of his jaw, or the raising or lowering of his eyebrows.

"What's that there you're drinkin'?" he said.

"A martini, sir."

"Now that sounds good. I think I'll have one of those too. But let's stop this sir stuff. I want this to be a friendly, frank meetin', and I'm a lot more comfortable with Earl than I am with sir." He winked at Henry then motioned to the waiter, indicating with a gesture of his hand that he would like the same to drink as his guest.

"Well, I hope I won't disappoint you," Henry said. "But not very much has changed since we last spoke."

Baldwin nodded and drew his lips tight, causing the skin around his eyes to wrinkle. "I know, I know," he said. "Things aren't much fun over at the Bureau these days." He looked Henry straight in the eye. "That's why I asked you to meet me here. I understand the kinda pride you have. I'm a proud ol' devil too. An' I thought meetin' in amiable surroundin's might change the tone a bit among your peers. I don't haveta tell you they'll all be talkin' about this over cocktails this evenin'."

Henry was forced to smile at Baldwin's portrayal of an old southern fox. "Believe me, I greatly appreciate the gesture. It's one of the very few I've experienced in the past six months."

Baldwin drew his lips together and nodded again. "I know that too," he said, looking Henry in the eye again. "But it's not all kindness, Walt. I'm a firm believer in the quid pro quo, and while I want very much to make things less difficult for you, I do want somethin' in return."

Henry just nodded. They were mature men who knew how the game was played and Baldwin's candor was no revelation.

"I been talkin' to Mark Slocum. By the way, what do you think of him?"

"Very fair, very smart, and I wouldn't want to meet him in a dark courtroom," Henry said.

Baldwin laughed. "Yeah, he's a tough little devil, isn't he? He really did a job on that ol' governor up in Maryland." Baldwin chuckled softly. "Sonofabitch deserved it, though."

The message was subtle but quite clear to Henry.

"Anyway, I was talkin' to him about you," Baldwin continued. "An he kinda feels you know a lot more than you're tellin' us, Walt. Now let's not pussyfoot about this. You're gonna havta go. There's not much question about that. Now I don't mean that in a criminal sense, understand me. If criminal action turns up, then it turns up. We'll play that straight down the line. I, for one, don't think it will, an' Slocum tells me it's still pretty much up in the air. But Walt, you haveta give us somethin'. You jus' can't keep on refusin' to talk about it. The only choice you leave us then is to fire you for failin' to cooperate with an official investigation. You know that's true."

Henry sipped his martini and waited while Baldwin lit an unfiltered cigarette, drew the smoke deep into his lungs, then expelled it. All about him he could feel eyes watching and he struggled to keep his face friendly and calm. He very much wanted the advantage of which Baldwin had spoken. He finished the last of his drink and motioned to the waiter for another.

"I still have the problem of reviewing the files," he said. "I can't open myself up to perjury because I simply mixed up dates or forgot incidents. Certainly you understand that."

"Forget those things," Baldwin said. "You just concentrate on the things that weren't covered by reports, the actions that were taken without orders." He stared at Henry, still smiling. "Now don't tell me those things didn't happen. I may be a country lawyer, but I'm no fool. I know there were times when our people went ahead without orders. Times when they extended their actions beyond the orders given. Now we're not gonna destroy the FBI for doin' what it was told. And we're not gonna attack ol' Mr. Hoover in his grave, or jump up and down about the mistakes of Edmund Norris or past administrations. Ever'body knows about that already, an it wouldn't serve any purpose at all. But Walt, the public wants action and damn, we're gonna give 'em some."

Henry's eyes hardened. Baldwin spoke as though he were trading horses, not men's lives. He was doing his *country lawyer* act as if no one knew his Durham law firm represented half the tobacco interests in North Carolina. And he was also pushing him, too hard perhaps.

"Let's assume there was some overzealousness," Henry began. "And let's also assume I knew about some of those instances. What we would be talking about would be the actions of very devoted men who were following established procedure, or at least believed they were. Now you have to understand circumstances. An investigator looking into the activities of a terrorist group—I mean legitimately looking into it—can come across an opportunity to gain some valuable insight into what is being planned, or who else might be involved. He *cannot* afford to wait five or six days for official approval because these opportunities are momentary things. They just don't linger on indefinitely. So let's say he moves. Improperly, perhaps, by strict standards. Imprudently, when you consider the risks involved. And certainly unwisely where his own ass is concerned. But these were men who were devoted to their jobs and they were dealing with people who were planting bombs, who were disrupting entire universities, sometimes entire cities. And occasionally people were dying because of them." He paused, returning Baldwin's intense gaze. "And now you're asking me to help myself by pointing a finger at those men and saying yes, so-and-so moved ahead too quickly; he took too much on his own authority and by doing so he technically violated the law. Maybe that would even be okay if the government also disclosed where the precedent came from, who established it, under what authority and why. Without that you end up with a select group of accountants and lawyers who happen to work for the FBI and who appear to have taken it upon themselves to become burglars. And how the hell do they defend themselves?" He waited again, watching Baldwin nod his head. "And we both know they did act under the highest authority, and if they went too far in some instances, I honestly believe it was because that authority wasn't definitive enough, perhaps intentionally so."

The waiter returned to the table and they halted the conversation long enough to order lunch. When the waiter had departed again, Baldwin smiled across the table at Henry. "You make a very eloquent argument, Walt. And in some ways you may be correct."

"Excuse me, sir." Henry interrupted. "We were faced with a constantly escalating situation and we were trying to stop it from growing. What if it reached the level it already has in Europe, where business executives and government officials are being shot down in the street? Where kidnappings become everyday occurrences? What if it still reaches that level? How far would our government go then?"

Baldwin looked at Henry with a concerned affection, almost like a father responding to an overzealous son. And the look not only appeared genuine, but appropriate, even though Baldwin was no more than a half-dozen years older.

"I think we would probably pull out all the stops. And I think we'd be justified in doing so."

He watched the satisfaction spread in Henry's eyes and paused to allow the full effect of his admission to set in.

"However," he added, "I also believe it would be wrong and was wrong to take that kind of action until . . ." he paused again . . . "until the situation fully warranted it. We're both lawyers, Walt. And we should understand better than most that even though we bend things at times, we live by a rule of law. If we don't, especially at our level, well then we might as well chuck the Constitution in the Potomac, 'cause that's where it would belong. Now you're critical of what I'm askin' you to do because I'm not willin' to burn, kill, rape, and plunder by exposin' all the mistakes and misadventures that were involved. Well, maybe you're right again. I'm not willin' to tear everythin' apart, and I am willin' to set some examples so that the message is got by all and this kinda thing doesn't happen again so easily."

"Do you really believe it's not going on right now?" Henry looked at him coldly. "You think it stopped with Norris? The players haven't changed, only the referee."

"It sure as hell better not be, Walt. The intelligence community has got to learn that it's a part of government, not a government unto itself."

They stopped talking as the food was served and throughout lunch concentrated on Henry's current status at the Bureau. Over coffee Baldwin again returned to his expectations of Henry, his mood slightly sterner than it had been earlier, but still friendly, sincerely so, Henry thought.

"Now, Walt, I don't have too much time left, so let me lay it out the way we're goin' to play it. As I told you we haveta have somethin' from you. We can't have you refusin' to cooperate and just ignore the fact that you are. Frankly, it's embarrassin'. You can limit what you talk about, and we can agree about that beforehand. Then, once your thirty years are in next January, you retire and go about your business. Now I'm not talkin' about any immunity. I'm assumin' you've been tellin' me the truth and you yourself never overstepped your authority. If all you did was overlook the misdeeds of others, then we'll consider that a sin of omission and treat it as such. Let me stress again that the scope of our investigation is going to be limited anyway." Baldwin drew a deep breath. "Now, on the other hand. If you decide you can't cooperate—and I'll respect your judgment on that—well, then we're goin' to fire you for failin' to cooperate. You'll still get your pension. We're not about to hold that over your head, although I know there's some boys in the Bureau who've suggested that. But you'll be leavin' under a god-awful cloud and that's not good, Walt. And I gotta be honest. If it goes that way, we're also gonna be lookin' a lot harder at your past decisions." He smiled across at Henry. "If it does go that way," he added, "I sure as hell hope we don't find anythin'. An' I mean that sincerely."

"I hope you don't too, sir. How much time do I have to make up my mind?"

Baldwin looked down at his nicotine-stained fingers. It was the first time he had failed to look directly into Henry's eyes.

"Why don't we say thirty days," he said. "It's November fifth now. Let's say December fifth. It's an important decision for you, and I don't think you should be forced to rush it."

He looked up and saw the expression on Henry's face and respected the way he fought to hide the pain. Twenty-nine years and I come along and give you thirty days, he thought. Must be like goin' to a doctor and bein' told you got cancer.

5

The golf had gone well; the shower had refreshed and he was pleased that his leg had held up after a full nine holes. Walking down the long, ornate marble hallway that led to the Alcazar Lounge, Edmund Norris was pleased with both himself and the day. The regular Friday golf game on the Breakers' course was something he looked forward to each week and he regretted only that his physical condition now limited him to the one day. His son-in-law walked at his side, still praising an approach shot Norris had made on the fifth hole. It had been lucky; his foot had actually slipped on the downward swing of the club, but he kept silent on the point. Praise for his once-acceptable game had become too infrequent for the luxury of honesty.

When they reached the Gold Room, Dalton Wilkerson automatically stopped. One of the two Secret Service agents who preceded them had already entered the room and the second remained at the door. The two agents who brought up the rear stopped, as usual, ten feet away from the open fourteen-foot double doors.

It was an idiosyncrasy of Norris's and they were all aware of it. He could never pass the room without stopping to admire its beauty, and his eyes brightened as he stood now in the entrance gazing into the massive room, nearly one hundred feet long and more than fifty feet wide. Stepping inside, he looked up at the elaborate gold leaf ceiling which had been copied from one in the Ducal Palace in Venice; he studied again the intricate diamond patterns formed by the plasterwork which subtly changed into graceful arches at the wall, forming navelike frames for the portraits of the historical figures, who before and after the Renaissance participated in the discovery of the New World, and whose images now encircled the room. Art and history blending into graceful beauty, he had often thought. Few cultures had ever rivaled the Italian in the ability to achieve that simple subtlety. At the far end of the room stood a great stone fireplace, so out of place in Florida, yet so necessary to the room itself, its overpanel depicting a globe turning on its axis bringing the Old and New Worlds together. Something we still have not achieved, he thought, as he often had before.

"Just marvelous," he said to Wilkerson as they continued down the hall, passing carved wooden tables and decorative chairs that were spaced at distant intervals along both sides of the smooth stone walls. "Have you ever read anything about the history of this hotel?" he asked.

Wilkerson grinned boyishly. Even at thirty he appeared little more than eighteen when he smiled. "No, I haven't," he said. He bent his head down and looked at the floor as they walked on, hiding the amusement that now filled his face. There had never been a need to read anything. On each occasion he had visited the Breakers he had done so with Norris, and each time he had also heard a detailed account of the massive building's architectural wonders. It was not that Norris was growing senile, he knew. It was merely that he brought so many people there and wanted each to appreciate the beauty that surrounded them; he simply forgot now whom he had told and whom he had not.

"It was built in 1925," he began. "There had been an earlier hotel, built at the turn of the century, but it was destroyed by fire. The Flagler family built it. Old Henry Flagler really, the railroad tycoon. The family still runs it along with several other hotels. The museum here was started by them too. The Flagler Museum over on Whitehall Way. It was originally their home." Norris gestured with both hands as they walked, the palms held up, moving in small almost indefinable circles.

"Anyway, they built the entire building, massive and elaborate as it is, in only eleven and a half months," he went on. "Amazing feat. It cost six million, even then. They had this fairly well-known architect of that day, a chap named Leonard Schultze out of New York, and he patterned the exterior, with those massive twin towers, after the Villa Medici in Rome. It set the tone for the entire area. That's why you see so many Italian Renaissance mansions here." Norris smiled, thinking of his own less elaborate home. But far more American, he told himself. "Well, at Flagler's insistence, Schultze carried the same theme throughout. That room we just left is a *copy*, an actual copy of one in the Ducal Palace in Venice. The Mediterranean Ballroom next to it is almost exactly like one in the Palazzo Deg'l Imperial in Genoa. I made a point of seeing them on my last official trip to Italy. The wops couldn't believe we had duplicated them here." He laughed aloud, thinking of the umbrage that had registered on Aldo Moro's face when he had told him, the words *American upstarts* written all over it. "All these small dining rooms we're passing on the right were taken right out of the Florentine Palace Davansate," he mispronounced the final "a", making it hard.

"They were really upset?" Wilkerson asked, laughing.

"Furious. They didn't say so, but you could tell. Very touchy about their possessions, those wops. The lobby here, with all those frescoes and the decorated vaulted ceilings. Well, that chap Schultze swiped that right out of the Plazzo Carega in Genoa. And that garden the lobby looks out on to." He laughed as he spoke. "It's a ringer for the inner gardens of the Villa Sante in Rome."

They started into the Alcazar Lounge and Norris stopped, taking Wilkerson by the arm. He chuckled again. "I almost forgot the fountain out in front. Moro was showing me the Bobli Gardens in Florence and there it was, right in the center of it. When I told him, he just ground his teeth and turned red." He laughed again. "It wasn't very good for Italo-American relations, but I couldn't resist it. He was such a pompous old bastard. Still, too bad about what happened to him."

The maitre d', having been informed of their impending arrival, led them to a table in the rear of the dining area which had been kept free of other guests. Two Secret Service agents sat at a table a discreet distance away, while another remained at the door and the fourth occupied one of the low swivel chairs at the end of the depressed bar. Their table was next to the window, overlooking the ocean. Here, as always, because of the breakers built into the sea, the water crashed against the beach below, almost reaching the retaining wall that rose above it. It was high tide and the beach had all but disappeared. Windows covered the length of the east wall of the room, absent only from the area directly behind the bar, and as Norris looked out now, seven brown pelicans flew past in their traditional V formation and it reminded him that Hall would call that evening. He looked back at his son-in-law and gestured again with his hand.

"This is the only room that wasn't stolen from someplace in Italy," he said.

Wilkerson looked around him and nodded his agreement. "What design is it?" he asked.

"Moorish," Norris said. "Old Flagler built another famous hotel called the Alcazar up in St. Augustine around the turn of the century. The old devil practically developed the east coast of Florida single-handed. It's the beauty of this country," he said, more to himself than to Wilkerson. He closed his hand into a fist for emphasis. "You can accomplish just about anything you want here, if you have the determination."

"And a few million bucks," Wilkerson said. He smiled at Norris affectionately, making himself appear younger again. A strand of unruly hair crossed his forehead and it made his slender face seem even longer than it was. He was boyishly handsome in an American sense and he had a thin, almost frail body that was perfectly proportioned for the natural-shouldered tropical suit he now wore. Normally he would have dressed more casually, even though his father-in-law seldom did. But the Breakers demanded at least a jacket so he had been forced to emulate Norris's penchant for formality.

The waiter took their order for drinks, after which Norris began to lecture again, chiding Wilkerson about his preference for Manhattans.

"There are only two drinks worthy of the name cocktail," he said, smiling. "The martini and the stinger. All the others are just for old ladies' luncheon clubs. I'm not talking about straight liquor, mind you. It's when you begin to mix them that the failure always takes place."

Wilkerson grinned at him again. There was no subject on which his father-in-law had not formed an opinion, he thought. But most of the political figures he had met were like that, his father-in-law, perhaps, only more so. They had grown close in the nine years since he married Norris's daughter, Emily. The media had often spoken of Norris's closeness to his daughter, about the degree to which he valued her opinion on serious matters. As always they were far from correct. It was he, not his wife, in whom Norris often confided, discussed plans with, and, in moments of anger, expressed opinions and concepts that would have sent the average journalist running to his typewriter.

"You seem in exceptionally high spirits today," Wilkerson said, thinking back to the suffering Norris had endured during the first two years of his forced retirement.

"Yes, things are going rather well, I think. At least I hope they are. It would be a welcome change," he said.

Wilkerson lowered his voice. "You mean with General Hall."

Norris nodded. "He's an ass in many ways, I know. But he's competent enough. Much better than that mental dwarf we have now, or that backward-thinking fool from California. With the proper guidance and a good staff, he'll do well. All we have to do now is see that he gets the chance."

"I never cared for him much," Wilkerson confessed. "I always thought he suffered a bit from tunnel vision."

Norris nodded again. "That's true. But he's growing and he has the toughness we need right now. He'll support our friends for a change. None of this nonsense about turning our backs on friendly governments because some rabble starts screaming they're oppressed. Look at the problems the Shah is facing now. And getting no support from us. Hall, at least, would put us back on top again, the way we were before the opposition screwed everything up."

"Have you talked about your role if he's successful?" Wilkerson's voice was a low whisper.

Norris imitated it. "Actually, he's willing to offer far more than I want," he said. "All I'm interested in is some type of roving ambassadorship, nothing formal, of course. Just something that will allow me to call upon old friends and advance policy." Norris laughed. "I'm too old for anything else. And the public would probably lynch us all if anything more than that was even suggested."

El Tiburón turned his head to the sound of Norris's laughter. He was sitting at the center of the bar, nursing a Scotch and water. Wally Rogers leaned his head toward him.

"It's like I told you, good buddy. That lyin' ole Nazi plays golf here every Friday and then usually eats lunch in here."

He had whispered the words but El Tiburón nudged him to be silent. He was conscious of the Secret Service agent six seats away, and he was concerned they had already exposed themselves more than they should. The surveillance had only begun the day before and he knew that as it continued they would have to work from greater distances to avoid detection. But he had wanted to be close to Norris this once. He wanted to get the feel of the man, come close enough almost to smell him, smell him sweat, know that he could get that close. Close enough to use the Graz Burya automatic, which was now safely hidden under the seat of their car.

The bartender approached them, inquiring about another drink. It was an unusual bar, El Tiburón noted, only table height with swivel seats the size of normal chairs. But the area behind the bar was depressed into the floor, bringing the level of the bar up to the bartender's waist on the service side and it gave patrons seated there the sense that they were being served by a dwarf.

"No, we have to be going," El Tiburón said. He studied the check, noting the three dollar price per drink. A sum that could feed a large family on rich, black bean soup, he thought. But the North Americans would never learn to limit their indulgences so the poor could be cared for. They even begrudged them decent food and shelter, preferring to have women and children forced into the streets as prostitutes.

He paid the check and he and Rogers left without looking toward Norris. The Secret Service agent at the door studied them, then looked away, satisfied with their well-tailored clothes, certain there was no threat present.

Halfway down the hall El Tiburón shook his head in disbelief. The opulence of the Breakers amazed him, and he recalled the drive up from South Palm Beach, the ocean to his right, the walled mansions of the wealthy to his left, seeming to go on endlessly.

"It baffles me that the poor have not risen up in this country and murdered all these people in their sleep," he said aloud. He looked at Wally Rogers' hulking face. "All the wealth here. All this indulgence while so many go hungry. Children walking through the snow in Harlem with holes in their wornout sneakers and these people have mansions that they use only three months a year. And still no one objects."

"They've been taught to believe it's the way things are supposed to be," Rogers said. "My daddy always told me that if I worked my ass off I could have one of those houses someday. He believed it. Liars like that ole boozehound in there made him believe."

"Yes. We're all taught to believe it. Get yours first. Let the others take care of themselves. Even the socialist countries accept it to a certain degree." He walked on silently, looking into the rooms that imitated the splendor of European selfishness. So like the Americans, he thought. Stealing the culture of others because they have none of their own. He had often thought that the Statue of Liberty, that hulking whore in New York harbor, should be replaced by an enormous Coca-Cola bottle. The grand symbol of American ingenuity.

They stopped near the exit.

"Is there some place we can sit outside inconspicuously along the route he'll take home?" he asked.

"There's a restaurant called Dinkel's at the corner of Poinciana Way," Rogers said. "They have an outdoor café in front and we could probably sit there and see them pretty good."

"They couldn't see us, though?"

"The café's around the corner. They'd havta be lookin' for us to notice."

El Tiburón smiled at Rogers' heavy southern drawl. He had never thought of Florida in terms of the deep South. For him it had always been a place for wealthy Jews and the bourgeois Cubans who had run in terror from Castro. But it was truly redneck country. The Blacks and the small smattering of Hispanics were clustered in filthy inland ghettos, which were ironically located on the western side of the railroad tracks that cut the area in half. Rogers had told him, as they had driven about the night before familiarizing him with the area, that until only a few years ago, Blacks had not dared to enter the center of any towns after nightfall. His own father, he had confessed, had often bragged how he and his friends would drive around in their youth searching out any Blacks who had broken that unwritten law. How comical, El Tiburón thought, that liberal New York Jews and anglophile Wasps had seized control of so much of what these crackers prized. They had been so busy persecuting the Blacks that they had surrendered control to the robber barons to safeguard their mania for segregation.

It was a short drive to the café and they had already eaten lunch when Norris's car stopped for a traffic signal at the intersection of Poinciana Way. Seated to face the intersection, El Tiburón could see Norris's mouth moving behind the closed rear side window of the car, see the clumsy gestures he made with one hand.

"There he is now," he told Rogers, whose back was to the intersection. "Talking away like an old woman."

"Jus' like I told you. He's livin' a very patterned life down here. Every mornin', real early, he walks along the dunes behind his house. But you'll see that tomorrow when we go out in the boat. A couple of times I saw him, he didn't even have any Secret Service agents with him. But even when he does there's never more than two."

The car pulled quietly away, and they fell into silence as two young women took a table in the previously deserted outdoor area. Rogers looked them over hungrily. He was a large, rawboned man, homely by almost any standards, with a round, moonshaped face that was intensified by brown, strawlike hair that he combed across his forehead. But his physique was powerful and finely muscled and it was noticeable even through the sport jacket he wore and for some reason it seemed to draw women to him.

"There's a fair-lookin' pair of pussycats over there," Rogers said. "We could do with a little recreation." He raised one eyebrow to indicate the possibilities. "Our friend ain't goin' anyplace else today. His Friday golf game always wears his old ass out."

El Tiburón shook his head, smiling at Rogers's eagerness. "Maybe later," he said. "There seems to be plenty of activity at that place we're staying."

"Oh, you bet your ass," Rogers said. "Divorcees and all kinds of young things. And everyone of them walkin' around in heat."

"Well, let's go back," El Tiburón said. "I want to work a while on the communiqué we'll use after the diversion in New York. But maybe after dinner you can cool a couple of them down."

6

P amela Norris sat at one end of the long sofa, sipping a drink and talking with her daughter who was seated on her left in a side chair. At the other end of the sofa, a full four feet from his wife, Edmund Norris stared at the flickering television screen, his son-in-law to his right in a second side chair. As a group they could have been likened to a set of bookends placed at the opposite edges of an empty desk, and the distance that separated them during these family gatherings was as real as it was physical at that moment.

The deep, reassuring voice of the television newscaster filled the sprawling family room where most of their time together was spent. He was speculating about the questions President William Lee Jordon might be asked in this unusual prime-time press conference, which he noted with undisguised annoyance was already behind schedule.

Norris snorted derisively, both at the speculation and the irritation. Jordan, like himself, like all recent presidents, had already determined precisely what questions would be asked. Certain *friendly* members of the media would have been called upon to raise specific topics, and they would do so because they knew those questions would evoke newsworthy answers that would make them appear *on top of it* to their editors back home. Any real questions would be left for the end of the conference, and he knew from experience that if Jordan handled the earlier topics well, drawing out his answers and provoking additional questions on the same topic, there would be little time left for subjects with which he was not prepared to deal.

"Do you think he'll say anything about running again?" Wilkerson asked.

"Some fool will *ask* because of his recent decline in the polls. But he'll avoid it. It's much too early for that," Norris said. "That's still a year away. But speculation about it, both the *if* and the *when*, will get him more coverage and voter interest than anything an out-and-out statement would produce. And I'll give him one thing. He's a damned clever politician when it comes to keeping up public interest, even for an incumbent president."

"Did I hear something favorable about Mr. Jordan?" There was a teasing quality in his wife's words and what seemed like a slight slur.

He had been warned by his daughter that Pamela seemed to be drinking a great deal lately, but he had not noticed it himself. He looked at his daughter now, but she did not seem concerned. Emily was beautiful and he thought she had become even more attractive since her marriage.

"I always give him credit when he deserves it," Norris said. "It's just that he gives me so little opportunity to praise him."

Dalton and Emily both laughed, thinking the remark witty, as did Norris himself. His wife only smiled.

Out of the corner of his eye, Norris watched her, trying now to remember if that was her first drink that evening. They had become close after he left office. He had needed her then and she had been there, helping him through difficult periods. But recently, since he had become more active again, there had been little time to spend with her. His relaxation now, his method of obtaining peace of mind, came from ornithology and his evening work in the bird room. He looked across to her now, wanting to say something that would please her, but she was deep in conversation with Emily so he did not. Watching her he realized she was still a fine-looking woman. Like him she had aged rapidly; it had seemed to happen quickly after he left office, within a year, certainly little more. There was loose flesh on her neck now and her once-slender figure had taken on some added weight along her waist and in the upper arms. But she still had the patrician bearing that had first attracted him, her chin held high, her straight nose slightly uplifted as she spoke. The hair was still blond, with some touches of gray, but of course it was treated to appear that way. Yes, she was still beautiful, only now in a matronly way. He smiled at himself for sitting there reviewing his wife's physical attributes like some young buck. A sixty-four-year-old woman.

He ran his hand inconspicuously along his own midsection and squeezed a handful of flesh, part of the small paunch he had developed over the past few years. You've slipped quite a bit yourself, he told himself.

"Daddy." His daughter's voice broke into his thoughts and he turned to her and smiled without reason. "Mother just suggested that we might rent a boat tomorrow and go out for a sail. You and Dalton could fish if you like, as long as it's one of those boats that keep moving, not one that just sits there in the heat."

"You mean one that trolls," Dalton corrected her.

"Whatever," she said with an indifferent tilt of her head.

"Would you like that, Pam?" Norris asked.

"I thought it might be nice, Ed. You know I always liked it when we went out on the presidential yacht, whenever I could get you to take me along."

He thought he had heard the slur again and he looked at her more closely, then decided he had been wrong. He chose to ignore her comment about the presidential yacht. She had been making slightly digging comments lately, but he felt she was just becoming a bit cranky in her old age. This outing she had suggested would be an opportunity to please her and he wanted to do that.

"Well then, we'll go," he said. "I've used a captain over in Rivera Beach before and I believe I have his name filed away." He smiled. "If I don't, I'm sure our Secret Service boys do. I'll telephone in the morning."

"No dear," his wife said. "Have one of the agents call and make the reservation in his own name. Otherwise the captain will start talking about it and there will be a dozen photographers there when we arrive."

"Yes," his daughter added. "And they'll find some way of accusing you of catching some endangered fish."

Norris nodded, then looked quickly back at the television screen where President Jordan could be seen entering the East Room of the White House to the polite applause of more than one hundred reporters. Norris cupped his chin between his thumb and index finger, allowing his elbow to support the weight of his head. He was frowning and his eyes narrowed as he watched Jordan smile toward the reporters. The scene brought back memories of his own press conferences and of the bitching that always followed from reporters who had not been called on and who had decided they were being persecuted. He was sure Jordan was experiencing the same complaints, and he wondered if any president had ever left office without despising those insufferable bastards. They were whores, who took anything they could get for themselves, then pointed a finger at others who simply did the same.

He listened as Jordan began with a prepared statement intended to assure those watching that the energy situation was well in hand. His advisors, he said, had found that heating oil reserves were adequate to meet needs throughout the winter and that OPEC would keep the promise, made the previous June, to maintain the twelve dollar and seventy cents price level. But again he urged the citizenry to use restraint in consumption, except where the physical health of the elderly or infirm might be compromised.

"I think I'll remain in Florida this winter. He's ignoring the fact that we could lose the Iranian supply if things don't settle down there," Norris said.

Dalton laughed, adding that he was glad he had relatives in the South that he could visit when the oil ran out.

"I wish you had known our President when he was just the junior senator from North Carolina," Norris said. "He was such a pragmatic, backstabbing SOB. He'd agree to vote with the Senate leadership and then go out and hustle his own legislative deals behind their backs. After a few years no one trusted him, but since he came from a locked-up state, all he had to do was keep the party leadership happy back home and the boys in Washington couldn't exert much pressure at all." Norris pointed toward the television screen. "Look at him now. Our knight in shining armor. And that aide of his, Cramer Lessing, is even worse. He'd sell out anybody, including Jordan."

"They both make me ill," Emily said. "They're both such fakes I don't understand why people don't see through the act."

Norris looked at his daughter. Her lips were pressed together indicating her annoyance. He could remember how she had pouted as a child and some of it still stayed with her. Her hair was still the same too. He had noticed it the other day when he had touched her head. Soft, silken, with hints of blond showing through the chestnut brown. She looked like her mother, he thought, the same high cheekbones and slender nose, only her face was fuller, the cheeks slightly chubby. Their figures were similar too, he had noticed that by the pool the other day, small and delicate but still attractive. There was nothing ostentatious about her body and he liked that.

Jordan's press conference droned on. There was nothing exciting in it, but there seldom was in these things and it was often more interesting to see what topics were being avoided. It had been interesting to note that Jordan had *led* with energy problems, it should work well to Hall's advantage, he thought. When they had spoken again the other day he was still edgy. Perhaps this would bring him to his senses, make him see how clear-cut the situation was. There were times he honestly wondered about Hall, whether he had the instincts needed for the Oval Office, the ability. But he was the *only* possible choice if his own aims were to be achieved, that much was certain. He would simply have to mold him into a bird of prey, bring out the instincts he was sure were there. Hall was like too many senior military men. He thought power, like war, was a game. But power had never been a game. It had *always* been a weapon.

The pool was on one side of the high, elevated patio and there were deck chairs and small tables scattered about. The end of the patio nearest the sea was enclosed by the final three feet of a cement seawall, and a group of people stood there now looking down at the beach ten feet below. There was a full moon and the people at the wall were waiting to see if the sea turtle eggs they knew were buried there would hatch that night. Inside the restaurant that stood at the northern end of the patio El Tiburón sat at the small bar sipping planters punch. It was the fourth he had had since dinner and the mixture of rums and grenadine and the touch of apricot brandy had left him pleasantly numb.

"Do you think the turtles will hatch tonight?" he asked.

The woman working the bar was named Beryl. She was middle-aged and British and she spoke with the clipped accent that always makes the English sound as though they have the answers to all questions.

"It's difficult to say. It could be tonight or tomorrow night, but when they do come out, we must turn off all the lights," she intoned.

"Why is that?" he asked.

"Because they'll get lost and die if we don't."

He smiled at the woman. She was attractive and she had been pleasant to him since he had arrived at the small motel of which the restaurant was a part.

"I don't understand what you mean, Beryl. I've never lived right on the ocean like this."

She placed a hand on her hip and looked at him like a school-mistress about to address her class.

"Well, you see, the sea turtles bury their eggs in the sand on a precise schedule to insure that they hatch during the full moon. Then the newly hatched turtles use the moon to find their way to the ocean. They follow the light, you see. If there are other lights it confuses them. One year we had to go down and help them. Quite a few had run up against the seawall out there, because of the lights on the patio. Now everyone turns their lights off when the turtles are due to hatch, and the people around here get very upset if someone doesn't."

He smiled and turned to look out the window where well over a dozen people had now gathered to await the event. All around the motel, which had been inappropriately named the Hawaiian Ocean Inn, there was a glut of high-rise condominiums with one- and two-bedroom apartments that ranged in price from fifty to more than one hundred thousand dollars. It was a playland for the near-wealthy and the successfully retired and the parking areas at most of the buildings looked like the used-car lots at Cadillac and Lincoln dealerships. They were self-indulgent people, he thought, people who gave little if any thought to those who had less than they did. But they were banded together here, determined to save as many sea turtles as possible. He began to laugh, the liquor finally having its effect.

"Why are you laughing?" Beryl asked.

He looked at her innocently. "I was just thinking of all the people in the world who don't have enough to eat and all of us here, who have so much, sitting around worrying about the turtle population."

"Well I don't think that's a very nice thing to say," she said. "We can't do anything about all those people, but we can do *something* about the turtles. And you better be careful when they hatch," she added. "There are very strict laws protecting them and the South Palm Beach police are very diligent about enforcing them. Last year they arrested a man for trying to walk off with one of the eggs."

He laughed again. "I promise you I won't kidnap any turtles," he said.

By midnight, when the restaurant closed, all of the turtle watchers had wandered away, more interested in finding an open bar than continuing their vigil. El Tiburón sat alone on the seawall, his feet dangling over the edge. He had spent the past three mornings in the small fishing boat they had rented, drifting far offshore near Norris's estate, studying his movements through a camera lens. The afternoons had been spent investigating other locations where he might be taken, and all had proved fruitless. An assault on the house, he had decided, was nearly impossible and far too great a risk. The golf course at the Breakers was not located well for an escape, and the same was true of the old Everglades Club in downtown Palm Beach, where Norris and his wife dined one evening each week. The only possibility was the beach behind the house during one of his early morning walks. Wally had been right. Norris had appeared there faithfully each morning shortly after sunrise, and his other movements also seemed to confirm the ritualistic nature his life appeared to have taken. He obviously had little concern for his own safety and El Tiburón suspected that those who guarded him would be equally lax. Already he could have killed him more than a dozen times and escaped without great difficulty. It was something any well-trained professional could have accomplished. The kidnapping would be more difficult, but he believed now that it, too, was possible. Only the escape route still had to be planned in detail and then he could leave. Wally would remain behind to maintain the surveillance and organize the equipment that would be needed. He, too, was a professional, well trained and disciplined and probably one of the finest rifle shots he had ever seen. He had amazed the Cubans with his proficiency while training there and the Chinese Tao-Pau, who had assisted the Cubans then, had presented him with the Russian-made Graz Burya automatic that was now hidden in his car.

He looked down at the beach. Still no turtles. People in the islands worried about the turtles too. The poor who lived along the coasts hunted them to sell to the restaurants that served the wealthy and the tourists. Go safely little turtles, he thought. Go all the way to Puerto Rico and Cuba and Haiti and maybe then these fools here with their misdirected concerns will have helped someone who is hungry.

He swung his legs off the wall and walked slowly across the patio to the stairs that led up to the two-room suite he and Wally now shared. He looked at his watch. It was twelve-thirty and Wally was still out prowling the bars in nearby Lantana hoping to get lucky with one of the pretty suntanned women who seemed to dominate the area.

Inside the room he opened his locked suitcase and withdrew the slender briefcase hidden inside. At the small desk he studied the communiqué that was now nearly complete. It would arrive at the New York offices of the Associated Press and United Press International late in the evening on Thanksgiving Eve, moments after bombs had detonated in ten Manhattan locations. By that time he and the others would be staying at this very motel, making final preparations for an act that would stun the world. He shook his head, knowing he must concentrate on the present. Tomorrow afternoon they would drive inland to the Everglades, to Wally's small fishing cabin near Belle Glades where Norris would be held. Before that, they would time the trip by boat from Norris's home to the location where the van they would use would be waiting; then time the entire trip across the flat, threatening interior, something Wally assured him would take no longer than fifty minutes. He felt the escape by boat would confuse those searching for them. Once the kidnapping was discovered they would first look to the small deserted Cays off the Bahamas, only forty-five minutes to the west. The small cabin was an unlikely place to hide and that was its advantage. He himself would have been more comfortable with a location in mountainous terrain, more suitable to his training. But there were no mountains in Florida and Wally knew the Everglades. He had grown up fishing there, living for weeks at a time in the cabin his father had since left him. El Tiburón wondered for a moment what Juan would think of the location. Juan, the *barrio* boy who was deathly afraid of snakes, though he would not admit it. It reminded him that he must telephone Juan tomorrow, find out what progress the others were making, reconfirm their commitment in his own mind. No, he told himself, it was not time to worry. It was a time to act, coolly and professionally in the manner he had been taught. He began to read the communiqué again, and he felt satisfaction as the names of the exploitive corporations and government officials he would soon attack appeared before his eyes. The marvelous ruse that would put fear in their hearts. But they were not important. And he realized, too, that even Edmund Norris was not important. He was only a symbol that could be used dramatically. His capture would give them power. They would turn him into a weapon they could then use for the benefit of many.

7

H e had decided to visit the old walled city the previous afternoon. The 727 had banked over Old San Juan exposing the moss-covered battlements of El Morro far below and the need to walk the ancient streets had risen within him. Originally, he had planned to meet Miguel south of the city in Rio Piedras, where they had been students together at the University of Puerto Rico. It all seemed so long ago now. He had not been in the old city since those student days and it had suddenly seemed important that he go there, walk the narrow, blue-stoned streets, perhaps even stop and eat asopao, or *calamares en su tinta* in La Mallorquina, the island's oldest restaurant, later perhaps even to sit quietly over a glass of Barrilito, the only rum his people had refused to export, the solitary item the Anglos had not taken away from them.

He had left the Caribe Hilton at eight o'clock and by eight-thirty, despite the insanity of the San Juan rush hour, he had parked his rental car in the Plaza de Colón under the watchful bronze stare of Christopher Columbus, Puerto Rico's first tourist. Looking at the statue, he had smiled at the thought. Almost five hundred years and still you are with us. He left the car near the plaza; he had decided to walk to feel the old city beneath his feet. It had not changed. The old Spanish buildings still remained juxtaposed with newer office buildings, stores, and curio shops, still untouched by the hands that had converted much of the island into a glass and steel nightmare. Much of the old seventeenth-century wall survived, surrounding the old city, benignly protecting it from intrusion that now came from within. Even the blue paving stones of the streets remained, having been brought to the island centuries before as ballast in the hulls of Spanish galleons.

Standing on the battlements of El Morro now, he looked out toward the sea where Drake and Hawkins had laid seige to the Spanish garrison in 1595. And still the city was under seige, both from without and from within. The two hundred acres of fortifications that comprised El Morro stood only as an assurance of the oppression that had existed through five centuries. The sea, one hundred and forty-five feet below, crashed against the stone walls, a constant reminder of the freedom in which others would not allow the island to bathe. He turned and walked back through the once impregnable bastion of colonial Spain which took more than two centuries to complete. A fortress built to keep others from taking what had already been stolen, its labyrinthine tunnels still holding the whispers of foreign soldiers forced to oppress a simple people. Along the castle walls lay the gift of the Americans, the strange golf course built by the now-departed Antilles Forces of the U.S. Army. Ingeniously constructed fairways replaced the ancient moat, that great gift of a northern culture that prized recreation above history.

Once outside the walls he wondered again if it would ever end, this strange need to dominate this dot of land one hundred miles long and thirty-five miles wide. Near the entrance to the fortress, he passed the Church of San Jose, the oldest place of Christian worship still used in the Western Hemisphere. It had been a *gift* from the Dominicans, who had brought their belief in Jesus to enslave the minds of his people, while still others had enslaved their bodies. His father had taken him to the church as a boy, to see the great vaulted Gothic ceilings, this rare survival of true medieval architecture transferred to the New World. For three and a half centuries the body of Juan Ponce de Leon had been buried there, before inexplicably being transferred to the Cathedral of San Juan Bautista only a few blocks away. His father had taken him to the cathedral as well and had shown him the many mementos of *los reyes Catolicos* displayed next to the glass case that held the remains of Saint Pio, the converted Roman centurion whose body had been brought there from the catacombs of Rome. What was this strange fascination the Catholics had with moving bodies about like pieces of lost luggage? His father had laughed when he had asked the question so many years ago. You must be patient with them, he had said. They have preserved much of the world's great art. And in gratitude for that we must allow them this morbid practice they find so necessary.

He smiled to himself, thinking of his father again. This afternoon he would travel to his grave in the mountains, the slight homage he felt was so necessary now before everything else began. He continued on, the history of this, his spiritual city, engulfing him. Just past the ramparts, at the foot of Calle San Sebastian, he passed Casa Blanca, intended as the residence of Ponce de Leon, but one which he had never entered, choosing instead to die in Florida searching out his insane dream of eternal youth. But the Spanish, and then the American military commanders, had used it for him as they had usurped so much else of the island's beauty. To the left of Casa Blanca was the San Juan Gate, the original entrance to the walled city, and beyond it, La Fortaleza, the official residence of the puppet governor. He walked quickly past the iron gate that guarded the entrance to the residence, keeping his eyes away from the two police officers who protected it from the people. But there was no need to look. He had toured the building as a young student, this half-palace, half-fortress with its marble floors and great mahogany stairway. He had stood in the terraced gardens and in the mosaic-studded chapel that had once been used for the storage of gold stolen from the people. No. There was no need to look now. One hundred seventy-one governors had lived there, thieves and usurpers all, and he did not want to see it again until a free Puerto Rican had walked through its doors.

He looked at his watch and quickened his pace. Miguel would be waiting, and like all revolutionaries, he would become nervous if the meeting was not held on time. Paranoia reigned supreme among them all, often with good reason. He moved quickly down Calle del Cristo, past the cathedral and on to the Cristo Chapel, built to mark the spot where a horse and rider leaped over the seventy-foot bluff in 1753—jumped and survived, so the disputed legend claimed. Next to the chapel Miguel sat on a shaded bench in the Parque de las Palomas, his back to the street, his eyes concentrating on the unobstructed view of the harbor. El Tiburón sat next to him and smiled.

"They tell me I can find Miguel Ortega Sanchez here," he said.

"In two more minutes you would have only found an empty bench," Miguel whispered in Spanish.

"Let's speak English," El Tiburón said. "I want to play the tourist speaking to the *nativo*, just in case we're noticed."

Miguel nodded. "You said it was important. I suppose that means a lot of trouble."

"A lot," El Tiburón said. He smiled again, watching his friend frown, his drooping mustache seeming to reach down almost to his chin as he did. He had not seen him in two years and then it had been in New York.

Miguel looked at him with soft, sad, brown eyes. "Well, nothing is easy anymore. What do you need? Guns, money, a place to hide?"

"A place to hide will do. But not now, and not just for myself." He looked out toward the harbor and waited, giving Miguel time to object. "There will be six of us. We are planning an action within the next few weeks, and if we are successful, the Yankee police are going to be looking for us everywhere."

"How will you come?" There had been no hesitation in Miguel's voice. He simply wanted to know how much would be needed.

El Tiburón smiled and squeezed his arm, keeping his eyes on the harbor. "We'll be coming from western Florida, probably by chartered aircraft to Key West. From there by boat to Cuba." He looked at him now. "Because of what we are going to do I think the Cubans will want us gone quickly. My plan will be to have us dropped ashore at night near Ponce. We would notify you of the time and place by radio."

"How long will you be here?"

"Three to five days. Four of the people will be Anglos and we can take them to a hotel like normal tourists. Juan Hernandez will be with me and we will go up into the mountains, somewhere in the Toro Negro Region."

"And after the five days?" There was still no concern in Miguel's voice.

"I expect we'll have to leave by then and we'll need transportation to Surinam. I have friends there and the new independent government is always happy to see tourists and ask no questions."

Miguel turned to him and El Tiburón could see a sense of pride in his slender, pockmarked face. "This is a major action then?" he said.

"The chances are good that we won't need you at all. But if we are lucky and we succeed, then we will." His voice was soft and it surprised him. He was speculating about his own destruction and yet his voice was gentle and even, almost resigned.

"I wish I could be with you," Miguel said. "Here we do nothing. We make threats to disrupt things like next year's Pan Am Games,

but we know even that will fail. The people don't believe in us any-
mo.e and they are right not to."

"When we finish, they'll believe again, even if we fail," he said.
"And you, too, will be proud. This will not be like the foolish rant-
ings of FALN."

"What do you do now?" Miguel asked. "Do you go back to New
York?"

"Soon. First I want to visit my father's grave in Lares."

Miguel shook his head. "Don't go there, Carlos. Stay away from
that region. The whole area is infested with police. San Sabastián,
Lares, Angeles, Utuado. They question anyone they wish; they hold
some people for days and you know what that means. They suspect
everyone of being a revolutionary. Recently, they were even searching the caves there and now they have men in civilian clothes moving
around, watching everyone."

"I have to go Miguel. But I'll just be another tourist with a camera around my neck. I'll be all right."

"You should have an Anglo woman with you then," Miguel said.
"The tourists always have women with them, fat, foolish women in
short pants."

El Tiburón laughed. "I don't have time to find a fat, foolish
woman in short pants," he said. "I have a rental car and I have a
false American identity that would hold up even if it were traced by
the police. I won't allow myself to be caught. Not now."

~~~~

He drove west out of San Juan, taking Route 2 through the towns
of Bayamon and Vega Baja. When he reached Manati, in the heart
of the pineapple country, he turned north on Route 681 and headed
for the coastal road that led to Arecibo. On both sides of the road
the pineapple fields spread into infinity and farther to the north lay
the grottolike Mar Chiquita beach, where the ocean crashed through
an opening in the high rock cliffs to embrace the crescent-shaped
shore. He had gone there with his father as a small boy. But more
often they had remained in the mountains, preferring to swim and
fish in the mountain lakes and streams, catching black mouth bass
and catfish with sharpened sticks and then diving into the cold clear
water to cool themselves.

Along the road to Arecibo, billboards announced the coming

baseball season and extolled the virtues of the Arecibo team, which, the billboards claimed, was destined to go the Caribbean world series. El Tiburón laughed, reading the signs and thinking how identical billboards would now surround other cities saying the same of their teams. Unlike most of his fellow Puerto Ricans, he had never been a baseball enthusiast. In the mountain country, the men, his father included, had preferred cockfighting, and throughout the November through August seasons, they would travel each Saturday and Sunday to the many *galleras* throughout the island. It had been years since he had been to a *gallera*. His father had always preferred the old Santo Gallo in Santurce, but now, he had read, most people traveled to El Muda for the air-conditioned comfort of the Club Gallistico.

It was midafternoon now and he was hungry. He had decided not to eat in the city, but had planned instead to stop at one of the many *lechoneras* he remembered along the way. But most now seemed to have been replaced with makeshift barbeque chicken places. The Anglo tourists no doubt preferring that to *lechon asado*, perhaps finding suckling pig roasted on an open spit a bit too native for their tastes. As a compromise he contented himself with two slices of *pan de agua* and coffee at a tiny roadside stand, telling himself that the more Spartan meal of the coarse native bread was more suitable for a revolutionary.

Not far from the stand, by the roadside, a young man stood next to a makeshift rack that held several dozen *jueyes* that he hoped to sell to passing tourists. As a small boy, he, too, had spent nights chasing the speedy land crabs with a flashlight, listening to the threatening snap of their claws as they struggled to escape. But he had never stood at the roadside in the heat of the day, hoping to sell them before they rotted in the sun. He looked at the man. He was close to his own age and he looked strong and able. But still he was forced to chase the crabs all night and then stand in the sun to beg enough money to put rice and beans in the bellies of his children. As he left the stand he drove slowly past the man, but avoided looking at him, trying not to embarrass him. The fine native bread and rich coffee sat heavily in his stomach and he wished he could have shared it with this man without shaming him. But there was no way. What was it the writers had called this island of his birth. *A cherished slum, the poorhouse of the Carribean*, and those painful words of Luis Muñoz Marín: *a land of beggars and millionaires, of flattering statistics and distressing realities.*

Anger rose in him, thinking of the honesty of the statement, thinking of the man who had made it, a man who then, as governor, offered the Anglo corporations tax-free status and low labor costs so the country could develop out of the sweat of the poor. It had been the same ever since the hated Treaty of Paris, when Spain surrendered control to the Americans. From one thief to another. Living off the misery of the islands, nearly three million people, while luring another million to the slums of New York. More cheap labor for the silk-suited filth who ran the corporations, men who were happy with the wage scale that allowed Puerto Rican children to grow up in the rat-infested streets of the *barrio.*

He forced himself to draw deep breaths, to control his growing anger. The anger had forced him to speed and that could only invite the attention of the police. He tried to concentrate on the billboards, which in growing number began to announce the Ron Rico rum distillery in Arecibo, promising, in English, courteous guided tours and ample complimentary drinks. The only thing it did not say was that *nativos* need not appear, but the people did not have to be told that. No, it was not just the outsiders who oppressed, who lived off the human misery that threatened to drown the island in the tears of its own poor. It was just easier to hate the outsider, even though he had been invited to bring his pain to the island. And when independence finally came, those who had invited the outsiders would run to Florida as the Cuban exploiters had run before them. And the good life would continue to be theirs.

Outside Arecibo he turned south and almost immediately began climbing into the lush green mountains. He was only twenty miles from Lares now and from the quiet grave of his father, nestled there in the foothills of Mount Guilarte. Already the air seemed cooler and smelled of the forest and it made the miles pass quickly. When the road ended at the junction of Route 111, he turned west and knew that Lares lay only five miles ahead. He had driven the road often, sometimes taking it to the western coast to the towns of Aguada and Aguadilla, where he would sit and listen to the residents of each insist that their town was the true place where Columbus first set foot on the island. It was an argument that had lived for centuries, and each town had erected its own monument to prove the validity of its claim. He laughed thinking of it now. His people were indeed mad and he loved them for their madness, just as his father had loved them for their simplicity.

It was three-thirty when he entered the sleepy village of his birth. He would not stop; he had decided that already. If Miguel was right about the police, he would not risk the chance of being seen and recognized by former neighbors and of then being forced to present his falsified papers to a police officer who had heard of his arrival and knew his true identity. Instead, he would drive on, moving slowly through the town, keeping his eyes straight ahead, like any other tourist passing through some insignificant village. At the intersection where the small post office stood, a man in a tan suit watched the car pass. Yes, there were police in the village. Wearing the suit was deliberate, intended to frighten with its implied authority. He watched in the rear-view mirror, as the man in the suit studied the retreating license plate. But it would be recognized as one belonging to a rental car and that should be enough to allay any suspicion. Just another Anglo out for a drive in the quaint countryside.

The town quickly faded in the distance and the mountain forest again swallowed each side of the road, filling the air with the sweet smell of new growth. The cemetery and his father's grave were only a half-mile distant now and he allowed the car to take on speed as it moved down a small hill. There was a sense of urgency in the pit of his stomach; he wanted to be there, to stand at the graveside and speak aloud to his father. They had been close for so many years, the simple artist and his son. He had not known his mother. She was only a vague memory, a soft, smiling woman who had died when he was four. Then there had been only his father. They had been together for the next seventeen years, before he, too, had left him, killed by the police who had beaten him with clubs during a demonstration for striking textile workers. He remembered with bitterness the days his father had laid in a coma, never to speak to him again. And he remembered the day after the funeral when he had left for Cuba for the training he would now use. And that was why it was important to be here, to explain aloud why it was all necessary, explain it to his father beneath the ground, not that he believed he would hear him, but out of respect for his memory.

A lizard rushed across the road and he braked abruptly to keep from crushing it beneath the wheels.

His father had never been a violent man, even his voice had been soft, gentle, like the breeze that cut through the treetops on a quiet evening.

"What's this, Poppi?"

"It is a present for you, Carlos. Open it."

"But it's a camera. Why did you give me a camera. I want to be a painter, like you."

"You can be a fine artist with a camera, too. You must learn to use it."

He smiled to himself as the car lumbered on. In the distance he could see the cemetery, rising gently upward behind a tight row of trees. A good way to let a ten-year-old learn that he lacks the talent to paint, he thought. And a gentle way to point him in a more suitable direction.

He parked the car along the road and climbed up through the trees and on to the sloping plane of the cemetery itself. His father's grave was at the rear of the cemetery, close to the edge of the forest, and as he approached it he could see that the small white wooden marker had almost been hidden by the fast-growing weeds. He knelt beside the grave and pulled at the weeds, clearing away the marker even though he knew it would be hidden again in weeks. The painted white wood had faded and chipped in places, and the name, Guillermo Rivera Soto, and the dates of his birth and death were now difficult to read. It was a simple grave for a simple man, and it was the kind he would want for himself when the time came.

"Perhaps soon, Poppi," he said aloud, smiling at the thought. "And if we were wrong and there is a God in heaven, then it will be you with your canvas and me with my camera, both of us making our pictures of the angels."

He had been squatting at the side of the grave for several minutes before he felt the presence of someone else.

The sound of the footstep behind him was almost imperceptible at first and still some distance away. He waited for the sound to come closer before turning, but even before he did, something inside him knew it would be the man in the tan suit.

When he turned, the police officer smiled down on him. His teeth were yellow from nicotine and the color seemed to jump out from beneath his bushy mustache. He was wearing a Panama hat that sat on the top of his round head as though it were several sizes too small. Carlos noticed that there was a dark stain on his blue necktie that also suggested sloppy eating habits.

"Mr. Rivera, you've come to visit the grave of your father. How nice." He spoke in Spanish and for a moment El Tiburón wondered if it were some kind of test or if he really knew his identity.

"Buenas dias, señor." He spoke the words hesitantly, like an Anglo might who had learned the language, but not too well.

The officer reached into the side pocket of his suit coat and quickly displayed his badge. El Tiburón noted the pleasure that showed on his face as he displayed it. He had found it to be true of every police officer he had ever seen, even those in the socialist nations, the immense pleasure they received in showing the symbol of their authority, like some fag displaying his penis in a communal shower, he thought.

"Some people back in the village were surprised when they saw you and you did not stop." He was still smiling as he walked around to the opposite side of the grave. El Tiburón stood and returned the smile.

"My name is Ortega," the police officer said. "I was curious myself about why you did not stop and then I saw your car parked along the road and I became even more curious. I did not realize your father was buried here."

"Yes." El Tiburón smiled again. "That's why I didn't stop. I wanted to come here first. I was going back to the village now, and then, perhaps, even drive up to our old house."

"You don't live in Puerto Rico now, do you?"

"No, I live in New York."

"What do you do there?"

"I'm a photographer. Mostly for magazines."

Ortega put the badge back in his pocket, then spread his legs and placed his hands on his hips.

"A lot of people around here thought you went to Cuba when you left," he said.

El Tiburón forced a laugh. "No. New York, not Cuba," he said. He started to move around the grave to be closer to Ortega.

"Some people said they thought you were with those pigs in FALN. Did you know that?" He had turned his body as El Tiburón moved closer so he was still facing him. They were the same height, but Ortega was much more muscular and he seemed cocky about his physical abilities. Somewhere, also, there would be a gun.

"You know how people talk. Anyone who attends college is FALN. They think all 25,000 students at the university belong to it."

He tried to smile again, but he knew it was not successful.

"I think that, too," Ortega said. He looked straight into El Tiburón's eyes and held the blank expression on his face. "Well, maybe just twenty thousand of them," he said, finally smiling.

For a moment El Tiburón was confused, then forced a smile himself. "Well, I think I'll go back to town and look up some old friends."

He turned to go, but Ortega's hand caught his arm.

"Why don't you show me some identification," Ortega said.

"But you know who I am."

Ortega nodded his head up and down and for a moment he reminded El Tiburón of those foolish plastic dogs that many Hispanics used to put in the rear windows of their cars.

"That's right. I know who you are. But I want to see who you say you are." He was grinning again, displaying all of his yellow teeth.

"My wallet is in my coat in the car."

"Then we'll have to go get it, won't we?"

He looked back at his father's grave. Even his pilgrimage of respect had been tainted now by this grinning fool with filthy teeth. He turned and started back down the sloping cemetery, displaying as much casualness as possible. Ortega remained a full two paces behind him. He was obviously not an intelligent man, but he was clever and his instincts for survival were good.

"It must be difficult working here in the mountains," El Tiburón said. "I can still remember how suspicious the people here always were, especially when dealing with someone from another region."

"I was born in Barranquitas," Ortega said. "It was much the same there, so I am used to it."

"Ah, yes. I knew a young woman at the university who came from Barranquitas. She was very beautiful. But I can't seem to remember her name now." El Tiburón glanced back over his shoulder, smiling. He could see the sense of pride that came to Ortega's eyes at the complimentary mention of someone from his village. Like most Puerto Ricans he was parochial, even as El Tiburón was himself, when it came to *his* mountain region.

"The women of Barranquitas are very beautiful," Ortega said. "The Indian blood there is very pure. They are not as fancy as some of the rich city women. And they don't have duennas following them to protect their virtue. The blood is enough."

He had removed his hand from the right pocket of his suit coat and El Tiburón suspected it was there that he kept his gun. Ortega seemed more relaxed now, and as they approached the trees that lined the roadway, El Tiburón used his thumb to free the end of the thin wire garrote that circled the inner waistband of his trousers.

Stepping through the trees he could see Ortega's unmarked police car parked behind his own and he glanced along the deserted roadway in both directions. It was a long straight stretch of road, clear for at least one hundred yards each way. He moved clumsily down the slight embankment, seeming to slip on the loose soil, using the graceless movement to free more of the garrote. There were small leather-covered loops at each end of the wire, large enough to insert three fingers into each. He fumbled in his trouser pocket for his keys, then held them out in an open palm toward Ortega.

"Do you want me to get the jacket, or do you want to," he said.

Ortega flashed his yellow teeth again. "You seem familiar with police procedures," he said.

"I see a lot of television in New York," El Tiburón said. "It makes all men experts."

"Except they can catch criminals in one hour," Ortega said.

"But they have to, my friend. That's all the time they have."

Ortega laughed at El Tiburón's joke. He seemed to have lost interest and paid little attention as El Tiburón opened the car door and bent over the front seat. The coat lay in the middle of the seat. He had wrapped it around his heavy Nikon camera to protect it from theft, and as he retrieved the jacket now he wrapped his fingers around the leather camera straps.

Ortega was lighting a cigarette as El Tiburón eased back out of the car, the jacket, with the camera hidden beneath, clutched in his right hand. The words, *cigarette smoking may be hazardous to your health*, flashed inexplicably through his mind as he turned, smiling, then swung his right arm across his body with all his strength.

A sense of confusion leaped into Ortega's eyes, then fell away with his sagging body as the camera crashed into his right temple. He fell heavily to the ground, his body turning so his face was against the loose dirt of the embankment. Before he could move El Tiburón was on him, straddling his body, his right knee pressed against the right pocket of his suit coat, feeling the hard metal of the pistol. He slipped the garrote around his neck and jammed his left knee into his back just below the shoulder blade. With the first upward pull of the wire he heard a low guttural gasp as the flow of air was cut off. Ortega struggled to reach his pistol, then fought desperately to turn his body, his feet and hands clawing at the ground, kicking up clouds of fine brown dust. He was strong and the adrenaline was surging through his body and in that first minute El Tiburón felt as though he were riding some wild animal. He leaned back against the garrote and jerked his hands back away from his body, tightening the wire. Ortega clawed at the wire with both hands, but it had already cut through the flesh and the tips of his fingers were now red with his own blood.

"That woman from Barranquitas was a whore," El Tiburón gasped. "She fucked everything, even large dogs."

He pulled again, leaning his head back, placing all his weight against the wire. He heard a gurgling sound and he looked and saw a bubble of saliva, turned pink with blood, rising from Ortega's mouth.

Keep the pressure on, he remembered. *A full two minutes. It takes a long time to strangle a man.* He leaned back against the wire even farther, feeling the sweat roll down his face and along his body. Ortega's body was moving more slowly now, in jerky, fading spasms.

"Were you one of them, Ortega? Were you one of the scum who killed my father, you filthy pig with yellow teeth?" His voice was a hoarse whisper, drained of energy, and he pulled against the wire again, grunting with the effort.

Ortega's body shuddered beneath him and his arms and legs jumped with the nervous spasms of death. Still El Tiburón pulled against the wire, counting off seconds in his mind, remembering his training, the time needed to kill with the garrote, the weapon of execution invented by the Spaniards to produce a prolonged, agonizing death.

The wire slackened in his hands and he bent forward, exhausted. Beads of sweat dropped from his face on to the back of Ortega's head. He pulled himself off the body and fell back against the embankment, fighting to regain his breath. He had to move, hide the body before a car came along the road, but he was too exhausted. He looked down at the dead police officer, watching his back for any sign of breath still in the body. A small pool of blood was inching its way outward beneath Ortega's neck. He pulled the wire free. It was red at the center and there seemed to be tiny bits of flesh mixed with the blood. He felt suddenly nauseous and he pulled himself up and wiped the wire on the back of the dead man's suit coat.

In the distance, back along the road toward Lares, he heard the grumbling sound of a failing automobile engine. He pulled at Ortega's body, almost hysterically, nearly jerking it off the ground. The police officer had parked his car so close to his own that the bumpers were nearly touching. It provided a perfect screen now, and he slid Ortega's body parallel to the car and crouched beside it, waiting. The sound of the engine grew louder; it had the low wheezing rumble of an engine near the end of its life and he knew it would not be a police car. He reached out and withdrew the pistol from Ortega's pocket. It was a small flat Barreta, a nine milimeter, deadly at close range, but useless otherwise. He would not use it, he told himself. Not unless he had no choice.

A battered pickup truck appeared in the distance. Its front fender was rotted away and it flapped comically as the truck struggled along the road. He crouched low, praying that it would not stop. If it was someone from the area, they would know the cemetery was there and they would not be curious about two automobiles parked at the roadside. He listened as the truck moved past, pressing himself against the side of the car, one knee on top of the dead officer. The sound of the engine began to diminish and as he peered out along the side of the car, he could see two children standing in the back of the truck.

He pulled Ortega's clothing open and searched the pockets for keys to the police car, then hurriedly opened the trunk. He rolled the dead officer over and felt the nausea rise in his throat again as he looked into the lifeless bulging eyes. His tongue was swollen and protruded from his mouth, obscuring the large yellow teeth. He turned the body over again and dragged it face down to the rear of the police car. The body was heavy, and he struggled with it, finally getting the upper half over the edge of the trunk. The inside of the trouser legs were wet with urine and the smell of excrement filled his nostrils as he grabbed the ankles and heaved the body into the trunk. The true smell of death, he thought. Not the beautiful scenes in Renaissance paintings, with angels and family hovering about the deathbed. Just the smell of shit and urine as the body gives up its final offering to a spiteful world.

He drove the police car west away from Lares, looking for a path that would lead into the forest. One hundred fifty yards down the road, where it began to curve south again, he turned into a narrow dirt path, gunning the engine, forcing the car through the heavy brush that scratched angrily against the sides. The car jolted through the underbrush and he could hear the body bouncing in the trunk as if resisting its final journey. Fifty yards in the path ended against a cluster of trees and he killed the engine and sat quietly, listening to his own heart pound against his chest.

He would not go to the village now; he would not visit the house of the old zango woman to buy the amulet he had wanted to bring back to Juan. He must leave the island quickly. It was doubtful the body would be discovered for a long time and he would obliterate all signs of the tire tracks leading back into the forest. By the time someone chanced upon the car, the trunk would have become an oven and little would be left of Ortega. There was time, he *could* remain but he would not. Too much had been risked already.

He climbed out of the car and threw the keys into the brush. His legs felt weak and he could feel them tremble as he walked. He took Ortega's gun from his waistband and threw it far into the forest, then stumbled forward along the path. Halfway to the road he dropped to his knees and his stomach convulsed uncontrollably. He was sick for several minutes.

8

Two weeks had passed since his meeting with Baldwin and throughout those tense, tedious days of concern he had found no way to save himself from the inevitable. He noticed his hands were trembling and he folded them in front of him so it would not be noticeable. Sitting in Mark Slocum's office now, waiting for him to complete a telephone conversation, Henry thought of the advice his own attorney had given him. *They're offering you a deal, Pat. And it may be the only way for you to get out of this with your reputation intact.* He tried to push the words from his mind, as he had since they were first spoken, but they kept returning. He watched Slocum as he dispassionately clicked off instructions to an unseen subordinate. The assistant attorney general's suit coat was draped over the back of a chair and the cuffs of his shirt were rolled up to the elbow. He was small and wiry, with unruly hair that stuck out at absurd angles, and his hard eyes seemed to dart about, making him look like a small gamecock, always ready for battle. Henry knew nothing of his personal background, but his reputation as a prosecutor, even though he was only thirty-five, was considered awesome by Justice Department standards. Probably a street kid who snuck in the back door of Harvard Law, Henry thought. In any event the prognosis of dealing with him would not be good, even though he had shown himself to be fair, perhaps even because he had.

Slocum put the receiver down and began to scratch at his head furiously, making his hair even wilder.

"I'm sorry," he said. "The distractions around here are constant. We have people who are afraid to think without getting authorization." He brought his teeth together as if biting something. It was the closest he came to smiling, Henry had noticed. "Well, you said you wanted to talk. I assume it's about your problems at the Bureau," Slocum said.

"I guess you know that I spoke with the attorney general a few weeks ago," Henry said.

Slocum only nodded and waited for Henry to continue.

"At that time he spoke about the need for me to cooperate in some way. That's where I'm stumbling right now." Henry unfolded his hands, then clasped them together again, realizing they were still shaking. "I'm just not sure to what degree I can. Without any records to rely upon, I mean. It's just damned difficult."

Slocum looked down at his desk and scratched at his head again. "He told you not to worry about the records, didn't he?" He looked up at Henry; his eyes were hard, but he did not seem unfriendly. It was as though he wanted to be helpful, but was being frustrated in the effort.

"But that doesn't leave me very much room, Mark." Henry could feel himself sweating beneath his three-piece blue suit. He was angry with himself now for even asking for the meeting. He was still looking for a way out, he realized, and there was none. He was fifty-three years old and he did not want to be thrown out in disgrace and Grant Desverne's words had plagued him for the past two weeks. *Nobody's hiring retired burglars these days.*

"Look. You've got a lot of room for movement. We all do." Slocum's voice was soft, reassuring. "Just tell us about the more recent things. Excesses you learned about after the fact. Things you weren't able to control at the time. Also give me anything from conversations at your own level. Indications that other supervisors had experienced the same thing, wittingly or unwittingly. We know you guys talk to each other."

"Not about things that can put our necks in a noose," Henry said.

"Just give me what you *can* in that area. But I want specifics about things in New York. The more recent things that you remember clearly. That's the least I can get away with, and I'm not bullshitting you."

Henry's face contorted and he could feel the bile rising from his stomach. He leaned forward in his chair, clenching his hands together until the knuckles were white.

"You're talking about pointing fingers at the men who worked under me. About times they went ahead because they didn't want to pass up an opportunity. What happens to *them* if I do that?"

Slocum looked down at his desk again as though he wanted to avoid Henry's eyes. Then he drew himself up and stared across the desk at him.

"That will be up to the Bureau. We won't recommend prosecution, but we'll leave discipline up to them."

"Jesus Christ, Mark. The careers of these men are already fucked up. Now you're talking about the possibility they could even be fired." Grant Desverne flashed though his mind. He was seated across the table from him, grinning like a young kid. His eyes became sorrowful as he listened but he tried to hide it, tried to keep the conversation light. *"Your assistant. And a very beautiful one, I might add. She almost fell off her chair when I asked for you."* There was laughter in the Italian restaurant. Then the faces of so many others, working together in New York, working hours beyond endurance, and later drinking together trying to forget how tired they were.

"I didn't say it was nice." Slocum's words seemed to come from a distance. "Look. Let's lay the cards out. I'd like to do it the way you want to. Point the finger at Edmund Norris and the others before him who did the same thing. Lay it all out, from top to bottom. But it's not going to be that way. The decision has already been made, and there's not a damned thing I can do about it."

"You know what you're asking me to do, *don't you?*"

"Don't talk about it. Don't even think about it. As far as this whole thing is concerned, we're all standing at the edge of a pond right now. And the pond is full of shit. Just think about it in those terms. That's the best advice I can give you. That, and to get the hell away from the pond."

Slocum sat watching. He knew it was over now, one way or the other. His instincts told him which way and the knowledge left him with a sick feeling for having been a part of it.

"It's not what I thought Baldwin was talking about," Henry said. "Maybe I just didn't want to think that was what he meant." There was anger in Henry's eyes now, not at Slocum or Baldwin or anyone in particular. "So I do that and then I walk," Henry said. "That's it, that's the deal."

"Not completely," Slocum said. "We will recommend an official reprimand. After the fact. After you've already retired. Failure to adequately supervise, or some meaningless bullshit like that. But that will be it."

Henry stood. "I can't give you an answer now. I just can't."

"There's no need to," Slocum said. "Take your time. There's two weeks still. Take all of it." He watched Henry leave his office, and when the door closed behind him, Slocum shook his head. "I should have listened to my mother and gone to medical school," he said.

Out on the street Henry moved like a well-dressed somnambulist, a junkie in a three-piece suit walking on the nod. When he reached his car he slid behind the wheel and sat there staring through the dirt-spattered windshield. The air was crisp already with the coming of winter. There was no place as cold as Washington in the winter. It was a wet, chilling cold and the Potomac became gray and ominous and seemed deeper than the imagination could grasp. In Vermont, there would be snow already and everything would be white and clean and the streets would be filled with the laughter of kids carrying skis. There would be brandy and warm fires. He could sit and talk to his wife before one of those fires, and they could laugh about her inability to handle skis. He and Mary had been happy in Vermont. It was the last time he remembered being happy. Poor dead Mary. She didn't have to worry about skiing anymore. His eyes filled with tears and he clenched his jaw, fighting them off. He sat quietly feeling his chest rise and fall beneath his clothing. She could have been a good skier if they had stayed there, he thought. Her car would never have struck that tree on that lonely Virginia road. He ran his hand along his cheek. It felt like the skin of a dead man made ready for burial. I could probably still ski, he told himself. It's been a long time, but I could probably still do it. It was like riding a bike, or firing a gun, or stabbing someone in the back. Once you learn how, you never forget. He clenched his teeth again. Outside the light was beginning to fade. Perhaps later it would snow. It would be like Vermont then. All that would be missing would be the purity. Perhaps he could walk in the snow. Perhaps he could even meet someone and they would sit and talk before a fire. Mary: close and warm and together and safe again. Perhaps they would joke about skiing and outside there would be children carrying skis over their shoulders and laughing. Perhaps he could take his revolver and put a bullet into his brain and be happy again.

9

The bulletin board was covered with enlarged photographs, broken down into sets depicting the various days Norris had been observed walking along the dunes. In each set two Secret Service agents were shown with him and in the close-up shots they appeared dull and sleepy. At the bottom right-hand corner of the bulletin board was the list of locations where explosives would soon be planted. The list was headed by the homes of New York's two senators, followed by the mayor's Gracie Mansion residence, FBI headquarters on East 69th St., the Mobil Oil and Chrysler buildings across the street from each other on East 42nd St., the General Motors Building on East 59th St., the American Bank Note Company on Lafayette St., the residence of New York's police commissioner, and St. Patrick's Cathedral.

El Tiburón studied the list, wishing he had time to risk ten more bombs. Too many who deserved recognition had been left out. He had considered a bomb at one of the offices of Puerto Rico's puppet government, but had decided against it. If a Puerto Rican national was killed it might divide the community, as the Fraunces Tavern bombing had years before. And this was to be an act of liberation, not vengeance. Death was not required in the placement of the bombs. Destruction, terror, and confusion were the goals.

He looked across the room where the devices were stacked neatly on a long table, each wrapped like a parcel, each needing only a simple adjustment to set the timing mechanism.

Earlier that morning, Wally Rogers had telephoned. There were no problems in Florida, no break in Norris's routine. They would all leave for Palm Beach the following morning, the devices distributed, the diversion set. He looked at the others as they sat quietly in the studio loft awaiting his instructions. There was an air of expectancy, of nervousness, and that was as it should be. This was not some terrorist prank, some pinprick on the leg of a powerful giant. It was a full assault on the power and dignity of the United States and it would be treated as such.

He smiled at the others; he could feel his heart beating and he was pleased with his own degree of tension.

"You've all studied the photographs and the maps," he said. "You all know the timing patterns we've established. Once we get to Florida, we'll have two days to familiarize everyone with the locations and then one day more to review everything. Wally has rented the boat and purchased a used van under a false name. The weapons are already in Florida, along with a box of grenades. The explosives will be planted here while we're traveling south. This is the last chance for anyone who does not want to be with us. I mean that. We cannot afford any last-minute problems, so, as they say, speak now or forever hold your peace."

"I got my piece," Juan said, reaching out and squeezing Norma's arm.

The others laughed nervously, but not too nervously, El Tiburón thought.

"Okay. Any questions?"

Richard raised his hand, forcing El Tiburón to smile.

"This isn't school, Richard," he said. "You don't have to raise your hand."

The others laughed again, but Richard ignored them. His eyes were intent, almost wild, as they peered out through his steel-rimmed glasses.

"I'm concerned about the ten minutes by boat to where the van will be waiting," he said. "That's a long time to be exposed, isn't it?"

El Tiburón nodded. "Yes, it is. That's why we'll use silencers to take out the Secret Service personnel if they're with him. Everything will have to be very fast, very military. But you've all been trained for that. You're not amateurs and neither are they." He smiled again. "But we're better," he added.

"You bet your ass we are," Juan said. "Man, what are you worried about? Shit. Five minutes, ten minutes. They never gonna know what hit them. What's the matter, man. You want to go home to your mama?"

"I'm not worried," Richard said. "The operation's important to me. I just want to be sure. I want to be sure we get him, that's all. I want that sweaty, lying, hypocritical bully right here." He extended one hand, palm up, like a claw.

"We're all nervous," El Tiburón said. "We should be nervous. It will keep us alert, make us ready for anything that happens."

"The cabin in the Everglades. How secure is it?" Norma asked.

"It's good. It's about a quarter of a mile from the southern tip of Lake Okeechobee, right in the glades, and it's isolated. The nearest town is Belle Glades and there's a lot of sugar cane planted near there, so you have a lot of Puerto Rican and Jamaican migrant workers, old-fashioned cane cutters. There'll be no problem about Juan or me moving around unnoticed. And if the rest of you dress like shit-kickers, you'll fit right in."

Carol leaned forward and began rocking her body back and forth. She seemed the calmest of all, the most eager to begin. "This town," she said. "What kind of pigs do they have there?"

"County sheriff's deputies and, from what Wally tells me, they're not much to worry about. Besides, he knows most of them. He grew up in the area and spent half his life fishing in those swamps." El Tiburón watched her expression, the hard look in her eyes. He would make love to her tonight, he decided. Purge himself before it all began.

"But what about us," she continued. "Those pigs may know Wally, but won't they be curious about the rest of us showing up there?"

"Every cracker in the area has a van or a camper of some sort," El Tiburón said. "And sooner or later they all end up fishing in the lake or those godforsaken swamps."

"Yeah, man. I wanted to ask you about that," Juan said. "They got those fucking alligators down there?"

El Tiburón nodded and tried to keep from laughing. He had pictured Juan's street-smart toughness when he had visited the cabin and he had wondered what his reaction would be when he saw the preternatural creatures that infested the area.

"Don't worry, I'll protect you, baby." Norma drew out the last word, affecting a Puerto Rican accent.

Juan grinned at her. "That's good, honey. Cause I don't want nobody to eat me except you."

Their laughter was interrupted by a knock at the door, and Juan jumped up and moved to the long table where his Stechkin machine pistol lay next to the explosives, his favorite toy that he cleaned religiously each day, keeping it ready to spit out one hundred and five rounds every ten seconds.

El Tiburón opened the door, then stood aside to allow three Puerto Rican teenagers, two boys and a girl, to enter. They were the first of the messengers, the first of the young children who would deliver the wrapped parcel-bombs to the well-placed maintenance people and security guards who would set the detonators and plant them.

He stroked the young girl's hair and asked if they were hungry. One of the boys said he was and Norma led him to the kitchen. He smiled at the other two and pointed to a bowl of fruit on a small side table. The packages would be safe for them to carry; he had no fear they would be hurt. They would not be set for detonation until they reached their final destinations. They were his children of destruction, his children's crusade, and he would take no chance with their safety. The youth and future of Puerto Rico, fighting for their homeland like the soldiers they would one day be.

"*Viva Puerto Rico libre*," he said to them.

The children called the words back.

~~~~~

It was midnight, and as they lay in bed, Carol pressed against him, rubbing her vagina against his thigh. Her breath came in short gasps and he could feel the heat from it coming in bursts as she ran her tongue against his shoulder. He raised her leg with one hand and slid partially into her, teasing her, allowing her to feel only part of what was yet to come. She strained her body, trying to capture more of him. He placed his hand against her hip, stopping her, then withdrew himself, and reached down, taking his penis in his hand and rubbing it against her.

"Oh, you bastard," she whispered. "I want it now. Now."

She arched her back, forcing her pelvis against him and he bent his head down running his tongue along her breast, circling the nipple slowly. She grabbed his hair, forcing his head hard against her breast, filling his mouth with it.

The window was open a few inches and a cold breeze drifted over them, but it was not enough and they were both perspiring and her body felt slick against him. She twisted violently, forcing him on top of her, trapping his legs from behind with her own.

"Give it to me now," she whispered. "Give it to me and I'll do anything you want."

He raised himself and stared down at her, smiling. Her small breasts rose and sank in rapid expectation and she reached up and pulled him to her, wanting, demanding. There was a high, soft moan as he entered her and her whispers became more rapid as she thrust herself against him, joining his rhythm to her own.

"More, Carlos, more. More, more, more, more, more." Her voice faded off, overtaken by the rapidity of her breath, until with a final, violent thrust she arched her back and cried out in pleasure, holding herself there for as long as she could, then sinking back and moving again, slowly, gently now, her breath shuddering with the joy of the final movements.

They remained next to each other, exhausted, the sweat drying slowly on their bodies. She turned to him and pressed her face into his chest, then pulled back and looked at him, her eyes gleaming.

"Do you know what I'm going to do when we get him to that cabin?" she said.

"What?" There was a slight smile on El Tiburón's lips as he watched her eyes gleam with pleasure.

She giggled. "I'm going to take off all his clothes and tie his wrinkled old body to a bed. Then I'm going to walk around the room naked and make that sexless old pig look at me. And I'll talk to him, tell him things I like to do. Nice things. Things he probably never did himself. Things he jerked off thinking about as a kid, but could never get anybody to do with him. And when his old prick jumps to attention I'll spit on it. I'll spit in his face. And then I'll do all the things I talked about right there in front of him with somebody else."

Her laughter filled the bedroom and the sound of it sent a chill through his body. He slipped out of bed and walked to the window and closed it. She was still giggling to herself when he returned to the bed. He believed what she said and the fact that he did disturbed him. There was a cruelty in her laugh that he did not feel toward any man, not even Norris, not even the man he had killed. Ortega's face flashed into his mind, the massive yellow teeth grinning out at him. The too-small hat sitting atop his round face. And then the eyes and the bulging swollen tongue, the smell of urine and excrement.

"Let's not talk about it now," he said. "We have to sleep, we have to prepare ourselves."

She slid against him again, pressing her body against his. Her body felt cold now and the muscles in her back seemed firm and hard, more like a man than a woman. He drew a deep breath and closed his eyes, but the yellow teeth returned. They were soldiers, not animals, he told himself. He would not allow the situation to degenerate. He would control it.

10

He sat in the bird room, his body sunk deep in the soft leather chair that was his favorite place, his perch as he called it. His foot was propped on the sofa table, easing an earlier attack of pain, and the elevated foot tapped at the air, keeping time with the music that flowed from two wall speakers. How appropriate. Arthur Fiedler playing Sousa. More than appropriate. Prophetic. His wife and his daughter and his son-in-law were busy discussing plans for the Thanksgiving feast. And feast it would be. He would wait to tell them at dinner, in a toast, perhaps. He could tell Dalton this evening. He would appreciate the importance of it more than the others. No, he would wait even for him. He would savor it alone until tomorrow.

He looked at the telephone beside him, still feeling the pleasure that had surged through him minutes before when Hall had called. The Falcon had finally emerged. In two days, actually less than forty-eight hours from now, Hall would begin his low-key questioning of administration policies using the exact format that he, Edmund Norris, had prepared. He smiled to himself. He had been smiling continuously since the telephone call. He had agreed to make the statement. *The* statement. Coming from a member of the military of Hall's standing, it would have maximum impact on the media and should catch the White House with its drawers down. He chuckled at the thought.

Hall had called to insure that his support could still be counted on. Counted on indeed, he thought. He had *prayed* for the decision. *Prayed* for it. It would be the beginning of everything, his only hope for it. He became serious for a moment. There would be calls to make after the announcement to firm up financial support. There had been promises from many, from the Shah, from Somoza, both of whom were in search of promises themselves. And the amounts would be substantial, but they would have to be funneled through others. Then all those bastards who caused so much humiliation would pay. Uncommon joy filled his face. He could not think of those things now. Just savor it all for the moment. Savor it. The work would come later.

He looked down at the mounted peregrine falcon that again threatened to spring from the sofa table. Even this stuffed dead hulk of a bird, this poor imitation, pleased him. Standing next to it was his latest acquisition, the coveted king rail, the secretive marsh bird he had only once been able to see in the wild. He reached forward, his fingers barely able to reach its long, slightly curved bill. The mottled feathers along its back glistened in the light of a single table lamp, its small glass eyes fixed in a downward gaze, as if waiting for a small fish to appear on the tabletop. It was the same size as the falcon, although it seemed heavier, more substantial, he noticed. *Rallus elegans.* Oh, how you frustrate us when we try to find you. Hiding in the interior marshes, letting us hear your deep grunting, but refusing to reveal yourself. He strained forward and stroked the rust-colored breast, then sat back and considered both birds together. Juxtaposed, they seemed to present a pleasing contrast. The bold falcon and the clever elusive rail, even the contrasting colors of slate gray next to the mottled brown seemed pleasing to the eye. His collection was nearly complete now, the mounted species, the color prints, the books, many of them rare. It would be a legacy of an intellectual pursuit begun late in life, and he was certain there would be many who would marvel at it, just as they had over Thomas Jefferson's cataloging of ninety-three Virginia birds in his *Notes on the State of Virginia.*

There was a light knock on the door. He stared at the dark wood, momentarily irritated by the disturbance. But nothing could spoil this evening, and he watched as the door swung away and Dalton entered grinning.

"Hidden away again, eh?" He ambled across the room, his slender body loping like a young animal, and sat on the leather sofa across from Norris. "You know, this place has an eerie feeling in this dim light," he said.

"Eerie?" Norris said. "I never thought of it that way. But I suppose it could. I guess I'm just used to it."

Dalton craned his neck toward the workbench where the partially dissected wing of the anhinga was still pinned. "What on earth is that?" he said.

"The wing of an anhinga," Norris said. "It's very unusual. I've been studying it. The species has no oil glands to preen its feathers with." He stood and walked to the workbench and picked up a leather bound copy of *The Audubon Field Guide* and began flipping through the color photographs in the front of the text. Dalton had come up beside him and Norris jabbed a finger at a photograph depicting an anhinga perched on a branch near a body of water, its wings extended, drying in the sun.

"See here. Unlike most birds they aren't able to secrete any oils so their feathers become saturated when they go into the water and they perch this way to dry them. It's almost as though God forgot that he made them as marsh birds."

He began turning the pages again, stopping when he reached another photograph of an anhinga, this one submerged in the water so only its head and long neck were above the surface.

"They can't float for the same reason, and they look like this in the water. The Indians in the Everglades call them the snakebird, because they look more like a snake when they're swimming."

"It's amazing the way you've taken to this study of birds," Dalton said. "You've really become quite an authority."

"You learn from the birds," Norris said. "If I had begun my studies earlier, I never would have had the problems I've been forced to live with." He raised one finger, shaking it. "Always watch the birds," he said. "Take the anhinga here. The alligators in the swamps often float near him, trying to convince the anhinga that their bodies are logs that the bird can rest on. But the anhinga is too smart. He's patient. He watches and he waits and sooner or later the alligator moves. Birds have traits to fit any occasion, any problem, any danger. They know how to survive. When a climate is unsuited to them they go somewhere else. Even man hasn't had the sense to do that. He tries to change his surroundings, adapt them to his own desires. The bird moves to new surroundings and makes them his own. He adapts rather than try to change the unchangeable. He outwits the things that threaten him."

"But birds are killed by predators," Dalton said.

Norris shrugged. "Even birds make mistakes," he said. He straightened his shoulders. "But the eagle usually dies of old age."

"That's the largest bird, isn't it?"

"No, the largest bird is the Andean condor. It's four feet long and has a wing span of eleven feet." His mind clicked. *Vultur gryphus.* "The smallest is the bee hummingbird of Cuba. It's less than an inch long." Click again. *Messisuga helenae.* "Did you know that Darwin studied birds extensively before writing his *Origin of Species.* Thoreau and Emerson used birds to build their philosophy of transcendentalism. Birds led to the discovery of the Hawaiian Islands, and Columbus followed pelicans to the New World. Jefferson, Benjamin Franklin, Aristotle, they all studied birds."

He was almost rambling, and Dalton reached out and touched his arm.

"I'm sorry. When I start on the subject I can't stop." He laughed uncomfortably. "But remember what I said. Always watch the birds. I wish I had begun studying them many, many years ago."

〰〰〰

Ten miles to the south, on the beach close to the water, they sat in a circle talking quietly, the sounds of their voices only a whisper against the noise of the surf. Above them and extending out over the sea, the sky looked like an ocean of small lights. When those lights disappeared they would begin, and life would not be the same for them again. It was something El Tiburón had explained carefully. It was something they all knew and understood and believed. To a person, they all wished that tomorrow would not come.

〰〰〰

In his small dark airless apartment in Georgetown, John Walter Henry slept quietly. Mary Roche's head rested against his shoulder, her sandy blond hair partially obscuring her face, her arm across his chest, holding him. The only light in the room came from the faint glow of a street lamp outside, and on the table next to the bed sat two glasses and a half-empty bottle of Scotch. His breathing was quiet and relaxed and there were children walking through the snow carrying skis on their shoulders and at that moment he could hear their laughter.

Part
Two

11

They walked slowly toward the dunes, their features barely distinguishable in the dim light of morning. Ahead, a slight mist drifted over the water and moved slowly toward the shore, leaving the grass of the rear lawn wet and slippery beneath their feet. There was a strong wind off the sea now, stronger than normal for the time of year, and beyond the dunes Norris could hear the surf striking the shore with unusual force, waging its endless battle with the beach, hissing and crashing against the sand and the sand responding, sending its army of stones and shells rushing after the water as it retreated. It was a minor war, he had often thought, each fighting to overcome the other and neither ever winning. The proximity of the ocean had always pleased him, but somehow during the *special* holidays—Christmas, Easter, and today, Thanksgiving—it had also seemed out of place; the palm trees, branches moving frantically in the wind as they did now, even more so. The two agents walked slightly behind him; they were still talking about the bombings in New York and that too seemed out of place. But it was so like them, like all policemen really. They always magnified these things and the people involved, gave them greater significance than they deserved, and in doing so, increased the importance of their own work. He smiled to himself. The stocky, bull-like agent he knew only as Frank was using the word *scumbag* over and over again. Cop talk. Always crude and almost never precise. He did not know the other agent's name. He was new to the complement that guarded him, a tall, angular young man with an out-of-date crewcut that seemed jarring on someone so young. Normally he worked in the guardhouse at the front gate. An incredibly boring job, Norris was sure. Checking cre-

111

dentials and recording the comings and goings of all visitors, a tin soldier in a business suit. But they were decent men, simply frustrated by their work. Like most men, they had entered a job expecting romance and excitement, and like most, they had found there was none, only tedious daily effort that was seldom appreciated. And to some degree that lack of appreciation was justified. Everyone knew the Service was made up of men who had not been accepted by the FBI and CIA. You simply did not have to be too bright to run alongside a car, and even less so to throw your body in front of a gun. But still it was necessary.

And you certainly don't make things easier for them, he thought. They're concerned about careers and pensions, and you like to take walks alone. He smiled to himself again, recalling the infamous story that every agent still whispered about. The romantic widow of one of his predecessors. The squeals that had come from her bedroom one night. The agent guarding her who had rushed in with his gun drawn, only to discover the sounds had been squeals of joy. The agent, as the story went, quietly holstered the gun and returned to his room and began packing his bag. Before he had finished, the call had come from Washington, reassigning him to a post on the other side of the country.

He stopped at the edge of the dunes and laughed out loud.

"Did you say something, sir?"

Frank had moved up beside him, and Norris looked at him and shook his head.

"No, nothing."

He stood there watching, unable to move as Frank's body flew backward, bouncing limply on the grass like some discarded doll. His forehead had suddenly exploded. It was as though a bomb had gone off behind his eyes. He looked toward the younger agent for some explanation, but he, too, had fallen, his face a mass of red, his one remaining eye staring up through the hideous color.

His body jerked backward and he could feel himself falling, his feet above him, his body sliding back along the dunes. His heart pounded in his ears and he could feel hands pulling him roughly, dragging him down along the sand. A hand clasped his throat cutting off all air, and then the face of a madman stared down at him, the wild brown eyes flashing unexplained hatred. There was a strange, square gun, a machine pistol, he thought, and it was pointed at his face.

"One move, pussy, and I kill your old ass right here."

The hand released his throat and he gasped for the air returning to his lungs. Another unseen hand jerked him to his knees.

"Now walk." The voice was a growl, animal anger.

There were others now, surrounding him. Two other men and a woman. A boat sped toward the shore, a small cabin cruiser like the ones that would soon gather beyond the reef to fish. Coming to help. The thought flashed through his mind like a prayer and then evaporated as quickly as it had come. He was pulled into the water, stumbling, falling; then, jerked to his feet again, he felt his bladder give way. They were on each side of him now; the boat slowed, turned sideways, and began to roll with the surf, its engines reversed, growling. They were pulling and pushing him, driving him through the water until the waves slapped against his waist, then lifting him, pushing him up as the man in the boat took his arm and began pulling him roughly over the side. He heard himself groan as he struck the deck, pain shooting up his side, his breath squeezed out again, then large hands pulling him up. Hard eyes staring into his face, strangely contrasted by a soft southern voice.

"You just get your ass down them stairs or I'll shoot it off. Right now." Stumbling, then half crawling. Three steps down into the small, cramped cabin where two benchlike beds ran along each side until they met in a V at the bow. The boat surged forward and again he nearly fell. The boat seemed to stagger, then shudder as a large wave hit the bow. From behind, a woman, the one from the beach, came down the stairs, a rifle cradled in the crook of her arm, her small eyes piercing, like a bird of prey.

"Sit." She seemed to spit the word out. More hatred. The rifle leveled at him now. Needlessly. She stood at the foot of the stairs, her body rocking with the motion of the boat. The boat began to move more rapidly, forcing her to sit, the waves bouncing against the hull with greater regularity, giving off the hollow thundering slap of water against fiberglass.

"You are a prisoner of war of *Ejército Mundo de Revolución.*" The woman smiled as she spoke and he tried to understand what she had said.

They are all insane. Slowly, with that thought, reason returned. His heart pounded in his ears and for the first time he realized he was trembling. It was the wet clothing, he told himself, not the fear he felt pushing through his body. He began to speak, to question the woman, then stopped himself, fearful his voice might tremble as well.

If they were going to kill you, you'd be dead already. Kidnapping. The word assaulted him like a blow to the stomach. It was impossible, but it was happening. It was all a vague, hideous blur. Everything had either happened too quickly or too slowly. He could remember falling down a long flight of stairs as a child, of reaching out, trying to stop himself, but unable to, just continuing to fall. It was the same now. Frank's forehead exploding, his body floating back like some ridiculous rag doll. He remembered now. He had felt wetness on his face. Had it been the blood from that explosion? He reached up and touched his face, feeling for something sticky, then he looked at his hand. Nothing. Of course not. If there had been blood the sea would have washed it away when they dragged you to the boat. The urine. You urinated in your pants. Was that washed away too? A violent shiver took hold of his body and he had to pull his shoulders up against his neck to control it. The woman seated across from him smirked. He wanted to ask her for a blanket, but decided he would not.

A young man came down the stairs. Tall, blond, his eyes intent. He stood over the woman.

"Is he all right?"

"He couldn't be better."

Their voices sounded distant to him.

The woman smiled up at the man. Her teeth were slightly uneven, Norris noticed, her nose slightly curved. She was small, but her heavy breasts made her seem larger than she was.

"How does it look?" she asked.

"So far, so good."

The man extended one hand. There was a walkie-talkie in it. From one of the agents Norris assumed.

"It's been quiet on this. Not a sound out of them."

"You think it got wet and went on the blink?"

"I made sure it didn't."

The woman's smile broadened. "I wish we could send them a little message. I hate to think of them sitting around worrying." She let out a low cackle.

The young man smiled, weakly, Norris thought. He seemed nervous. He turned abruptly and climbed back to the deck. Norris arched his shoulder to control another wave of trembling. The boat continued to slap the water. Just sit and be quiet. And for chrissake try to stop shaking. The woman continued to stare at him, her face filled with a mixture of contempt and pleasure. He looked into the barrel of the rifle. The bore opening seemed to grow larger as he stared at it. He had seen this kind of contempt, this hatred before. It was not new. But those people never had guns.

It had been the same earlier on the beach, and even now El Tiburón could still feel the churning in his stomach. He took a deep breath. It had begun. Finally. And so far it had worked. Out beyond the diminishing wake of the boat he could no longer see the bodies of the two Secret Service agents they had dragged down the dunes out of sight of the house. He looked at the walkie-talkie again, then adjusted the squelch to assure himself it was working. It seemed fine, and still there was nothing. There had been no activity as they fled; no other agents had appeared. It had gone smoothly, ridiculously so, and now it would be a success even if everything else fell apart. Even if they were caught they could kill Norris, and that in itself would make it a victory.

He tilted his head back and let the spray off the water soothe his face; he flexed the muscles in his legs. They were still stiff from the hours of waiting. Two and a half hours. It had seemed like days. Hugging the ground, waiting, watching for the muzzle flash from Wally's rifle, knowing it would be small because of the silencer. Waiting to move quickly, hoping he would not miss and force a noisy bloodbath. Just lying there tense and tight, unable to hear your own breath because of the sound of the surf, but still hearing your heart pound in your temples. He breathed deeply again, filling his lungs with the sea air.

He looked at Wally's back as he guided the small, speedy Crisscraft toward the Palm Beach inlet where they would turn back down the intercoastal and head for the small dock where Carol would be waiting with the van. Wally seemed completely at ease, he thought, totally in control. Incredible shooting. Even with the fine Russian sniper scope he had used, two head shots from the moving deck of a small boat was more than he had expected. The Tao Pou who had trained them in Cuba had been right. There were few in the world who were better with a rifle. He glanced about the small deck. Juan sat grinning at him, his eyes still blazing, and El Tiburón remembered how, for a moment on the beach, he had feared Juan would kill Norris and it had frightened him and he had almost grabbed him from behind.

Richard McGovern moved next to him at the stern of the boat. The wind was whipping his Afro-styled hair back, and the spray from the water clung to his wispy beard and spotted the lenses of his steel-rimmed glasses, making him look even wilder and more unkempt than usual.

"Is there anything on the radio yet?" Richard's eyes seemed electric, even through the spotted glasses.

"Nothing. It's like they were all asleep back there."

Richard grabbed his wrist. "Man, we did it. And it was easy. I can't believe how easy it was. Wait until those fools in FALN hear about this." He leaned his head back and let out a whooping cry. Juan immediately let out a second. All of them, even Norma, seemed totally unconcerned, and yet El Tiburón could still feel the churning in his own stomach, the slight tightness in his chest. He adjusted the walkie-talkie again and held it up to his ear. Still nothing. Richard was right. It was all just too easy. That was what was wrong, what was bothering him.

The boat sped down the intercoastal, ignoring the lower speeds demanded on the inner waterway, staying well into the channel, away from the hidden sandbars, slowing only when they moved under the Flagler Memorial Bridge and again under Royal Park Bridge and then just to avoid the chance that the bridge tender on either might notify the Coast Guard of a speeding boat. Beyond the Royal Park Bridge, in the distance, he could just make out the small dock where the black van was parked. Carol would be sitting on the dock fishing, or at least pretending to.

El Tiburón moved up next to Wally and focused his field glasses on the dock. She was there and she was alone. He scanned the area. There were two small transient hotels across from the dock, used mostly by elderly guests. There was no activity; not even a car moving along the palm-lined macadam of South Olive Avenue. He continued to scan the area, looking for any sign of a trap, any indication that something had gone wrong. As they drew closer he could make out the features of Carol's face, watching them eagerly as they approached. There was no fear, no concern, only anticipation, and as the boat moved to the dock she dropped the fishing rod into the water and jumped to her feet.

The dock was ten feet above the water and it obscured the boat from the roadway above. El Tiburón climbed the ladder that led down to the water while the others waited below, the engines of the boat still running in case escape proved necessary. Carol moved quickly to his side as he stepped up onto the dock.

"Did it work?" Her face seemed to be holding back the pleasure she was waiting to release.

He smiled and nodded. "He's below."

She glanced about the deck of the boat. "Where's Norma?" There was a sudden look of fear on her face.

"She's below with him." He smiled at her again. "There were no problems. Is everything all right on this end?"

She reached out for him. "Everything is beautiful."

He pushed her gently away, then smiled again. "Let's move it. Open the back of the van."

He turned and waved the others up. Wally killed the engines and began stuffing the weapons in a large canvas bag while Richard went below to help Norma with Norris. They came up the ladder quickly. Even Norris seemed to move spryly, with Wally behind, the palm of one immense hand planted firmly against his buttocks, pushing him. Within seconds they were in the van, Wally at the wheel, El Tiburón next to him, the others crowded in the back behind a row of empty cardboard boxes that kept them out of the view of any oncoming traffic.

The van turned west on Route 98 and began the forty-five minute drive through the flat marshy terrain that led to Belle Glade, the small, impoverished farming community that sat at the northeast corner of the Everglades and only minutes more from Wally's isolated cabin.

In the rear of the van Carol sat staring at Norris, his wrists now taped behind his back, more tape spread across his mouth.

"He looks different than I thought he would. Sort of withered and old," she said.

"What'd you expect, baby. He's just a dried-up old pussy." Juan grinned at her, then reached out and pinched Norris's cheek, causing his eyes to squeeze shut.

Carol gave him a hard look. His choice of terminology offended her. Juan was a crude pig and would always be one, she told herself.

"He doesn't look like the big powerful man who ordered the deaths of so many good revolutionaries, does he?" Richard stared at him as he spoke, then leaned across and spat in Norris's face. "Before this is over, I'm personally gonna cut your shriveled old balls off."

El Tiburón leaned across the empty cartons. "Take it easy back there. Let's not get carried away with ourselves. We have a long way to go before we're clear of all this."

"I'm not getting carried away. I've been waiting to do this all my life." Richard glared at Norris, then struck out with his foot, catching him solidly in the thigh, producing a muffled groan from behind the tape on his mouth.

"I said, knock it off." El Tiburón's eyes were filled with rage.

"You do what you're fuckin' well told, Richard." Wally's voice boomed through the van, carrying all the intimidation of his brute size.

"He deserves to get his ass kicked." Norma's voice was soft but firm. "But they're right, Richard. It should wait till later."

"Heah, what's the matter with you people. We just pulled off the biggest fucking snatch this mother-fucking country every saw an' you're all fighting with each other. Now you behave yourself, Richard." Juan smiled across at him. "Later we'll kill his ass."

A tremor caused Norris's shoulders to shake and it brought a gleam to Juan's eyes. He motioned toward Norris with his head.

"Besides," he said. "You're gonna scare his old ass into a heart attack."

Richard laughed, as did the others. All except Carol. She rested her head against the side of the van and crossed her arms. He looked so *old.* Her feelings at that moment puzzled her. It seemed as if it were only months ago that she had demonstrated against this man. It was much longer than that, of course, years now, but it didn't seem so. And a few years before that you wouldn't have cared if he had horns and a tail. She glanced across at Norma. And you were probably out collecting money for Hadassah, she thought. She bit her lip and looked at Norris again. He just didn't seem like the same man, sitting there shaking, all tied and gagged. All about her the others were jabbering like children, talking about the success of the mission, how it would blow the minds of the rival FALN. It was just beginning to fix itself in their minds, in hers. They had done it, they had taken him, this man who had been president and whom they all hated. It was just that it didn't seem like the same man; that's what bothered her. Perhaps it was because she hadn't been there on the beach; hadn't seen him with his bodyguards with his protected house in the background. It annoyed her that she no longer felt the need to humiliate him. It was an indication of weakness that defied her training, marred her worth as a member of the group.

Norris let out a small groan.

"Shut your mouth," Carol snapped.

Her voice was low and bitter and it caused the others to stop talking for a moment and stare at her.

The van moved easily through the flat, dull cityscape of West Palm Beach and out past the international airport. From there, almost immediately, the level of population began to fall away and the land itself seemed to be gradually swallowed by spreading vegetation, almost as though the Everglades beyond was already reaching out, ready to extend itself, to claim anything that someone else did not fight to keep. There were windows on the sides and rear of the van that were mirrored on the outside, but provided a clear view from within. The others had not traveled the road before. Only El Tiburón and Wally had studied the route to the cabin. Now the others seemed transfixed by the change in the terrain, the gradually increasing stretches of nothingness, broken only by small communities of battered shacks that looked as poor as the shell rock roads that led into them; marked, like all areas of the poor, by the occasional Gospel tabernacles that offered hope where hope did not exist.

Minutes passed with little more to see than a canal running parallel to the road, and along it occasional Black children or old women fishing with long cane poles.

"It's like something out of Uncle Remus," Norma said. "Probably the only decent food they can afford."

"Damn good fishin' in those canals," Wally said.

Juan leaned close to the side window. "What's that floating out there in the canal, man?"

Wally glanced in the rear-view mirror and grinned. "'Gator, probably."

"Alligator?" Juan craned his neck trying to keep the retreating object in sight. "I thought those suckers were all way back in the swamps."

"Ain't a piece of water in the whole damn state that ain't got 'gators in it," Wally said.

"How the fuck you people go swimming then?" There was a look of willful disbelief on Juan's face.

"When I was a kid we usually took a dog with us," Wally said. "Otherwise we'd just keep a watch out, but a dog was best. 'Gators seem to prefer dogs to people. Lose a lot of damn dogs down here though." He glanced in the mirror again and watched Juan shaking his head.

"Nice fucking place you people picked for us to hide out in," he said.

"Long as we keep the cabin door shut at night, they won't bother us none. Gotta keep an eye out for snakes, though."

"Don't worry baby. I'll protect you," Norma teased.

"Fuck," Juan said.

Wally glanced at El Tiburón and began to laugh quietly. "We'll be goin' through Loxahatchie in a minute," he said. "You remember that place. Nothin' but a handful of watermelon stands and shacks and two general stores. Don't blink or you'll miss it. After that comes that ol' Lion Country Safari and that's the last bit of civilization we're gonna see until we hit Belle Glade. And like you saw, that ain't much more than a piss-poor town surrounded by sugar cane fields.

El Tiburón turned and looked back at Norris. The former President was sitting in the middle of one of the two benches they had placed along the sides of the van. His shoulders were hunched up and he was staring at the floor and he seemed much smaller now than El Tiburón had thought he would. Sitting there in his wet clothes he did look old and shriveled. El Tiburón turned back to the road. The terrain had changed again, the heavy vegetation suddenly yielding to low, barren swampland that seemed to stretch endlessly, the deep black soil threatening in itself. In the distance, cattle could be seen grazing on the thick-bladed swamp grass, many with large white birds perched on their backs waiting for insects to be flushed into the air.

"Look at those crazy, fucking birds," Juan said.

Norris raised his head brought back to life by Juan's words and looked back over his shoulder out the side window. For a moment he wished he could hear the hoarse croaking of the cattle egrets, or even explain to the others how the birds had only come to the western hemisphere early in this century, crossing from Africa to South America, then spreading north until their range reached southern Canada by the early 1960s. His mind clicked. *Bubulcus ibis.* Orange bill and legs. He felt a stab in his shoulder and turned back to find Juan glaring at him.

"This ain't no sightseeing tour for you, pussy. You keep your eyes on the floor."

"We got trouble." Wally's voice was crisp and professional.

"What is it?" El Tiburón reached inside his loose-fitting shirt where a Graz Burya automatic hung from a shoulder holster.

"Sheriff's car behind us, flashin' his little ol' red light," Wally said. "I was pushin' it a bit, so he probably just wants to give us a ticket, but everybody in back better hit the floor and get ready in case we gotta kill his ass."

Juan pushed Norris to the floor and crouched over him, pressing his machine pistol against the back of his head while the others moved up low behind the empty cardboard boxes and began pulling weapons from the canvas bag. Slowly, Wally eased the van to the shoulder of the road and glanced at El Tiburón, who now held the heavy Russian automatic along the side of his right leg.

"How many?" El Tiburón asked.

"Just one."

Wally watched the patrol car through the side mirror, then turned to El Tiburón and grinned. "No problem," he said, drawing out the first word. "I know this ol' boy. Known him all my life."

He leaned his large head out the window and grinned back at the approaching deputy.

"You such a hard ass now that you givin' tickets to your friends," he shouted.

The deputy pushed the brim of his Western-styled uniform hat back on his head and returned the grin from a deeply suntanned face.

"Well I'll be damned," he said, moving up beside the window. "I ain't seen you in years, Wally. Where the hell you goin'?" The deputy had a protruding Adam's apple that danced along his throat as he spoke.

"Bass fishin' out in the glades." Wally turned to El Tiburón and pointed a finger back at the deputy. "This here's ol' Jim Grady. He used to be a good ol' boy till he decided he was Wyatt Earp." He looked back at the deputy, still grinning. "This here's a buddy of mine from Miami who don't believe the size of the bass we got out in them swamps."

The deputy smiled across at El Tiburón. "Buddy, you're in for some mighty fine fishin'." He looked back into Wally's still smiling face. "Your folks still got a cabin out there?"

"Folks passed away, but I reckon that ol' cabin is still there, unless the glades swallowed 'er up."

"Well, damn, it's been good seein' you again," the deputy said.

"But you take 'er easy on that gas pedal. More'n likely there'll be a radar trap this side of Belle Glade. Those boys out there jus' love to catch folks rushin' out to Lake Okeechobee. It'll cost fifty dollars if they grab ya."

"I'll sure do that. An' thanks for the warnin' Jim. Good seein' you again."

Wally watched the deputy amble back to his patrol car, then glanced across at El Tiburón as he eased the van back on to the road. "Shit," he said.

Juan let out a low laugh from the rear of the van. "Man, you sure can talk like one of those cracker fuckers," he said.

"I am a cracker, you little Puerto Rican bastard. Been one all my life." His face broke into a broad grin. "Sure am glad we didn't have to kill that ol' boy, though. Known him since I was no higher than a monkey's ass."

Norris was still on the floor, his eyes pressed shut. For a moment he had hoped, but it had been hope mixed with the fear of renewed violence, and now all that remained was a deep sinking feeling, a need for surrender, for peace. He did not want to move. He felt as though he could remain there on the filthy floor of the van until all life simply evaporated from his body. Beneath his head he could hear the wheels against the pavement, and the sound heightened the sense of movement, making it seem as though the van was hurtling along at an uncontrollable speed. Rough hands forced him to move. He struggled up and fell back on the bench and looked into the face of the young blond man who stared at him from the front seat. His body ached and he felt a sudden anger begin to rise within him. He would survive this, he decided. He would not allow himself to be robbed of all he had planned.

"Are you all right?"

Norris stared into El Tiburón's face. The voice was gentle, but the eyes were cold and unyielding. He nodded in reply to the question. This was the leader, that much he could tell. And it was this man who could keep him alive. He would have to discover what kind of man he was dealing with, he decided. Exactly what kind.

12

She was already awake when he opened his eyes. Her elbow was propped up, holding her head above him, the sandy blond hair hanging loosely along her face as she looked down at him, smiling.

"What time is it?" Henry asked, his voice thick and raspy.

"It's still early. Why don't you sleep some more." Mary Roche smiled, then leaned down and kissed his forehead. "It's Thanksgiving. We don't have to go in this morning." She spoke with her lips still against him, then raised her head and smiled again.

Beneath the partially removed sheet her firm breasts swayed slightly as she ran one hand softly against his chest. There was a tenderness to her touch, something, he realized now, he had always suspected was part of her, even though there had been no overt indication of it during their daily contacts in his office. It had been something beneath the surface, unspoken but there, and when they had met accidentally in the small bar near headquarters it had suddenly emerged, together with his need of her.

Perhaps it had been the nervousness, the fear he had no longer been able to control, arousing some maternal instinct. But that made no sense. She was twenty-seven. He had learned that last night. Twenty-six years his junior. She had only been three when Mary, his Mary, had been killed.

"Why did you come with me last night?" he asked.

"I've wanted to, almost from the beginning." She toyed with the hair on his chest, avoiding his eyes. "Last night you seemed to need me. Not just need a woman, but need *me*." She looked into his face again, expectantly, awaiting some confirmation.

123

He pulled her down to him and held her and felt her press happily against his body. He kissed her hair, taking in its aroma, remembering.

He had gone to the bar the previous evening simply because it had a fireplace, and he had taken a seat near the fire and had ordered brandy. He had not known she was there, not until she had come up beside him. Later they had sat quietly together, staring into the fire, and then she had simply taken his hand and they had left the bar together.

"If the old man was still alive, he'd probably be taping this conversation and getting ready to fire both of us," he said.

She giggled. "There's a joke at the office that claims there are two agents assigned to guard his grave to make sure nobody rolls back the stone."

She raised her head and looked at him impishly. "Are agents allowed to make love to each other now that he's gone?" she asked.

"Only if they're boys and girls."

"Well." She smiled, drawing out the word. "I think we qualify."

She leaned down and kissed him, moving her leg across his, pressing herself against his thigh.

Her body was warm, firm but soft, almost fragile at that moment. It sent a tremor through him in a way he had not experienced in many years and although he knew it was all foolishness, it was a foolishness he wanted. He had always laughed at men his age, comforting themselves with young women, struggling to be what they would never be again. But he did not care, not now. He wanted her close to him. He wanted to hold Mary in his arms. He wanted it and he needed it.

She kissed him softly, slowly at first, and gradually he could feel the passion building within her, shown through gentle but urging movements of her body, the rapidness of her breathing. She ran her hand slowly down his body, reaching for him, taking the rigidness she had produced gently in her fingers, making everything but her body suddenly flee his mind.

They made love slowly, deliberately, taking turns giving pleasure to each other and receiving it. Then they lay quietly in each other's arms allowing the pleasure to recede in its own time.

He took a cigarette from a pack on the nightstand that he had bought the night before in a moment of depression. He had given up the evil weed almost four years ago, taking up a pipe to satisfy his taste for tobacco. He drew deeply on the cigarette now, feeling a slight guilt, and watched as the smoke billowed, cloudlike, in the shaft of light coming through the window. Mary lay on her side against him, her head in the notch of his shoulder; her breathing was soft and relaxed.

"What made you join the Bureau?" he asked, surprised by the new relaxed tone of his own voice.

She stirred slightly, making a more comfortable nest out of his body.

"I studied accounting at Northwestern," she said. "I always had this passion for working with figures. Then I graduated and found that even being at the top of my class wouldn't get me into a good firm." She sighed sleepily. "I didn't have the right physical equipment, I guess. Anyway, they tell me things are different now, that women are at a premium, but it wasn't the case five years ago."

"But why the Bureau?"

"After a year of frustration I heard about it and thought I'd try for an appointment. And here I am . . . " she paused, then laughed, "working as an agent, but really as a secretary."

He ran his hand through her hair. "Believe me, it's me not you. I don't need either an assistant or a secretary. The problem is that you're assigned to someone who isn't given anything to do, so you end up answering the two or three phone calls I get each day."

"It will change." She stroked his chest.

"No. It won't change, not for me. It will for you after I leave. Then you'll get some interesting work . . . hopefully."

"You're going to leave, then?"

"I won't have much choice in the matter."

She hesitated, as if deciding something. "I've heard talk about it, but I never asked. I didn't feel I had the right to." She waited again. "Did all those things really happen?"

He smiled to himself. "Yes, they all happened." And a lot more, he added to himself. "But they happened under orders. That's what they don't want to admit now."

"I don't know if I could follow orders like that." Her voice was sleepy and there was no criticism in it.

"There was a trust then. A belief in what you were doing and why. I'm afraid that doesn't exist anymore. If you ask an agent to do something even slightly covert now, he wants it in writing. And who the hell can blame him."

She breathed deeply. "That's not really what I mean." She paused. "I guess I really believe in civil rights. That there are some things that shouldn't be tampered with. The things that Norris did really went against my grain. I guess that sounds silly."

"Only when you're face to face with the alternatives," he said. His voice had a weary tone now and he realized he did not want to pursue the conversation and he wondered why he had begun it in the first place. "Do you think you'll stay with the Bureau? As a career, I mean? Now that the Norris people are no longer in control?" He smiled slightly at the naiveté of the premise.

"I doubt it," she whispered. "If I ever got into the tax end of it, I might. But I think I'll probably leave soon."

We both will, he thought.

They were quiet again and he started a second cigarette, annoyed with himself for doing so. He looked about the bedroom. It was a dumpy room, like the rest of the apartment, and he knew he would not be sad to leave it. Then back to New York. Or, perhaps, Vermont. The thought of being there pleased him, heightened his sense of calm. He looked toward the window, trying to see if it was snowing. The evening before the skies had seemed threatening, but now, in the early morning, it appeared bright and sunny. A nice day for a holiday. He looked toward her, only able to see the top of her head resting against him.

"Do you have plans for today, for Thanksgiving, I mean?" he asked.

"I was going to drive to Maryland, to my parents' home, but I'd rather stay with you," she said. "Unless you have plans yourself."

He stroked her, allowing one hand to drift lightly over the soft down of her lower back.

"I don't have any plans," he said. "But I don't want to keep you from yours."

"They're not important," she said, pressing against him again. "I know a quiet little restaurant out in the country in Virginia. It's very romantic and rustic, and it would feel very much like Thanksgiving there."

"It won't do your career much good to be seen with me," he said.

She pressed against him again, rubbing her cheek against his shoulder.

"Will you take me there?" she asked.

He held her close to him and stroked the back of her head, letting his fingers enjoy the softness of her hair.

"I'd like that very much," he said.

He could feel her smiling although he could not see her face.

"But let's stay here like this now and then make love again. Then we can go, later in the afternoon," she said.

When the telephone rang fifteen minutes later they were still holding each other. The sound of the telephone had erupted like an alarm, startling him, making him feel like a schoolboy who had been caught and who suddenly knew he would be punished. He swung his legs over the side of the bed and felt immediately foolish, sitting there naked with a young woman beside him, about to answer the phone.

The message burned into his mind like a branding iron, and he could hear himself answering in a distant voice.

"I'll be there immediately," he heard himself say.

He held the receiver in his hand until the humming sound of the dial tone brought him back.

"Jesus Christ," he whispered.

Mary drew up beside him, placing a hand on his shoulder. "What is it?" she said.

He shook his head to clear his mind. "We have to go into the office right away."

"Why? What's happened?"

"Edmund Norris has been kidnapped."

13

He stood at the window staring blindly into the garden that stretched out before him. The window, one of three directly behind a large mahogany desk, ran from floor to ceiling and the thick bulletproof glass gave off a green tint in the morning sunlight that tinged his face with a sickly pallor. President William Lee Jordan did not turn when he heard the door to the Oval Office open behind him. It would be Cramer Lessing bringing him the latest update on the Norris kidnapping; it was something he was not sure he even wanted to hear.

It had been a difficult year and it was getting worse; only the prospect of peace between Israel and Egypt had brightened it. He shook his head slightly, thinking of what lay behind and ahead. A faltering economy, escalating problems with OPEC, a recalcitrant and rebellious Congress and even rumors of a primary fight that could be lost. And now this sonofabitch has to go and get himself kidnapped.

He turned to face Lessing, his hard blue eyes glistening.

"What new excuse have those idiots in Secret Service come up with now," he snapped.

Lessing glanced down at his shoes and noticed he was standing on the large presidential seal ringed by a circle of stars, that dominated the center of the blue carpet. He stepped off the seal as though avoiding any disrespect to the authority it represented.

"They're pretty sure now that he was taken away by boat," he said, studying Jordan's reaction. "It seems they found a cabin cruiser tied up at a dock on the intercoastal waterway about two and a half

128

miles from the house. It was rented, probably under a phony name, and there were some spent shell casings on the deck. They're pretty sure they'll match up with the bullets that killed the two agents. The bad news is that they didn't find the boat for an hour to an hour and a half after they think the kidnapping took place. So the kidnappers had a good head start. What makes it even worse is that the place where they found the boat is only a half mile fom West Palm Beach International Airport." He paused before continuing. "What it means is that they haven't a goddamned idea where they might be now."

Lessing had delivered the information with the staccatolike efficiency he knew Jordan preferred, and he watched as the President turned back to the sickly green light of the window.

"Pretty sure. They think. What the hell does that mean? I'll tell you what it means. It means they don't know what happened or what can be done about it."

Jordan had clasped his hands behind his back and was nervously drumming the fingers of one hand against the air. He turned and walked to his desk and seated himself in a high-back swivel chair and continued to drum his fingers on the desk.

Lessing remained standing. He watched Jordan through narrowed eyes, believing it demonstrated the intensity of his interest. He was six feet tall, with the body of an athlete that had begun to go to seed. His mouth was expressionless; even when pleased he rarely smiled.

Jordan looked up at him. "Sit down, Cramer. We've got to figure out what the hell *we're* going to do."

Lessing took an upholstered side chair and continued to watch Jordan's reactions. The President's eyes were hard and intense, and years of working with the man had taught him to move cautiously at these moments. Still, he knew the man's priorities, for they were his own as well.

"We're between the rock and the hard place," he began. "Politically we're short on time. Right now the press has no idea what's going on. We've kept the local police out of it to avoid the possibility of a leak. All of our own intelligence people have been alerted and are gathering their forces now. The head of each office will be here in half an hour."

Lessing drew a deep breath, waited for some response, and then continued when none was forthcoming. Like Jordan, his speech patterns became more southern, what he liked to think of as down home, when speaking about political problems.

"I figure we have an hour and then we have to make an announcement. The people at the FBI feel there'll be some kind of ransom demand, probably delivered to the two wire services. If that happens before we're ready, we can hold them off for an hour or two, but only if we brief the wire service people here and demand secrecy. So our big problem is how to explain what happened and what we're doing about it. Then we have to consider how we're going to react to any demands these bastards make and how it's going to look politically if we don't react the right way. This damned thing is going to have more impact on the public than an assassination because it's never happened before. And, if we let them kill that SOB without making it look like we tried to save him, we're going to turn an acknowledged sonofabitch into a damned martyr."

Jordan leaned back in his chair and stared coldly at Lessing. "It would have been a helluva lot simpler if they had just shot him," he said.

Lessing's expressionless face moved slowly up and down in agreement. "We also have the Norris family to contend with," he said. "The reports from the house indicate that all hell's breaking loose there. My last report was that Mrs. Norris hasn't taken her hand off the scotch bottle, and the son-in-law and the daughter, who were there for Thanksgiving, are ready to bust a gut. I think a personal call might be wise."

Jordan placed both palms on the desk and pushed himself up. "And who do I speak to? The slightly inebriated former first lady or the frantic daughter?" He moved to a long mahogany table behind the desk, picked up a sheaf of papers, looked at them, then dropped them back on the table.

"I'd suggest the son-in-law," Lessing said. "Just so we can honestly say we've been in contact and are offering the *personal* support of the President and the first family."

Jordan turned and stood quietly for a moment, folding his arms across his chest. He was a small, slender man, no more than five feet eight inches tall, and because of it he always took care to avoid standing next to taller persons when photographs were taken. He had a pleasant, almost gentle face when he smiled, but it was something reserved for public appearances, and his features were hard now and accented the heavy lines around his eyes and mouth. He ran a hand against one side of his thinning, sandy-gray hair, then looked sharply at Lessing.

"What if we sent the first lady to be with Mrs. Norris? Wouldn't that be viewed as a gesture of unusual support? Perhaps even as a Christian act?"

Lessing rubbed his chin and narrowed his eyes to indicate his intensity of thought. "Some of the pundits might say we were upstaging the Norris family . . . for political reasons. Maybe we could have her say something about including the Norris family in the first family's prayers. Something like that might be better, I think."

A touch of irony flashed across Jordan's face. He held both hands out at his sides, gesturing toward the subdued splendor of the Oval Office. "Here we are, in what's supposed to be the most powerful office in the free world, and the best solution we can come up with is a few quick thumps on the Bible."

He returned to his desk and sat heavily in his chair, then looked across at Lessing. "You're right. It's the best way," he said, looking down at the desk. "How is the statement coming?"

"The entire speechwriting staff is working on it now under my supervision," Lessing said. "We should have a first draft for you within the hour. I've told them to keep it short and to the point, a minimum of detail, with the proper balance of outrage and concern. It will avoid any hard line that might produce drastic action on the part of the kidnappers and still leave our options open."

"All right. What's next then?"

Lessing smiled for the first time. The mundaneness of conversations within the Oval Office always amused him. Not because they were that way, but because of his own constantly reoccuring naiveté in expecting them to be something more. They were simply frank business discussions, no more and no less than those that might be held among executives of any major corporation. The simple weighing of the advantages and disadvantages of decisions that had to be made, with an underlying emphasis on personal survival.

"We have to think of how we plan to conduct the investigation, the chance of a rescue and the sticky problem of how we deal with any ransom demands," he began.

"Ransom is out," Jordan said. "I don't see how we can agree to any demands given what we've said in the past when other countries were faced with similar situations."

"Well, that leaves us with two alternatives," Lessing said. "We can flat out refuse and accept the consequences, which could be disastrous politically. Or we can give the appearance of negotiating, stall for time, and hope that our people can find him. I think the chances are slim that they can, but if we can induce them into protracted negotiations, it would at least appear that we made every effort to save the man and maybe even allow us to shift the blame for any failure to the impatience of the kidnappers. But we sure as hell better catch them afterward."

"We'll be using all the combined services." Jordan's words had taken on the tone of full command.

Lessing nodded. "FBI, Central Intelligence, all branches of military intelligence, Secret Service, and, of course, the special military unit the army has trained for this sort of thing. The head of each, along with the attorney general, should be gathering right now in the Security Council conference room."

Jordan nodded, then rubbed his fingers in slow circles against his temples. He was quiet for several minutes as his mind retraced the conversation, seeking flaws in the steps he would take. He looked at Lessing for a moment without speaking. He hated to rely on the advice of others; he secretly distrusted the necessity of it.

"There's one thing, Cramer. I think we need one person to head up the entire operation. Now this is going to necessitate giving that person extraordinary authority. A helluva lot more, in fact, than I care to give anyone. But I don't see how to avoid it. It will also have to be someone whom the public, the press, and especially our *loyal* opposition, will accept. And that means a great deal of expertise in this area and I don't know who the hell has that. We just haven't had former presidents kidnapped often enough."

Jordan leaned back in his chair and stared into his now steepled fingers. "I've given some thought to the attorney general, but frankly, I don't think he's foolish enough to accept. If this thing is fouled up, the person in charge is going to have to bear a great deal of the responsibility, both immediately and historically. There's a certain scapegoat factor involved here, and if worse comes to worst, we may be forced to employ it. I'm afraid the attorney general will see that immediately."

Jordan righted his chair and rested his forearms heavily on the desk and looked directly into Lessing's face.

The trace of a smile formed on Lessing's lips and he reached into the folder of papers on his lap and withdrew a single sheet.

"I've given that some thought," he said, pleased by his own anticipation. "What I have here is a list of five names with a brief synopsis of background information on each." He handed the sheet to Jordan before continuing. "You'll notice I've put a small check next to the name of one of these people and I think you'll find he meets *all* the criteria you mentioned, especially the last."

Jordan read the list carefully, then reread the checked name again. He leaned back in his chair again and looked across at Lessing, smiling and shaking his head.

"You're a devious man, Cramer. That's one of the things I truly appreciate about you."

Lessing returned the smile.

"You think he'll take the job?"

"It will give him a chance to save his own neck. The only one he'll ever get."

Jordan nodded his head, still looking into Lessing's face. "You think he can pull it off?"

Lessing shrugged his shoulders. "I don't personally believe that anybody can, unless they get awful lucky. But he's a true believer and he knows how to play it down and dirty. And, most important, he's got a stake in the results so I think he'll try like hell."

Jordan slapped both hands on the desk. "Let's go to our meeting," he said.

14

T he cabin was sturdy but from the exterior seemed battered and weatherworn, little more than a collection of old wood built on stilts to escape the fluctuating water level of the Everglades; something that might easily collapse and slip into the high marsh grass that surrounded it on three sides. There were two rooms, sparsely furnished but adequate, and a small storage area with a curtain serving as a door. Norris had been placed in the cramped, airless storage room. The cabin had no electricity and the room lacked even a window. The only light came through a small hole in one wall, where a knot had fallen from the ancient planking that had been used to cover the exterior of the building. Like the rest of the cabin, the room was filled with the overriding smell of rotting wood.

Norris sat in a chair in the six by six foot room, his hands still taped behind his back. Only the gag had been removed. His wet clothing had only partially dried in the dank heat and his body still trembled uncontrollably. From the other room he could hear voices, joking complaints about the condition of the cabin, one voice louder than the others, the voice of the man with the threatening wild eyes, the one they called Juan.

Other sounds intruded. The incessant chirping of insects. The occasional call of a bird, calls he vainly tried to identify, wished that he could seek out, locate, and confirm, if for no other reason than to maintain his sanity.

The curtain was pulled away. The tall blond man stood in the doorway, his face partially obscured by the absence of light. Norris's shoulders shook again and he fought to control it.

"How do you feel?" El Tiburón said, his voice intentionally soft.
Norris nodded, afraid his own voice would tremble if he spoke.
El Tiburón turned to go.

"My hands," Norris said, surprised that his words sounded
steady. "I can't feel them. The tape is too tight and it's cutting off
the circulation. I have gout and that's bad for me, especially without
my medication."

El Tiburón crossed the short distance to the chair.

"I'll remove the tape," he said. "But you'll have to stay in this
room. If you come through the curtain, you'll be shot. Is that understood?"

Norris closed his eyes and nodded.

El Tiburón gently turned Norris in the chair and knelt behind
him and began unwrapping the tape. The light was obscured as Juan
appeared in the doorway.

"Hey, man, what are you doing that for?"

Norris could not see Juan's face clearly, but he could feel the intensity of his eyes, the unmistakable sound of anger in his voice.

"We want a hostage, not a sick old man to worry about." El Tiburón had not looked at Juan. He removed the last of the tape from
Norris's wrists and felt him cringe as the hair was ripped away.

"We're going to end up killing the old bastard anyway." Juan
snorted and turned abruptly away from the doorway.

El Tiburón stood and looked down at Norris. "Open and close
your hand for a few minutes. It will help get the circulation going
again."

Norris automatically followed the instructions. "Is that true?
What he said about killing me?"

"I have no interest in killing you, unless I have to."

"That isn't what your friend said."

El Tiburón squatted in front of Norris and looked directly into
his eyes. He could hear the heavy breathing and he knew the man
was frightened. It annoyed him that he was causing fear in an old
man and he had to remind himself who the man was.

"We're making demands of your government as conditions for
your release," he said. "If they're met, we'll keep our word."

"What are the demands?"

El Tiburón's jaw tightened. "That's none of your business. The
only control you have over your life right now is by doing as you're

told. If you do that, you won't be hurt."

Norris lowered his eyes; there was a slight tremor in his shoulders.

"Take off your clothes," El Tiburón said. "I'll see if there is something else for you to wear. If not, I'll get you a blanket."

"Thank you."

El Tiburón turned to go and Norris reached out and touched his arm lightly, stopping him.

"I don't understand why you're doing this. I'm not important anymore and I haven't done anything to you people." His voice was just above a whisper, trying to keep his words from the others.

"You've caused harm to millions of people, *Mister* President," El Tiburón said. "Now I'm going to do something *for* those people, by making your government pay to get you back, *or* by killing you. One way or another you are going to free my people in Puerto Rico, the same people you denied freedom to, the same people you allowed your corporations to exploit."

Norris began to speak, but El Tiburón waved his hand. "There's no negotiation between us," he said. "You have nothing to bargain with. Now take off those clothes."

Norris stood and began removing his suit, which was now little more than a limp bundle of rumpled cloth.

"It can't do any harm for us to talk," Norris said, shivering. "I don't mean negotiate, but just exchange views, ideas."

El Tiburón looked at him and smiled, amused by the suggestion. "I'll talk to you, *Mister* President. Perhaps later I'll talk to you. But I'm afraid you won't like what you hear very much. The views of *Ejército Mundo de Revolución* don't exactly coincide with yours."

"One of the women used that name before. I don't recognize it."

"It translates as the World Army of Revolution, or what your right-wing tabloids call WAR."

Norris stared at him, his lips moving almost imperceptibly. El Tiburón took his clothing and walked through the doorway, pulling the curtain behind him. He had displayed a certain arrogance with the man and it now annoyed him. He felt it cheapened him.

Norris dropped back into the chair, now wearing only his underwear. He wrapped his arms around his shoulders. The irony of it, the goddamned irony, he told himself.

When El Tiburón entered the main room of the cabin carrying Norris's clothing, Juan sneered at him.

"Are you going to take his clothes out and have them cleaned and pressed?" he snapped.

El Tiburón ignored him, turning to Wally. "Are there any old clothes here that he can wear?"

Wally shook his head. "Nothin' at all, ol' buddy. I got an old horse blanket, though."

"That will do." He looked at the others individually. "I don't want a sick man on our hands. I don't want to have to worry about getting him medicine. If they agree to our demands we are going to have to return him, and I don't want to let the entire operation fail because we were foolish enough to let him die on us." He looked at each of them again. "Getting the demands, that's the important thing now. We can always kill him, we will always have that option. My concern is for the people of Puerto Rico, not that old man in there." He looked at Juan and the look carried the accusation of his words. "To get the most for our people we must keep him alive . . . for now. If there's disagreement, we can discuss it, but bickering about how we deal with him can only cause friction among us that we don't need. I'm not asking you to be nice to him, just to keep him alive."

Wally stepped forward with an old army blanket that seemed to intensify the rotting smell in the cabin.

"It's all I've got," he said.

Norma took it and allowed it to unfold in her hands, then held it out giving it a mock appraisal.

"Not exactly Christian Dior," she said. "Certainly not what he's accustomed to." She grinned at the others, then turned to Carol. "Would you like to help me dress him?"

Carol felt momentarily uneasy, then forced a smile. "I'd love to," she said. She glanced over her shoulder at El Tiburón. "Shall I make him some tea?" she said, immediately regretting the comment.

El Tiburón stared at her, his eyes hard and uncompromising. "I think something to drink would be good for all of us," he said.

Carol's face reddened and she turned abruptly and started for the storage room. Norma followed with an exaggerated walk, causing her heavy breasts to sway back and forth.

Juan turned his back and stared out through one of the small front windows.

"Shit," he said.

Richard moved up beside him. El Tiburón stared at their backs, his face showing his rising anger. He looked at Wally. The large hulking southerner winked at him. His jaw was set firmly.

"Everybody's gonna do jus' what they're told," Wally said. "An' I'll help you see to it."

Juan looked back over his shoulder and glared at the man who was easily twice his size, then looked back out the window. Fucking asshole cracker, he thought.

"Shit," he said again.

Norris was still huddled in the chair, hugging his shoulders when the two women pulled back the curtain. He looked from one to the other and felt more naked than he was.

He seemed very small sitting there, and the loose flesh along his chest and arms seemed to hang like melted wax. Carol felt the uneasiness return as she looked down at him, and she staggered slightly to one side as Norma brushed by her.

The blanket hit Norris in the chest and tumbled to the floor.

"Put it on," Norma snapped. She walked slowly around the chair, looking down at him, then stopped and lifted his chin with the index finger of one hand. "If you're a good boy, maybe we'll do something else for you." She looked at Carol. "You think he can still get it up?" She laughed, then looked back into Norris's face. "How about it? Can you still get it up?"

Norris turned his head to the side and looked down at the floor. He reached down and picked up the blanket and drew it around his shoulders. These people are animals, filthy animals. Exactly the kind of filth you've always fought.

Norma laughed. "I think he's playing hard to get," she said.

Carol stepped up beside her, remembering her own plans for Norris's sexual embarrassment and feeling suddenly sickened by them. Sickened now by Norma as well. She placed her hand on Norma's arm.

"Let's leave him alone," she said.

Norma looked at her sharply, her surprise showing in her eyes.

"He's just a pathetic wrinkled-up old man," Carol tried to explain.

"He's a murderer," Norma said.

Carol felt rising guilt and the accusation in Norma's eyes cut her.

"I know he is," she said. "It's just that it makes me sick to my stomach to be in the same room with him." She turned to go and Norma's voice boomed out behind her.

"You hear that you dirty old bastard. You make this woman sick."

El Tiburón listened from the other room. There was nothing he could do, or would do, about verbal abuse, he told himself. The man deserved it and all he would fight for was to keep him alive for as long as necessary. But the tensions disturbed him. They were urban guerrillas, not terrorists, not criminals. They must act like what they were and remain united and the others would have to understand that. He would have to make them understand. He looked at Wally. The big southerner's eyes were fixed on the storage room.

"Someone has to contact New York and have the communiqué with the demands delivered to the wire services," he said.

"You want me to go into town and make the call?" Wally glanced back at the storage room as he spoke, then toward Juan and Richard. He was concerned about trouble if El Tiburón were left alone.

El Tiburón nodded his head. "It will be better," he said. "You can move about the town more easily right now. And I want to talk with the others. There are some things that have to be understood. But first we have to set up our perimeter. It shouldn't take long and then you can leave."

For the next hour they worked together as professionals for the first time since the assault. El Tiburón remained in the cabin, guarding Norris and watching the others through the front and rear windows. Wally and Richard began with a safety line running from one stilt at the rear of the cabin out to a dense patch of forest seventy-five feet to the rear, where one of two small rowboats had been hidden. The line would be slack and would lie beneath the foot of water that covered the marshes behind the cabin. Access to the line could be gained through a trap door in the cabin's main room, and under the cover of night the line would provide a direct escape route to the boats and the deep tropical forest beyond.

On the long narrow stretch of solid land that led down to the front of the cabin, Carol, Norma, and Juan flailed away with machetes, cutting the heavier foliage at the outer edges, creating an open killing ground to any frontal assault. They then laid a low trip wire, fifty feet from the cabin, which stretched across the open area, then ran along perpendicular lines to the cabin itself, where the ends were attached to clusters of tin cans forming a crude alarm system. An identical trip line was laid by Wally and Richard in a semicircle along the sides and rear of the cabin, set at a level three inches below the water. The final precaution involved four plastique charges, each set one hundred feet from the four corners of the cabin, the detonation wires running along the ground and up through the trap door where they could be quickly wired to the detonators inside. The purpose of the explosives was twofold: to cause heavy casualties among a large assault force, and to create the diversion that would be needed for any escape. But they all knew there would be no escape if they were found. The precautions were more psychological than real.

Inside the cabin, El Tiburón moved from window to window watching his five comrades work. They moved quickly and efficiently as they had been trained to do. He smiled to himself, thinking of the backgrounds of each and the evolution that had taken place. Norma Epstein swung her machete like the best of peasant women, and her effectiveness with a carbine fired from the hip would have shamed the average member of the U.S. military. It was a far cry from her well-to-do upbringing on Long Island's North Shore. But that was true of each of them, even Juan with his background on the mean streets of the San Juan *barrio*.

He watched Carol longer than the others, taking pleasure in her fluid movements, the agile dexterity she brought to each physical task, whether assembling a trip wire or furiously making love. The inaneness of her midwestern background had disappeared in college; she had made the transition from a frivolous teenager to a woman whose passions were dominated by conviction and thought, and the raw nerve she had often displayed had repeatedly amazed him.

Her husband, Richard, by contrast, was an enigma. Working now with Wally, himself the consummate guerrilla, he was, perhaps, the coolest of all. His expertise with explosives was unquestioned, and when moving about with plastique and wire all the intellectual woolliness that normally surrounded him disappeared. Even his wild, unkempt appearance seemed to change. He was a perfect technician who became difficult only when he abandoned his small-town good sense for endless philosophizing.

El Tiburón relaxed, watching them. They were working again as they should. That alone would help ease the tensions that had grown steadily since the assault. It would now be his job to maintain the level of professionalism that would be needed. Reason, patience, and strength, he told himself. It was what he had been trained to do, to lead others with effectiveness, to bring them together as a single-minded force.

Later that afternoon, Edmund Norris sat quietly inside the storage room, trying to hear the conversations now going on in the outer room. He had heard someone leave; he had heard the engine of the van as it drove off. Now a meeting was taking place and at times he could hear the heated voices of the man they called Juan and another man. There were softer voices too. The blond man and the women, he thought, but he could not hear what was being said. He wanted to move closer to the curtain but his fear of reprisals, if caught, kept him from doing so. The occasional chattering of his teeth interfered with his ability to hear and he clenched his teeth trying to stop it, but it proved useless. The blond man had indicated that they would talk, and if he kept that promise, there was hope. And there was one other thing he could do that might save his life. But the irony of it still disturbed and frightened him.

15

The conference room normally reserved for the National Security Council was located in the basement of the White House and, like the Oval Office, it seemed to have a power of its own. It was a stark, rectangular room, relatively small and designed exclusively for work. The heavy walnut paneling that covered all four walls lacked the distraction of a single painting or photograph. The only break in the monotonous paneling came at the foot of a long conference table, where dull brown draperies concealed a projection screen built into the wall. In all, it gave the room an effect that defied diversion of thought.

When the President and Cramer Lessing entered at 9:45 A.M. five of the ten upholstered swivel chairs around the conference table were occupied. Attorney General Earl Baldwin had placed himself at the foot of the table. To his right sat CIA Director William Horton and White House military advisor, General Robert Levy. Directly across from them were FBI Director Jonathan Morgan and Morris Chase, director of the Secret Service. Of the five clustered at one end of the table, only Baldwin seemed out of place. His baggy, rumpled suit was an obvious contrast to the perfect tailoring of the others. Only he failed to show the correct one and a quarter inch of cuff from the sleeve of his suitcoat; the only distinctive mark in his dress was the presence of cigarette ash on his necktie.

When the President seated himself at the head of the table, with Lessing to his left, a gap of empty chairs separated them from the others. Jordan glanced quickly around the room. Each man had brought a senior aide, who now occupied identical swivel chairs that lined the walls along the length of the table. They, too, seemed clus-

142

tered away from the President, as though not wishing to bridge the gap between the professional and political ends of government. Jordan noticed the distance with disdain. He folded his hands in front of him almost as if preparing to pray and stared down the length of the table at Baldwin.

"Earl, what is the situation now?"

"We are in one helluva mess, Mr. President," Baldwin drawled. "I believe the reports on exactly what happened speak for themselves. We've had a major breach in security that's difficult to explain. On the other hand, we are fairly well agreed that we're dealing with one of several radical groups who have had the capacity to accomplish just this kind of assault for several years now. Right now we're forced to wait on their demands to determine exactly which one we're dealin' with." Baldwin allowed his weathered face to soften slightly, then peered at the President over the top of his old fashioned spectacles, looking more now like the academician than the small-town southern lawyer. "You know it's amazin' something like this hasn't happened before," he added.

Lessing leaned forward and cocked his head toward Baldwin. Listening to the attorney general seemed to intensify his own southern accent. "Earl, you're not trying to excuse this abominable breach in security by telling us we've been lucky in the past, are you?"

Morris Chase stiffened under the indirect attack and Baldwin avoided the Secret Service director's eyes. Instead he smiled at Lessing. He had known him for more than ten years now and during that time he had learned to both admire and despise his ruthlessness.

"I don't think *anyone* here is interested in excuses, Cramer. We're all aware of how bad it looks and how important it is that we salvage as much as possible. One thing I think we should be considering though. And that is that we handle this in such a way that we discourage other groups from trying something similar in the future. It also might be nice to try and get Mr. Norris back alive."

"All right. Let's stop the infighting, right now," Jordan said. "There's no question we have to investigate how this happened. The public is going to expect that. The question now is how we catch these people, how we keep ourselves from looking like total fools, and whether we *can* keep Norris alive in the process. Let me tell you this at the outset. I don't believe we can agree to any ransom demands. Past statements preclude that. We can appear to negotiate if we have to, to give ourselves time, but that's all." He paused and looked at each man individually. "There's one other criterion. That sonofabitch is not going to become a martyr or a hero. And it's going to be the responsibility of everyone here to see to that."

"Excuse me, sir." Jonathan Morgan had pivoted in his chair. His heavy, round face carried all the severity he had learned to invoke in his years as a judge. Now as director of the FBI it served him equally well.

Jordan stared into the smooth, slender face of the gray-haired former jurist, annoyed by the interruption. "What is it," he said.

"I must warn you, Mr. President, that if we adopt too rigid a set of guidelines, we are going to impede our chances of getting President Norris back. And we may very well be making him a martyr in doing so."

Jordan leaned back in his chair and began drumming the tabletop with his outstretched fingers. The display of annoyance was noted by all at the table.

"I've discussed the situation with our top kidnapping experts within the Bureau," Morgan added. "They advise me that under no circumstances should we close the door on any demands that may be made, or even appear to be negotiating in bad faith. Time is on our side, not theirs. If we can convince them to extend any deadlines they may set, we increase our chances of success with each additional hour. After all, sir, we do have the full resources of the government at our disposal."

"That does not appear to have done us much good up to now," Lessing said.

William Horton's hard gray eyes carefully studied the President's reaction to Lessing's words. The CIA director's sharp Anglo-Saxon features gave no hint of his own position, nor did he wish it to. As the son of a former U.S. senator, he had served in the CIA immediately after his graduation from Harvard, before going on to various posts in the diplomatic corps. Now at fifty-three, he had returned to head the massive intelligence-gathering network. All of his training had taught him one thing: caution.

Horton extended his hand, which held a cigarette in a black cigarette holder. "Mr. President, if I may interject one point." He smiled slightly as Jordon nodded his approval, then continued. "We at CIA feel it is safe to assume we are dealing with political radicals. Therefore, any demands made will, in all probability, require political solutions. This, in itself, will give us justifiable cause for delay. Let us imagine, for example, that they fall back on the old cliché and demand the release of so-called political prisoners. Since we have few in federal prisons, this would necessitate the cooperation of the governors of the states involved and that alone could create certain delays. Any broader philosophical demands could simply be agreed to and then rescinded later."

"What makes you feel these people are political radicals?" Lessing said. "Couldn't they just as easily be Black militants or a group of lunatics like the ones who kidnapped Patty Hearst? In that case we might find ourselves dealing with some outlandish social demands that could not easily be rescinded, isn't that true?"

Horton placed the cigarette holder between his teeth, tilting it slightly upward, almost reminiscent of Franklin Delano Roosevelt. "We certainly can't rule out any possibility. But studying what took place tells us certain things. First, this was an extremely well-planned operation. This in itself implies some guerrilla training. It also presumes a great deal of prior surveillance of Norris's habits." Horton allowed himself a small smile. "Now perhaps you're not familiar with the area of Palm Beach in which Norris lives, Cramer. I think the very nature of that area would preclude the continuous reappearance of any gentlemen of color. I think we can exclude any foreign group for the same reason."

"I would agree," Morgan added. "The consensus seems to be that we will find ourselves dealing with a group similar to the Weather Underground, or something of that ilk. Nice, clean-cut, well-spoken white kids, who've probably been trained in any of a half-dozen different Communist countries."

Jordan brought his hand down on the table. "Gentlemen, we are wasting time speculating about whom we're dealing with. Let's talk about *how* we're going to deal with this. Mr. Chase, you've been very quiet. What has the Secret Service been doing *since* this disaster?"

Morris Chase's bulldog face reddened. His entire career had been spent in the Secret Service, and he considered any failure by his men a personal one. He shifted his short, stocky body toward the President. There was a slight film of perspiration on his upper lip, and he spoke in a clipped monotone.

"At present, nearly every Secret Service agent based in Florida is in Palm Beach or is enroute there. Only skeleton crews remain at the various offices. The same is true of most Florida-based members of the FBI and CIA. In addition, every office of those three agencies has been placed on full alert throughout the country; all leaves have been cancelled; and joint investigations are being conducted into the whereabouts of all known members of radical groups. We also plan to bring in people from other states. In all we are contemplating a combined force of slightly more than seven-hundred men to conduct the investigation and search. That figure does not include technical and scientific personnel. I have also asked General Levy to make military personnel available where needed, including military air transport."

Jordan turned his attention to Levy, whose hatchet face and large hooked nose had always reminded Jordan of the eagle on the presidential seal. He was dressed in civilian clothes rather than the Army uniform he preferred, and like most military men, he wore the best of suits badly.

"General, what about this crack antiterrorist unit we have stationed in North Carolina?"

Levy drew himself up before speaking, his words coming with dull military precision. "They're on alert, sir. We're preparing to move them to the naval base at Pensacola, which would then be used as a jumping-off point."

"Just a moment, General," Jordan interrupted. "What role are they playing right now in finding these people?"

Confusion spread slowly across Levy's face. It seemed to begin at his jutting pointed chin, move to his mouth and eyes and then upward to his high, receding forehead, where furrows suddenly appeared. "Sir, the role of the unit would involve the capture of the terrorists, not the task of finding them."

Jordan stared at him incredulously. "How the hell do you capture somebody if you don't find them first. And what the hell good is a crack antiterrorist unit if they don't have the capacity to find terrorists?" he snapped.

Levy stuttered. "Well, Mr. President, it was always assumed that the intelligence and investigatory agencies would locate, and that we . . ."

"Jesus Christ," Lessing's words carried the full expression of his disgust. He looked at the President. Jordan's normally cold blue eyes were angry and there was the slight movement at one corner of his mouth that came only when he was close to rage.

"Sir, I think it's time we took some positive action," Lessing continued. "I feel we must have one person in charge of this investigation who will have *full* authority over all aspects and *everyone* involved. Otherwise we're going to have everyone operating on the basis of what *they* think their role is." Lessing had looked at Levy as he spoke the final sentence, then quickly at each of the others. Now his eyes returned to Jordan.

"That may be the first sensible thing I've heard today," Jordan said. He looked at each man at the table. "Do any of you have any suggestions?"

There was an uneasy silence.

"I feel the responsibility rests with the Secret Service," Chase finally said. He spoke the words hesitantly, then deepened his voice, adding what he hoped would be viewed as resolve. "As the head of the Service I'm willing to assume personal responsibility."

"I should think the Secret Service has done quite enough already," Lessing snapped. "And I truly doubt if the public would be very happy to have the Secret Service in charge of cleaning up its own mess."

Chase stared at Lessing, his eyes wide, his face crimson. "You have a question of morale as well," he said. "To remove the Service from responsibility now would be to hold it up to public ridicule. May I remind you that two of our men died resisting this assault?"

"And may I remind you that the assault should have been stopped?" Lessing snapped back. "I assure you that *no one* will remove the Service from responsibility."

A slight smile appeared on Jordan's lips. Lessing and Chase were squared off like two mongrels in a dog pit. As always, Lessing had proved the perfect foil, pricking subordinates just enough until they moved into the desired position.

"Now hear. Let's just curtail all this."

Jordan's southern accent had broadened several degrees, giving him the calm, folksy air of a wise old southern patriarch. At the opposite end of the conference table Baldwin noted the change. In the years he had known the President he had seen the technique applied often and he knew it was tantamount to a mugger asking his victim for a cigarette before striking out with his blackjack.

Jordan smiled openly for the first time since entering the room. "Now both you gentlemen have made some very valid points." He looked warmly at Chase. "Morris, you have my full confidence, and I assure you that the courageous efforts of those boys who gave their lives will receive very prominent mention in the address I plan to make to the nation later today. If I recall correctly, I believe a similar attack was made on Harry Truman at Blair House some years back and that some agents died heroically then, too."

"But *they* stopped the attack," Lessing interjected.

"Yes, that's true," Jordan said, nodding. "But we're dealing with a much more professional type of terrorist now, Cramer. Aren't we?"

Lessing inclined his head in agreement but maintained the look of disdain that now seemed permanently fixed on his face.

"Now Cramer has a point too, Morris," Jordan continued. "The public is going to expect a full-scale response and they're going to get it. Now, as I see it, Bill Horton is probably correct about the type of person we're dealing with. That means political terrorists as well as kidnappers. It also means we need someone with expertise in both areas. Now I'm going to write a name on a piece of paper and pass it among you for your comments."

Jordan wrote the name slowly, then handed the paper to Lessing, who appeared to study it intently before sliding it down the table to Levy, who also read it without any apparent recognition, then passed it to Horton. When the note reached Baldwin, he glanced down the table at Jordan, then passed the note to Morgan. The FBI director's face showed the first clear sign of emotion. His facial muscles tightened, and as he passed the note to Chase, he turned to the President.

"I disagree completely," Morgan said.

Jordan's face hardened again. "Why, Jonathan?" he asked coldly.

"As you're well aware, sir, we have asked Mr. Henry for his resignation because of past activities. To put him in such a position of responsibility now could place the Bureau in a very embarrassing light."

Jordan leaned back in his chair and looked around the table. "Any other comments? Any suggestions?"

"I think Jonathan has a valid point," Baldwin said.

Jordan looked down the length of the table and slowly began drumming his fingers on the surface. "Well, Earl, to be honest, the first name I considered was yours as head of Justice. But in all fairness, you're not an investigator, are you? Then I considered Jonathan as head of the FBI. But, again, as a former judge, he's not an investigator either and would simply have to appoint someone beneath him to run the actual investigation." Jordan sat upright in his chair. "But *I'm* going to do the appointing in this case, and whoever gets the job will carry the full weight and responsibility of that appointment. Now if you gentlemen disagree, I'm willing to consider other candidates. But they will have to have extensive knowledge of terrorist activities—and I believe we all agree that Mr. Henry qualifies there—and they must also have experience in dealing with kidnappers. Now, unless I'm wrong, Mr. Henry's years in the FBI, twenty-nine years, I believe, also qualifies him there. However, if Henry is unacceptable and we have no other suitable candidate, then it will *have* to be one of you gentlemen." Jordan waited, allowing the silence of the others to fill the room, noting that even Chase had not renewed his offer.

"Are you sure Henry will want the job?" Baldwin finally said.

Jordan smiled. "I'm a great believer in the principle of creative tension," he said. "Simply put, that means that good and talented men react best under extreme pressure. Mr. Henry has a great deal to gain from this assignment and I believe he's a talented subordinate." Jordan waited again. "Then if there are no other suggestions, I assume we're agreed." He turned his gaze on Morgan. "Jonathan, I'd like you to ask Mr. Henry to join us here immediately."

Morgan rose and walked to a telephone located on a small table next to the concealed projection screen. As he did a member of Lessing's staff entered the room and handed him a long sheet of telex paper. Lessing read it quickly then passed it to Jordan. "Just a moment, Jonathan," Lessing said.

Jordan read the telex slowly, then looked at the others. "It appears we have the demands of the kidnappers, gentlemen. They were received by the wire services a short time ago. It would also appear our assumptions were partially correct." He paused, reading the telex again. "Our adversaries appear to be Puerto Rican according to their demands. They call themselves *Ejército Mundo de Revolución.* Does that mean anything to you gentlemen?"

"More commonly known to the media as WAR," Morgan said, still standing next to the telephone. "They're a splinter group of the FALN, but up to now they've been content with the usual terrorist activities, bombings, robberies, things of that type. I'm afraid I don't know much more about them."

"Well, it would appear they are no longer content with the usual terrorist activities," Jordan said. "Hopefully, Mr. Henry will know a bit more about them, or at least have the capacity to find out."

"I'll get Henry here," Morgan said, picking up the telephone.

As the call was being made, Horton scribbled a note on the yellow pad set out before him, tore off the sheet of paper, and turned to hand it to the senior aide seated behind him. The aide stared into Horton's eyes, his face as expressionless as his superior's. Horton turned back to the President. "What are the demands, sir?" he asked.

"Actually, they're rather simple and to the point," Jordan said. "First, we are to abandon our announced plan for a plebiscite on independence in 1981 and move it up to February of next year. Prior to that plebiscite, all U.S. troops and other federal personnel must be removed from the island. Secondly, the United States must guarantee continuance of its two billion dollars in yearly welfare payments for the next ten years, with accompanying increases based on cost of living figures. Third, the United States must impose penalties on U.S. corporations operating on the island if they fail to develop job-training programs for the people there, or fail to follow certain guidelines. Essentially those guidelines call for Puerto Ricans to be paid the same wages as their American counterparts, as well as the establishment of management quotas that would increase each year until ninety-five percent of all management positions were held by Puerto Ricans at the end of the ten-year period. That's basically it, minus all the revolutionary didactics."

Horton took a long drag on his cigarette. "Very clever," he said. "What they're asking is that we remove the primary obstacle that has kept the people from voting for independence, namely their dependence on welfare, and also that we sweeten the pot for the working class by holding out the promise of higher wages and opportunities for advancement that don't now exist. We do all that and we end up with a socialist government that will be in the other camp by the time the ten-year period is up, if not sooner. And one that will be prepared to run its own industry. Very cute indeed."

"And in return we get Edmund Norris back," Jordan said. "Now that's one hell of an offer."

"There is one good point," Horton added. "It gives us the opportunity to delay, to appear to be working out the many problems and seeking agreement from the various parties involved, the Congress, the corporations, the present government on the island."

Jordan leaned back in his chair and stared out over the heads of the others. "And if they do kill Norris, we have the inaction of others to blame, don't we?" he said at length.

Morgan walked slowly to his chair. "Mr. President. Mr. Henry is on his way."

Jordan rubbed his hands together. He could now see the first indication of hope in an altogether bad situation.

16

T hey descended the steps of the White House together and silently entered the rear of Morgan's waiting limousine. Normally, Henry
would have preferred to walk the few short blocks to FBI headquarters. But Morgan never allowed himself to be publicly exposed. Unlike Hoover, he accepted the need of the bulletproof limousine and
the two accompanying FBI agents who constantly guarded him.

They had not spoken since the meeting with the President had
ended, other than Morgan's suggestion that Henry return in his car
and Henry's acceptance. There had been little warmth during the
meeting, other than the President's false assurances of his confidence
and support, and Henry had recognized that for what it was. He was
still slightly numb. He had suspected the purpose of the summons
when he received the call from Morgan, but not the extent of the authority he would have. It was an opportunity for personal survival
beyond anything he could have hoped for or would have considered
possible. He smiled to himself. And it also provided all of them with
the perfect scapegoat. So be it, he told himself.

The limousine moved slowly down the long drive toward Pennsylvania Avenue. Morgan looked straight ahead as he spoke.

"There's no need for me to go into the kind of pressure that will
be on you *and* the Bureau over the next few days or weeks," he said.

Henry glanced at him, momentarily taking in the cold aloofness
of the man, then looked straight ahead himself.

"I realize I would not have been your choice for the job, Jonathan. But that's really a moot point. I'm going to need the full support of everyone involved if the Bureau *and* I aren't going to end
with the shitty end of the stick."

Henry could feel Morgan stiffen as the gauntlet was dropped back in his lap. Neither man looked at each other. Just two people staring straight ahead, wishing they were with someone else, Henry thought.

Several moments passed before Morgan answered. He was collecting himself, Henry decided, avoiding any expression of anger.

"With the broad-based authority you've been given, you should have no problem. Certainly not from us. As the President said, you're to have full access to everything you want." He paused, gathering himself again. "Even I don't have that," he added.

They were quiet again. The car swung into Pennsylvania Avenue, heading into the bright sunlight, itself a blatant contradiction to the events that had already taken place.

"What are you going to need immediately?" Morgan asked.

Henry suppressed a smile. "I'll need everyone who worked with me in the special unit in New York reassembled here by the end of the day."

He could feel Morgan stiffen.

"They're the people who know the territory best, Jonathan," he added. "I don't have time to train new people."

"I'd prefer that we keep that as quiet as possible, for the sake of the Bureau," Morgan said. His voice had grown even colder than before, and he continued to stare straight ahead.

"I plan to have as little involvement with the press as possible. I have no objection to having one of the press relations people assigned, if you wish."

Morgan nodded. "That might help. What else will you need?"

"I'll want to choose some technical people and some specialists from headquarters, and I'll want final approval of anyone brought in from other offices. I also want all the old files on radical and suspected radical groups." He looked at Morgan, holding the stare until the FBI director was forced to turn toward him. "And I won't accept the bullshit that went down at the meeting. I know damn good and well that neither the Bureau nor the CIA ever shredded those files as ordered."

Morgan turned away and stared out the side window. "You'll have them before the day is out," he said. "Anything else?"

"Just one thing. Keep Malcolm Welch off my ass. If he sticks his nose into one thing, I'm going to scream bloody hell." Henry hesitated, then chuckled to himself. "No, just tell Malcolm that if he pisses me off, I'll ask that he be assigned as my assistant."

Morgan laughed and turned back to Henry. "You're a sonofabitch," he said, still smiling.

"That's exactly what the job calls for, isn't it." His smile faded. "If I roll craps on this one, I'm back in the shithouse, Jonathan. If not . . ." He looked Morgan in the eyes.

Morgan nodded. "As much as I'd like to see you tossed out on your ass, I hope you make it, Pat."

Henry smiled at the use of his nickname. "So do I, Jonathan, for both our sakes."

~~~~~

At 1 P.M. William Horton sat behind his massive modern desk at CIA headquarters. The office was the largest of any within the government, slightly larger than a tennis court and something that Horton had always felt adequately measured the true power of the position. On the opposite wall, a massive television screen projected the image of William Lee Jordan as he solemnly advised the nation of the Norris kidnapping. The President's voice was soft and even, his face grave but firm. Though not mentioning the demands, it was acknowledged that the administration had been contacted by the abductors and that every measure was being taken to assure the former President's safe return.

Slowly, Horton placed a cigarette in the black cigarette holder. He turned to the senior aide seated to his right, then placed the holder in his mouth, leaving the cigarette unlit.

"Touching sense of concern our President has, eh?"

The aide nodded, still watching the screen. "What do you think of this fellow, Henry?" he asked.

"A wise political choice. Knowledgeable, yet vulnerable. Still, I would have preferred someone like Chase or Baldwin. This chap, Henry, knows the field and that's always troublesome."

"What do we do when he asks for assistance?"

Horton lit the cigarette and allowed the smoke to drift slowly out of his mouth without inhaling it. "We give it to him. Personnel, material, technical advice."

"Files dealing with WAR?"

Horton inhaled heavily on the cigarette. "We have no such files. They were destroyed. If he persists, give him the memoranda, what little there was, that we received from the Bureau and explain that somehow they missed being shredded through some internal foul-up. But under no circumstances is Henry or the White House to be given anything substantive. That could only bring irreparable damage to the Agency. And for the good of the nation, the Agency must survive." He paused, drawing heavily on the cigarette again. "Even if it means that Norris does not."

The aide turned and looked at Horton. He was a small, painfully thin man with an unusually broad mouth that dominated his slender face. His name was Dwight Farragut and Horton had often mused that it should have been Ferret, based on his appearance alone.

"I can foresee only one problem," the aide said.

"I can't foresee any," Horton said.

"There's the question of Norris himself."

"Why should that be a problem? I would think that was academic."

"What if he discloses information?"

"To whom? The members of WAR?"

"Yes. Precisely."

Horton smiled broadly. "My dear Farragut, how well do you know the former President?"

"Not well at all, sir."

Horton returned the cigarette holder to his mouth. "I assure you, Edmund Norris, despite his many blunders in the past, has no penchant for suicide. Besides, I doubt very seriously that he's still alive. The gentlemen who took him may be revolutionary idealists, but they're not fools. They know damn well their demands will never be met." He shook his head sadly. "They also know it doesn't matter. Just by taking him and making those particular demands, they've beaten us. That whole island will be a hotbed of revolutionary pride for years to come. And after we catch them and kill them, which we assuredly will sooner or later, their pictures will be hanging on the walls of every Puerto Rican shanty from the Bronx to San Juan."

"What if we didn't kill them?"

"Oh, no. That would be far too dangerous. The only slight hope would be to get them and also manage to get Norris back alive, and, as I said, that's highly improbable. But it is an amusing thought. Edmund Norris telling the world about the terrors of abduction. Somehow I can't quite picture our former President as the new Patty Hearst."

They both laughed at the idea.

17

He had heard them arguing late into the night, but only the angrier statements had been intelligible. Jordan had addressed the nation on television, that much he had understood, but they, these madmen, had only heard brief news reports on a portable radio. He had not heard those broadcasts, only the arguments that followed. Insane arguments. Irrational statements answered in calmer, less concerned tones, but even that had been only an assumption. "He's laying a three-card monte game on us, man." The words had been shouted by the small, wild-eyed man, he had thought, but there had been no way to be certain. The voices and murmurs had been a contradictory jumble, confusing, and as such, frightening. Cacophony, like the sounds of the birds in his aviary at dawn, individual clarity, combined discord, only the more violent, the strongest identifiable. He had hoped the analogy would not prove true. Then there had been quiet and he had huddled in a corner, waiting for someone to come, his leg extended, trying to ease the pain. It had been nearly dawn before sleep came. The sounds of the birds had begun outside, and it was only then that the terror had left him.

The room was airless, hot, suffocating when he awoke. The old blanket wrapped about him had left him bathed in sweat. The cold of the previous day, whether produced by fear or by the saturated clothing, was no longer with him. Only the oppressive suffocation of the room. The pain in his leg was gone, but he knew it would return without medication, the knee and ankle would begin to swell as the level of uric acid increased. He removed the blanket and fumbled in the dim light for his underwear. It had dried in the stifling heat and

156

he pulled it on, covering himself. Outside the sounds of the Everglades crept through the cracks in the wood. He moved to the wall where a knothole had fallen from one plank and knelt before it, peering out. The light was blinding—the sun seemed directly overhead—and he was forced to remove his eye several times to accustom it to the shocking change. He placed his ear to the hole, listening. Insect sounds overpowered all else. Then it came, distant at first, then closer. A series of deep resonant notes, a low beeping, more rapid toward the end. He pressed his face against the wall, straining to take in as much terrain as possible, searching for some movement, some obscure flash of color. It was there, in high grass, barely visible to the right of his line of vision. He pressed his face harder against the wall, struggling for a few more centimeters of vision. The king rail, moving away, moving in the wrong direction, the mottled brown body slipping from view.

Light flashed behind him as the curtain over the doorway was pulled back. He turned his head and saw the outline of the man.

"What are you doing, trying to crawl through the hole?"

There was humor in the voice, the blond man's voice, the one with the absurd name, or title, or whatever.

"I was trying to see what was outside," Norris said.

"Not a helluva lot." He stepped forward. There was a bundle under one arm. "I have your clothing. All dry now."

"It's so hot in here," Norris said.

"You don't have to wear them. I just thought you might want to."

"May I go into the other room? There's no air."

"Yes. I want to talk to you anyway."

Norris struggled with his trousers, feeling dull pain return to the joints of his leg. He put on the wrinkled, white shirt. It still held the smell of the sea.

"May I have my shoes?" he asked.

"No shoes. We don't want you going for a stroll."

The humor was still in the voice, but the light was too dim to make out the facial features, to determine the intent.

Norris followed El Tiburón into the main room. Only the large, hulking man who had pulled him into the boat was there, seated in front of a window, an expressionless stare in his eyes. He was naked from the waist up and he seemed even larger and more powerful than he had the previous day. The others were not there, and as he looked about he could not see them through the open door that led to the other room behind him.

"Sit down," El Tiburón said, motioning toward a table and chairs in the center of the main room.

Norris sat clumsily, attempting to keep his bad leg extended. "Where are the others?" he asked.

Amusement flashed across El Tiburón's face. "You don't seem to understand. We're not here to answer your questions." He looked at Norris for a long moment, then broke into a grin.

"Man thinks he's here on a vacation," Wally said. "Hot damn, honey. I assure you you ain't." He stood and swaggered across the room, taking up a position across from where he had been, in front of another window.

El Tiburón sat across the table from Norris. "How do you feel?" he asked.

"My leg's bothering me. As I explained yesterday, I have gout and need medication to control it."

"I'm afraid we can't help you. Is there anything else you can do to ease the pain?"

"Just stay off it. Keep it elevated, when possible. Watch my diet."

El Tiburón smiled again. "Well, I don't think you'll have much problem staying off it. We don't plan on you taking any long walks. As far as the diet goes, you tell me what you can eat and we'll do what we can."

"Jus' like a fine ol' restaurant," Wally said.

Norris stared at the tabletop, his hands in his lap. He felt helpless, even more than in the worst days of the past, and the sense of humiliation bordered on the pathetic. He looked across the table, gathering his pride.

"You said you wanted to talk to me," he said softly.

El Tiburón studied him, momentarily admiring the man's quiet display of strength.

"Your President was on television yesterday, and while he didn't reject our demands, he was somewhat obscure. That's not a healthy situation for you. So what I'm going to ask you to do is help us make it healthier. I want you to tape-record a message that will be played to a local radio station over a telephone and then mailed to your home. The message will be written for you and you will record it exactly that way. In the background a local news broadcast of the radio station will be playing, so it will be clear to everyone, your family included, that you are alive and well for the present. That should give some comfort to your family, as well as serving our purposes. Do you agree?"

Momentary anger flashed in Norris's eyes. "How humiliating is the message going to be?" He hesitated, then snorted derisively at himself. "That doesn't matter. Of course I'll do it. I want to stay alive."

El Tiburón felt admiration for both the initial display of courage and the pragmatism. "I assure you it won't be humiliating," he said. "Just a simple statement of facts, the most important of which will be a deadline by which our demands must be met."

"What's the deadline?"

"Seven days. Starting tomorrow."

Norris snorted again. "I hope your demands are simple, because this government couldn't get a check written in seven days, I assure *you.*"

"I hope you're wrong, because that's all the time they're going to have."

"What are the demands?"

El Tiburón withdrew a folded sheet of paper from his pocket, opened it, and pushed it across the table.

Norris held it a foot and a half away from his eyes, struggling to focus on the typewritten text. When he returned the paper to the table, he shook his head. "I don't know," he said. "If the government of Puerto Rico and the Congress don't agree immediately, it could take months."

"The government of Puerto Rico does what it's told. If your own Congress wants to issue your death warrant, that's their choice." El Tiburón's voice had become harsh for the first time.

"Mr. . . . ." Norris hesitated, making a circular gesture with one hand, searching for the name.

"El Tiburón."

"Mr. El Tiburón. I assure you that you've already frightened me with the probability of my death. I'll make your recording and I'll do as you tell me. And I assure you I'll start counting off the seven days."

Norris had spoken the words softly, but with an unmistakable defiance that brought a slight smile to El Tiburón's lips.

"Good," he said, waiting before going on. "There's one other thing. They've appointed someone to head the investigation of your kidnapping, and although they didn't say so, he's sure to run an extensive rescue operation. It's a man named John Walter Henry, an assistant director of the FBI. Would that be the same man who ran your police state operations against revolutionary groups in New York?"

Norris nodded his head. "I would assume so."

"That's fascinating. The revolutionary groups there used to refer to him as Pig Number One. He's quite expert, if I remember correctly." He grinned at Norris. "You had trouble remembering my name before. I assume you don't know what El Tiburón means in Spanish."

Norris shook his head.

"It means the shark." He grinned again. "And, Mr. Norris, if you drop a pig into the waters of the revolution, the shark will devour it."

"Eat his ass right up," Wally shouted.

Norris glanced from one to the other. "I prefer to think of Henry as a bird," he said.

El Tiburón laughed. "Oh, yes. The great American eagle."

Norris shook his head. "No. Perhaps a pelican."

El Tiburón hesitated, temporarily confused, then broke into laughter again. "That's right, isn't it. They eat fish." He leaned across the table. "But they don't eat sharks."

"I'm thinking in terms of a very large pelican," Norris said.

"You got some pair a balls, old man," Wally said.

El Tiburón studied Norris intently, his amusement mixed with admiration, somewhat confused by the fact that it was. It was something he had not anticipated. His hatred for the man's principles had blinded him to the fact that he might be able to admire the man as a person, his sense of inner control and power. But why not? He undoubtedly would have admired Stalin in the same way, even though he, too, had been an oppressive monster. You destroyed the man not because you hated him as a man, but to stop the execution of the principles. Tyrannicide, pure and simple. But there were things to be learned, even from tyrants, he knew. Means to achieve power. Methods of manipulation that could only be learned from practical application. He leaned back in his chair.

"Tell me. What do you think of our demands?" he asked.

Norris looked into his eyes, trying to ascertain if the question was the start of another humiliating game. He shrugged his shoulders.

"Come now. Tell me," El Tiburón said.

Norris was confused by the question. But an answer would keep him out of the hot, airless storage room. It would also provide the opportunity for dialogue that might even be extended. He drew a deep breath.

"The principles are fine," he began, watching for any show of annoyance. "They show a certain naiveté about the operation of government, this one anyway, especially with regard to its ability to control business in a realistic sense." He hesitated, then continued. "Tell *me* something. Do you truly believe that given all your demands, the Puerto Rican people will vote for independence?"

El Tiburón's eyes widened and it sent a tremor through Norris.

"They will," he said, rising from his chair and turning his back to Norris. He turned back abruptly. "The only thing that has stopped it, subverted it, is the dependence your government and your corporations have forced upon them. You have never understood the soul of the Puerto Rican people, the passion they feel for their island homeland. You see them only as something exploitable because they are a simple people."

He began pacing the floor. Norris watched him, frightened by the intensity that had suddenly erupted.

"History lesson, *Mr. President.*" He snapped out the words like a man whose life had been challenged. "In 1952, when your damnable commonwealth was forced on the people, 18.9 percent voted for independence. In 1964 another 2.7 percent voted for that freedom and in 1976, still another 6.4 percent joined the cause." He glared at Norris. "And all in spite of the fact hat 53.3 percent of my people are forced to live on your damned food stamps. Do you realize that in your wretched, impoverished state of Mississippi only 12.5 percent of the people are dependent on food stamps to *eat.*" He jabbed his finger in the air. "You take away the yoke of commonwealth and leave the carrot of food stamps and my people will rush to freedom. You give them a chance to control the fourteen billion dollars of industry, earn equal wages with equal opportunities for advancement, and they'll run from you. You think they don't know why you want them? You think they believe you want five million *spics* as first-class citizens? You think *they* don't know that what you really want is the off-shore oil, the tax-free industry, the cheap labor? You think they don't understand they're the fifth largest U.S. market in Latin America? Shit, *Mr. President*, they know those things. But they also know that they don't *eat* unless you allow them to." He pointed out the window. "I wish I could take you a few miles from here, into the stinking *barrio* in that filthy little town. I'd like you to see the people who come here to cut cane and pick vegetables. We're your new slaves. We just don't have to wear chains on our legs. Our chains run from Washington to San Juan in the form of forced dependence."

He rested his hands on the back of his chair. His breath was coming quickly and his face mirrored the rage inside him. He took a deep breath, allowing the rage to pass, then slowly returned to his chair.

"We spics were always passionate politicians," he said. "Excuse the diatribe." He leaned forward again, resting both forearms on the table. "Go on. Tell me what you think."

"I don't want to anger you," Norris said.

El Tiburón waved both hands in the air. "You won't anger me. I want to hear your views." He smiled, more at himself than to put Norris at ease. "I'm sorry for the outburst. It wasn't directed at you personally."

Norris looked into the handsome, smiling face. It was almost boyish now. Everything had become a contradiction. He had not realized the man was Puerto Rican, but it was obvious that he was. And now he was apologizing to someone he had kidnapped and treated brutally, this same man who had coldly murdered two Secret Service agents, now concerned that he had been rude.

Norris folded his hands, his face took on the stern look of the knowledgeable instructor. "Let us assume," he began, "that a vote for independence becomes a reality, either because of the actions you have taken or at some future date. First of all, Congress would not be obligated to continue any form of financial aid. It would, no doubt, do so to some degree. But that would undoubtedly be based on certain concessions from the new government. Here I'm talking about trade agreements, military installations, things of that nature. Should they concede to your demands under pressure, those agreements could be altered or rescinded at any time. If, however, it came in the form of a treaty with a new and legitimate government, it would certainly be honored throughout the period in question. There you have one flaw in your demands."

Norris waited for some reaction, but El Tiburón only nodded. "Secondly, there would be no way for this government to stop island-based industry from simply folding their tents and leaving Puerto Rico. As you said, they are there because of the tax incentives, because of the relatively cheap labor force and the favorable market conditions. Any new government would probably have to offer similar incentives. Now I'm not defending the exploitation. I'm merely pointing out that business, by its very nature, *is* exploitive."

"They can't take their factories with them," El Tiburón interjected.

"No, they can't. But if I remember correctly, the current real unemployment rate in Puerto Rico is at least thirty percent. If anything, more industry, not less, is desperately needed. And if the factories were abandoned, who would operate them? You yourself admit there's a shortage of trained managerial personnel."

"A new government could obtain aid from friendly nations."

"That's true. But you'd have to be sure that the facilities could operate as efficiently *just* to maintain the current economic level. The last figure I recall was that individuals and interests on the mainland took more than one and a half billion in profits out of the island each year. That amount is just a little more than half of the welfare costs alone. Therefore, any new government, sooner or later, would either have to double the industry, or operate at twice the efficiency that presently exists. That, I'm afraid, might require a similar exploitation of the work force."

El Tiburón began to speak, but Norris raised his head, stopping him. "Please just let me finish," he said, smiling. "Now let us assume that certain foreign powers provide technical assistance to help develop the island's natural resources. They, too, will want trade agreements, military concessions, political alliances."

"You have a question of philosophy as well."

"And you, of course, are not a capitalist."

"Is any sane man today?"

Norris smiled. "Only those who have been successful at it, or hope to be."

"There is no hope for my people through capitalism."

"Probably not. Not for several generations, at least. But remember one other thing. There's not that great a difference between those who seek to dominate socialist countries and those who seek the same thing in the capitalist world. It's like the difference between the politician and the merchant. The politician seeks power to achieve wealth and comfort. The merchant seeks wealth and comfort to achieve power. And similarly, there's very little difference between the socialist politician with his dacha on the Black Sea and the Wall Street banker who manipulates government. Somehow those beneath either always lose. Tell me, do you think Premier Castro has ever dined on caviar while many of his people went to bed hungry?"

El Tiburón's jaw muscles tightened. "It does *not* have to be that way."

"No, it doesn't. But somehow it always seems to happen."

"It certainly did under your regime."

There was a harshness in El Tiburón's voice, but Norris could tell it was more defensive than aggressive.

"I never denied my Machiavellian approach to both politics and economics," he said. "I always understood that power was the only justifiable end in politics. And that meant that goodness equaled efficiency and that any efficient way of acquiring, consolidating, and expanding power was good. Any inefficient way was bad."

El Tiburón laughed.

"You may laugh," Norris said. "But your own actions in themselves indicate a somewhat pragmatic approach."

"Yes, but for the good of the masses, not the few," he snapped.

"That's only an excuse for the practice."

"And I suppose you would justify exploitive capitalism in the same way?"

"Yes. The only desirable end in economics is the production of goods and services and the accumulation of wealth. I simply feel capitalism is more efficient in accomplishing that."

"And more brutal."

"Perhaps. But socialism, when practiced in the extreme, thwarts initiative and ambition. Only artists and mad scientists, I'm afraid, produce for the sake of the work itself."

Anger flashed in El Tiburón's eyes; his lips curled. "You make it all sound so glib. Do you really believe I'm that naive. You sit there spouting your artificial classroom political explanations, giving none of the guts of what really happens."

He stood and backed away from his chair, pointing a finger at Norris, his lips almost a snarl now. "When you talk about the benefits of capitalism what you really mean are the real estate swindles pulled off by the friends of those in power who then pass a share of the benefits back in quiet little loans that never seem to be repaid.

When you talk about diplomacy you mean the gifts exchanged by dictators, jewels passing from one strongman to another, quiet sanctuaries where a monster can hide in luxury after the people he's ravaged have risen up against him. The old quid pro quo, keeping it all in the club, because every strongman knows that his turn may be next. And in the meantime, fuck the people, because they're all just fools."

Norris leaned back in his chair, allowing his silence to play against the younger man's words. "Perhaps my greatest failure was that I didn't protect myself well enough," he said. "You say I'm rotten like any other politician." He shrugged. "But you have to include the Castros and the Maos of the world as well. Power isn't wielded by nice little men. The social fanatics and the saints are just tools for the people who do wield that power. But the power and the spoils that go with it stay with those who have the guts to be pragmatic. And that just might be in the best interests of mankind in the long run. History has shown that saints have been some of the most ruthless murderers. And it's also shown that they achieved the least for mankind."

"So you prefer to be one of the saintless shits," El Tiburón said.

"I prefer to achieve." And so does he, Norris thought. Perhaps he even admires the very fact that I could do what he accuses me of. Yes. He studied the younger man in the ensuing silence. Perhaps he *can* be led. But cautiously, carefully. I only wish he were under my power as I'm now under his. But it's his power now. So be cautious. Even disagree cautiously.

El Tiburón shook his head, the anger gone now. "Philosophically we'll never agree. To you it's a question of efficiency, to me it's intent. You'll never see the value of the government-owned automobile plant that produces cars because the people need them, rather than to grab profits."

"It's also a question of results," Norris said.

El Tiburón smiled at Norris. The old man was sitting there in his rumpled shirt and trousers, barefooted and unshaven, looking more like a Bowery bum than a former world leader. And here we are debating the values of communism and capitalism, he thought. Pure madness. He truly thinks of himself as the gunfighter, the football hero. All the things he could never be, but can now fantasize about because of the real power he held. He shook his head.

"All right. Enough philosophy," he said. "Since I'm forced to deal right now with your capitalist republic, what is your overall view of the demands?"

"I hope they succeed," Norris said.

El Tiburón threw back his head and laughed. "I'm sure you do," he said.

"I only wish you had excluded all the revolutionary jargon," Norris added.

El Tiburón stared at him. "Why?"

"It will give some people an excuse not to deal with you seriously. It also gives them an out if the negotiations fail. They can simply brand you all as wild-eyed revolutionaries."

"We are wild-eyed revolutionaries," Wally interjected.

El Tiburón raised his hand toward Wally. A look of concern had flashed through his eyes. "Those words were intended for my people. *They* understand what I'm saying."

"That doesn't alter the fact," Norris said. "When you start talking about imperialist domination, colonial politicians and stooges, and capitalist exploiters, you're raising the hackles of the conservative element in the Congress and across the country. If you're going to get what you want, the support of those people, even if it is just tacit support, is going to be needed."

"You can't change revolutionary principles and facts to satisfy your opposition. Especially just to make things more comfortable for them."

"Not even to achieve what you want? What happened to one step back, two steps forward."

El Tiburón turned to Wally and extended both hands. "Look at this man," he said. "Now he's teaching Lenin." He turned back to Norris, shaking his head over the unbelievable nature of the conversation. "I think this is all I can take for now," he said. "You'll have to go back inside your room."

Norris winced at the idea. "Would you mind if I just looked out the window for a while." He hurried on before El Tiburón could answer. "It's just that I'm very interested in ornithology and the birds in this area are quite exceptional."

"Ornithology? Sheet," Wally said.

El Tiburón stared at Norris. Taken by surprise again, he thought. "You can look out the back window for a while," he said. "But close it first. And don't try to open it again. Understood?"

Norris nodded. "Thank you." He rose slowly from the chair, his eyes searching El Tiburón's, seeking some sign of success or failure in this first confrontation.

El Tiburón smiled and motioned toward the rear room with his head. He watched Norris struggle forward and limp toward the back room.

"And don't forget to tell me what you can eat," he called after him.

He placed his elbow on the table and cupped his chin in his hand. He glanced up at Wally, then back at the table, and slowly shook his head. He was glad the others had not been there.

~~~~~

The old team had gathered.

Henry's strike force was now headquartered in a large suite of offices on the top floor of the Executive Office Building adjacent to the White House. Each agent there had once been part of the antiradical unit in New York. The only exception was Mary Roche, whom Henry had requested both for personal reasons and because he felt she could be trusted.

The offices were Spartan, set off only by the elaborate plaster work of the building's interior. But there the austere nature of the operation ended. There was an extensive telephone network, a direct tie-in to the FBI computer center, duplicating and recording equipment, a full clerical staff, and most important, a record room which now held the Bureau's complete files on all radical organizations potentially connected with WAR, some three truckloads.

Henry's own office was small by choice. The largest of the offices in the suite had been utilized to house the records. But the space was adequate, and at his personal request, it had been equipped with a standing American flag and an FBI seal. It had been a touch he had not been able to resist.

Seated there now with Grant Desverne across from him, Henry could feel the blood coursing through his veins. The months of forced inactivity had left him feeling like a well-trained runner whose race had been canceled. Now he was functioning, even if it was in a job no one in their right mind would have wanted. No one but him.

"The full complement are in place in and around Palm Beach,"

Desverne said. "We have some decent partial prints from the boat and the shell casings found on deck, but nothing good enough for match-ups without possible suspects to compare them against. Checks at the airport have ruled out an escape by air. There simply wasn't any private air traffic at that time and no reports of any seaplane or helicopter activity on radar. Even if they were flying low, the Coast Guard air patrols would have spotted something. They blanket the area because it's a major air drop for drugs. Since there's little question we have the right boat, we can rule out any escape toward the keys off the Bahamas as initially feared. So. . . ." He drew the word out.

"They're still in the area, somewhere," Henry said.

"Best guess is a hundred-mile radius," Desverne said. "It's still a lot of territory."

"Too much. But it's what we've got."

Mary Roche entered the office carrying a computer printout one quarter of an inch thick. She placed it on Henry's desk, then leaned over and explained the coding alongside each name and address.

Desverne placed his fingers against his lips, hoping it would be viewed as the involuntary act of a man deep in thought, not someone hiding an irrepressible grin, which it was. Mary Roche's long, silky hair hung down along her cheeks and her soft rayon blouse was unbuttoned much lower than the Bureau would have considered proper.

If he hasn't yet, he certainly should, Desverne thought, tilting his head slightly for a possible glimpse into the parted rayon. He definitely should.

"How many names in all?" Henry asked.

"Two hundred and forty-two. But the list also includes university relationships, professors and other students the subjects were close to, attorneys, relatives and close friends, where available," Mary explained.

"How many hard subjects with known radical backgrounds, active or inactive?"

"Eighty-three, seventy-one with known addresses."

"Henry nodded, then looked across the desk at Desverne. "Dez I want full surveillance on the seventy-one and tracers placed on the remaining twelve. In addition, do the same for relatives, former attorneys, and any university ties that are shown as having been close. Those names are coded "A-2", the primary subjects, "A-1". Cross-

check for military records on the primary subjects, as well as for updated criminal records. NCIC* should be able to provide that within
a few hours. On all A–1 and A–2 subjects I want the whole shot.
Wiretaps, mail and physical surveillance, investigations into recent
travel, credit information, employment information, and, if applica-
ble, medical data, any girlfriends, wives, hookers they might go to,
everything. Also check for any licensed weapons, any past history of
experience with boats, and any recent travel to the Palm Beach area.
I want agents to have teletype photos of all primary subjects for use
in canvassing every motel and hotel within a twenty-five-mile radius
of Palm Beach. That's a smaller area than it sounds like, since just
about all of them are within spitting distance of the coast. Get new
photographs where needed, if someone's grown a beard or shaved
one off. Also I want reports on major crimes in every large city east
of Chicago over the past two months. Deal only with actions against
government or corporate individuals or buildings. We know they
used those bombings in New York as a ruse, but they may also have
been involved in other actions as well that could give us a clue. Include Puerto Rico as well. The whole damned island. I want the photos shown in every hotel there, as well." He paused, thinking. "Oh,
yeah, one more thing. I want a list of traffic citations given out in
the Palm Beach area during the thirty days preceding the kidnapping
and every day since it happened. And I want it continued each day
until we catch them. Feed the names of the vehicle owners into the
computer for comparison against every name on the list, including
known aliases. On rentals, get the names used with the rental agencies. We'll also need the normal crosschecks of any fingerprint files
of all two hundred forty-two against the partials found on the boat.
We'll undoubtedly only end up with probable comparisons, but at
least that'll be a start."

"Sounds like we're back in business again," Desverne said.

"We better be, or we can kiss Edmund Norris good-bye." He
glanced up at Mary. "I'm going to need constant updates on everything that comes in. You and Dez are going to have to collate it all.
Dez will issue orders to the various offices of all combined agencies.
Help him wherever you can." He studied Mary's expression for a
moment, then broke into a grin. "I don't think Mary really approves

*NCIC—National Crime Information Center, which provides computerized
criminal information to police agencies throughout the nation.

of all this, Dez. She's a firm believer in civil liberties."

"So am I," Dez said, smiling up at her.

A hint of red showed in Mary's cheeks. "I just never realized we could get so much information on so many people this quickly," she said.

Henry patted the computer printout. "We couldn't if we didn't have this to start with," he said. His eyes darted back to Dez. "That reminds me. What's happening with our request for files from CIA?"

"We're getting a lot of bullshit. They insist their files *were* shredded as ordered. I told them to look again."

"Bullshit is right. They haven't followed a presidential directive for the past twenty years, unless it suited their own policy. Look. You go there personally. See this character Farragut that Horton has assigned to assist us, and tell him in no uncertain terms that the shit hits the fan unless he stops screwing us around. Don't worry about repercussions, there won't be any."

"Did I ever worry?" Dez grinned.

"No, you never did. That's why you live in Omaha." Henry returned Dez's smile. He still felt a lingering guilt in dealing with the man. The temptation to turn on him for self-preservation had been real. He put it out of his mind.

"Before you go to CIA headquarters, get the instructions out on the teletype. If you get any negative feedback, you just tell those bastards that everything is per order of the President and that they can confirm that with Cramer Lessing at the White House. You should enjoy doing that."

"I almost hope they object," Dez said, standing to leave. "I'll keep you posted on any reactions. You might enjoy it too."

Mary started to follow Dez out the door, but Henry stopped her. She took the chair across from him.

He leaned back and folded his arms across his chest. The sleeves of his shirt were rolled up to the elbow, exposing the sinewy muscles of his forearms. He tried to make his features as unbusinesslike as possible. He very much wanted her to understand.

"I know this is all new to you," he began. "I also know it's something that was never talked about at the academy. But it's not new. It's not something that I invented. It's been going on for a long, long time and with good reason." He stood and walked over to the window and looked out. It was raining, and below, people were hurrying across Lafayette Square struggling with umbrellas against the wind.

"You don't have to explain to me, Pat," Mary said.

He turned around and leaned back against the windowsill. "I want to," he said. "For several reasons." He returned to his desk. "People often become offended when they find out the Bureau has been keeping tabs on some university president or prominent professor or scientist or writer or whatever. But a lot of these people end up one day being proposed for sensitive government jobs. What they don't know is how long it takes to run a really thorough background investigation when you start from scratch. There's no way we could do that prior to a nomination or a Senate confirmation hearing or even before someone started to work. So we have files because we have to know something about these people beforehand. In the case of radicals it's simply been a question of future self-preservation. It was never just protection against bombings and robberies. For a long time now, we've anticipated this type of thing happening. Everything's pointed in that direction. After the Patty Hearst fiasco, we expected a rash of similar actions. Personally, if that had been successful, or at least if the kidnappers hadn't met such a grisly end, I think it would have happened. But it's still a very real probability, even forgetting about Norris. Do you know that right now you can't find a major corporate executive, especially among the oil companies, who hasn't taken some security measure, whether it's a bodyguard, defensive driving for his chauffer, electronic security for his home, or whatever. Some have done all of it, and a number of companies even have full-time consultants who teach corporate personnel how to deal with ransom demands. Some former agents are making a bundle doing just that." He patted the computer printout again. "This, right here, tells me we were right all along, especially now."

Mary looked at him, her eyes soft, fascinated by his intensity. "Pat," she said. "I won't question you. It just takes some getting used to."

Henry laughed softly. "Is that all you have to say after this great lecture I've just given you?"

She nodded her head.

An hour later Mary Roche was still thinking about Henry's words, about the man himself. There was a temporary lull in information coming in and she sat at her desk, her mind removed from the moment. He was such a gentle man, such a contradiction to the work he did. She had found herself thinking of him often, even be-

fore that night they were together for the first time; since then, even
more so. Sitting before that fire the first night, he had told her about
Vermont, about the intrinsic beauty there. She had never been to the
New England states, and she had doubted it could ever be as beautiful as he had described it. He had spoken about it as though it had
some magical sense to it, some purity that did not exist elsewhere,
and she had decided he had romanticized it in his mind to satisfy
some inner need. But everyone had those needs; she knew she had
them as well.

She found herself wondering what it would be like to go to Vermont with him, and she shook her head, driving away the thought.
But he didn't seem so much older when she was with him. She was
only reminded of the fact because he mentioned it so often. Perhaps
she wouldn't have liked him when he was younger. Perhaps he had
been brash and overly sure of himself then, like so many of the men
in the Bureau who were her own age. All cockiness, regarding themselves as supersleuths, looking down on those in other agencies, and
especially those in the police. But she doubted he had ever been like
that. He was too patient, too understanding. Just the way he had tak-
en time to explain things to her. It hadn't been necessary. Certainly
he didn't have to explain his actions that way, and surely not to her.
And they had been out to get him, to force him out of the Bureau,
to destroy him.

A sudden surge of protectiveness rose within her, forcing her to
smile at her own foolishness. And how would you protect him? she
thought. But all the same she knew she would want to, would do
anything to try. And what did that mean? What did it mean about
her feelings toward him. He excited her, his gentleness aroused her
passion, as did his sense of strength. But the feelings she felt were
more than that. How much more she wasn't sure. He'd laugh at you
if you fell in love with him, she told herself. No. He wouldn't laugh.
He'd be gentle with you even then, especially then.

She drew a deep breath and stroked her hair absentmindedly.
Just being with him now is the important thing. Now, when he needs
you. She wondered if he would still need her that way when it was
over. God, she thought. If Norris hadn't been kidnapped, it might
be over now. Inwardly she was surprised at herself, realizing that she
was pleased the kidnapping had taken place. Both for his sake and
your own, she thought. Just stay close to him, she told herself. Let
things happen naturally, or not happen. Stay close to the gentleness

and the strength. But, God, I don't want to lose him. Not now, not so soon.

"I'm going over to Langley, now."

Dez's voice brought her back, and she looked up at him startled by how deeply she had slipped away into her own thoughts. Her eyes blinked slightly as she looked up at him. He was grinning at her.

"Having naughty thoughts?" he quipped.

She tilted her head defiantly to one side. "I always have naughty thoughts," she said.

"Don't let Pat find out you're doing it during working hours."

She felt the redness coming into her cheeks. Dez looked into her face and broke into a broad smile.

18

Nine o'clock and already the heat was oppressive. But at least it was no longer just the dark, suffocating storage room.

He was seated before the window in the rear room of the cabin, wishing now that they would allow him to open the window. It was absurd. He stared into the dense foliage, thick tangles of lush vegetation, broken by occasional stretches of open marsh grass, each forbidding in its own way. The sounds, the endless heat, the occasional movement that only made one uneasy at the thought of what it might be. Five thousand square miles of it, stretching from the southern end of Lake Okeechobee down to the dense mangrove swamps at the tip of the peninsula; infested with every threatening form of life known to the continent. He shook his head. And they're afraid I'll escape into it, when a man one-third my age wouldn't last an hour on foot.

He glanced about the foliage, the rich greens and browns that seemed to cry out with life in this airless, dire, repellent place. And yet so beautiful, while every animal out there lived in fear of the sounds of others that might prove larger and more powerful. Not unlike the people in this cabin, he thought. All trapped from without and from within. They *were* frightened, just as he, too, was. It showed in their eyes during lapses of bravado. But that was something that only made them more dangerous.

He found himself wondering if these people were truly willing to die for this insane cause of theirs. Certainly they had considered it at the outset. It had probably seemed romantic to them then. But just considering it and. . . . He shook his head again. It was foolish to even think about it. It must be assumed they were willing to waste their lives. Anything else would be false hope, nothing more. They had not tried to hide their identities from him. Yes, they were prepared to die. How stupid human beings were. The greater his exposure to them, the greater his disappointment. The lesser animals showed much greater intelligence. They, too, would fight for what they held to be theirs. But when that fight proved hopeless they would move away to begin again. Even an animal protecting its brood would surrender when it knew the battle was lost. Survival. Only man had not yet learned the overriding necessity of it.

His body froze. In the distance he could hear a soft, low, guttural bark, like the scolding of a squirrel, a sound almost indistinguishable from the mangrove cuckoo. His eyes searched the denser thickets where he knew the shy, secretive jay-sized bird might be. Any movement would reveal it, even the smallest flash of brown and white plumage. *Coccyzus minor, thirty centimeters, ranging from southern Florida through the West Indies and from Mexico to northern South America, Insectivorous.* Noise came from behind, disrupting his thoughts. They were arguing again. Outside the soft barking seemed to fade, then was gone. Even the birds were abandoning him today. His breath had quickened in the momentary excitement. Beneath his clothing he could feel the perspiration forming rivulets along his body. Disgusting oppressive heat. The odor of his own body. Perhaps they would allow him to wash. He ran one hand along his cheeks, scratching softly. They had no right to keep him filthy. Damn them. Damn them all. And the tape recording, the damned tape recording. It was only after he had made it that this maniac, who called himself the shark, had said he could use the rear window during the day. Had it been that beneficial to them? Had he sounded as pathetic and desperate as they wanted?

He stared blindly into the patch of dense forest off to his left, trying to remember the words he had read, trying to recall if the sound of his voice had remained as firm as *he* had wanted.

This message has been prepared for me by the members of Comando Central of Ejército Mundo de Revolución. That much had been fair. It would be understood that everything that followed had been someone else's words. He struggled to remember, but the sequence seemed jumbled. *In the background you can hear a news broadcast being played. This is being done so you can be assured that I am alive and well at this time. It is now nine P.M. on the twenty-fourth of November. You have seven days to meet the demands pre-*

viously sent to you. If those demands are not met, I will be executed at exactly nine P.M. on the evening of December first. There will be no extensions of this deadline. He was certain his voice had faltered then, but he had not been allowed to listen when the recording was replayed. *My captors wish to assure the American people that they have no desire to harm me. Their only interest is in securing justice for the people of Puerto Rico, who have been denied independence and forced to live under the oppressive exploitation of Yanki corporate interests. They are not the enemies of the American people and only ask for Puerto Rico what each American citizen asks for himself, the right of self-determination and economic opportunity and freedom. In addition, they seek continuance of federal assistance for a limited period of time in the form of reparation payments for the years that those rights were denied. They wish to point out that this assistance is far less than that given in the past to nations who engaged in unsuccessful wars against the government and people of the United States. I shall now read the demands which the President of the United States declined to reveal to the American people yesterday.* The demands had been the same, but the wilder rhetoric had been eliminated. This man, this shark, had been far more clever this time, but even more important, he had listened. He wondered if any meaning could be attributed to that.

Outside, the piercing sound of insects seemed to intensify. The sun had risen over the eastern line of trees and it reflected angrily on the marshes to the west, catching the water that lay below the high grass and sending out flashes of light. In the center of the marsh there was a small pond, no more than fifty feet across, and the bright yellow glow of the sun spread out, engulfing all but its outer edges.

He turned at the sound of footsteps. The one they called Juan was standing in the doorway, his face sullen. He had the strange weapon in one hand, the machine pistol, but he made no move forward.

Norris felt himself swallow. His mouth had become dry at the sight of the man. There was a sense of brutality that seemed to permeate his being, some irrational need to cause physical pain.

Juan looked down at the weapon, then back at Norris.

"You like my gun, old man?" He held the machine pistol up, the barrel angled toward Norris's head. "It's a nice gun, man. A Stechkin machine pistol. You ever hear about it? Shoots one hundred five rounds in ten seconds. One little squeeze of this finger and your whole fucking head looks like a piece of Swiss cheese."

There was a flash of humor in his eyes, but his mouth was still hard. Norris looked down at the floor, forcing his eyes away from the weapon and the man.

"But I can wait," Juan said. "Your government ain't gonna give up nothing for a piece of shit like you."

Norris continued to stare at the floor.

"Look at me when I talk to you," Juan shouted.

Norris raised his eyes. The man's mouth had twisted into pure hatred.

"How are the birdies today?"

"I haven't seen any," Norris answered.

"Isn't that too bad. Maybe I should put you back in the storage room, then you won't have to worry about your little birds, you old faggot."

"I'd like to stay here."

"I'd like to stay here." Juan imitated his words in a high whine. "But you don't have nothing to say about that right now. The people who want to be nice to you are gone. Wally went to deliver the tape. And your friend went for a walk with Carol. All you got now is me and the others."

Norris stared at him, fighting to control his fear. *Lanius ludovicianus, the loggerhead shrike. Impales its prey—a small bird, or mouse, or insect—on a barbed wire fence or thorn, then tears it apart, sometimes waiting for it to die a slow, agonizing death.* They even look alike. Dark and threatening. A black mask for a face.

Juan grinned at him. "Go ahead and watch your little birds, asshole." He watched Norris's shoulders tremble and his grin widened.

Norris turned back to the window, squeezing his eyes shut. Insanity, insanity, insanity. He had to make sure he was not left alone with this man, *Lanius ludovicianus, the butcher bird.* There was no hope with this madman.

Juan walked back to the table in the main room and seated himself across from Richard McGovern. His chair was angled so he could see Norris and his eyes continuously flashed toward the room. He picked up an oil-laden cloth and gently wiped the barrel of the Stechkin, stroking it as though it were too fragile to be handled roughly. Norma sat in a wooden chair, looking out one of the front windows; there was an M–16 carbine across her lap.

"What's he doing in there?" Richard asked.

"He's watching the birdies," Juan said. He looked back in the room, his face darkening. "I'd give anything to kill his fucking ass," he said.

"I'm sure you'll get the chance," Norma said.

Juan looked across the room at her. "Why you say that?"

"They'll never give in to save him," she said.

"Then why the fuck are we wasting our time in this fucking place?"

Norma shrugged. "We have to try for the people, right?"

"She's right," Richard said. "There's too much fucking money involved. They'll never give up that kind of bread. Not for him or anybody. Even if they promise to do what we want, they'll just try to fuck us later."

"Then we ought to kill his ass now," Juan said. He dropped the cloth and ran his hand along the weapon, feeling the smooth, oiled surface. "I don't understand how you people think."

"We agreed to wait," Norma said.

"You fucking agreed. I didn't agree to shit." He stared into the rear room. Norris's back was still to him, hunched in the chair. "I don't understand this shit. Since when we have rules we have to play by? We oughta kill his ass, dump him in that fucking swamp and get the fuck out of here. We shoulda done that in the first place and jus' told them that more of them would get their asses killed unless we got what we wanted."

"Well, it's too late for that now. We're committed, right?" Richard looked toward Norma for some confirmation.

She nodded again.

"Man, you're all fucking crazy. Who says it's too fucking late," Juan snapped. "We can always change things. Who says we can't change our fucking minds?"

"We just sent off the tape," Norma said. She got out of her chair and came over to Juan, then leaned down and kissed his cheek. "If we kill him now, we look like a bunch of crazies. Carlos is right about that. If he dies, it has to be because they let him die. It's a question of propaganda, lover."

"I'll tell you, the idea of turning him loose burns my ass too," Richard said. "I never thought about that part of it before. Just the idea of taking him was enough then. This is different. Nobody's going to understand if we send him back." His face had taken on a pensive look that seemed intensified by the steel-rimmed glasses and wispy beard. He always appeared to be pouting when thinking seriously, and it gave him the look of an intellectual seven-year-old.

Norma looked down at each of them. "You're both too fucking much," she said. "Last night we decided to do it this way and now, twelve hours later, you start talking about wasting the old bastard."

Juan picked up the cloth again and began stroking the machine pistol. "So maybe I think we made a mistake," he said.

"It's this goddamn place," Richard said. "It's getting to all of us. It's so miserable here. The bugs and the heat. I'm starting to feel like I'm the prisoner."

"But it's a perfect place. Wally was right about that. They're looking for Puerto Rican freedom fighters and the last place they're going to look is in the heart of redneck country." Norma stroked Juan's hair. "Come on, baby. Keep cool. It's just six more days and it'll be over."

The door to the cabin opened and El Tiburón stood there with Carol behind him. A guilty look flashed across Norma's face. She had left the window, the one post that was to be occupied twenty-four hours a day. She turned and walked quickly back to it.

"I'm sorry," she said. "I was only gone for a minute."

El Tiburón walked to the table. He could feel the tension in the room and decided not to make an issue of the lapse in security. He looked into the rear room. Norris was still facing the window; his arms were resting on the windowsill. He appeared even smaller, more frail.

"Any problem with him?" he asked.

"He gives me a problem when he breathes, man."

He gauged the sound of Juan's voice. There had been no release of the growing tension since they had arrived at the cabin and it was beginning to show. They needed diversion if discipline was to be maintained.

"We should get some reaction to the latest communiqué on the news tonight," he said.

"Yeah, more bullshit," Juan said.

He placed his hand on Juan's shoulder. "We'll go see," he said. "There's a small bar in the *barrio* in town that Wally told me about. They have a television there. We'll go watch the news. Two people can stay here, the rest of us will go. We'll have a few beers and we'll listen."

"Who stays?" Richard asked.

There was a note of dissatisfaction in his voice. El Tiburón had immediately thought of taking Carol and Norma with them. It would provide the release needed. But he did not need jealousy to contend with as well.

"I was thinking we'd divide it up each night," he began. "Juan and I one night. You and Wally the next. Juan and I can make it in the *barrio* place, you and Wally in one of the Anglo bars that he knows. The women would go each night because that would make everyone less conspicuous. Does that make sense to you?"

Richard shrugged.

"If you mind, Juan and I can go tomorrow," he said.

"I don't care," Richard said. He was staring into the top of the table.

El Tiburón knew he was lying, but it didn't matter. Juan was far more volatile, and he knew he had to get him out of the cabin to keep things under control. Wally could handle Richard and he would do his part and stay away from Carol for the next few days. He would not risk that additional problem.

~~~~~

Even the early evening darkness could not hide the filth and poverty that marked the small city of Belle Glade. Standing on the outskirts of every hint of commercial prosperity were the ramshackle cabins of the poor, clapboard structures built on stilts, leaning to one side or the other in apparent defiance of gravity. In the center of the oversized town the poor were clustered together on filthy side streets, each marked by small dirty shops and dimly lit bars, streets where the people mingled on the sidewalks with bottles of beer in their hands, trying to escape temporarily the cramped apartments above with their broken windows and faded plastic curtains.

As the van moved slowly through the main streets Carol McGovern found herself counting the storefront churches that seemed to compete with Dixie Fried Chicken and MacDonald Hamburger shops, each offering their own recipe for poverty, only the churches identifying those whom they chose to nourish, their signs specifying Haitian, Jamaican or Puerto Rican salvation.

The large sign on the outskirts of the city had identified it as the *Winter Vegetable Capital of the World*, but now the streets spoke of the price of that prosperity. Carol McGovern had been raised in a midwestern city and she recalled her parents' constant complaints about the rising cost of food and her own lack of thought during those years about the denial of human decency for those who gathered it. It was the insoluble problem of capitalism. Deny the poor so the majority can eat.

"I hate this place," she said. "It's everything I hate about my country."

El Tiburón smiled, keeping his eyes on the road ahead. "It's good to see it," he said. "It makes the struggle real."

"It just makes me feel helpless," she said.

The van turned into one of the dingy side streets. Along the sidewalk in front of the Ebony Bar and Lounge, Jamaican and Haitian men were gathered together in a rainbow of colors. Bright green and yellow trousers mixed with pink and orange shirts, as the men stood and postured like impoverished peacocks. Farther down the street Puerto Rican men imitated their Caribbean peers in front of the Blue Bell Bar, their eyes darting suspiciously toward the black van as it eased to the curb.

"Is this it?" Norma asked, taking in the threatening dark eyes watching her from the sidewalk.

"It reminds me of Avenue A," Juan grinned. "We better sit by the window or we'll come out and find everything gone but the steering wheel." He giggled. "You know what the Anglos say, how every Rican is born with a monkey wrench in his hand."

El Tiburón laughed at the truth in the humor.

"Speak Spanish when we get out," he said. "We won't have any trouble, then."

Inside the bar the smell of *chorizos* and old grease mingled with the odor of stale beer. A half-dozen men sat at the bar, their features obscured in the dim light, their voices hushed, suspicious of the strangers. While the others took a table near the grimy front window, El Tiburón went to the bar and ordered beer and a plate of *chorizos* from the small wiry bartender. The idea of eating food from what he was sure was a filthy kitchen sent a tremor through his stomach, but he knew the gesture would put minds at ease.

The bartender smiled when the order was given, showing a mouth half empty of teeth that seemed to match a large scar on one cheek, his badges from years of work in tough *barrio* bars. When the beers were served without glasses, El Tiburón took them without question and asked if the television set could be turned on to the news. The small man eyed him suspiciously and El Tiburón immediately understood. He was asking for favors before offering any display of paying and he reached quickly into his pocket and pulled out a ten dollar bill. The bartender flashed a second smile, then hurried off to turn on the television set before returning with the change. When El Tiburón returned to the table, leaving fifty cents behind on the bar, he was certain he had not only won the bartender's favor, but also his protection should their presence be objected to later.

When the bartender brought the spicy Spanish sausage to the table both women winced slightly, each fighting to hide their repulsion. El Tiburón smiled to himself and quickly reached for a piece of the sliced reddish brown meat. Eating among the poor in a public place was often harder than risking physical danger, he mused. It was not like eating in the mountains or in the home of a simple villager. There was a different level of poverty in the *barrio* of a foreign country. There was a sense of uncleanliness brought about by defeat.

The *chorizos* were poor, old, and stale. He caught Juan's eye, then looked at the plate of food and again at the women. Juan's eyes brightened immediately.

"Eat," Juan said, reaching out and grabbing a piece of the stale sausage. He watched as Carol and Norma each took a piece. He waited until they had both begun chewing. "If you cook them in enough grease you can't taste the cockroach shit," he whispered.

Both men laughed at the reactions. Carol's eyes bulged and Norma began to gag.

"Some revolutionaries," Juan whispered. He picked up a slice of meat and tasted it, wrinkling up his nose. "Come to think of it, they didn't use enough grease this time," he said.

When Walter Cronkite's solemn face appeared on the bar's black and white television screen their playfulness ended. El Tiburón could feel his stomach knot as the newscaster began his report with the Norris kidnapping.

"At nine A.M. this morning," Cronkite began, "the terrorist group known as WAR telephoned a Palm Beach, Florida radio station and played a tape-recorded message that federal authorities believe was made by former President Edmund Norris, who was kidnapped from his home Thanksgiving morning. The message reiterated the terrorists' previous demands and set a deadline of seven days for compliance if the former President is to be returned alive and unharmed. Here is that message."

As the newscaster's voice trailed off, a photograph of Norris appeared on the television screen and the slightly garbled message played over it. When the message ended the report shifted to a filmed interview with the radio station manager whom Wally had contacted by telephone. The manager, a short plump man with a weathered face like a walnut, expressed his belief that the contact had indeed been real. He also confirmed that the news program played as background to the recording had been identical to the one broadcast by his station the previous day.

When the cameras returned to Cronkite's fatherly face, he began a recapitulation of the kidnapping, describing in detail the brutal deaths of the two Secret Service agents, the earlier bombings in New York, and ending with the formation of the strike force now headed by Henry. The newscast then switched to a prerecorded interview with Cramer Lessing at the White House, during which the presidential aide assured his interviewer that *all necessary steps* were being taken to see if the demands of the kidnappers could be met. Lessing stressed, however, that the demands required complex negotiations, not only with the Congress and government of Puerto Rico, but also with the heads of numerous corporations whose tacit approval would be needed to honestly guarantee full compliance.

"The members of this WAR group must recognize that Puerto Rico could become foreign soil if the plebiscite they want is successful. That in itself might limit the ability of the United States government to enforce the corporate regulations they have requested without the cooperation of the corporations involved," Lessing added.

Cronkite then offered a synopsis of Henry's controversial background in dealing with terrorist groups in New York, and ended by pointing out that despite those allegations he was undoubtedly *the* expert on terrorism in the FBI today. As the cameras turned to a filmed interview with Henry, El Tiburón stiffened in his chair.

The picture flickering across the screen showed Henry, in shirt-sleeves, perched on the edge of a desk in a crowded Washington office. Behind the desk was an attractive woman, her face intent on him as he spoke, her look of admiration, obvious. In the background men and women moved about in a flurry of activity.

Henry answered the questions tersely, stating only that *some* initial progress had been made, but declining to elaborate or to predict any hope for success within the limits of the deadline. When asked about the number of agents assigned to the investigation, he offered the interviewer an incredulous look and snapped that it was "adequate to the situation."

As Cronkite began his summary of the story, El Tiburón leaned back in his chair and looked at each of his companions.

"What do you think?" Carol whispered.

He smiled at her. "I think we have a hard man looking for us. But I don't think he has a chance in hell and he knows it."

His voice had been barely audible and it had forced Juan to lean across the table to hear. "I still don't believe that bullshit about trying to meet our demands. They're stalling," he whispered.

"It doesn't make any difference," Norma said. "We still have the old man."

"The important thing is that the demands are out in the open," El Tiburón said. "Our people know what we're trying to do now. Now their support will come. And the people of this country know too. Just think how pissed off those assholes in FALN are right now."

"You think the American people will want their government to give up the island?" Carol asked. "They can get pretty hardnosed and there are still a lot of people who are against the Panama Canal treaty."

"But we're not asking them to give anything up. Just to move up the plebiscite two years." He grinned at each of them. "I think most of them will be happy with the possibility of getting rid of a lot of spics."

They laughed.

Juan leaned across to Norma. "You don't want to get rid of all us spics, do you baby?"

"I'll let you visit," she said. "Late at night. But only if you wash."

"Did you notice the way that woman was looking at that FBI pig?" Carol said.

"Hey, even pigs get laid," Juan said.

"Don't underestimate the man," El Tiburón said. He hesitated, thinking back to an earlier conversation. "He believes in the efficient use of power and he has a lot of it to use efficiently right now."

"What the hell does that mean?" Juan asked.

"It means we move carefully."

"And we stick to the deadline, right?" Juan's eyes were intent, insistent.

"Completely," El Tiburón said. "Unless it's to *our* advantage to change things."

"No." Juan had raised his voice for the first time and it had startled everyone at the table.

El Tiburón stared into his face. "We don't close off *our* options," he said. "And that includes killing him tomorrow if it proves necessary, or a month from now if that's best. You don't achieve victory through rigidity or irrational anger."

Juan's face was blazing now and El Tiburón softened his voice and leaned toward him, speaking in Spanish.

"We need each other's support, my friend. If we move against each other we help them."

"He's right," Norma whispered. "Things have to be done collectively or we lose our strength." She turned her eyes to El Tiburón. "But that also means the will of the majority."

"Agreed," El Tiburón said. He looked at each of them and smiled. "Now let's drink some beer and relax. We've earned that much today."

Juan leaned back in his chair and looked at each of them. His face was still filled with anger.

~~~~~

At eleven o'clock Henry was reviewing reports. He was seated on the sofa in his apartment, the papers spread out before him on the floor. Mary Roche came out of the small kitchen and moved up behind him, a glass of Scotch in each hand. She sat on the arm of the sofa and extended one hand.

"I thought you could use this," she said.

Henry looked up at her and accepted the outstretched glass. His face seemed drained of color and there were deep circles under his eyes.

"I don't understand what they're up to," he said.

"What is it you don't understand?"

He picked up the transcript of the tape recording. "The change in tone. It's almost as though two different groups were involved."

"I don't understand what you mean."

Henry slapped the transcript against his hand. "All the didactic nonsense is missing on the tape recording. All the revolutionary jargon."

"Maybe Norris refused to repeat those things."

Henry looked up at her, then leaned back against the sofa. "It's possible, but I just don't see him pressing them that way. Something's happened to make them move more cautiously. Either that, or they're having second thoughts. I just don't know. But I've got a gut feeling that something is happening that could give us an edge. If we only knew what the hell it was." He sat up again and stared down at the papers on the floor. "I've gone through every damned communiqué this group has ever sent out and there's nothing like this in any of them. The only other possibility is that somebody there believes they can really get these damned demands through. If that's the case we just might be able to stall them with the right scenario."

Mary reached out and ran a hand along his hair. "Seven days isn't enough time, is it?"

"Not by half. Not unless they really screw up, and as of now they haven't made one mistake. At least not any I've been able to spot, and I've gone through everything, dozens of times."

"Then all we can do is wait," Mary said.

"That's about it."

She slid down next to him on the sofa. "Good," she said.

Henry's features softened. "Are you propositioning your boss, lady?"

"I certainly am, sir."

He pulled her toward him and felt the warmth of her face against his. She's been sitting there just thinking about it, he told himself. The thought was the first reassuring one he'd had that day.

~~~~~

William Horton was also working. He was pacing the floor of his massive office listening to Farragut's final report of the day. He stopped in the center of the office and began rocking back and forth on the balls of his feet.

"Are they sure?" he asked.

"As sure as they can be without the original tape to work from."

Horton shook his head and began pacing again. "I'm disappointed in these chaps," he said. "Based on what they did earlier, I thought they were smarter than that, more professional."

"Perhaps they just kept him alive long enough to have this one recording made."

"Perhaps. But we can't risk it." He walked back to his desk and lowered himself thoughtfully into the soft leather. "I want our people to do everything to find out who these people are. We have to find out before Henry does, no matter what the costs."

"That could be dangerous for Norris," Farragut said.

"Norris doesn't matter to us now. He's a liability, and he's a dangerous one," Horton said. "The longer he's alive, the greater the chance he'll try to buy his way out with information."

"I'll take care of it immediately," Farragut said.

~~~~

Wally and Richard were playing gin rummy. He could hear their playful banter coming from the main room. The heat in the storage room was unbearable and he had stretched himself out on the floor near the curtained doorway to take advantage of the air that filtered in beneath it. He had discovered the slight breeze earlier when he crawled up to the curtain to hear the news broadcast on the portable radio. The report had not been encouraging.

Six more days, he told himself now. Six more days and then one last chance at survival. Hopefully, it was a decision he would not have to make.

19

The tape recording arrived in the mail at eleven o'clock, bringing on long, angry arguments with FBI agents at the house, and it was past noon before the Norris family was able to hear it. The effect was devastating, a mixture of relief and renewed fears.

The sound of Norris's voice had filled the large living room where they had gathered so often. There had been traces of fatigue and fear, but also a firmness that was almost defiant. Emily had rushed from the room, weeping, when the tape ended. Pamela Norris had not moved from the long sofa, the only display of emotion a slight trembling of her lips. Dalton had remained with his mother-in-law, certain she would need the greater amount of comfort.

"Don't worry," he said, seating himself next to her. "We're going to get him back."

Pamela Norris continued to stare straight ahead, her chin slightly uplifted, the patrician bearing that had first attracted her husband still very much in evidence. She did not seem to be looking at anything in particular, just staring, her mind fixed on something distant, perhaps something in the past. Dalton watched her, wondering if she had heard his words.

She turned to him and smiled faintly. "Please fix me a drink, Dalton," she said. Her voice, too, seemed distant, removed even from her request.

He walked to a small side table and selected the bottle of Glenfiddich he knew she preferred and poured an ample amount over ice. She accepted the glass without looking at him and he sat beside her again, brushing the ever-present unruly strand of hair from his forehead, then waiting quietly, not really knowing what to do next.

Moments passed before she spoke again, this time without looking at him.

"I think you should see how Emily is," she said.

He rose without answering and walked quickly to the long hallway that led to the guest room. His wife was on the bed, staring at the ceiling, her eyes red, her small breasts rising and falling rapidly. He sat beside her and stroked her shoulder.

"They're going to kill him," she whispered. "I know they are. Those bastards, those dirty bastards."

Emily seldom used coarse language and momentarily it surprised him. He wanted to tell her it wasn't true, that her father would be ransomed or rescued or something, but he could not.

"All we can do now is wait and pray for him," he said, immediately recognizing the banality of his words.

"We can do more than that," she said. Her jaw was set firmly and her eyes suddenly became angry. She looked very much like her father at the moment. "We can go to the media. We can tell them how Jordan isn't doing enough, how they're abandoning him because they hate him."

He continued to stroke her shoulder. "We can't do that. Not yet," he said. "There's no proof they're not trying, not while they have the strike force working on it."

"All they have are people here trying to keep us from finding out anything. Look what they did with the recording." She was breathing rapidly now, her anger growing.

"That was because of fingerprints," he said. "And stupidity. I'll call Cramer Lessing and tell him if it happens again, and if we're not given assurances that the right things are being done, that we'll go to the public."

"It won't help," she said, turning on her side. "Nothing will help." She began to weep again.

When he returned to the living room Pamela Norris was gone; the only sign that she had been there was a crumpled handkerchief on the table next to the sofa. Dalton looked into the adjoining rooms without success and the Secret Service agents he questioned could only assure him she had not left the house. When he entered Norris's office suite in the seaward wing of the house, he noticed the door to the bird room was open. As he entered, he could see her standing in the aviary, her back to him.

"Mother," he said softly, as he came up behind her. "Is there anything I can get you?"

She did not speak for several seconds. She held her drink in both hands in front of her and slowly rotated her head, searching the wire enclosure. The air was still, as were the birds, but as he looked around he could see the various species watching the intruders.

"I think we should free them all," she said. "I never approved of this, caging them this way. But Edmund always felt it was justified. He always said there was much to be gained."

Dalton shifted his feet, his long, slender body seeming to emphasize the awkwardness he felt. He brushed his hair from his forehead and moved up beside her. She continued to look out into the aviary.

"It might be upsetting to him, to come home and find them gone," he said.

She remained silent, then absentmindedly sipped her drink. "I wonder how it could be done," she said. "There's no door to the outside. I suppose they would have to be caught somehow, then placed in a cage and taken outside."

From high in the aracaria came a low croaking sound.

Dalton drew a deep breath and excused himself. The tension was driving everyone to the point of a breakdown and he was certain it was due to the absence of any real information. He went straight to Norris's desk and picked up the private telephone and dialed the White House. Three minutes passed before Cramer Lessing came on the line.

"Dalton, I'm so sorry. My secretary should have interrupted me. I was on another call." Lessing was using his softest southern lilt and Dalton found it especially grating.

"Cramer, I'm calling to express the concerns of the family over the total absence of information we're getting. It's having a serious effect on everyone here, and it could cause some very unfortunate repercussions."

There was a palpable silence, before the soft seductive cadence began again. "I assure you, Dalton, everything is being done. You all know as much as we do right now. The investigation is in its infancy, but it is moving ahead and we expect things to begin to break soon." He paused, but only for an instant before rushing on. "Now I don't want you to assume that I'm talking about something major within hours. But I assure you we're throwing everything we have into this. And, as you know, those resources are considerable."

"Cramer, you're not telling me a damned thing. We have to have regular information here. There has to be *something* to keep the family's spirits up, if at all possible. Otherwise, I think you're going to find public statements being made that are not going to be helpful."

"That would be very unwise," Lessing said. The lilt had disappeared; they were talking business now.

"Then make sure the family receives regular, realistic, and comprehensive reports," Wilkerson said.

"I'll do what I can," Lessing said. "But we have to be sure the information remains very tightly held."

"Oh, for chrissake, Cramer. Do you really think we're going to leak it and jeopardize the man's life?"

Pamela Norris walked slowly into the bird room, then stopped and turned in a circle when she reached the center. The room was dark. So forbidding, she thought. Such a strangely dark place. She walked slowly around the room, studying the prints on the walls, the mounted species that stared at her from the tops of tables and from fixed positions on the walls, their eyes seeming to look in all directions at once. The room was like a human soul filled with pain. Some accumulation of suffering that had finally found expression. "Your dark side revealed, Edmund," she said aloud. There were so many things she did not understand, had never understood. She had understood the pain and the suffering, not only his, but her own. Suffering that was not supposed to be hers, but was. And the doubts, the questions that were never answered. She wondered now if it might not be better if he did not return.

Dalton entered the room and she looked at him and smiled. "Dalton, do you like this room?"

His long slender face seemed confused. "I never thought about it, one way or the other," he said.

She nodded her head slowly. "No, neither did I, I suppose," she said.

20

Henry puffed quietly on his pipe, listening as Cramer Lessing ranted on. It was the second call from Lessing that day and the only difference was that it was slightly more demanding than the first. Henry looked at his wristwatch. It was two o'clock. At this rate Lessing would call twice more, he decided. He picked up a folder from his desk. The telephone was cradled between his chin and shoulder, freeing his hands for the reports he was scanning. Lessing's voice droned on, ignored. When he finally paused for breath Henry responded.

"All I can do is repeat what I told you before. As soon as we have something concrete, you'll be advised immediately. If I told you anything else I'd be telling you less than the truth."

Lessing's voice erupted immediately. At every pause Henry simple interjected a "yes," or "I understand," and continued to search the reports on his desk for something new or promising. Lessing had not yet reached the point of threatening to replace him. Perhaps he understood that the bluff would be called. Or perhaps he merely realized that he could not afford to lose the only scapegoat the administration had.

The door to Henry's office opened and Grant Desverne hurried in, appearing eager, almost excited. Henry interrupted Lessing in midsentence.

"Cramer, something just came up. I'll have to get back to you." He stared patiently at the ceiling, listening. "I don't know if it's important, but I assure you if it is I'll get right back to you." He replaced the receiver without waiting for a reply. "Asshole," he said, then looked across at Desverne.

"The White House getting on your ass?" Dez asked.

Henry's lips curled up in a tight smile. "They're trying," he said. "You have something?"

"We just might, but it's still pretty sketchy."

Henry could feel his pulse quicken. All investigations began with something sketchy; they had already gone through half a dozen similar reports. But at least the system was functioning, and sooner or later there would be something. He hoped it would be sooner.

Desverne took a chair opposite him and opened a manila folder on his lap.

"We just received a report from Puerto Rico in response to our request for information on all unusual criminal activity," Dez continued. "Seems they found the body of one of their people yesterday. He'd been dead quite a while and stuffed in the trunk of his own police car. But the autopsy showed he'd been garroted, not your normal way to get it from the usual criminal."

Henry stood and walked to the window, keeping his back to Desverne.

"They found the cop's body in the forest outside Lares which has always been a major hotbed for island radicals. Their investigation came up with the fact that shortly before he disappeared he followed some guy out of the town whom he suspected of being FALN."

Henry spun around, eager now for more. "Who was the guy?" he asked.

"Name's Carlos Rivera, about twenty-eight. His father was killed several years back during a labor demonstration. Probably by the cops. He was a fairly well-known painter, and after his death the kid disappeared. The book on him was that he went to Cuba, but it was never confirmed."

"Did we ever have anything on him?"

"We started a file on him based on the P.R. police reports at the time. Several years later the name Carlos Rivera came up in connection with FALN in New York, but there was nothing definite, so we added it to his file as a probable."

Henry could feel his blood coursing now. "Is he on our master list?"

Desverne broke into a grin. "He sure as hell is," he said. "Not much more information, but the cops in P.R. have come up with a photograph. It's old—from his college yearbook at the University of P.R.—but it's something."

Henry moved quickly across the room and took the photo from Desverne. He stared into the young, smooth-featured face. "He doesn't look Puerto Rican," he said.

"A lot of them don't. But he's the genuine article."

"Any aliases or associates?" Henry continued to stare at the photograph, as though burning the face into his mind.

Dez blinked, an involuntary action that came when he was excited. "No aliases, but a probable associate, providing it's the same Rivera in the New York FALN report. A guy by the name of Juan Hernandez, also Cuban-trained and a definite in FALN. I have a photo of him, too."

Henry took the second photograph, a police mug shot from New York; he held it next to Rivera's. "What was he arrested for?" he asked.

Dez checked his notes. "Assault. It was reduced to harassment and the sentence was suspended. We learned later that he was represented by a lawyer with ties to FALN, but by the time we found out, Hernandez had disappeared. He gave a phony address when he was arrested and nobody bothered to check. It was a typical screwup in the New York court system, and to be honest, we never chased him down at the time. It didn't seem worth it."

Henry returned to his chair, still studying the photographs. "Well, we're going to chase him down now. Both of them." He placed the photographs on the desk and leaned back in his chair. "We'll do the whole shot on these two, just in case," he said at length. "Telex the photographs to our people in P.R. and have them check every hotel, car rental agency, and airline. I want it done immediately, with reports back before the day is out. The same in the Palm Beach area. Don't spare the manpower. I also want to pull out all the stops in New York. Have them contact every skell, every hooker, pimp and junkie in the P.R. community that we've ever dealt with. Have them call in all paid informants, past and current, to get any possible addresses on either of them. Then I want full activity on those locations. Thorough searches, prints, interior photographs, everything. And don't take time for warrants. Just tell them to go in and do it under the same authority. Also get complete computer printouts on each of them. Social Security checks, military, the whole works. Use the NCIC computer as well as the Bureau's. If either one of them ever pissed in the street I want to know what street it was and where."

Desverne headed for the door, then turned back to Henry and grinned. "You gonna tell the White House?"

"Fuck them. I'll tell them when I'm ready," he said. "Just get moving and have Mary help you and get anyone else you need."

It was seven o'clock before the first reports came in. Henry was still in his office, staring down into Lafayette Square. Winter had settled on the capital, and as always, one could almost see the cold. He found himself thinking of Vermont again, a more pleasant cold, where the harshness of winter was softened by the beauty of the surrounding countryside, the unmarred snow and the spirit of activity it produced among those who lived there. Here, there were only the barren trees and the stinging air. People hurrying to escape it, remaining indoors whenever possible, an entire city held captive by the elements. There was no purity here. Not like Vermont.

He turned from the window as the door to his office opened, and from the look on Desverne's face, he knew something had happened.

"We're hitting on all eight cylinders," Dez said. He moved quickly to Henry's side and handed him a telex report, then began explaining the information as Henry read it.

"Carlos Rivera was registered at the Caribe Hilton under the name Carl Rawlings. It's a typical m.o. for radicals, using the same last initial and first name whenever possible. We have positive confirmation from three separate hotel employees. He remained three days, rented a car under the same name, using a New York driver's license. The address on it was phony. He flew in and out under the same name, the dates of which coincide with that cop's death. He flew in from Miami and the flight out was for New York. That places him in Florida during the time surveillance on Norris must have been taking place, and then back in New York before that rash of bombings." Desverne's eyes were blinking, and Henry could hear the excitement in his voice. It matched his own pulse rate.

He drew a deep breath. "It makes a fairly good circumstantial case for the cop killing," he said. "But it's still only a probable for the Norris thing." He looked up from the telex. "But it's a damned good probable," he grinned. "What do we have from Palm Beach?"

"Nothing, yet," Dez said.

"We do now." Mary Roche's words hit the room like gunfire, and they both turned to her as she hurried toward them, smiling.

"Carlos Rivera was registered under the name of Carl Rawlings at the Palm Beach Hawaiian Ocean Inn in South Palm Beach for a two-week period prior to the trip to Puerto Rico," she said, handing Henry the latest telex. "He used the same phony New York address he used later with the car rental agency in Puerto Rico. A woman bartender there remembers him. Apparently he got into an argument with her about sea turtles or something, and she was quite emphatic it was the man in our photo. There was another man with him, a large, blond American, about the same age. He registered under the name of Walter Richards, so I've already begun cross-checking the master list for names and photographs starting with the initials W.R."

Henry grinned at her, then looked at Dez. "The lady learns fast, doesn't she? Next thing you know she'll be pulling her own burglaries and mail openings." His grin widened as he watched Mary's cheeks redden. "Anything on the kind of vehicle they were using?"

"Only that the desk clerk thought is was a rather commonplace sedan," she said. "He didn't bother to fill in the information on the registration card."

Henry shook his head. "You don't kidnap somebody in a sedan." He turned back to Desverne. "Check all truck and van sales and rentals in the immediate area, prior to the snatch. Use Rivera's photograph *and* the description of this Richards guy. We may get lucky and find he used the same alias, but I doubt it. Have our people pay special attention to any vehicles rented or purchased under names beginning with the initials C.R. and W.R. Also check for stolen vehicles, although I doubt they would have taken that kind of risk. I also want a computer rundown on all traffic tickets and parking summonses. Cross-check registrations against the tickets and again, key in on those initials."

Mary and Dez hurried toward the door and Henry shouted after them. "And get those clowns in New York moving; as of nine o'clock tonight, we only have four days left."

Henry returned to his desk and picked up the photographs of Rivera and Hernandez. He put them back on the desk, then lit his pipe, still keeping his eyes on the two faces. Everything seemed to fit, almost too conveniently. A dead cop in Puerto Rico. One unexpected mistake. He continued to stare at the faces. Be the right people, he told himself. Just be the right ones.

~~~~~

They sat in a small alcove on the second floor of a Mexican Restaurant on East 49th Street, just off Second Avenue in Manhattan, two business associates enjoying a quiet dinner together. One man was short and fat, with a round Hispanic face and heavily oiled, straight, black hair. The other was approximately the same age, in his late forties, dressed in a conservative tweed suit, his horned-rimmed glasses and thinning gray hair complementing a soft gentle face. Only his hard blue eyes seemed in contrast to his appearance.

"The Company would like whatever information you can obtain as quickly as possible," the man in the glasses said.

"The contacts with my government were always discreet on both sides," the Hispanic said. "It was as it should be. Domestic trouble was being purchased, not the identities of the persons causing it."

"I understand that. But certainly there were methods of contact, through personal newspaper advertisements or whatever. We would like you to attempt to make such a contact now."

The fat man shook his head, filling his mouth with a slice of cactus covered in a rich creamy sauce. "Normally, contact was made by WAR's people," he said. "Even during the best of times, our attempts to contact them were not always answered."

"But you will try."

"Of course. But the entire matter must be handled with extreme discretion on Washington's part. My own position, as you well know, is difficult. If my own cover was jeopardized there would be no question of the outcome."

The man in the tweed suit smiled warmly. "My friend, I assure you we would never allow that to happen. All parties concerned would be eliminated, both among the people here and among the kidnappers. Nothing would ever find its way back to you."

The waiter brought a tray laden with food and they stopped speaking as he spread it before them. The fat man's eyes widened as a steaming plate of *mole poblano* was placed in front of him. Food was something even more important to him than business. He smiled at the man across from him.

"Have no fear," he said. "Arrangements will be made. It may take time but I will not fail you. Now let us eat. The food here is extraordinary."

Later that evening William Horton received the report on a private line in his office. Time was the only factor now, he realized. But that was so often the case. He would have Farragut contact Henry's people in the morning to determine his position in the race now underway. Carefully, he fitted a cigarette into the black cigarette holder and placed it in his mouth without lighting it. He was attempting to give up smoking on orders from his physician.

Part Three

21

He was short, fat, and bald with only tufts of unruly brown hair sticking out above his ears and it all combined to make him look slightly ridiculous. As he strode spryly into the office, dressed in a shapeless tweed suit, his face bright, Henry was reminded of someone's bachelor uncle in from the country for a visit.

Kermit Knutsen was joining the investigation at Lessing's insistence. As chief of the Political and Terrorist Psychology Section at Walter Reed Army Hospital, he was considered one of the nation's leading authorities on the psychology of terrorism, exactly the kind of help Henry did not want to be saddled with at the moment.

The two men shook hands, and Knutsen took a chair directly in front of Henry's desk. He sat there with his feet and knees together, his hands clasped in a ball in front of him, his body leaning slightly forward. His sanguine face was beaming, filled with obvious delight at being part of an active investigation in his field of expertise, not relegated to a study of data after the fact. Henry looked at him and drew a weary breath.

"I imagine you've looked over the material," Henry said.

"Of course, of course." Knutsen began rotating the thumbs of his folded hands. (Tweedle Dum and Tweedle Dee, Henry thought). "I've studied both sets of demands, the circumstances of the kidnapping and the data you've assembled on your potential suspects. Fascinating material and a highly volatile situation."

Henry leaned back in his chair and pressed the thumb and index finger of one hand against his eyes, rotating them gently. "Yes, we know that," he said. He looked across at the cherubic psychologist again. "Dr. Knutsen, is there anything you can . . ."

"Oh, please," Knutsen interrupted, "call me Kermit. It will make working together so much easier. And may I call you John?"

"My friends call me Pat," Henry said, noting the confusion the information produced in Knutsen's slightly bulging blue eyes. He placed his forearms heavily on the desk. "Now, as I was saying." He exhaled loudly. "We have one concern and one only, and that's getting President Norris back *alive*."

"Of course, of course," Knutsen said, nodding his agreement.

"Good," Henry said with growing impatience. "Now, Kermit, is there anything you can tell us, from what you've seen so far, that can help us either in locating these people, or in telling us how best to deal with them, either during this period of negotiation or during any rescue attempt."

Knutsen's thumbs spun wildly. "Yes, I think I can. Yes. Fascinating, as I said." His eyes seemed to bulge farther from his head. "Tell me first, have you had much exposure to this kind of situation before?"

"I've had a great deal of experience with kidnappers and terrorists. My only involvement with the two combined outside of skyjackings was a peripheral one in the Patty Hearst case. But I've studied most of the situations in Europe, the Middle East and South America, if that helps at all."

"Yes, of course it does. But in recent years we've learned some rather interesting things, and while our studies are still in the hypothetical stage, I believe we may have stumbled on to a key factor in dealing successfully with this kind of situation."

Henry leaned back in his chair, realizing now that Knutsen intended to impart his information at his own pace, in his own way. Silently he cursed Lessing.

"Tell me, are you at all familiar with the Stockholm syndrome?" Knutsen began.

Henry nodded. "I've heard the term."

Knutsen flashed a broad grin that made his cheeks puff up like a chipmunk. "This could very well be the key," he said. Almost like a rubber ball suddenly set in motion, Knutsen's round body rose from the chair. He clasped his hands behind his back and began pacing Henry's office as he spoke, the professor returned to the lecture hall. "Simply put," he began, "we have discovered that when terrorists or bank robbers or the like hold hostages for an extended period of time, a bond develops between the captors and the captives." He turned toward Henry and raised one finger, shaking it in the air. "This is a mutual bond, you understand. In some cases, the attachment of the captives for their captors has become so strong that they have threatened rescuers with assault, have agreed to marry their captors, visited them in jail, and, in certain situations, actually set up legal defense funds for them." He clasped his hands behind his back again and resumed pacing. "Even more important for us, there have also been cases where the attachment of the captors to the hostages has been *the* major factor in saving their lives."

Henry was growing impatient; he wanted Knutsen to get to the point. He began to speak but the psychologist raised his hand stopping him.

"The syndrome was first noted a little more than five years ago when a group of bank employees in Stockholm were held captive for five and a half days by a cornered bank robber." Knutsen's bulging eyes seemed to twinkle with delight. "Toward the end of that siege, one of the women captives actually telephoned the Swedish prime minister and complained that the bank robber was providing the hostages with their only protection from the police outside. Fascinating, is it not?"

Henry nodded wearily. "Yes, it is. It's all quite interesting, Kermit. But my problem is a bit more immediate, and to be blunt, I need something more than theory right now. I have to find a way to rescue Norris and I have to know how to keep them from killing him before I do. These people have already demonstrated a slight tendency toward violence."

Henry's sarcasm brought a smile to Knutsen's lips.

"And the Stockholm syndrome is your answer, Pat. And it may be your only answer. Let me break it down for you so you understand completely."

Henry held up his hands in surrender and Knutsen returned to his chair, pulling it closer to the desk, increasing the sense of importance of what he was about to say.

"It is not surprising that these terrorists have already killed. In fact, I would have been surprised if they hadn't engaged in some form of violence." Knutsen glanced about Henry's office, taking in the Spartan furniture, the standing American flag, the massive FBI seal. The smile returned to his lips. "I realize you feel that I'm excess baggage that's been foisted on you, Pat. But I honestly believe I can help. If you'll only hear me out, I promise that if you still don't agree, I'll stay out of your hair from that point on."

Henry selected a pipe from a rack on his desk and began filling it. He smiled at Knutsen. "Sorry if I've been rude, Kermit. It's just that my time seems to be at a premium these days. Please go on."

Knutsen rubbed his hands together. "Well, as I was saying, I'd be quite surprised if some element of violence had not been attached to this whole affair. Psychologically, members of radical groups who are taking on a powerful government or corporation suffer from a subconscious feeling of impotence. To overcome this feeling they often turn to an initial exertion of power, a way of showing they have force and are willing to use it. But after that power has been demonstrated, that feeling of inferiority usually subsides, except when they are threatened again, or in the case of seriously disturbed persons."

Knutsen leaned back in his chair, becoming all business as he warmed to his subject.

"As you know, Pat, seventy to eighty percent of all hostage deaths occur at the end of a siege, during attempts at rescue. Otherwise, hostages are rarely killed by their captors after the third day of captivity. And this is due to the Stockholm syndrome. There are, of course, variations which I will explain, but basically the premise holds."

"Tell me about the variations first," Henry said, interested now for the first time.

"Well, that's the unfortunate part. It includes the variables that will force us to continue working, at least partially, in the dark. It seems that terrorist groups are being trained in this phenomenon of the Stockholm syndrome, are actually being taught ways of avoiding it."

"How do they do that?" Henry puffed repeatedly on his pipe, leaving a heavy cloud of smoke between himself and the psychologist.

"Quite simply by not allowing the human factor to develop. It's really quite simple. The easiest way is to have two distinct groups among the captors. One group that guards the captive, and a second that avoids all but the most minimal contact. Then, when the time for killing arrives, members of the second group can do it without major personal conflict." Knutsen's eyes brightened. "It's really a very old principle cleverly reapplied. Just as one soldier can kill another rather cold-bloodedly in war, he might find it quite difficult to kill the exact same person if he had sat and talked with him, joked with him, played chess with him. Killing a person he had become familiar or even friendly with would be far more difficult, unless it involved a so-called crime of passion."

"You're saying that once you get to know someone, it becomes more difficult to kill?" Henry removed the pipe from his mouth and grinned.

"I hope I'm not to take that smile personally, Pat?" Knutsen said.

"I wasn't thinking of you, Kermit. I was thinking of the man who sent you."

Knutsen laughed. "Yes, Cramer Lessing can be a bit trying. But that would fall into the crime-of-passion category."

"What other variables are there?" Henry asked.

"Only two more, really. But first, let me point out that I don't think the one we just discussed applies to our situation."

"Why?"

"Well, assuming we are correct about the number of captors involved—five or six persons. There simply would not be enough manpower to provide the necessary division of labor. We must assume that given the circumstances of the kidnapping itself, these people are reasonably professional and well trained. That would mean they have at least two people guarding Norris twenty-four hours a day and the numbers needed for that just wouldn't allow for a more isolated killing group. The other two variables, however, could apply. The first would involve dehumanization of the captive himself. Keeping him bound and gagged and isolated would tend to make him less of a person to his captors. This is why the more common criminal kidnapper, the one seeking a financial ransom, often finds it easy to kill his victim, even after the ransom is paid. He has kept the victim bound and gagged and blindfolded to avoid escape or identification later if he's captured by the police. He then finds it very easy to kill that person, who is no longer a person at all, but merely a package." Knutsen paused and drew a deep breath. For the first time there seemed to be a look of concern in his eyes.

"The third and final variable is even more problematic," he continued. "It involves the psychopath and the egomaniac. If, within the group of captors, we have a psychopathic killer—one who enjoys killing for the pure pleasure it gives him—we then have a variable beyond our ability to control or manipulate. If we have an egomaniacal terrorist, we have a similar problem, only slightly less severe. The egomaniac would be susceptible to the Stockholm syndrome, but that susceptibility could not be guaranteed. This type of person is a deliberate captor who sees his captive as little more than a poker chip to be used in achieving his end. And unfortunately, he is quite willing to execute his hostage to achieve that end."

Henry rocked back and forth in his swivel chair. "Do any of our suspects appear to fit into those categories?"

"There simply isn't enough data on them right now for me to make an intelligent evaluation," Knutsen said. "Hopefully, your men will come up with more, providing these suspects are the kidnappers."

Henry hesitated. "The second variable," he said at length. "Wouldn't they have Norris bound and blindfolded to keep him from identifying them later?"

Knutsen shook his head. "I don't think so, for two reasons. First, Norris is not a young man; he has a severe case of gout and, according to your report, probably does not have any medication with him. If he were constantly tied up, he would undoubtedly be in a great deal of pain. Based on the tape recording I listened to, I don't feel that he is. Second, these people are highly political, dedicated to a cause to a fanatical degree. Based on their demands, I would even go so far as to say they view themselves as potential martyrs to that cause, revolutionary heroes, if you will. Their primary concern is not keeping Norris from being able to identify them. Their primary concern is in getting their message across. We've done some rather extensive research in this area, in some widely varying cases. The Hanafi confrontation here in Washington and the Moluccan train attacks in the Netherlands, for example."

Knutsen pulled his chair even closer to Henry's desk. "Do you remember that Croatian terrorist in New York in 1976? Planted a bomb in a locker at Grand Central Station that killed a police officer. Then he hijacked a Chicago-bound jet."

"Very well," Henry said. "I was the head of the New York office then. His name was Busic, or something like that, wasn't it?"

Knutsen nodded, smiling. "Zvonko Busic. Extremely intelligent. Extremely dedicated to his cause. In studying him we found some fascinating things. Basically he was a man who abhorred violence. He was a man who wanted his hostages to respect him. And even more important, he was a man who wanted the world to understand his actions, understand his cause, so he would be viewed as a patriot, not as an animal. In short, he was a sensitive fanatic. And I'm afraid this is where our government has made a major mistake in this whole Norris affair."

"Mistake?" Henry spoke the word with considerable concern. He knew there had been blunders before, during, and immediately after the kidnapping. But since the investigation had begun, he knew of no mistakes.

Knutsen nodded, almost solemnly. "When it was decided not to release the demands—the first demands, with all their didactics in-cluded—we denied the captors their very real need to explain their cause." He raised one finger into the air again to emphasize his point. "The best strategy we have right now is to force them to delay their deadline, to extend it, and thus to give the Stockholm syndrome a chance to be firmly established. The longer the delay, the greater Norris's chance for survival. And the better your chance to find him. If we broadcast their message to the world, we not only inflate their sense of importance, we make them believe they are advancing their cause *and* enhancing their own image among the people of the world. And in doing so, we give them a reason to postpone their deadline."

"The administration does not want to advance their cause, or in any way make them look like heroes," Henry said.

"The administration also doesn't want Norris killed, I assume," Knutsen added.

Henry paused, unsure of the correct answer himself. "I would as-sume not," he finally said.

He and Knutsen stared at each other, each silently recognizing the very real uncertainty of the answer. Knutsen sat back in his chair and nodded.

"If it was up to me," he said, pausing before continuing. "If it was up to me, I'd even arrange demonstrations in support of the kid-nappers and make sure they received broad media coverage. Tell me, Pat, do you honestly think you have any chance at all of finding Nor-ris before the deadline?"

"I doubt it. There's a chance, but it's almost infinitesimal."

"Then what choice do we have but to play up their demands?"

Henry shook his head, then turned his chair so he was facing the window. Outside, the sun was almost directly overhead. Half of another day gone already, he thought.

"How could we do that without seeming to acknowledge the validity of their charges?" he asked.

Knutsen hesitated. "You yourself could go over the charges and demands in briefings with the media and then discount them in some way. Perhaps even in response to some prearranged question. That would satisfy their need to get their message across and also direct any antagonism away from Norris and toward you. The denunciations would have to be carefully worded, however. But I believe I could help you with that."

Henry continued to stare out the window. "I'll talk to Lessing," he said.

"Then you feel I might be able to help?"

Henry turned his head toward the round, cherubic face now grinning back at him. "I'm damned glad to have you, Kermit. You'll receive copies of all reports, but I'll have to ask that you only discuss them, and your opinions, with one person. Me. We have some internal problems that you're not aware of. But I'm sure you'll pick up on them very quickly."

When Knutsen left, Henry called Mary into his office. His face seemed dark and she wondered if the funny looking little psychologist had given him some bad news.

Henry tapped his fingers on the desk. "This Knutsen character," he began. "He's to get copies of reports I receive and any new communiqués that come in. But I want you to keep an eye on him, watch what he does with the stuff he gets, for the first few days anyway. I want to know if he's making copies of things and taking them out of here."

She seemed puzzled and hesitated for a moment. "You think there's something wrong with him, Pat?"

"I don't know if there is or not. I just want him watched for a couple of days, that's all."

There was an edge to his voice, and he was still tapping his fingers on the desk. She had not see him like that before.

"I didn't mean to question you," she said. She smiled at him. "It's just that he seemed like such a lovely little man and he was sent over by the White House. Before he came in he was telling me about . . ."

"I don't care if he was sent here by Jesus Christ." Henry's voice cut her off and he watched the smile disappear from her face, replaced now by a startled uncertainty. He ignored it.

"I just didn't realize you didn't trust him," she said. Her face had colored and she seemed hurt and annoyed.

"I don't trust anybody that I didn't ask to be part of this," he said.

She stiffened slightly. "I'm sorry. It just seems a little paranoid to worry about someone sent to help." She watched his face and regretted the words as soon as she had spoken them.

He placed both palms on the desk and leaned forward, almost as though he was about to propel himself over it. "You just listen to me for a minute. This is *not* a subject for debate. I think you're confusing our personal relationship with our business relationship. In this office, I expect every agent to follow orders without question. And that includes you."

Mary's back seemed to straighten and her chin rose slightly. "I'm sorry," she said.

Henry lowered his eyes and shook his head. "Look, Mary. Maybe you don't understand, but there are people who resent the fact that I'm involved in this and who would love to see me fall flat on my kisser. Those people don't give a damn about Norris, but I do. And not just because it means saving my own butt. I don't want these bastards to get *away* with this. And I'm not taking any chances with anybody walking in here and screwing this thing up because it's in their interests to have it turn out that way. I worked under that man, and I believed in what I did then. Can you understand that?"

"I understand. I'll do exactly as you said." She was staring over the top of his head. Her mouth was tight.

He filled his cheeks with air and blew it out slowly. "I'm sorry if I was abrupt, but I don't have time for hurt feelings either. Just take care of this for me . . . please." He added the final word as an afterthought and watched her as she left the office. A bit stiffly he thought.

He leaned back in his chair and screwed the knuckles of his index fingers into his eyes. Shit, he thought. Murphy's Law. This whole operation seemed to fall under it. He stared at the door, wishing he had not allowed her to leave that way. He'd buy her a drink when they were finished tonight, if there were any bars still open. Say something nice to her later, just in case, he told himself. He stuck his lower lip in his mouth and began sucking on it. She was probably right. He probably was being paranoid. But in this business, especially this time, it was the only way to fly. The telephone rang, and Mary and everything else disappeared from his mind.

22

The pickets walked in a haphazard line along Pennsylvania Avenue in front of the White House. At the head of the line, Rabbi Philip Leshin, a longtime friend of the former President, carried a simple placard that pleaded: Save Our President.

It was the second day of the group's vigil and already the number of people demonstrating had doubled. Unlike most demonstrations, those who populated this line of march were middle-aged and well dressed. Several carried signs identical to the rabbi's and occasionally there were chants urging Norris's safe return. Otherwise, the demonstration seemed more like a prayer vigil, which was the description Leshin had offered during his repeated interviews with the media. Within the White House the "Save Our President" group had already been dubbed SAP, by way of a not-too-subtle change of the possessive pronoun to a present indicative verb.

~~~~~

"That is the most piss-poor idea I've heard this week." Cramer Lessing glared across his desk at Josh Carling. "Are you tellin' me you actually endorse the request?"

Carling stared back at Lessing, unconcerned. As White House press secretary he was used to being growled at. If it wasn't the President or Lessing, it was a member of the media who had been deceived or denied some request, or a cabinet member whose ego had been bruised by some presidential slight. It was simply part of his job: being the bearer of annoying requests and unwanted information.

"Cramer, I don't endorse anything. I'm simply explaining that it

211

might get favorable media coverage if we agree to it. It also might add to the growing hysteria if we don't." He relaxed his long, slender body, waiting for the verbal explosion he expected. His handsome, angular face remained emotionless.

"I don't see what possible good it can do to let that crazy, politically motivated sonofabitch meet with the President of the United States just because he's walkin' up and down in front of the White House with a bunch of demented assholes."

Lessing's voice had been surprisingly calm and his choice of expletives brought a slight smile to Carling's lips.

"If the President simply assures him that every effort is being made to get Norris back, he'll hold a press conference and repeat that for us."

"We've already said that," Lessing shouted, ending the calm.

"And having somebody else say it again can't hurt us. It can only be a plus." Carling ran a hand through his short blond hair. "Certainly you can see that."

"And what if that sonofabitch goes out there and says we aren't trying hard enough?"

"Now why the hell would he do that, Cramer?"

Lessing jabbed his finger in the air, in the direction of Capitol Hill. "Because that bastard is being manipulated by some of those conservative sons of bitches in the Senate, that's why. They're already sharpening their knives up there, just hoping we'll foul up in this thing so they can use it against us. They don't give a damn about Norris. You know that as well as I do."

Carling rubbed his chin and grinned. "There's an old saying up on the Hill. We eat together. We drink together. We visit each other's homes. Then one of us stumbles and falls and we eat him."

"Well nobody's gonna eat *us*," Lessing snapped. "You tell him that the President appreciates his goddamned prayers, but is just too busy handling the crisis to meet with him."

"Don't you think that decision ought to be made elsewhere?"

"It's my job to decide what he's bothered with and what he's not bothered with," Lessing snapped.

Carling rose and started for the door, then stopped and looked back at Lessing. The paranoia of the office was all too obvious, but it was also a tool to be used. "If we lose this one there's going to be a lot of blame spread around, Cramer. It's not a good time to make a mistake in public relations," he said.

Lessing's eyes narrowed. "You'd love to see me fall on my face, wouldn't you?"

"I'm not your enemy in this, Cramer. You know that. Hell, I haven't seen my wife since this whole thing started, and from the looks of things, no matter how it turns out, I'm gonna be stuck in this mausoleum until Christmas. Now what do you want me to do? Give you honest answers, or just jerk you off?"

Lessing stared down at the papers on his desk and began rapidly tapping a pencil against them. "All right," he said. "I'll tell him, and I'll tell him your opinion." He looked up at Carling. "Along with my opposition."

"I'll try and have some good news the next time I come around," Carling said.

Lessing watched him close the door behind him. "I doubt it," he said aloud as he began sifting through papers on his desk.

He leaned back in his chair and stared at the papers. Off to one side were the notes he had taken during a telephone conversation with Henry. The word, *madness*, had been scratched across the bottom and underlined three times. He placed the notes in a leather folder along with Rabbi Leshin's written request to meet with the President and various informational queries from unfriendly members of the House and Senate. Moments later he was hurrying along a corridor headed for the Oval Office, ignoring those he passed, noting only that the palms of his hands were sweating.

Inside the Oval Office, the President looked exceptionally haggard, the lines around his eyes seemed to have deepened, and Lessing noticed he was smoking a cigarette, something he had not done in years. He took a chair alongside the President's desk and opened the leather folder on his lap.

"They're driving me back to these things," Jordan said, holding the cigarette out in front of him, then snuffing it out in an oversized ashtray. "What's the bad news at *this* hour, Cramer?"

"I'll start with one small ray of hope," Lessing said. "Henry's people have come up with some suspects that are being investigated now. They expect to know if they were involved or not by the end of the day. They're no closer to finding out where Norris is being held, but they're still convinced it's somewhere in Florida. To be perfectly honest, I don't feel he's telling us as much as he could."

"Have you assigned one of your people to his staff? Jordan asked. Jordan began drumming his fingers on the desk. "Seems our Mr.

Henry knows how to play the game, doesn't it."

"He's also come up with a request. He wants to play up the terrorists' demands with the media," Lessing interjected.

"What for?"

Lessing blanched and folded his hands tightly in his lap. He leaned slightly forward. "Well, it seems one of our top psychological people from Walter Reed has advised that it's our one hope in getting the deadline extended."

"Who the hell brought a psychologist into this damned mess?"

Jordan's face had reddened with abrupt anger, and as Lessing watched him he could feel the perspiration begin to flow into the palms of his hands again.

"I'm afraid I sent him over there," Lessing said.

Jordan stared at him for several moments, his mouth slightly parted. "Whose side are you on, Cramer?" he finally asked.

Lessing shifted nervously in his chair. "I didn't intend for him to get involved in this way," he said. "I just thought his evaluation of the terrorists and this WAR group in general might be useful to us if anything went wrong later on." He began to stutter. "I mean, some way of explaining our inability to negotiate with those people, if it turned out that we couldn't get Norris back."

Jordan shook his head and stared down at his desk. "I do not intend to help propagandize the cause of these maniacs," he snapped. "You make sure Mr. Henry understands that."

Lessing shifted again in his chair, drawing Jordan's gaze back to him. "I may have inadvertently misrepresented Henry's position," he said. "He didn't actually request permission to do it. It was more in the form of an advisory. But he assures me it will be done in a way that will not make it appear that the government supports their views." Lessing had rushed the final sentence and now hurried on before Jordan could object. "The idea is to satisfy the need of these people to get their message across and thereby give them an excuse to extend the deadline. According to the psychologist it will also focus attention on Henry and away from Norris, in other words make Norris less of an enemy to these people."

Jordan sat quietly, staring into the eyes of his senior aide. "Tell me something, Cramer," he said at length. "Does it appear to you that we're losing control of this situation?"

Lessing twisted in his chair again under the President's sarcasm. "Well we did give him rather extensive authority."

Jordan nodded. "And unfortunately he appears to know how to use it, doesn't he?"

"I'll veto the whole plan, then," Lessing said.

Jordan shook his head. "No. Let him go ahead. Just emphasize the need for caution. We can't afford to get two million Puerto Ricans all riled up for independence. There's too much at stake economically. And we can't afford to have these terrorists become martyrs anymore than we can afford to make Norris a martyr. Make sure he understands those are the guidelines he has to operate under. Now tell me the rest of the day's unpleasantness."

Lessing looked back into his leather folder, trying to decide whether Rabbi Leshin's request or the various informational demands from opposition members of the Congress would prove less troublesome. He decided to combine it all into one unpleasant package.

Jordan listened, then lit another cigarette and drew on it heavily. "You know, Cramer, in ancient times messengers who brought bad news to their king used to be put to death. Until now I never understood the wisdom in that custom." He drew on the cigarette again. "You deal with the good rabbi yourself. That should be punishment enough. Assure him every step is being taken to rescue his beloved President and ask him to keep rallying support among the nation as only *he* can. And if there's any statement to the press, you make sure either you or Josh are there with him. I don't trust him any farther than you do."

Jordan snuffed the cigarette out and promptly lit another. "As far as the requests of the loyal opposition in the Congress go, you just remind our friends that we need their support at this time, not their political maneuverings. You also remind them that this administration still controls the federal purse strings and we're not beneath applying a little pressure of our own in their home districts. And you make sure they understand I intend to have a long memory about all this."

Jordan stared at the newly lit cigarette and shook his head, then crushed it out in the ashtray.

23

He had spent most of the afternoon talking with Norris in the rear room of the cabin and Carol had watched him, troubled at first by the intensity of his interest, then gradually wishing she could also be a part of the discussion. It was strange and it confused her, and she wished that everything could be as simple and clear as it had been when it all began four days ago.

Four days, she thought. Four days since they plucked him from the beach. Three since they issued the demands. And four more now until the deadline. She looked around the room. Wally was seated near the window, a rifle across his lap, his eyes scanning the bleak terrain that seemed even more ominous now that the sun was setting. Norma was seated at the table, her head propped in both hands as she stared into the book she had bought the previous day. It was a battered copy of John Fowles', *The Collector*. Norma had found it in a rack outside a secondhand furniture store, and Carol thought again now as she had then what an odd choice it was, given their situation.

She looked at her wristwatch. Juan and Richard had been gone for more than an hour now, off to purchase a small, battery operated television set to help ease the monotony in the cabin. And God, it was monotonous. Sheer boredom, broken only by the possibility of a sudden attack. At times, almost wishing that attack would come, if only to break the tedium of one, hot, dreary hour slipping into the next without change. They had thought the radio would be enough, but it wasn't. Perhaps the TV set would be, but she doubted it.

She looked at Norma again, hunched over her book, her large breasts brushing against the top of the table. She smiled to herself.

Years before she had prayed for large breasts. How old had she been then? Twelve? Thirteen? Then the fashion had changed and her long, lithe body had become desirable, worthy of notice. Women worried about such ridiculous things. They were taught to. But so were men, some men at least. Juan with his tight trousers, always posturing so the outline of his penis could be seen, sure in his mind that the indication of its size would be an irresistible attraction to any woman.

Norma shook her head as she read. She was an animated reader, often shaking or nodding her head, at times even making faces. So bright, so committed, Carol thought. They had been as close as sisters for several years now. No, closer than sisters. And that one evening, months ago, as close as two women could ever be. Carol shook her head, driving the memory away, then looked back into the rear room. Norris had his back to her. He was speaking. She could tell by the concentration on Carlos's face. When she had gone into the room earlier to see if he wanted coffee, they had been talking about birds. No, Norris had been talking about them, lecturing almost, and Carlos had seemed fascinated.

Birds, she thought. Perhaps the heat was getting to them as well. The various species that inhabit the Everglades. She smiled at herself, realizing how much she would like to listen instead of keeping her post by the window.

Carlos's face. So attentive when he listened to someone, so absorbed in what they said. Such a concerned man. It had been days since they had slept together and she realized now how much she missed it. She had been with Richard, but that was different. He was so intense, he concentrated so completely on what he was doing, never losing himself in her, never responding with abandon. She loved him. She loved all of them really. Each in a different way. They were a family, much more so than the one in which she had been raised.

The revolutionary family. What typically trite, sophomoric claptrap. You're getting to be like Richard, she thought. Poor Richard, still trying to look like Leon Trotsky, with his wire-rimmed glasses and bushy hair. Yet, without him you would have grown up with your cheerleader mentality. Probably be driving a stationwagon through some Chicago suburb with two kids screaming in the back seat. She looked out into the threatening gray haze that now dominated the marshy terrain. It almost sounds good, she thought.

The lights of the van brought her back. Instinctively she reached for the rifle leaning against the wall, then left it there as she recognized the van as theirs. Juan and Richard jumped out, Richard holding the small, transistorized Sony above his head.

"They're back," Carol said, then looked out the window again and watched her husband tuck the television under one arm and continue toward the cabin with an exaggerated Charlie Chaplin walk. She turned from the window. El Tiburón was standing next to Norma.

"They seem to be in a good mood," Carol said. "Nothing like an idiot box to satisfy the TV generation. I'll bet they'll be watching cartoons tomorrow morning."

"It beats watching the alligators eat the snakes," Norma said.

The door of the cabin swung open and Juan entered with a flourish.

"¡ Arriba!" he shouted, raising one hand in the air, then bringing it across his waist, bowing, then swinging it back toward the door. "I want to present the Television Man, who now brings you the mos' important of capitalistic tools, somethin' to dull your brain an' make you wanta buy more soap an' dog food an' deodorants than you ever thought you needed."

He stepped back as Richard entered with the Sony held above his head with both hands, like a priest elevating the Eucharist.

Juan folded his hands in prayer. *"Per quem haec ómnia, Dómine, semper bona creas, sanctí ficas, vivi ficas, bene dícis, et praestas nobis."*

"Shit, Juan. Don't tell me you were an altar boy," Norma quipped.

"Of course I was, baby. I used to look down the ladies' dresses when they closed their eyes and stuck out their tongues for communion."

"He also used to steal the altar wine," El Tiburón said.

"How about the poor box, Juan?" Wally asked.

"Hey, man. You think I'm sacrilegious or somethin'? But I did try to feel up a nun once."

They were all giggling like schoolchildren as Richard placed the television set on the table. Juan strutted in front of it, still grinning. He looked into the rear room and saw Norris sitting there. The smile faded from his face and he looked angrily at El Tiburón.

"Hey man, how come that prick is out of his closet?"

"You can't keep him locked in that sweatbox all day and keep him healthy," El Tiburón said.

"What the fuck do I care about his fucking health." Juan spun away and stamped over to the window.

Carol looked at each man in turn. For a moment the tension had been broken. But only for a moment. Juan was such a mental midget, such an asshole, she thought.

"Hey, let's try this thing out," Wally said.

The others were quiet. He snapped on the set and began adjusting the knobs and aerial. An image of Bugs Bunny appeared on the screen and they all began laughing again. Even Juan, despite himself.

~~~~~

When the evening news went on the air at seven o'clock no one was surprised to find the Norris kidnapping still the dominant story. They gathered around the small screen intent on every word, the set placed so even those standing guard at the windows could watch. Walter Cronkite's face was solemn, almost severe, and it seemed to offer his personal disapproval of the kidnappers and when the group was described as the *most wanted* terrorist band in the world today, El Tiburón felt a surge of uneasy pride and he glanced at the others, trying to gauge their reactions.

Neither he nor the others fully grasped the reality of what they had done. He realized that now, but even the realization failed to alter the fact. They were isolated from the reaction of the average person; the images on a television screen and the statements printed in newspapers were only shadows of that reaction and as such lacked the necessary impact.

Cronkite was comparing WAR's action with the Red Brigade's taking of Aldo Moro, stating flatly that it had been far more devastating because it had turned the undisputed leader of the free world, the United States government, into a seemingly helpless victim.

The statement brought a whoop from Richard, followed by a sophomoric exchange of hand slaps with Juan. They still did not understand, El Tiburón thought. To them it was a dangerous game, but still a game. They did not understand the political realities, as he understood them, as Norris understood, as those who now hunted them understood.

Norma made an *oinking* sound that produced a wave of giggles and brought El Tiburón's eyes back to the small flickering screen. Henry was sitting on the edge of a desk, as he had in the earlier broadcast. Near him, watching intently again, was the same woman he had noticed before and there was the same activity, the same constant movement of bodies in the background.

Henry began by reviewing the demands, and the very words seemed distasteful to him, but his eyes remained emotionless, his demeanor calm. Very much a professional, El Tiburón thought. Just as it should be.

"Is the government prepared to meet these demands?" The voice of the interviewer was low, intentionally solemn, manufactured, intended to impress his audience.

The camera moved in for a tight shot of Henry's face.

"The government is doing everything in its power to attempt to meet the rather *extensive* demands this group has made." There was a slightly mocking tone in Henry's voice now. "There are several things that should be understood, however. First, while there is undoubtedly some support among a radical minority in Puerto Rico, the demands of this group in no way reflect the attitude of our Puerto Rican citizens. WAR, as these people like to call themselves, has proclaimed *itself* as spokesmen for the Puerto Rican people. But to my knowledge they have no such mandate."

Henry had added the final words with a slightly mocking smile.

"Secondly, there is a rather strong body of opinion which holds that the demands made by this group are little more than a ruse, a way of excusing an outrageous crime that was never in any way intended to help the people of Puerto Rico. I think that's rather clearly shown by the complexity of the demands and the unreasonably short time period we've been given to execute them. These demands, after all, involve decisions that rightfully belong to the Commonwealth of Puerto Rico and its legally elected officials, the Congress of the United States, and a host of independent corporations, the operating officers of which must by law consult their various boards of directors before entering into the kinds of agreements that are being demanded."

"But the demands are being pursued?" the stilted voice of the interviewer asked.

"Most certainly. And they're being pursued with every conceivable shortcut in mind. But there's only so much that can be done. The duly elected government of Puerto Rico, for example, is rightfully concerned about giving in to these people, who they fear plan to stage a Cuban-styled revolution if they're successful in forcing room of the cabin. From her post at the window Norma Epstein could not hear their conversation, but from the intensity she could see on El Tiburón's face, she knew it was not idle talk. His nostrils seemed to flair slightly as he spoke. He's laying the law down to the old man, she thought. He had been strangely silent after the news broadcast; he seemed to withdraw into himself. But that was not uncommon. They were much alike, she thought. Only *he* did not find it necessary to hide his withdrawal, to live behind the mask of an extrovert. But he had not been raised as an outcast in his own country. He wasn't a Jew, wasn't forced to live with the condescension of the tight-assed little Wasps who considered Long Island their own little preserve. She smiled inwardly. And Juan accused her of being anti-Semitic. Anti-Zionist, yes. Anti-Israel, yes. But never against her own people. Only the ones who opposed reform and necessary change. She trembled slightly. Asshole, she thought. You sit here in a goddamned oven and you start shaking. But it was natural to be frightened. You'd have to be a fool not to be. She looked at Juan and Richard seated next to each other, staring at the fuzzy images that moved across the minuscule television screen. If the shoe fits, she thought.

Richard turned with her stare and stood and walked up to her.

"Man, that little screen is murder on my eyes," he said.

"So don't watch it, dummy."

"It still beats sitting around counting the fucking mosquitoes."

Norma laughed. "Is that what you do?" She motioned with her head toward the table. "I finished *The Collector* if you want to read it."

"I already read it," he said. "You have anything else?"

She shook her head.

Richard looked back into the rear room. "What the hell does he spend so much time talking to that old bastard for?"

"Who knows? Intellectual curiosity, maybe."

Richard nodded. "I suppose." He looked at Norma. "It's funny, isn't it," he said, lowering his voice. "Seeing Norris here like this. It's like he's a different dude. You know what I mean?"

She smiled. "A three-day growth of beard and grungy clothes make a difference, don't they?"

"It's even more than that. It's like it's hard to see him ever having all that power. I have to keep reminding myself about all the shit he pulled."

through a vote for independence, by whatever means, l
gal."

"Is there any indication that the Cuban government
group?"

"To our knowledge there is no outside support for t
whatever. There have been no expressions of support, only
nation or silence."

"And in the meantime, Mr. Henry, your strike force is
ing to locate President Norris and his captors?"

"With all possible vigor."

"Can you tell us how that investigation is going?"

"All I can tell you is that we do have suspects and we f
investigation is into a positive, rather than a negative, phase f
first time. Beyond that I will not speculate further."

"Shit," Juan shouted. "You got shit, motherfucker, an' you
it."

El Tiburón stared at the screen as Cronkite's image reappe
and began to recap Henry's cautious indication of progress. He
had seemed to look into the camera as he spoke about the suspe
almost as though he had been speaking personally to those he kn
would be watching. Words spoken with defiance. El Tiburón's ja
tightened and he felt sudden anger at the sense of failure that seem
to be rising within him. He wanted to turn and shout at the other
Tell them to shut their mouths, find a way to drive the cocky over
confidence from them. They were acting like children, like fools.

~~~~~

The television lights went out, leaving behind the dissipating
waves of heat they had generated. Henry turned and walked back to
his office, stopping outside the door where Knutsen stood waiting.

"Well?" he said.

"The gauntlet has been dropped. Exactly as it should have been.
Now we just have to hope that I knew what I was talking about."

"Let's also hope I know what the hell I'm doing," Henry said.

~~~~~

It was ten o'clock and the night noises of the Everglades seeped
into the cabin, playing strange background to the dialogue of an old
Humphrey Bogart movie that now dominated the front room. El Tiburón sat alone, talking quietly with Edmund Norris in the rear

"Why don't you talk to him about it?"

Richard made a face. "Besides, it already drives Juan crazy that we even let him out of that fucking storage room."

"Fuck him," Norma whispered.

El Tiburón walked up beside them unnoticed. "Who are you planning to fuck?" He was grinning at her.

"You," she snapped.

"You sure I'm not too much man for you?" He fought to repress a smile.

"Oh, shit. Now I have to take macho shit from you too? Isn't it enough I get it from madman Jose over there?" She lifted her chin toward Juan, expecting him to turn. He was too enraptured with Humphrey Bogart. Norma looked back at El Tiburón. "You looked like you were giving the old man a hard time."

All mirth left El Tiburón's face. "Just asking him some questions," he said.

"About what?" Richard asked.

"Henry. I wanted to know more about him."

"What's to know? He's tryin' to bury our asses," Richard said.

"That's why I want to know as much about him as I can."

"You think he was being straight? About having suspects, I mean?" Norma asked.

"It doesn't make much difference whether he was or not. Sooner or later they would have identified us, or at least some of us. I'd just like to know more about how he thinks, how he works, the kind of support he'll get. There's a lot of conflict, a lot of jealousy in their intelligence community."

"You're afraid he'll find us, aren't you?" she asked.

El Tiburón shook his head. "Not unless we fuck up. Without mistakes it would take them six months to find us here."

"Well, I don't know about you, honey, but this gorgeous female doesn't want to be here that long."

He leaned over and kissed her forehead. "Neither do I." He grinned at her. "You want to go get a beer?"

"Sure, if we don't go to that sleazy place we went to before."

"We can go to that redneck bar near the canal that Wally and Richard went to."

Norma picked up the rifle and handed it to Richard. "You're on duty, my love," she said.

"Bring back a couple of six-packs," he said.

〰〰〰

It was eleven-fifteen when the reports finally arrived from New York and the slight smile on Henry's lips gradually grew into a broad grin as he read them.

"Some piece of luck," Dez said. He was seated in Henry's office watching his reaction. He, too, was smiling.

"And it all started with a hooker?" Henry asked, shaking his head in disbelief.

"The sins of the flesh. This guy, Juan Hernandez, couldn't keep his pecker in his pants. He kept bragging about this big loft he and his buddy had in Soho, promising the broad that he was going to throw a big party and invite all her friends. She thought he was full of shit, but when our people started showing his and Rivera's mug shot around West Broadway, sure enough, people knew them."

Henry began flipping the pages of the inventory of items found in the loft. He shook his head again. "From the excess gunpowder found on the floor, the place must have been a damned bomb factory." He allowed his eyes to continue along the list. "And a map of Palm Beach. Now isn't that curious." He looked up at Desverne and smiled. "Okay. Now we know who. All we need to know now is where."

He leaned back in a chair and picked up a photograph that showed Rivera, Hernandez, and two women and a third man. "Do we know who these people are yet?"

"I'm running the photo and all the prints we picked up now," Dez said. "If they've ever so much as spit we'll know by morning. Our people are also moving that picture through Soho for anything they can get. First names, nicknames, anything. It's only a question of time."

Henry nodded. "So's finding them. But how long do you think it would take to show their pictures to everyone within a hundred-mile radius of Palm Beach? We still need another break. And a lot more time."

〰〰〰

"You seem worried," Norma said.
"I am." He smiled at her weakly.

They were seated in a corner booth near the jukebox, allowing the howling endless blare of country music to cover their words. He sipped his beer, keeping his eyes on her.

"Are you going to tell me why, or is it a secret?" There was a teasing quality to her words, but beneath it he could hear the hint of fear his admission had produced.

"What did you think of that interview with Henry tonight?"

"You mean the part about the suspects they have?"

"No. That doesn't matter. I'd expect him to say that, whether he had any or not. I mean the part about our demands."

She shrugged her shoulders. "They're starting to make excuses. Trying to cover their asses, I guess."

"They're doing more than that. They're trying to box us in."

"What?" The concern was clear in her voice now. She had misunderstood his meaning and he reached out and took her hand.

"I don't mean physically," he said, squeezing the hand to reassure her. "I mean philosophically. They know they can't find us in time and they don't think they can meet the demands within the deadline we set, so they're trying to throw the blame back on us, to erode our support with the people."

"I don't understand. There's no way anyone will believe them. They'll know it's shit."

He shook his head. "Who knows what people will believe." His eyes snapped back to hers. "Don't you see. The way he phrased it. The government is *willing* to meet the demands. They're *trying* to work things out. But we, *WAR*, don't want them to. *We're* making it impossible. And now, if they don't meet the deadline and we kill Norris, there will be people who will always believe that they could have had freedom, that they could have had the economic opportunities we asked for, if only we had given them more time."

El Tiburón slapped his palm lightly against the table. "He's very clever, this guy Henry, or whoever it is who's behind him."

Norma stared at him, her eyes widening slightly. "So what is it you want to do, extend the deadline?"

His eyes remained on the the table.

"Right now I'm not sure what to do. But I know that Juan would never stand still for any extension, even if it was the right thing to do. Maybe the others wouldn't either."

She was quiet for several moments, thinking. He sipped at his beer again, not sure himself what to say next. Norma glanced about the long, narrow room. The bar was crowded with men still in work clothes and women obviously dressed for an evening out, an odd mixture of battered denims and tight slacks. Norma looked at them through the layers of smoke turned a ghostly blue by the lights behind the bar. Slowly, she pushed herself up and offered El Tiburón a half smile.

"I'll be right back," she said, turning and walking the short distance to the ladies room.

Inside, another woman was standing before the greasy film-covered mirror reapplying makeup to her face. She appeared to be in her early twenties and her short blond hair was arranged in a massive array of tight curls and when she finished with the makeup she began pulling at individual rings of hair, snapping them into the desired positions. Norma stood before the mirror and ran her hands through her long, dark hair. The hair was dirty and there was a sticky feel to it. Days had passed now since she had been able to wash it. Drinking water for the cabin was brought in by bottle and she had not been able to bring herself to use the swamp water on her hair. But she would have to, she thought.

"Really crowded out there tonight, ain't it, hon?"

The woman was smiling at her and there was a trace of lipstick on her teeth.

"Sure is," Norma said, returning the smile.

The young woman bounced out the door, moving, Norma thought, as though she had springs in her shoes. It had been a long time, several years now, since she herself had enjoyed the mindless pleasure of being frivolous, of caring no more about her surroundings than the personal enjoyment to be usurped. She leaned forward, resting her head against the grimy mirror. Just below the bottom edge of the mirror several lines had been written on the wall in various shades of lipstick. Norma stepped back and stared at them. *Junior sure can do it*, the first read, followed by *"Don't I know it,"* and *"All day and all night."* Junior certainly had his admirers, she thought, smiling to herself at the idea of what Junior himself would think were he to read his reviews. She turned to go, then turned back to the mirror and looked at her reflection. The fear shows, she thought. It covers your face like a veil, no, a mask. She felt inept. Frightened and inept, a small child caught with its hand in its mother's purse, knowing something fearful was about to happen, sure of it, but unable to alter the reality. Instinctively she knew he was right. It was correct philosophically. But it also smacked of disaster, and she could feel that just as plainly; it was deep inside her. For a moment she was a young girl again, walking along the winding road in Glen Cove that led to her home, passing the country club and watching the other girls walking ahead of her, turn in, going to the club their fathers belonged to, the club her father could not join, feeling again the isolation and loneliness; the temptation to follow them, to be accepted by them and the self-hatred for feeling those things. She drew a deep breath and hurried through the door. She would not be tempted by her own fears or the isolation imposed by others. She would be true to the fight, true to herself, no matter what the outcome. A shiver went through her as she reached the table and sat down. He was staring at her, then a smile formed on his lips.

"The idea of extending it frightens you, doesn't it?"

She nodded her head.

"It frightens me too," he said.

"If it turns out to be the right thing to do, we won't have much choice, will we?"

"I suppose not," he said. "But it won't be easy."

She shook her head slowly, looking toward the bar again. The blonde from the ladies room was hanging on the arm of a muscular young man in a tattered workshirt. *Junior*? she wondered. But nothing in your life has ever been that easy, she told herself.

~~~~~

Richard and Wally were watching the late movie from their posts at the front windows. On the floor, along opposite walls of the front room, Juan and Carol were asleep on sleeping bags. A slight breeze came through the open front windows and the night sounds of insects challenged the dialogue of the movie.

"This movie sucks," Richard said.

"Ain't nothin' else on but Johnny Carson," Wally answered with a shrug. He was squeezing a black rubber handball in one hand and it caused the muscles of his forearms and biceps to move rhythmically. He looked down at the movement then transferred the ball to his other hand and watched the muscles in that arm move as well.

Richard asked him, "Don't you ever get tired of exercising?"

Wally shook his head. "When you're big like me, it all turns to fat easy, if you don't keep at it."

"Man, but you never stop," Richard said. Stupid jock, he told himself.

They were quiet again, their attention returning to the movie. After a few moments Richard grunted in disgust and turned toward the window, staring out into the blackness that seemed to stretch on endlessly. Yet, despite the dark, no shadow or movement could be missed. Earlier, he had jumped to his feet when a silent shadow had moved fifty yards out setting off the trip wire alarm. It had been a deer, quietly foraging in the high marsh grass, and despite its silent movements he had spotted it easily when the alarm sounded. He smiled, thinking of it now. It had scared hell out of him and he had almost fired. Only his training had made him delay. He looked back across at Wally. He was staring at the television set, his lips slightly parted like a small boy mesmerized by something strange and new.

"You think we're gonna have to take him out?" he said. When Wally looked toward him, Richard motioned toward the storeroom where Norris now was.

"Sooner or later," he answered.

"What do you mean, sooner or later? You think we'll extend the deadline?"

Wally shrugged. "Who knows. What difference does it make?" He grinned. "What's the matter, don't you like it here in the swamps, boy?"

Richard ignored him, thinking to himself that only a madman could like these swamps. "Have you talked to him at all?" He motioned toward the storeroom again.

"Nope. Don't have no interest in talkin' to him."

Richard hesitated. "I'd like to talk to him. Maybe tomorrow."

"No sense in talkin' to somebody you're gonna blow away," Wally said, his eyes again fixed on the television screen.

"Maybe we won't have to," Richard said.

Wally grinned, still looking straight ahead. "Actually, it'd be more fun to jus' take him a couple of miles into the glades an' leave 'em there. Nobody'd ever find his ole ass again." He chuckled to himself. "Mean country back there. Mean."

Behind the curtain that closed off the storage room Norris sat listening to the muted conversations, the words partially obscured by the television set. There were two among them who were dangerous now. The one called Juan and this big, constantly grinning country boy. Somehow they had to be blunted, their instincts to kill him thwarted. The others had to be won over, but he knew he was a long way from doing that.

Juan was the key. The country boy was a follower, he could be swayed by the strongest and that *could* be Juan if things became difficult for them all. Then he might convince them that violence was the safest alternative. Somehow Juan would have to be neutralized, gotten rid of. Tiburón could control the others. Somehow he would have to get him to see that.

It was as it always had been. In the end he had to protect himself from those who wanted to do him harm. The faces of those who had tried in the past flashed through his mind, causing his lips to tighten. There had been many, but few had succeeded and many of those who did had been repaid later. Even those who were his friends could never be truly counted on, *never*. It always had to be he himself. Not a peep from Hall on any of the news broadcasts. He was probably hiding under his bed, waiting to see how it all turned out before exposing himself. And that fool, Rabbi Leshin, just using it all to get his name in the newspapers, to add to his scrapbook. More photographs for the wall of his office. He snorted. But you used him, too, at times. But that's what fools are for.

He thought of his family. There had been little word from them either. He knew he could count on Emily, he had always been able to, and Dalton would be loyal because of her. He wondered about his wife, though. She had been a pain in the ass in many ways. Always questioning him, never willing to accept what he said on face value as Emily had. And that was what loyalty was. Accepting the necessary lie as well as the truth. Pamela had never been able to do that. But she had helped him. Her mere presence had made him acceptable to many who did not want him. And she had suffered and was probably suffering now. Or perhaps this was the chance for all her suffering to end.

He ground his teeth. It has to be you, he told himself. All your old friends in Washington will simply use this to further their own aims. It's always been that way. Anyone can be sacrificed to political ends. Tiburón. Right now you can trust him. You could teach him so much. He knows that. And he doesn't want to harm you. The others may force him to, but he doesn't want it himself. You must use that instinct, develop and nurture it as much as you can.

Outside he heard the van pull up in front of the cabin. Tomorrow, he told himself. When your mind is clear.

24

It was snowing, and already the accumulation was heavy. Henry stood at the wide window staring out through the heavy white flakes that floated toward the ground seven stories below. The window faced a park and the untouched whiteness stretched out toward the river, unmarred and peaceful. It was six-thirty, too early for the intrusion of people, too cold, the snow too heavy even for the occasional runners who normally moved along the paths. It was a different view, nearly a mile from his own apartment, and somehow it seemed even farther. They had begun using her apartment to avoid the reporters who had started to congregate in front of his building like vultures in search of carrion. He had never cared much for news people; he viewed them as obnoxious, demanding, a nuisance that should be avoided. Hoover had realized that and had imposed sanctions against those who dealt with them. But the new rulers of the Bureau had changed that. Part of the new openness they wanted to project. He sunk his hands into the pockets of his robe, brooding for a moment, then distracted by the sound of her movements behind him, the feel of her arms slipping about his waist, her body pressed against his back. She rested her chin on his shoulder and looked out the window.

"It's beautiful," she said. "Was it supposed to snow today?"

He shrugged his shoulders slightly. It had been days since he had given his attention to anything but his work. The days had simply blended together. There had also been a sense of tension between them since the argument about Knutsen and he wanted an end to that. He had been foolish and had treated her badly. He turned to her and suddenly smiled. She was naked and he placed his hands on

231

her hips and gave her a look of mock disapproval.

"Do you always stand in front of a window like this in the morning?"

"There's no one out there. Why? Does it bother you?"

"Not at all. Now I know where I'll go jogging in the mornings," he said.

She slipped her arms around his neck and moved against him, kissing his face lightly. "It's too cold to go outside for exercise," she said.

He ran his hands along her back, feeling the warmth of sleep that still clung to her, adding to her softness. The smell of her was warm as well, and like the snow outside, it seemed to remove him from the immediate, give him a sense of momentary peace.

Soon it would all be over, now only the result was in question. Then peace would not be a momentary thing, not an illusion like the snow outside waiting to be transformed into a gray mire. Vermont came to his mind again, as it always did when there was snow. The feel of Mary against him now made him realize how much he wanted her to be with him when it was over. But it was something he would wait to tell her. He wanted it all to end with a victory. It was like an athlete playing his final game, counting off the minutes before what he had lived with so long came to an end, seeking one final memory that would make the years seem worthwhile.

She leaned back and smiled up at him. "What are you thinking about?"

"You, actually."

Her eyes brightened, then turned coy. "Naughty thoughts, I hope."

"Very nice thoughts."

She stuck out her lower lip, imitating the pout of a small child. "Too bad." She turned, taking his hand and leading him back to the large brass bed that dominated the room. Gracefully, she slid onto the bed and coaxed him down next to her. He glanced at the night table, noting it was six thirty-five.

"We have time," she said. "Besides, it will help me to work at peak efficiency."

He lowered his face to hers. "Anything for efficiency," he said.

Her body seemed to erupt as he came to her, a soft, twisting violence that he had not known for many years, perhaps had never known, and he lost himself in it, hearing only the rapidness of her breath and his own.

When she ushered Knutsen into his office two hours later, he could still feel the warmth of their lovemaking, and his eyes remained on her now-clothed body, thinking back to her bedroom, the softness, the gasps of pleasure they had both uttered.

Knutsen was looking at him oddly and he realized that his lips had curved into a smile. The old boy must think I've lost my mind, he thought.

"You seemed quite pleased with yourself this morning," Knutsen said.

"Yes. I don't know why," Henry answered.

Mary turned in the doorway and smiled, making it hard for him to keep the smile from returning.

"It's the snow, I guess. I was posted in Vermont early in my career, and a new snowfall always seems to have that effect on me."

"You never would have struck me as a romantic, Pat," Knutsen said. "But then, you hide your feelings very well. Part of the training, I suppose."

Henry leaned back in his chair, wishing he could tell the chubby little psychologist that it was simply a question of making love to a beautiful young woman. "No analysis, please, Kermit. What have you got for me?"

Knutsen rubbed his hands together, then opened a manila folder on his lap. "I've done an analysis of our two terrorists. I assume that's all right."

Henry leaned forward. He placed his elbows on the desk and steepled his fingers, waiting for Knutsen to continue.

"A strange alliance, these two. They would seem to be total opposites destined for conflict and yet from what your men in New York have found it would appear they are quite close." He paused to light a large cigar, taking care to make sure it was drawing properly. "You must understand, of course, that the information I'm basing this on is not the most scientifically ideal. But it's all we have."

"What are you basing it on?"

Knutsen drew heavily on his cigar, expelling the smoke slowly. "As far as Juan Hernandez is concerned, we have his arrest record in New York as well as a rather extensive juvenile record from San Juan. Added to that are the interviews with people who knew him in New York. Carlos Rivera, conversely, has no police record, other than the scraps you chaps put together on his possible involvement with the FALN. But the interviews your men conducted with old neighbors who knew him as a boy and young man, and with professors at the University of Puerto Rico, paint a rather good picture. Add to that the people who knew him in New York and we get a reasonably clear image. There's not enough on either to assure a high degree of accuracy, mind you, but it's a good starting point."

Henry remained silent, knowing that Knutsen would take his own route to the essence of the conversation. He still found if difficult to trust him fully.

"I would guess that it was Rivera who wrote the communiqués, was the leader of the group. Of course it could be one of the others we haven't identified yet, but I would tend to discount that possibility. Rivera is not the kind of personality who could easily yield to someone else. He's too bright, too innovative in his thinking. He would be the type who would manipulate the wills of other less dominant figures. And he would also be highly competitive. I would guess that he has an enormous ego, but a well-hidden one, perhaps even from himself." He smiled across at Henry. "You're going to laugh at this one. He probably thinks of himself as a father figure to the others, and he also has a highly developed sense of morality. His own sense of it, of course. But that's largely true of most moral men who are also intelligent. Hernandez, on the other hand, is Mr. Hyde in full bloom. If he were the leader of this group I would recommend that we start saying prayers for Mr. Norris's soul right now. There's an exceptional streak of cruelty in this man that seems to have been there from his very early years. Did you know he was once arrested as a young boy for setting fire to an older cousin? Apparently the older boy had demeaned him in front of his peers, and young Hernandez waited until he was asleep that night, then poured lighter fluid on his blanket and set it afire. He then supposedly stood there laughing as the other boy screamed in pain. Nearly killed him according to the report."

"Nice kid. I suppose he has a high sense of morality as well."

Knutsen laughed. "No, our Mr. Hernandez has the morals of a goat, I would say. A rather maladjusted goat."

"Do you think this Rivera can control him?"

Knutsen stared toward the window, chewing on his cigar. "It's hard to say, Pat. From what I gather, there's a rather strong bond between them for some reason that escapes me completely. But Hernandez is not an intellectual sort. He responds to outside stimuli and Rivera may just be clever enough to realize that and control him that way. But Hernandez is also unpredictable. He has a psychopathic personality from what I'm able to gather and, put simply, that means he might respond favorably or adversely to a given stimulus. One simply never knows."

"What about the game plan we've initiated? Have you found anything that would indicate we're doing the wrong thing?"

"As far as Hernandez is concerned, anything we did or didn't do could be wrong. Assuming I'm right, and Rivera is running this show, I think we're on target. One thing though, Pat. I've got to have information on the others. We've got to know about them, if they're likely to side with Rivera or Hernandez if it comes to a showdown. Rivera is clever enough to yield to the flow of the moment to maintain control. He's the kind of person who looks toward the broader picture, takes his one step back in order to achieve two steps forward, so to speak."

"Hopefully, we'll have something on that before the day is out," Henry said. "Christ, we better have. I've practically got the entire New York office doing nothing else but running around with pictures of these people, not to mention half the fingerprint lab here in Washington going over the latents we picked up in that goddamned Soho loft."

He stood and walked to the window. Outside the morning snow had been turned into a filthy grime. Only the snow on the limbs of the trees in Lafayette Square retained any illusion of beauty, and that was very much an illusion. He turned back to Knutsen.

"So you think we at least have a shot at getting them to postpone their deadline." He spoke positively, insisting on an affirmative answer, almost willing it.

"Yes, we have a shot," Knutsen said. "How good a one we won't be able to tell until we know more about the others. And we'll know even better when we get their next message. That will be the real test."

The telephone intercom buzzed insistently and Henry glanced quickly at his watch. Nine o'clock. Time for Cramer Lessing's first call of the day. The bastard's like clockwork, he thought, glaring at the telephone and wishing he could afford to ignore it.

"That'll be your friend at the White House," he said. "Tell me something else, Kermit. Do you think these bastards would do a deal? Lessing for Norris?"

"Not even with a couple of draft choices thrown in," Knutsen said.

"I was afraid you'd say that."

When he picked up the receiver, Mary's voice purred across. "It's you-know-who," she said.

"Thanks a lot," he snapped back, then punched the blinking button on the console. "Good morning, Cramer. What can I do for you?"

Lessing's self-important voice boomed across louder than necessary.

"The President is interested in these suspects of yours. What can I tell him about them?" He had used the word "President" as though referring to some deity who should bring the listener trembling to his knees.

Henry eased back in his chair and grinned across at Knutsen. "You can tell him that we've confirmed who the leaders of the group are and that we're now following up leads that hopefully will tell us where they are. But that part is still up in the air."

"Well, who the hell are these people?" Lessing snapped.

"I'd rather not go into that," Henry snapped back.

"What the hell do you mean, you'd rather not go into it. Are you telling me you don't intend to inform the goddamned President of the United States who the hell these people are?"

Lessing was shouting, and Henry held the receiver away from his ear. Across from him, Knutsen covered his mouth so his laughter would not be picked up by the telephone.

"I'm not saying that at all, Cramer. I'd just prefer not to discuss the names over a telephone line, that's all. We're not getting a helluva lot of cooperation from CIA. If anything they're spending their time *watching* us instead of helping us."

"Well, what the hell do you expect," Lessing snapped. "You know what they're like. They spy on everybody. They even spy on me, for chrissake."

"I understand that, all too well. But it doesn't help me. If we're going to be successful in this, I have to guard against leaks. The last thing I need is to have the names of the people we're looking for show up in the press." He glanced across at Knutsen and winked, then listened to Lessing's prolonged silence.

"Then I guess it will have to be a personal briefing." He fumbled with the calendar on his desk. "How do you look for four o'clock?"

"I'll be available any time you want to come by," Henry said.

"Come by?" Lessing's voice had risen again, and Henry thought he could almost hear the grinding of his teeth. "I want you over *here*. Believe it or not, we have a few damned things going on here too."

"I'm aware of that, Cramer. But I have slightly more than seventy-two hours to win or lose this thing and I can't take an hour out to brief you at the White House. I just can't have people sitting around, if something breaks, waiting for me to give orders."

"You know you are really pushing too hard," Lessing said.

"That's not my intention. I'm trying to do the job I was asked to do by the President." He used the same inflection Lessing had with *President*. "And we both know whose ass is going to be burned if I don't."

Lessing was silent again, only his angry breathing audible. "I'll send someone to you at four. And I want complete information."

The receiver, still in Henry's hand, buzzed benignly. He stared at it for a moment, then looked across at Knutsen.

"He hung up?" Knutsen asked.

"Indeed, he did," Henry said.

"He can be a difficult adversary, Pat."

"It doesn't matter. Win, lose, or draw, I'm out anyway. It's just a question of whether I leave gracefully or with a foot halfway up my rump. And our friends from WAR will make that decision, not that pompous little ass on Pennsylvania Avenue."

Knutsen smiled broadly. "There is the question of achieving one final success, isn't there?"

"Don't analyze me, Kermit. Analyze them. You can study me when all this is over."

~~~~~

Lessing paced his office like a wounded animal. His jaw was clamped tight and his hands were thrust deep into the pockets of his trousers. His jacket was off, displaying the image he preferred, of someone who worked hard in shirtsleeves.

In his outer office, Rabbi Leshin was waiting and would now have to be seen. The information he had sought from Henry had been intended to appease the rabbi, to give him something in confidence that would have gotten him off the back of the administration, and he realized now that to have done so could have been a mistake. But still, Henry had no right to treat him with disdain, and he would not forget that he had. But there was nothing to be done about it now and probably never would be if he succeeded. The feeling of impotence that knowledge produced was intolerable to him.

He spun on his heels and buzzed his secretary on the telephone intercom. "Have Rabbi Leshin come in," he said, omitting any courteous amenities. He walked to the door and opened it, his hand extended in a warm handshake. He was smiling.

"Rabbi, it's so good to see you again. The President wants you to know how sorry he is he couldn't see you personally, but I'm sure you realize what a difficult time this is for him."

Leshin only nodded. He had a face that seemed chiseled from stone. Not a hard face, but one that seemed weathered and wizened, surrounded by a shock of unkempt white hair, which together with the oversized curve of his nose made him look slightly predatory. He took a chair opposite Lessing's desk and waited for him to be seated. Lessing was still smiling, but as he began to speak, the rabbi raised his hand.

"Before we begin, I think you should know that I've been in touch with members of President Norris's family and they are deeply concerned and distressed about Mr. Henry's remarks on television last night."

The smile faded from Lessing's face. "I don't understand," he said. "I would have thought they'd have been pleased by the progress that's been made."

"What progress? He was challenging these killers, telling them the government couldn't meet their demands. Attacking them. The only thing he could have achieved is to arouse their anger and place the President's life in greater danger."

"He's trying to get them to be reasonable," Lessing said, extending his upturned palms. "We need more time to find them."

"Finding them will just get the President killed. You should be giving them what they want and saving this man. That's what the family wants. That's what the nation wants. We have to save the President, not worry about catching these people. Later we can catch them and punish them."

"Rabbi, I assure you that's what we want. But even the United States government doesn't have the power simply to snap its fingers and agree to things that legally involve the decisions of others. Certainly you understand that?"

Leshin shook his head, making his nose wave like a baton. "No," he said. "There can be an agreement in principle. This could appease these terrorists. And then details could be worked out later."

"Rabbi, let me remind you that this administration has repeatedly declined to give in blindly to terrorist demands and it has urged and supported the same action by other governments in similar situations. Need I point out the Israeli position with the PLO?"

"That's a different situation. They are trying to destroy a legitimate government, take land that rightfully and historically belongs to the Jewish people. This group is asking for certain social changes . . ."

"They're not asking for anything," Lessing interjected. "They're holding a former President of the United States hostage and *demanding* we do certain things. We must try to find them and punish them for the crime or we'll only be inviting more of the same. There is a great deal at stake here."

"A man's life is at stake. A great man who has served his nation well. And this man Henry appears to be prepared to abandon him."

Lessing drew a deep breath. "What would you have us do?"

"Replace this man with someone who's interested in saving the President, not just in catching criminals."

I'd love to do nothing better, Lessing thought. "Rabbi, to do that would only make the situation worse. It would put us back days and virtually guarantee we could not locate these people. Mr. Henry, I assure you, is the best-qualified man we have. If anyone can succeed, he can."

"You're not listening to me." Leshin leaned forward, placing his hands on the edge of the desk. "First we must get President Norris back. Then we can worry about catching these people. Your Mr. Henry has the priorities reversed, and he made that obvious to the family last night."

The family be damned, Lessing thought. And damn this pain in the ass as well. He stared down at his desk and slowly shook his head. "Rabbi, we need your support in this, not your interference. And the same is true of the Norris family."

The rabbi's face tightened. "Interference," he said. "I'll relay that view to the family. But you should know they are now prepared to issue a public statement concerning the handling of this. And it will not be favorable, I assure you."

"If that's done it will only serve to jeopardize the former President's life." Lessing forced a smile with more difficulty than showed. "Now, perhaps interference was the wrong word. But we need your support, not your opposition. The people handling this are experts. They know what they're doing. They have already determined the identities of the terrorists and are very close to locating them. I assure you that nothing will be done to endanger the former President's life. But certainly you realize that we must locate them to insure that they don't kill him even if the demands are met. These are not trustworthy people. They've already killed, and we have no doubt they're willing to do so again." He waited, giving his words time to take effect. "Now, please, help us. Keep the family from making any statements that will harm what we're trying to do. Give us some support among your people and in the press."

"How can I promise you support unless I can be sure you'll meet the demands and save this man?"

"Everything will be done," Lessing said. "No options have been closed off. The only variable beyond our control is the terrorists themselves and that is precisely why we must locate them. More than anything else, the President wants to guarantee President Norris's safety."

"I must have assurances for the family."

"You have them. You may tell them and the media—in fact I'll join you in talking with the media—that no options have been closed off, that we are working to meet the demands, and will meet them, given adequate time. I'll stand beside you as the President's representative while you say it."

The rabbi's eyes brightened; the thought of his own image flickering across television screens throughout the nation played through his mind. "Perhaps that would help," he said pausing again. "At least it would counteract what this man Henry has done."

Lessing breathed deeply, the warm smile returning. "We need your help very much," he said. "And I know the President will be deeply appreciative, knowing we have it. If you want, I'll have my secretary notify the press corps that a joint statement will be issued."

Leshin nodded. "One thing. Who are these people? What do we know about them?"

Lessing twisted in his chair, not wanting to admit his own ignorance. "I'll be receiving a full briefing on that at four," he said. Noting the surprise on the rabbi's face he hurried on. "The President is handling this personally, you understand. And all information comes to him first to avoid any possible delay in making decisions."

"I see," Leshin said. "I'm sure the family will be relieved to hear that."

Lessing pulled several sheets of paper from his drawer and picked up a pen. "Let's just make a few notes on what we want to tell the press and what's better kept just for the family," he said.

~~~~

Knutsen and Henry sat side by side reading the reports that had just arrived. It was one o'clock, and Henry's half-eaten sandwich lay forgotten on his desk as his eyes moved rapidly over each page.

"What do you think?" Henry asked.

"Followers," Knutsen said. "But interesting followers. I wish we had something on this other one, the one who was in Palm Beach with Rivera."

"Apparently he wasn't part of the group in New York. At least no one recognizes his description and we don't have a photograph or fingerprints to work from."

He picked up a group photo that had been found in the Soho loft. It showed three men and two women, seated in a semicircle on the floor, the quotation of Augusto Sandino hanging on the wall above their heads. Henry studied each face. The fingerprints of all five had been in the apartment and there was no question in his mind now that all had been involved and that finding them was merely a question of time. Again, the same problem. Time. He placed the photo between himself and Knutsen.

"Did you notice the quotation on the wall behind them?" he asked.

Knutsen nodded and read it aloud. " 'Everyone dies sooner or later. All that is important is how one dies.' Not extremely profound," Knutsen added. "Do you have any idea who said it?"

"I had Mary check it. It was an old friend of our government, General Sandino. He drove the marines out of Nicaragua in 1933, then was bumped off by the Somoza family. The Sandinista movement is dedicated to him."

"And now our friend Rivera wants to drive the marines out of Puerto Rico," Knutsen said. "That would fit the ego pattern quite well actually." Knutsen picked up the photograph and tapped his finger against Rivera's face. "Highly intelligent chap," he said. "From what I can gather, very controlled and disciplined as well. I would say he is our leader, unless this other man, our unknown factor, is. But based on the reports from that motel in Florida, I would guess not."

"And the others?" Henry asked.

"Well, we know about Hernandez, and nothing has developed to change that evaluation. The two women are bright, the Epstein woman more so than Carol McGovern, but I would say each could be led by a powerful personality. The Epstein woman would be slightly more difficult, I would say. She would probably have to be consulted on proposals and brought around to the correct way of thinking. Both women come from very moral backgrounds, strong religious upbringings. But then, that was true of Hernandez as well. His mother was a devout Pentecostalist, so I don't know how much credibility to give that factor. But, excluding Hernandez because of his psychopathic tendencies, I would guess that the women would at least subconsciously resist the cold-blooded killing of a helpless captive."

"But they could be manipulated into doing it." Henry stated the premise flatly.

"Exactly. It would depend on the will of the leader or the group as a whole, majority rule, so to speak."

"What about him?" Henry said, pointing toward Richard McGovern.

Knutsen tapped the face of the image. "Perhaps the most interesting of all. Again, highly bright, a very mathematical mind, according to his college records. But for some reason intentionally subservient. I would guess something rather disastrous happened to our friend McGovern, something he himself possibly doesn't remember or never recognized as overwhelmingly significant. But it has made him a follower, even though he should have been one who led. These old reports on his activities in SDS are fascinating, Pat. He repeatedly yielded to the wills of much lesser minds, seemed to satisfy himself with the repetition of jingoisms, rather than true revolutionary thought, almost as though he didn't trust his own reasoning. He could be struggling desperately to conceal it from the others, afraid to reveal too much of himself for fear that that, too, will be discovered. But that's a fairly wild guess on my part."

"But he's the one with some stability. He's married to this Carol woman, isn't he?"

"Yes, but that means nothing. He's living among a group of men and women who are in constant fear of being caught, so the pressures on him are extreme. Given this added personal pressure he, too, could become an unstable variable."

Henry took the photograph back and stared at each face individually. Knowing who they are and what they look like, he thought, in a sense adds to the frustration. But Knutsen's analysis of what they're like and how they think, helps. Even if it's wrong, it makes it easier to deal with. He still had difficulty trusting Knutsen, but now found himself using his advice like a crutch. Grasping at straws, he told himself. Although he *was* beginning to like the old boy.

He picked up a handful of documents, rough drafts of old communiqués, handbills and the like, and began leafing through them. "What do you make of this?" he asked, handing one to Knutsen and pointing to the signature.

"El Tiburón," Knutsen said. "That means the shark in Spanish, doesn't it?"

Henry nodded.

"The name of the leader, I would guess. But it surprises me. I wouldn't expect something quite that dramatic from Rivera. But then, it could have been recommended in his training, a method of identifying oneself in a communication without using a traceable name."

"How would you feel about releasing that name, Kermit? About identifying the leader of the group as El Tiburón?"

"But that name's been used in connection with the group in the past, hasn't it? I saw it on other communiqués I've reviewed from previous incidents."

"Yes, but I was thinking that it might titillate the media and also give this guy the kind of public recognition you said he wanted."

Knutsen began rubbing his hands together, as if stimulating his own thoughts. "It might," he said. "It just might do that. It might also achieve that other objective. To rivet his attention and animosity on you rather than Norris. But I wouldn't reveal his true identity. That might throw him into a panic. Make him run for cover. And that might prove fatal to Norris." He began tapping his fingers together. "It would have to be very carefully worded," he said at length. "But I think you may have struck on something there, Pat. Is there anything among all these papers that gives you a clue as to where they are?"

"Afraid not," Henry said. "They're still in Florida, I'm sure of that. But God knows where. Knowing who they are increases our odds, though. Every relative, every friend, every previous employer or person they've ever had contact with is being watched. We're monitoring their phones, their mail, even how many times they go to the john. But we need a break. We need to have them contact someone. And there aren't too many days left for it to happen."

"Do you think they'll have to?"

"I don't know. Everything was planned so damned well up to now, I'm just not sure. I've been racking my brain trying to figure out some way to force them to make contact, but I can't think of anything that will work. They're too clever to respond to any round-up of associates, and anyway, my guess is that they've kept pretty tight security on everything. Our people haven't found anything that would indicate that any of their friends know where the hell they are."

Knutsen began pulling on his nose. "How to force them to make contact," he said. "A fascinating problem. Perhaps one of the individuals has someone in his background who might draw him out individually. A relative, a close friend." He shook his head. "No, you're right. They're too disciplined, too well trained. And frankly, too damned smart to be duped that easily."

"So all we can do now is go by the numbers and wait," Henry said.

"And we can try this El Tiburón thing with Rivera," Knutsen said.

~~~~~~

"Why should we trust any fucking thing you say?" Norma's voice was sarcastic and cutting.

"You shouldn't," Norris said. "No more than I should trust anything you say to me." He looked from one to the other. They were seated in front of him in a semicircle in the rear room. Only Juan was missing. He was standing guard at the window in the front room, unwilling to join—even though El Tiburón had offered to stand watch in his place—angry that the others had even wanted to listen to Norris.

"Have you ever considered the idea that we're all captives here together?" Norris asked.

"You're a prisoner," Richard said. "We can kill you and leave here any time we want." He spoke the words firmly, but there was a lack of conviction in his eye. Norris nodded toward him.

"That's true, but you would have to sacrifice your objectives and you would still be hunted. The ideal solution is that I live and you get what you want."

"Fuck you." The shout came from the front room, causing the others to glance back to where Juan stood at the window. His sallow complexion seemed to glow with anger and Norris looked away, avoiding the madness in his eyes.

"You're saying we're captives as much as you are," Carol said. "I don't accept that."

Norris extended his palms to her. "No one person, or group of people, controls anything completely, no matter what his position of power is. Circumstances dictate to a certain degree for a certain period." He hesitated, then smiled. "It's probably not the right subject to bring up, but as you all know, the situation in Vietnam passed through the hands of several presidents and none was able to make any dramatic changes when they first approached the problem."

"Bullshit," Wally snapped. "Nobody wanted to change nothin', that's all."

Norris steepled his fingers in front of him and stared down into them. "I assure you everyone wanted things to be different there. It just couldn't be done."

"You just got your asses kicked by the people," Norma said.

"Let me try to explain it differently. When any leader takes control of something, whether it's a government or a corporation or whatever, he cannot change things immediately to suit his own objectives. There are always standing agreements that exist, policies that have been established. In government, especially in the interrelationships between governments, sweeping changes simply cannot be made every time there's a change in administration. If that happened, no one would be willing to enter into any long-term agreements or understandings. They couldn't afford to do it, not if everything was contingent on an election every few years, or on the life expectancy of any one man."

"Revolutions change governments and policies all the time," Richard said.

"Yes, they do. But you seldom see any long-term comprehensive agreements with those nations. It's also why large governments pour so much money into small emerging nations to keep them as stable as possible."

"Usually at the cost of the people of those countries," Carol said.

Norris smiled. "Governments don't operate on the basis of political philanthropy. They operate for their own benefit, much in the same way you are now. I doubt you've given much thought to those who will lose employment or opportunities if Puerto Rico is free."

"We're concerned about the *people* of Puerto Rico, the majority," Norma said. She had snapped the words out without thinking. She hesitated, then her mouth tightened. "We have to work for those who have the greatest need," she added.

"No," Norris said. "You have to work for those you are trying to serve. And any time you gain advantage for one group, you create disadvantage for others. And you can't change your positions radically without warning, or no one will be able to trust what you say. That's why I say we're all captives to your demands to a certain degree. But there's a lovely irony to it all. You believe in your goals and you want to be successful in them. But for complete success, I have to live, which certainly is not a high priority consideration for you. On the other hand, I don't believe in your goals, but I very much want to see them succeed."

"It's too bad we can't blow your head off and get what we want too." There was a sneer on Norma's face.

"And it's too bad my government can't tell you all to go to hell and keep me alive at the same time," Norris said.

El Tiburón smiled inwardly over the expressions on their faces, the defiance, the uncertainty. The willingness to listen, the unwillingness to trust. He loved each of them. They were his children. Even the one who had not joined in. Even Juan. Unbendable Juan. His problem child. Wally, too, was not interested in listening, but he had joined them, out of respect for him.

He had suggested they talk with Norris. Urged them to, without really appearing to do so. He thought it would ease the tension. Give them a better understanding of it all. And Norris was good. But then, he had had a great deal of practice. He would not change their thinking, their idealism. But he would cause them to wonder, and in doing so, he would make them easier to lead.

"How much can we trust your Yanki government?" Richard asked. "How can we be sure they won't promise us what we want and then renege on it when they get you back?"

Norris studied the young man's face, the wild bushy hair and unkempt beard. Unstable, he thought. Someone who lives on the edge, always frustrated, never certain of his own destiny, or even if he has one.

He nodded his head. "I would trust them no more than they trust you, *can* trust you, from a political standpoint. But more so now than if and when they agree."

"What's that supposed to mean?" Carol asked. "It sounds like your typical double-talk."

"What it means is that they'll be looking for a viable excuse not to agree," Norris said. "But it will have to be one that will be acceptable to the public. It will have to be one where it appears *you* have caused the negotiations to break down, not them. Once they agree, they're trapped. To renege then would not only solidify the Puerto Rican desire for independence, but it would make it impossible to negotiate with any future group seeking demands under similar situations."

"But that's also a reason for them never to agree, isn't it?" Norma snapped.

"Yes, it is. That's what makes it a poker game right now. And unfortunately, I'm part of the pot."

"You really want us to believe you're on our side, don't you?" Carol asked.

Norris shook his head. "I'm not on your side. I only want to see you win this hand." Norris paused. "For my own sake," he added.

"So you're the one who's trapped, not us," Richard said. "You're doubly trapped. You're trapped in this cabin and you're trapped in our goals."

Norris drew out the moment, letting Richard's words register with the others. It was what they wanted to believe. "I suppose that's true," he said.

Richard grinned at the others. "Well they can't win this poker game. Not as long as we have him," he said. "They can just lose."

He stared at Norris. "Because we can always kill you," he said.

"Kill your fucking ass anytime we want." The words were shouted from the front room.

There was a pleased look on Juan's face. The mere mention of killing, Norris thought. It was all it took to please him.

El Tiburón stood. He would end the meeting on that note. "And you must never forget that, *Mr. President*," he said. "These are committed people, dedicated revolutionaries. Never doubt that."

He looked at each of them, noting the pleasure his words brought to their faces. And they are my children, he thought. And it is up to me to guide them.

25

He climbed the stairs of the abandoned warehouse slowly, listening to the barely distinguishable sounds of the interrogation that was underway on the second floor. When he reached the door of the room he stopped, taking time to clean the lenses of his horned-rimmed glasses. A muffled scream came from the room. He eased the door open and stepped inside. The boy was seated in a chair, hands tied behind him, and there was blood flowing down one cheek from a deep gash above his eye. The heavyset Hispanic turned as he entered, then brushed back a strand of black, oily hair that had fallen on to his forehead. They had not seen each other since their meeting in the Mexican restaurant and they nodded formally.

He grasped the lapels of his tweed suit coat and studied the boy for a moment. He was fourteen or fifteen, certainly no older, he decided.

"Well, what have we here?" he said.

"Our little *muchacho,* here, was one of the people who planted the explosives the day before the kidnapping," the Hispanic said. "Fortunately for us he bragged about it to some friends."

The agent looked across to another man standing by a shuttered window. He, too, was from the Company, a hard, young man with neatly trimmed hair and expressionless eyes.

"Has he told us anything?" he asked, directing his question to the younger man.

He shook his head. "He's stubborn. But we haven't been at it long yet. He will."

The older man turned to the Hispanic. "None of the other contacts worked?"

"Everyone has disappeared," he said. "I have tried every possible method of communication, but everyone has gone underground."

The man in the tweed suit nodded his head. "I suppose that was to be expected." He walked over to the boy and cupped his chin in his hand. "That means you're all we have, young man. So if I were you I'd tell us what we have to know and save yourself a great deal of pain."

The boy stared at him without expression. He had a thick Afro haircut that spread a full four inches from his head, and it accented his deep brown-black eyes and sallow complexion.

"Doesn't he speak English?" the older man asked.

"He speaks it," the younger man said. "He's just stubborn, defiant."

"That's too bad, son." He turned his back and walked back toward the door. The sound of the Hispanic's fist striking the boy filled the small empty room.

"Where are they?" the Hispanic shouted.

"I dunno." The boy's words came in gasps and then broke into a small cry as the fist slammed into his face again.

The older agent turned and stared back at him. Blood poured from his nose and he was gasping for air through his mouth. Broken nose, he thought. "Use the body more," he advised the Hispanic. "If you break his jaw, he won't be able to say anything."

The Hispanic grabbed the boy by the shirt and yanked him to his feet. The boy's leg's buckled as he was slammed against the wall.

"What's his name?" the older agent asked.

"Sito," the younger agent said.

The older agent walked over to the wall and leaned against it next to the boy. "Be smart, Sito," he said. "Sooner or later you'll tell us what we want to know. Save yourself pain. I have a boy your age. I don't like to see you hurt this way."

The boy's lips trembled, but his eyes spit hatred.

The Hispanic took a knife from the pocket of his suit coat and pressed a button that sent the blade snapping open.

"Maybe I'll just cut his balls off," he said. He placed the knife point under the boy's chin and pressed upward until a slight trickle of blood ran down the edge of the blade.

"How would you like that, Sito? No more pussy ever. Maybe you never had any yet. And maybe if you don't tell me what I want to know, you never will."

The boy's eyes widened, the earlier hatred replaced by fear. The Hispanic pulled back the knife, then drove his knee up in the boy's groin.

"Tell me," he said, as the boy's body lurched forward in pain.

The older agent chuckled to himself. "My friend. How can he talk when you do that? Christ, he can hardly breathe now, let alone tell us anything."

The Hispanic slammed the boy back against the wall and pressed the knife against his throat, holding him there. "Take his pants down," he snapped at the younger agent. "I'm going to cut one ball off."

The boy twisted to free himself, but the blade of the knife held him in place. "Don't do it, man. Don't," he said, as he felt his pants yanked down to his ankles.

"Then tell me," the Hispanic growled into his face.

"I dunno where they are. I really don't."

The older agent leaned forward. "What do you know, son?" His voice was almost soothing.

"I jus' know where they usta live. But they ain't there no more."

The older agent glanced up at the Hispanic. There was a slight smile on his face. He looked back at the boy. "Where is this place, Sito?"

"It's down in Soho. A loft on Spring Street."

"What's the number on Spring Street, Sito?"

Tears began to stream down the boy's face as he mumbled the number.

"Sit down and rest, Sito," the older man said, then watched as the boy slumped to the floor. He motioned to the others with his head and turned and walked back to the door.

"I think he's telling us all he can for now," he said as they gathered around him. "We can probably get the names of other associates from him now without too much difficulty, but I doubt they will know where these people are. They're professional, and I would imagine they're keeping to strict security procedures." He looked at the younger agent. "Check out this loft, but very discreetly. The Bureau's people may have located it already, so check for surveillance first. If you see any, skip it and report back to me. If not, I want everything of value brought in and I want prints taken."

The Hispanic motioned with his eyes toward the boy. "What about our little friend over there?" he whispered. "He has seen me, and that is dangerous for me."

The older agent nodded. "Yes, it's dangerous for us as well. But perhaps his passing can be useful to us."

"Who do you want to do it?" the younger agent asked.

"I think you had better. We'll keep it a Company function." He looked hard into the younger agent's face, as if deciding whether he was capable of what he would be asked to do. Anger seemed to flash in the younger man's eyes over the expression of doubt.

"We'll need to have his passing be quite public," the older agent said finally. "Since the New York press pays little attention to Black or Hispanic deaths, unless they are fairly sensational, I think mutilation of some sort would be best." He rubbed his chin for a moment, thinking, then went on. "And I want something found on his person, some papers or something, that would identify him as having some involvement with some Puerto Rican liberation organization. Perhaps our friend here could come up with something. Let's not make it WAR material, however. That would be too obvious."

The Hispanic nodded.

"Good. Also, as a safeguard against the Bureau covering it all up, there should be a call to the wire services claiming to be from WAR and charging that our friend Sito was the victim of torture as part of the government's efforts to find Norris."

The Hispanic's eyes widened. "When our friends in WAR hear about this, won't they retaliate?"

"They just might do that," the older agent said.

He turned to go, then stopped in the doorway and looked back at the younger agent. "Let me know about any new developments immediately," he said. "Oh, and there's no reason for the boy to suffer too much. The necessary work can be done after he's dead, unless that proves to be impossible. But try."

26

The rain fell heavily on the roof of the cabin, striking with near-thunderous force and causing them to speak louder than they normally would. They had both been disappointed by the rain. It had driven the birds to shelter, ending any chance to continue their discussions of the various species that thrived in the marshes outside. El Tiburón looked toward the window, noting how the sheets of water made the glass appear like an old disfiguring mirror. He marveled at the roof and walls of the rotting old cabin, which did not leak despite the endless assaults of drying sun and drenching water.

"I'm afraid we'll be seeing no birds today," he said.

Norris looked toward the window and nodded, running one hand along his cheek. They had permitted him to shave that morning and the skin felt smooth; clean for the first time in days. An odd luxury, cleanliness, he thought. But still very much a luxury.

"They'll be out when it stops. And they'll be very active, very hungry."

They were seated on the floor, El Tiburón, Indian-style, facing Norris, whose back was against one wall so he could extend his leg. From the other room they could hear the television set, its volume turned up to overcome the sound of the rain.

"Your friend Henry was on television again this morning," El Tiburón suddenly said. He watched the interest intensify in Norris's eyes, but he didn't speak.

El Tiburón waited to see if he would. "It seems you're becoming the forgotten man in this whole escapade."

Norris's eyes blinked, surprised at the word chosen to describe his imprisonment, then he snorted. "Does that surprise you? I've told you their interest would be far greater in capturing you, than in rescuing me."

"It seems to be even more than that." El Tiburón smiled slightly. "He used my name during an interview this morning."

Norris seemed startled, causing El Tiburón to laugh. "Not my real name. The same one you know me by."

Norris's jaw tightened and he concentrated on the wide boards of the floor. "Perhaps they're trying to frighten you and force you to act so the whole question of the demands can be forgotten."

"I thought of that at first myself. But there was more to it. The way he looked as he spoke. The tone of his voice. It's a personal battle for him, one he wants very much to win." He paused for a moment, then smiled again at Norris. "He's a strange man, Edmund." They had begun using familiar names with each other the previous day and, while it had surprised him at first, it now seemed quite natural.

"*Cyanocitta cristata,* Tiburón," Norris said.

El Tiburón cocked his head.

"More commonly known as the blue jay. That raucous little bird with a scream almost identical to the red-shouldered hawk."

"Ahh, so I get a lesson in birds anyway," El Tiburón said. "Tell me the analogy."

Norris looked at him with humor. "There is one you know. There *always* is. Very handsome bird, the blue jay, very proud, very brave, but often disliked because they chase smaller birds away from feeders, protecting those goods for members of their own group."

"So the smaller birds come looking for their right to life and the jays keep them from it," El Tiburón said.

"For as long as they can. Sooner or later the smaller birds band together and come in force and then the jays let them have what they want. What's really amazing, though, is how the smaller birds then let the jays stay among them, accept them, never seem to remember the persecution they inflicted."

El Tiburón laughed. "I wonder if Martin Luther King ever thought of Hoover as a fat old blue jay," he said. "Tell me, Edmund. What do the jays do when a bigger bird comes to protect the smaller ones?"

"Large birds never protect smaller birds. They only prey on them, one way or another." He watched the smile fade from the younger man's face and hurried on. "But the jays also hate to have larger predators in their territories. They become very violent and angry and try to drive away the competition, the threat to their dominance. It's often easy to find a hawk or a roosting owl by following the screams of blue jays nearby."

"Do these birds do any good?"

"By accident sometimes. They're very secretive birds, very protective of their possessions, and often they bury seeds and acorns to keep them away from other birds, so they can have them for themselves later. But often they forget where they've buried them, and in doing so, they inadvertently become planters of trees."

El Tiburón rose and walked toward the window. "Your friend Henry is certainly planting seeds right now," he said, adapting the analogy to his own use.

"He's not my friend, you know," Norris said. "In fact, right now, he's probably more of a danger to me than you are, Tiburón."

He turned back to Norris. "Yes, I know. And in doing that he also endangers everything good I want to accomplish."

"The main problem is that the forum is limited. It's tilted in his favor. A way has to be found to respond to him more frequently."

Suspicion flashed in El Tiburón's eyes, and Norris noticed it.

"I know," he said. "It's dangerous, the exposure makes you more vulnerable."

"And you too. If they find us and attack," El Tiburón said.

Norris nodded. "And me too."

El Tiburón paced the small room for several minutes, then sat across from Norris again.

"You realize that I cannot extend this deadline unless they make concessions," he said.

"I know. The others wouldn't go along."

"The majority would. But not all. And I can't afford to divide the group at this time. The only chance I have for success is in unity."

Norris pressed his lips together, causing his heavy jowls to sag along the line of his chin. "You're learning one of the great lessons of leadership," he said. "There will always be people who will choose a leader and then refuse to accept or recognize his right to make decisions. There will always be people who will resent the fact that someone else is leading them, making decisions for them, even when they're decisions they don't want to make themselves." He smiled across at him. "You have Juan and Richard."

"More so, Juan. But also the possibility of Richard. He might side with him. It's hard to tell about Richard. But that surprises me. I thought you would have been more concerned about Wally."

"I was initially until I thought about it and until I spoke with Richard this morning. Wally's the type who does as he's told. He'd kill, or not kill. It doesn't matter to him. Richard questions, and he questions himself more than anything. People like that are erratic."

"I hadn't realized you'd been observing us so closely."

"There isn't much else to do. Besides, I have been slightly concerned about this *escapade*." He used the same word El Tiburón had, but with an appropriate degree of irony.

"It's strange how much we think alike, isn't it?" El Tiburón said.

"Not so strange. People who choose, or are forced into positions of leadership, have to make hard decisions, do things that normal people don't understand, find difficult to accept. It takes a certain type of man to be that kind of person."

"I disagree with much of what you did. You realize that, of course." El Tiburón's voice was calm, but traces of resentment still came through.

"And I don't agree with much of what you hope for the world," Norris answered. "Perhaps it's a question of different generations. Perhaps I'm trying to hold on to the past too long and you're trying to achieve the future too quickly."

"The future has been long overdue," El Tiburón said. He paused. "Tell me. Why do you offer me advice when you oppose my goals?"

"I suppose none of this seems real to me," Norris began. "The setting, aside from the birds, certainly isn't. And I suppose it's the intellectual curiosity I have about the exercise of leadership. The successful dealing with problems. I failed to deal with certain of mine and since then failure in others has never held the same satisfaction it once did." He lightened his tone of voice. "And, of course, I have a rather personal interest in the outcome of this thing."

El Tiburón folded his arms in front of his chest. "I would not like to have to kill you, Edmund. It seems senseless, even though I know it may be necessary."

"I wouldn't favor it either, Tiburón."

They both chuckled over the obvious foolishness of the remarks.

"Tell me. How would you deal with my problem?"

"With them?" Norris said, nodding toward the outer room.

"Yes."

"I'd get rid of them." He watched the younger man's eyes widen with surprise. "I don't mean eliminate them permanently," he added. "That would hardly be practical, given the circumstances. I would find something else for them to do, something that would remove them as irritants, stumbling blocks. At least in the case of the most dangerous obstacle."

It was not necessary for Norris to mention Juan's name for each of them to understand of whom he spoke.

"We have been close for a long time. Too long, I'm afraid. In many ways he's like a wayward brother to me."

Norris shrugged and the gesture seemed to hold a sense of condemnation. "Ché and Castro were close, weren't they?"

El Tiburón looked at Norris, then at the floor.

"You know, of course, that Ché became a threat to Castro. He wanted to expand the revolution into South America, and Castro did not. At least not immediately. And Ché also rivaled Castro in popularity, was equal in stature as a revolutionary leader, and as such was a personal threat as well."

"So Castro sent him to Bolivia and abandoned him," El Tiburón added.

"Not really abandoned him," Norris said. "Just let him go off and pursue the goals he was so passionate about. If Castro had followed his advice, he never would have been able to consolidate his control over Cuba as he eventually did. Ché was threatening that primary objective as well as threatening Castro's leadership. Castro made a pragmatic decision and the major goals he had for Cuba were achieved."

"At the sacrifice of Ché," El Tiburón said. "I'm not prepared to sacrifice my comrades."

"Are you prepared to sacrifice your goals?" Norris asked.

Anger flashed in El Tiburón's eyes. "I'm prepared to sacrifice nothing. Only you, if necessary."

He stood and began pacing the room again, then stopped and looked down at Norris.

"I didn't mean to snarl at you," he said. "I want to send a communiqué to Henry and I'd like you to help me with it. Will you?"

"Yes, of course." Norris looked toward the window. Outside, faint rays of sunlight were beginning to appear and the rain seemed to be easing. "It looks as though things are about to clear up," he said.

El Tiburón turned his face to the window, then listened to the diminishing sound of the rain on the roof. "Yes. Maybe the birds will come out now," he said.

He walked to the window and wiped away the slight mist that clouded the glass. Out in the marshes everything was still, but in the distance he thought he could hear the faint chirping sounds of birds. He breathed deeply, pushing away the anger he felt rising within himself. Norris came up beside him.

"No sign of any yet?"

"None," El Tiburón said.

They stood together at the window watching for the first sign of movement that would soon come, occasionally wiping away the mist caused by their breath.

"You're angry because you know I'm right," Norris said.

"No," El Tiburón said. "I'm angry because I want you to be wrong."

27

"The reaction should be interesting," Horton said. "And, hopefully, quite swift."

He placed a cigarette in the black holder, lit it, and blew a shaft of smoke up and out across his desk. The agent watched him through his horned-rimmed glasses, taking note of the affectedness of the gesture. He had never liked the Ivy League types who seemed to run the Company these days. They were invariably men without field experience who looked down on those who had it. It had been different when he joined the Company. The old OSS boys were still running things then and they had been a different breed. They could do it themselves if they had to; they had done so during the war. He looked at Horton, smiling inwardly as he did, wondering exactly what the smug expression would change into if he was forced to *finalize* Sito himself.

"When do you think the package will be found?" Horton asked.

Package. What a delicate way to refer to the mutilated body of a fourteen-year-old. "Very soon," he answered. "We didn't want it to appear that it was left to be found, so naturally we made it seem as though some effort was made to conceal it. Shortly after it is, the appropriate calls will be made to the wire services," he added.

"Yes. It has to be fairly fast," Horton said. "I don't want Henry to have time to gag the media on this." Horton drew deeply on the cigarette holder again. "It's actually quite an ingenious move, I think. It's the simplicity of it that makes it so."

The agent nodded, wondering which genius in the humint section had dreamed it up. "You said there was another facet you wanted acted on," he said.

259

Horton smiled, then reached out and plucked a folder from his desk. "We need better information on Henry's movements, plans, etc., and to date he's been quite effective keeping us boxed out." He handed the folder across his desk. "But I think this will solve the problem for us."

The agent opened the folder and stared down at the eight by ten photograph inside, then read a brief synopsis. "What's his connection with Henry?" he asked.

"He's been assigned to assist him. Rather a good choice, too," Horton said. "Our friend, there, is one of the top experts on the psychology of terrorism living today."

The agent dropped his glasses to the edge of his nose and peered over them, studying the round, jovial face of Knutsen, the wisps of unruly hair, the almost boyishly smooth features. He had little faith in theoretical scientists. Those who developed drugs or serums that had a practical use were acceptable, but the others who simply gathered statistics and formulated conclusions were of little value, he had found. Now Horton appeared ready to waste his time with this one.

"What is it we want of him?" he asked.

"It's our understanding that he has immediate access to everything that comes into Henry's office. Almost as soon as Henry does, in fact. We, of course, want that information immediately. We also want it understood that Henry is to get as little assistance as possible in locating these people. He is only to get those things we approve first. All other information is to be given to the Company instead. In short, we want the edge his expertise might provide so we can be sure to reach them first."

The agent stared at him, expressionless. "You're assuming then that our ploy with the young boy won't work?"

Horton toyed with his cufflinks momentarily. "No, actually I'm rather hopeful about that, especially with that extra touch your man added to it. I simply want us in a position of advantage if it doesn't." He stood and walked out from behind his desk, stopping in the center of the large office. "It shouldn't prove very difficult," he said, keeping his back to the agent. "Read on."

The agent leafed through the dossier until he reached a familiar manila envelope marked *pressure point*. He opened it, his eyebrows rising as he did. When he looked up at Horton there was a slight smile on his lips. "No, I don't think I'll have any trouble convincing him at all," he said. "Tell me, how did someone with this in his background ever end up in such a high position at Walter Reed."

Horton turned back to the agent, the cigarette holder now fixed between his teeth. "The information was developed years ago by our people in Oslo, where Knutsen grew up. It came to light during a routine background investigation prior to his being offered a position in the government. A decision was made then to file it away for future use. It was a decision, I might add, made by a previous director, so it will not hurt the Company, as it exists at present, if it's now revealed." He smiled at the agent. "Quite a good decision, really, don't you think?"

One of the OSS boys, still producing benefits, the agent thought. "Quite good," he said.

"See him this evening at his home," Horton said. "Simply explain what we want and what the alternatives are. There's no reason for him to know our objectives."

~~~~~

Kermit Knutsen arrived at the small Georgetown row house that he rented shortly after nine o'clock, his briefcase crammed with reports he would use that night to further clarify his psychological studies of the terrorists. After dropping his briefcase and topcoat in the small room he used as a study, Knutsen waddled into the kitchen trying to decide what to prepare for a light dinner.

There was not much to choose from, he decided, staring into the open refrigerator. An omelette, perhaps. With cheese, onion, and mushroom. He shook his head. It was precisely what he had eaten the night before. Or was it two nights ago. He couldn't be sure.

The sound of the doorbell forced the mundane decision from his mind. He looked up at the kitchen clock. Nine-twenty, an odd time for callers, he thought. But then, nothing had been quite normal since this assignment to Henry's group had begun. He moved quickly down the long hall that led to the front door, the unwieldiness of his bulky body causing him to sway slightly from side to side.

Set within the heavy oak door was a smaller door that allowed Knutsen to inspect any visitors. He unlocked it and swung it open, then raised himself on his toes so he could peer out. The opening had been built for a giant, he thought, as he did each time he was forced to use it.

"May I help you?" he said.

The man outside smiled and held up a credential case, the emblem on which Knutsen immediately recognized as the Central Intelligence Agency. He looked the man over closely. He was in his mid to late forties, about ten years younger than Knutsen, himself, and the horned-rimmed glasses he wore belied hard, piercing eyes. Yes, he thought, he looked the part. He had dealt with the Agency in the past and had always been amazed at how much they all looked alike.

"Just a moment," he said, closing the small door and struggling with the two locks and safety chain that made up his elaborate but inadequate security system. He swung the heavy door open and offered a welcoming smile.

"I'd like to speak to you for a moment, professor," the agent said.

"Oh, does this have something to do with the strike force?" Knutsen asked.

"Yes, sir, it does. May I come in?"

Knutsen shook his head at his own absentminded rudeness. "Yes, I'm sorry. Please do. I just got home myself and I'm afraid my mind is still in a bit of a muddle." He ushered his guest into the hall, then pointed to the small spartan room off to his left. "Why don't we use my study?" he said.

The room was illuminated by the solitary light of the desk lamp, which left the bookcases along two walls and the various diplomas and framed scientific awards that covered the remaining two partially hidden in shadow. Knutsen sat behind his desk, and his visitor took the lone leather wing chair opposite him, pushing it back slightly so he too was partially obscured. Knutsen squinted out at him, trying to see his face more clearly.

"Well, what can I do for you?" he asked.

"Well, it's really a question of what we can do for each other," the agent said.

His voice was flat and emotionless, but that, too, was typical of the type, Knutsen thought. "Ahh, it's nice to hear you'll be doing something for me," Knutsen smiled. "What is it?"

The agent reached into his coat and withdrew a bulky white envelope and passed it across to Knutsen. "This," he said.

Knutsen tilted his head sideways and arched his eyebrows with amusement as he took the envelope, then opened it and withdrew photocopies of the *pressure point* document. He began reading, then looked up at the agent, his face now absent of color.

"Read it all, professor," the agent said.

Knutsen stared back at the collection of data, his mind not believing what he saw, yet, nevertheless, bringing him back thirty-eight
years to his days as a student in Oslo, forced from his mind long ago,
discarded, forgotten. He read on slowly, rereading every third or
fourth paragraph, noting the emphasis placed on things, often without justification. Yet damning all the same, no matter what the emphasis, no matter how it was applied. He looked across at the man
partially hidden in shadow.

"But these were things that happened when I was a student, that
I was only a party to as a student. They weren't things that I initiated." His mouth had become suddenly dry and it gave his voice
a croaking sound.

The agent removed his glasses and began cleaning them with a
handkerchief. "I'm aware of that, professor, and so is the Agency.
They've had these documents for many years now. Ever since you
were investigated for your first government post." He replaced the
glasses, adjusting them on his nose.

"Then all this is known to the government and obviously it has
made no difference. The circumstances are understood."

There was a pleading tone to his words that he could hear clearly
himself. Across from him the sound brought a slight smile to the
man's lips.

"It's known to the Agency. No one else," he said. "And, hopefully, it will remain that way. That's what I meant when I said we
could do something for each other."

Knutsen drew a deep breath and stared back at the documents
now spread out on his desk. "And what is my part in this unholy
bargain?" he asked.

The agent crossed his legs and held one knee in his clasped
hands. He began to speak in a flat staccato voice, an unbroken string
of words, like a machine spitting out facts without emotion. "It's
very simple professor. As you can see, the documents you have are
photocopies, which you may keep for your own reference. The origi-
nals must, of course, remain where they are. I assure you they will
continue to be classified under the highest security and will never be
made public, either here or in your homeland. As a consideration for
this you will perform a simple service. As you're no doubt aware,
Mr. Henry is not being very open with the Agency. He has his own
reasons for this, I'm sure, but, nevertheless, we would like better information than we are getting. That we expect from you. We're well

aware that you have access to all incoming information as soon as it is received. Each time you get it we expect notification in detail, along with whatever action is under consideration by Henry."

Knutsen's features had deteriorated even further; his face had become a cadaver's, the flesh sunken and pliable like putty. "Is that all?" he asked.

"Not quite. In addition to that you will be asked to clear any recommendations to Henry through the Agency. In short, you will make your recommendations to us and we, in turn, will tell you whether or not to relay them, or something entirely different."

"Why would you want to impede the investigation? Why place a man's life in jeopardy this way?" The question suddenly sounded as foolish as it was. Why dredge up a man's past, torture him with memories of a time that was torture enough in itself? What reason do these men have for anything?

"That's really a moot point, professor. I assure you our reasons are justified and have the best interests of the nation in mind. That should suffice."

Knutsen continued to stare at his desk. "The best interests of a nation come in many versions," he said.

The agent across from him was silent. Knutsen continued to look down, then slowly reached out and grabbed a handful of the papers, gripping them so tightly that the edges crumpled in his hand. He held them up and stared out across the desk.

"This happened thirty-eight years ago," he said. "I was twenty years old when these things occurred. A child, forced to be a party to things beyond my control."

"I have no doubt of that, professor. But you were, nevertheless, part and party to certain illegal experiments conducted on innocent victims by the Nazi occupation forces."

"I was party to nothing," Knutsen shouted. "I was a student, one of many, forced to observe the experiments, forced to write down data and collate figures. We had no choice. We either observed and assisted or we became victims of these experiments ourselves." His eyes had filled with tears; the sound of screams thirty-eight years old rose in his mind as though they were coming from the hall outside his study.

"Do you realize how many times I wept. How many times I vomited; went to sleep shaking with fear and loathing. What do you think it was like for a child of twenty to watch healthy men and women pressured and tortured until their minds snapped and they became nothing more than pitiful laboratory animals. Forced to record their demise day by day, and all of it simply because they were Jews or Catholics or members of the underground. My God, man. Do you know that four of my fellow students killed themselves to escape the horror of it?"

"But you didn't, did you, professor?"

"Is that my crime? The crime of survival?"

"You never made known your activities after the war, did you?"

Knutsen breathed heavily. "No. No, I didn't. The mood of the country was not very conducive to discussing anything that involved the Nazis, whether or not it was voluntary or otherwise. And it was something those of us involved very much wanted to forget."

"You must admit, professor, that your explanation has very much the ring of Nuremberg to it."

Knutsen's face filled with anger, momentarily returning it to life. "No, not Nuremberg. It has the ring of Auschwitz, of Dachau, of the people who were forced to stack the bodies, to dig the graves, lest they join those they buried."

The agent leaned forward, allowing his face to come into the light. His eyes were hard and cold, eyes that would accept no explanation, no reasoning. "I don't believe you'll find the signatures of those people on reports, on data accumulation sheets, professor. There is a great difference between slave labor and scientific observation, scientific assistance."

Knutsen's features had fallen again, his death mask reimprinted on his face. "Why do you think I've devoted my studies, my life, to combatting terrorism?" he whispered. "I, as few men before me, understand what it becomes. The bestiality of it, whether imposed by a small group of fanatics or by a government." He looked up at his visitor as he spoke the final words, then lowered his face into his hands.

"I assume our conditions are agreed to, professor?" The agent waited, watching the older man's unmoving figure. "Well, professor?" he added after several moments had passed.

"Yes, of course," Knutsen mumbled through his hands. He remained motionless. "Please get out of my house."

"Certainly," the agent said. "I'm leaving a telephone number on your desk. It's the number you'll be expected to call whenever necessary. I expect that will be several times a day. Please use a public telephone."

Knutsen heard his footsteps retreat down the hall; the door open and then close softly. He remained motionless for several minutes, his face still buried in his hands. Despite the sounds of the man leaving, when he finally looked up he almost expected to see him still seated across from him. He stared into the now-empty chair, telling himself it had not happened. Kermit Knutsen, war criminal, he thought.

"Yes, you should have killed yourself like the others," he whispered.

The face of a young woman came to him, her mouth contorted, the once-sensitive blue eyes screaming out with the terror that racked her mind. Trembling blue lips, a face forced from his memory years ago. Back now, perhaps never to leave him again.

He started to rise, but fell back into his chair, his legs, like his mind, unable to function now. The trembling began in his hands and spread up his arms into his shoulders, then through his body. *Dear God.* The soundless scream filled the room, billowing into each corner, each crevice until the force of it could be felt against his body, pressing him down, crushing against him with its weight.

Several blocks away the agent stood in front of an old townhouse on Wisconsin Avenue N.W., studying a menu afixed to a plaque outside. The food was Indian, a favorite of his since a posting there almost fifteen years ago. He lowered the horned-rimmed glasses on his nose and peered out over them. Yes, he thought. He would begin with an order of *samosas*, something he had not had in years. He smiled at the thought. He had not realized how hungry he was.

28

"**H**ow the hell did this happen?" Henry held the telex sheet in both hands. He was staring at it, unwilling to accept the consequences it could produce.

"No one knows. It took everyone by surprise." Desverne stood with his hands on his hips, a worried, almost frightened look on his face.

Henry looked up at him and the fear seemed to transfer from Dez's face to his own. "Could one of our people be responsible?"

"Christ, I don't see how. The only thing I can think of is a split between WAR and some other group. Maybe the idea is to pressure them into killing Norris."

"We've got to stop this from getting out," Henry said.

"Too late, Pat. It went out on both wire services. Reporters got to some uniformed cops at the scene who apparently blabbed," Dez said.

"Even the part about the message and the stuff found in the kid's pockets?"

"Everything."

"Jesus Christ. Then NYPD is going to have to disclaim the information. There's no other way."

Dez stared at the floor. "They can't do that either, Pat. The reporters got confirmation from the medical examiner's office."

Henry returned to his desk and dropped into his chair, the telex still held tightly in his hands. "Contact the top news people at both wire services and see if there's anything they can do to kill the stories. Explain what this could mean." His eyes sharpened with anger. "And double-check with New York. I want to know if anybody at all had contact with this kid. I don't want to say we never talked to him and then have some smartass reporter come up with a dozen eyewitnesses who saw him having tea with two of our people."

"Sure, Pat. But Christ, it couldn't have been one of our people." There was an uneasy look in Desverne's eyes that matched the feeling in Henry's stomach.

"Whether it was or not, the whole fucking ball game could be over because of it, both for us and for Norris." He placed the telex on his cluttered desk and smoothed the edges where his hands had held it. "Tell Knutsen to come in too," he said.

He selected a pipe from the rack on his desk and carefully filled it from a leather pouch. When the pipe was drawing properly he stared at the telex again, still unwilling to accept the information.

Sito Miranda, male Hispanic, fourteen years old. He shook his head. The body had been found in a Soho playground, only two blocks from WAR's loft, the hands and feet bound. Multiple fractures of both arms and legs; the face beaten until it was almost unrecognizable. Cause of death, loss of blood from severed genitals. One word carved into his abdomen, *kidnapper*. Puerto Rican liberation handbills among personal effects.

The door to his office opened and Henry had to look a second time to recognize Knutsen. He was wearing the same clothes he had the previous day, only now they were more rumpled than usual. He seemed to have aged in the past twelve hours; his eyes had the glazed look of someone who had not slept in days and it was obvious he had not shaved.

"You heard?" Henry said.

Knutsen blinked. "Heard?" he said.

"From the look of you I just assumed you'd heard about it."

"About what, Pat?"

He sat clumsily in the chair opposite Henry and took the telex copy extended toward him. He read it slowly, then closed his eyes. When he opened them again they were filled with tears.

"Dear God. They really want the man dead." His voice was barely more than a whisper.

Henry stared at him, the word, *they,* hitting him with a jolt. "Who do you mean, Kermit?"

Knutsen seemed to stir slightly and his face clouded for a moment. "Whoever did this, this thing." He seemed to snap back to life for a moment and he leaned forward. "The kidnappers, Pat. They musn't learn about this." His voice was almost pleading.

"It doesn't look as if we'll be able to stop it. The story's gone out already. We're trying, but it doesn't look good."

The life seemed to drain from Knutsen, disappearing as quickly as it had come. "Then they've won," he said.

Henry leaned forward, still unable to comprehend the physical and mental decline in the man. He wondered for a moment if Knutsen drank. "Kermit, you're making me nervous. You keep saying *they* as if you're talking about some particular group."

For a moment Knutsen's mind cleared and he wanted to blurt everything out, tell Henry, warn him. But he could not. He could not face talking about his past, explaining the terror he felt, the sense of being trapped by things long forgotten, of being a tool in the hands of others, just as he had been thirty-eight years ago, a coward unable to act. He remained silent, his mind clouding over again. Henry continued to wait.

"Kermit. Christ, man, what is it. You think it was our people who did this? Is that it?"

"You don't think that's possible?"

"Not for one minute do I think that," Henry lied. "It had to be some rival group, trying to force WAR's hand. It's the only thing that makes sense." He realized he was taking Desverne's explanation as his own, but it was the only one he could accept.

Knutsen still didn't respond.

"Kermit, look. I have to know how to respond to this, how to keep these people from blowing, if they hear about it. And I need you to help me." He wanted to reach out and shake him. "To top everything off we have a new communiqué that arrived this morning." He picked up the two-page message and dropped it on Knutsen's side of the desk. "It was stuck under the door of a small Palm Beach newspaper," he added.

Knutsen stared at the communiqué for several moments, then finally reached out and picked it up. He looked up at Henry and opened his mouth to speak; his jaw trembled slightly and he turned his eyes back to the communiqué.

"Kermit, what the hell is wrong with you today?" Henry said.

"I didn't sleep well." He continued to look at the communiqué but the words blurred before his eyes and his mind repeatedly flashed to the face of the man who had visited him the night before. Henry's voice came to him from a distance.

". . . We just don't have the time, damn it. You have to snap out of it and get cracking."

"I'll take these to my office and begin," he said. "I'll try to have something for you within the hour."

He raised a hand to his lips absentmindedly, and Henry noticed the hand was trembling. Alcoholic tremors, he told himself.

"Can't you do it here, now," he snapped.

Knutsen's eyes blazed to life again and his entire body seemed to quake. "I'm not a machine. I'm a man," he shouted. "I'm a scientist, not one of your bully boys who follow people around, spying on them, threatening them."

His entire body seemed to radiate anger. No, more than that, Henry thought. Fear. He sat back in his chair and stared across the cluttered desk. Behind Knutsen, Mary stood in the doorway. She had entered the room at the moment of the outburst and now seemed frozen in place, glancing at each of them. Henry noticed the shock in her eyes and wondered if his own registered it as well.

"All right, Kermit. Do it your way. Try to have something as soon as possible." He spoke softly, then watched Knutsen struggle to his feet and move toward the door, passing Mary almost as though she did not exist.

"What was that all about?" she said as the door closed behind him.

Henry exhaled a cloud of smoke and dropped his pipe in the ashtray on his desk. "Damned if I know," he said. "The only thing I can think of was that he was on a bender last night and is hung over. But I got a terrible feeling it's more than that."

"When we got in this morning he was already in his office. He looked as though he'd been there all night." She walked across the room as she spoke, stopping in front of Henry's desk. "When I saw him in there, Pat, I thought he was talking to himself."

"Have any of our people given him a hard time?"

"Not that I know of," she said.

"What the hell was he talking about? Bully boys? Spying? Threatening?" He looked up at her, not really expecting an answer. "Christ, I haven't got time for personnel problems now."

"Well, there's one problem you won't be able to avoid," she said. "Cramer Lessing just telephoned to say he's on his way here and has to see you immediately."

Henry squeezed his thumb and index finger into his eyes. "Shit," he said.

∿∿∿∿

Lessing entered the office like a man being pushed by raging winds and there were signs of fear in his eyes that told Henry what had prompted the visit.

"What is this all about?" he said. "The White House is being deluged with questions about this kid in New York and there are some very ugly implications being made."

He did not sit but instead began pacing the office and when Henry failed to respond he turned on him in anger. "For chrissake, answer me."

"I wish I could, Cramer. I just found out about it myself and I'm still trying to piece together all the facts."

Lessing seemed to age in front of him; the color momentarily left his face and he seemed unsure of himself. Then his eyes hardened. "So it could have been one of your people," he said.

"It could have been a member of the White House staff for all I know, Cramer." He could feel the sneer on his face, the uncontrolled anger that flew from him.

"That's not even funny," Lessing snapped back.

"Neither are your goddamned insinuations. Where the hell are your fucking brains. You think some agent grabbed this kid, interrogated him, tortured him, and killed him, then dumped his body in a playground with a message carved into his belly and liberation handbills stuffed in his pocket?"

Henry was shouting and it had brought the color back to Lessing's face. "Don't you dare speak to me that way. Who the hell do you think you're working for?"

Henry glared at him, then spoke in a near whisper. "I'll show you." He picked up the telephone and pressed the intercom button. "Mary, please come in here with a steno pad," he said.

"What do you think you're doing?" Lessing said.

"Watch," Henry snapped.

When the door opened, Lessing wheeled around. "Young lady, you won't be needed," he said.

"Cramer, you say one more word and I'm going to get out of this chair and knock you on your ass," Henry said.

Lessing's jaw dropped open and he stared back at Henry in disbelief.

Mary seemed to hesitate and Henry noticed that she was nervously twisting the steno pad in her hands.

"Please sit down," he said, waiting for her to take the chair across from him. "Take a letter to the President, this date. Dear Mr. President. Because of constant and repeated interference from members of your staff, and especially Mr. Cramer Lessing, it is no longer possible for me to pursue the kidnapping of former President Norris with any hope of success. Paragraph. Therefore, it is with deep regret that I resign from my present post. This resignation is to be effective immediately, so that whomever you choose to succeed me will have as much time as possible to launch an adequate investigation. Hopefully, this person will be able to work effectively with Mr. Lessing and members of your staff in a way I have found impossible." Henry paused, then added: "one final paragraph. Please also be advised that I am requesting immediate retirement from the Federal Bureau of Investigation and sign it *sincerely*." He added the final word with a low growl. "I'll need five copies. One for the President. One for our files. One for myself. And one each for immediate release to both wire services. Please have the letters on my desk in twenty minutes. I want to get the hell out of here as soon as I can."

Mary seemed to stagger slightly as she stood, and Henry waited until the door had closed behind her, then looked back at Lessing. "That's who I work for, Cramer. The man who'll get that letter in thirty minutes. Now get the hell out of my office before I throw you out."

Lessing's complexion changed from red to ashen to near white. "You can't do this, not now," he said.

"I just did, Cramer. Doesn't your brain function even to that degree?"

Lessing stuttered. "But it's going to look like you're running from this thing, this killing in New York," he said.

"I don't care what it looks like, Cramer. When this thing is properly investigated, I'm positive no one involved with my staff is going to be found responsible. And if someone is, then I'm just going to say that I couldn't be a party to that sort of thing. You see, Cramer, there's no way this can be tied in to any orders I gave."

Lessing held both hands out. "Let's just calm down for a minute. There's no reason to do this."

Henry leaned back in his chair. "There's every reason, every reason in the world. What I said in that letter is true. I have hours, just hours to succeed, and every day, five times a day, I have to deal with you or some asshole on your staff. And it takes time away from what I'm doing just so you can be reassured that your fat little political butt is being protected. You've made success impossible and I think the President should get someone you trust, so the investigation can proceed without constant interference. Now good-bye, Cramer."

Henry picked up his pipe and jabbed at the bowl with a pencil, removing the residue ash to get at the tobacco still beneath.

Lessing walked to the edge of the desk. "What do I have to do to get you to stop this madness?"

Henry hesitated, taking time to light his pipe. "You mean you still want me in this job?" he said.

"Of course I do. You know full well how disastrous it would be if you left now and in this way."

"It wouldn't be a disaster for me at all, Cramer. And the White House would get what it's been after for months. My resignation from the Bureau."

"Please," Lessing said, trying to force a smile. "Just tell me what I have to do to avoid it?"

Henry puffed away on the pipe, enjoying the new found subservience of the man. "There's nothing you can do about the letter. It will be written, with all copies held by me. The next time I receive a telephone call or interrogatory of any kind from you, or any member of your staff, the letters go out as stated. In other words, Cramer, stay out of my life and let me do my job, or else."

Lessing reddened again. "What am I supposed to do if the President wants information?"

"Do what you usually do. Lie to him, make something up. Or, if you choose, tell him exactly what I said. I just don't give a damn what you do. I suggest you content yourself with figuring out how you're going to get me when all this is over."

"Very well," Lessing said. "But just one thing before I go. How are you going to handle this thing in New York with the media. At least tell me that."

Henry shook his head, then laughed quietly. "You never learn, do you? All right, this one last time. But I mean it. It's the last time." He drew a deep breath. "I'm just as shook up about this as you are, but not for the same reasons. *My* concern is what those six terrorists are going to do when they learn about it. And it doesn't seem as though we can stop that. Therefore, I'm going to issue a statement that I'll put together as soon as you *leave*. It will indicate our suspicions that some rival terrorist group is trying to force action against Norris. I'll also raise the possibility that some right-wing element may have overheard the kid talking favorably about the kidnapping and taken action against him. In any event I'll make it clear that all efforts are being made to find the murderer. I'll also include any other recommendations I get from Kermit Knutsen. He's working on that now. Does that answer your question?"

"I don't think you should ignore the suspicions people might have about the government being involved. I think it should be dealt with directly, and then denied, of course."

"That's up to Knutsen. I've got to follow his advice on that. My main concern has to be the reaction of the terrorists. Public suspicions, whatever they are, will have to be dealt with later. But you can help me. If the White House exerts pressure on the media to play this thing down, we'll have a better chance of keeping Norris alive. If we don't do that the ball game is over anyway, and we all lose."

Lessing nodded. He had the look of a beaten man and even though it was a pleasant sight, Henry knew he would spend a great deal of time trying to find a way to even the score.

"Promise me one thing," Lessing said. "Let me know as soon as you can about any new developments. The President has to be kept informed to some degree."

"No problem, Cramer. As soon as I can tell you something without harming the investigation, I will."

"Thank you," Lessing said, as he started for the door.

Henry watched him. *Thank you*, he thought. Now isn't that a pisser. He leaned forward, placing his forearms on the desk, the feeling of satisfaction already waning. If they don't buy what you say and they kill Norris, Lessing will be sharpening the ceremonial sword before the body is even cold, he thought. But he would have done that anyway, he told himself. You were always the fall guy, no matter what.

The door to the office opened and Mary's head was suddenly thrust forward, her body still outside. "Is it safe to come in?" she said.

He grinned and beckoned to her.

She moved across the room tentatively. "He didn't look happy

when he left," she said. "Are you really going to send those letters
out?"

"You type them up and stick them in your purse. If we get one
more phone call from that SOB, we mail them. He understands
that."

She broke into a grin. His use of the word, *we*, pleased her. "If
they're never sent, can I have a copy to keep?"

"Why?" he laughed.

"I may want to write a book about this someday," she said. "And
I'd like to devote an entire chapter to the castration of Cramer Lessing."

"If we don't find Edmund Norris, and find him alive, you'll see
just how castrated he is," Henry said.

"Tell me one thing, Pat? Would you really have hit him?"

"I would have ordered you to," he answered, slightly embarrassed. "Now, would you do me a favor and see if Kermit has anything for me yet." He raised a hand. "But be gentle with him, smile
a lot. I need him too much right now to have him going off the deep
end."

"You trust him now, don't you?" she said.

"Not completely. But I like him. And more important, I need
him."

When she had gone, he stretched his arms out, then rubbed his
fingers into his eyes. It would almost have been worth it, had Lessing
actually called his bluff, he thought. Just to sign the damned letter
and get the hell out, get away from the insanity of the whole operation. He rubbed his fingers into his eyes again. Why the hell
couldn't you just practice law like everyone else in your class? You
could be making out wills for wealthy old dowagers, filing divorces
and bankruptcies, or closing nice, fat, real estate transactions. He
smiled at his own thoughts. And you would have climbed into a bottle years ago with the boredom of it all.

The door swung open again and Mary crossed the room with
what looked like a report in her hands.

"Kermit's gone," she said. "He gave this to his secretary and just
walked out without a word."

"Gone? Where?" he asked, taking the papers from her.

"He didn't say. She said he just handed it to her and walked
away and hasn't come back."

"Well check again. He probably just went to the men's room or something." He glanced at his watch. "It's only ten o'clock. He couldn't have gone to lunch. Check his home if you have to and tell him I need him. But gently," he cautioned again.

The report was inexpertly typed, obviously done by the man himself, and the typographical mistakes and other errors had been left uncorrected. The subject matter began with the latest communiqué, but the tone of Knutsen's analysis seemed somehow disjointed, rambling, and as Henry read it, he knew he would have to clarify several items.

This newest of the communiqués from WAR would appear to be following the pattern we had hoped to achieve, although further development is still needed. You will note the concern that appears to be an inherent part of the accusation leveled against the government for its "refusal to act promptly on the justified demands of the people of Puerto Rico." It is obvious that our attempt to place the burden of responsibility for any failure in achieving those stated demands back on the shoulders of WAR, has proven a success in their eyes. Further, the references to you, personally, as the engineer of this "shameful attempt," and the references to your "ineptness" and your "preference for rescue rather than necessary capitulation" indicates that you are beginning to become the primary target of their anger, thus making the situation a bit safer for former President Norris. But now you must do more. You must respond immediately to the communiqué. You must read their attack and counter it by stating flatly again and again that they are refusing to provide the patience needed to see that the demands are met. You must imply, without actually saying it, that they are unwilling to await a solution because they want to run for cover themselves, rather than allow the demands to be met. This escalation of the argument, again reasserting their apparent abandonment of their own goals for the Puerto Rican people, combined with a gentle accusation of cowardice should work. If, by the next communiqué, they have not agreed to an extension, then an open accusation of cowardice and abandonment of their people should be made. Hopefully, this will work, since the deadline will have been reached by then.

On the matter of the child in New York, I cannot even hope to predict a reaction. Such a horrible act. So insane for a society that professes itself to be God-fearing, decent, and humane. Their reaction, I fear, will be much like my own. One of anger, hatred, sickness of heart. Their response may indeed be violent and our only hope is to

*direct that violence away from Norris; to accuse others, to insist that
it has been done by those who care not for his safety. I would also suggest that the actions of WAR in kidnapping the former President,
must be held, in part, accountable for the death of the child, who, had
not terrorism been used to accomplish an end achievable by other
means, would be alive today. It might also be suggested that members
of WAR are suspected of committing the crime themselves, so as to
provide an excuse to cut even shorter the time period they have set.*

*I wish I could offer you more. But the death of this child has cre-
ated a variable that cannot be calculated. It may, perhaps, produce the
contact with those under surveillance we had hoped for. May God help
us all if that is the price we must pay for success. Be careful how you
phrase your words and be especially careful for yourself.*

Henry sat stunned, staring at the rambling report which had not
even been signed. What in hell is the man talking about, he thought.
It was written as though Knutsen would be unavailable to help prepare the statement, unavailable if and when other communiqués
were received. Jesus, he thought. *He* was quitting, walking out on it
all.

Mary returned to the office.

"He's still not back and there's no answer at his home number,"
she said.

"Well, keep trying. I've got to get in touch with him. In the
meantime send Dez in here."

~~~~~

It was eleven o'clock when Knutsen walked through the doors of
the Old Ebbitt Grill on F Street N.W., just east of the White House.
The barman appeared annoyed and glanced at his wristwatch. Knutsen looked at his own, noting the time.

"I'm sorry," he said. "I guess I'm a bit early."

He sat at the otherwise empty bar and meekly ordered a martini.
He had spent the previous hour walking along the tidal basin,
breathing the clean, cold air, thinking of his boyhood in Oslo and of
the arctic chill that would sweep across that city like the breath of
death itself.

He had never cared for Washington in summer, he thought now.
The oppressive humidity that saturated the air and made it hard to
breathe. The constant sense of griminess that the heat produced, al-

ways feeling wet and unclean. But who was clean in this city, or in any seat of government for that matter. They were *murderers all,* and he was one of them, had always been.

He rubbed the palms of his hands together. They were cold but also warm with the blood that was on them, would always be there, as it had been since his days as a student. He was like the rest. This man who called himself the shark, so ready to kill to achieve his personal goals. And Henry, prepared to end that life, should he be lucky enough to find him. And Norris had certainly killed. And the man who now occupied the Oval Office. And for years now, he knew, he too had been part of the *killing game,* a man hidden behind the guise of scientist, helping others in their death war.

He gulped at the martini, feeling the rush of alcohol come to his blood, the only warning the slight burn of the gin. Every man needed his narcotic, he had always known that to be true, even though men of his profession spent their lives trying to purge others of their dependence on that very real need. Life without a pain-dulling influence was like major surgery without an anesthetic, something for those who possessed that towering strength that was never intended for man.

The barman took his glass and mixed a second drink, and he brought it to his lips as soon as it had settled on the bar. He had not been drunk for a long time, his work, his studies, had served as his anesthetic. Years ago in Oslo that had been true as well. That woman, all those years ago, who had begged him to take her life. What was her name. He could not remember now. He could only remember the fear-filled eyes, the contortions of the face. The endless drugs and the gradually intensified shock treatments and, finally, the surgery that removed all that was human, or had ever been.

"You make a very good martini," he said to the barman.

He was standing behind the bar, leaning over a newspaper, a cigarette in his mouth. He looked up and nodded, then went back to his paper, his hard, craggy face showing no pleasure in the compliment. He does not wish to talk, Knutsen thought. Especially not to someone who has intruded upon his leisure before he had been prepared to work. But there were others who wanted to talk, who anticipated his conversation, and this man, this mixer of drinks . . . yes, even he, would be impressed by who those people were.

Before he left his office, before he had handed the report to his secretary, he had stared at his telephone, thinking of the number in his pocket. Then he had left, passing numerous pay phones outside, the ones he was expected to use when reporting to his new masters. But all men have masters, he had told himself. The poet lives in dread of disfavor from his publishers, his critics, the readers of his work. The actor lives with endless fear of his audience, the minister of his God. Man was taught to fear, for otherwise he would kill those who assaulted his life, tried to make it meaningless. What would happen if poets began murdering those who rejected their work? There would be many more books of poetry published. He laughed out loud at the idea. The barman glanced at him, displeased with what he heard. Laughter has no place in a bar in the morning, and those who laugh must have a reason. Those who laugh to themselves must be watched, for they know something others around them do not and that makes them dangerous.

"May I have another, please."

There was a slight rise of one eyebrow. Disapproval again, Knutsen thought. You are not well thought of by this man and that is not good. We all know that a man must be well thought of by his fellow creatures. He must also be loved by dogs and children, and he must never have sinned or faltered in any way because good people did not admit to those things.

The telephone rang and the barman picked up an extension hidden under the bar. Knutsen could feel the perspiration rise to the surface of his skin, the realization that he was trapped, discovered in his momentary hiding place. He gulped at his drink, prepared to run. The bartender replaced the receiver and walked back to his newspaper, glancing at him. Would he be allowed to leave, or had they called, telling him to keep that man at the bar in place until help arrived. He reached into his pocket for money, but instead his fingers found the piece of paper with the number on it. It had come into his hand as though it had a will of its own, to remind him of what he must do if he were still to be loved by the dogs and children of the world. The bartender left his newspaper and walked toward him.

"Another?" he said.

Knutsen shook his head, his eyes staring into the barman's, seeking some sign. There was none and he turned, moving back toward his paper.

"Yes, I think I will," he said. You must wait and see, he thought. See what they will do.

An annoyed expression flashed across the barman's face and he took the glass with an exaggerated gesture.

Very clever, he thought. But it won't work. All I have to do is telephone and everything will be all right. I have the number, you see.

His hand trembled slightly as he raised the glass. It was the alcohol, he told himself. Not used to it. Too much too fast. When you stand up you'll feel it even more. No, the number was no good now, its magical powers were no more. He had not done as he was told. He had violated the pact, the agreement with the shadowy man and the others who had agreed to keep silent. Such a small price had been asked of him. One life for another, a choice he had made before, made when he was young and strong and filled with ideals. And despite the personal torture he had known, the guilt and doubts that had racked his mind, it had been an easy enough choice to make. Survival was indeed a simple principle for men of principles.

He reached back into his pocket, fumbling for the money he knew was there. He withdrew a crumpled handful of bills and placed them on the bar, taking care to straighten them out one at a time. There was a ten, two fives, and four singles, a total of seven bills, the patron number of gamblers, the winner on the dice table, unless you had already begun the game. And the game had started. He stood and walked toward the door, leaving the money behind. See, I'm a good person, a generous person. The barman will be sorry when he sees the money left behind, the generous nature of the person he has not treated well.

Outside, the cold washed over his body, as it had years ago in Oslo. The streets were still fairly empty, the luncheon crowds still inside, enjoying the warmth of their offices. He reached into his pocket and withdrew the slip of paper with the phone number, crumpled it and let it fall from his hand. Button your coat, his mother had always told him. He did so now. Across the street two men sat in a parked car and the one behind the wheel glanced at him, then looked away. Watch, he thought. Watch and see that your killing game is almost ended. He looked into the street and saw the truck moving toward him. Quickly he stepped off the curb.

There were tears in Mary's eyes and Henry came to her and placed his arm around her shoulder. He looked at Dez and he too seemed shaken. They stared at each other, each man knowing what the other thought.

"Use as many men as you need," Henry said. "But I want to know everything."

He walked Mary to the window. The door opened and closed as Desverne left and they stood there alone, not really looking at anything.

"He was such a sweet little man," she said. "Did you know that he brought flowers to all the women in the office a few days ago. Just a couple of beaten up roses for each one. He said it was a bit of chauvinism he couldn't give up." She looked up at him. "You think he killed himself, don't you?"

"I hope it was only that," he said.

She looked at him, shocked by what he had said, the insensitivity of it. Then the words took on a new meaning. "Pat, you don't really think someone killed him?"

"I don't know what to think right now. I just want to find out."

"But it doesn't make sense," she said.

"The kid in New York doesn't make sense either." He left her at the window and returned to his desk. "I want you to go out to his house and talk to his neighbors. Take somebody with you who can open the place up and go through everything. Look for anything he wrote, anything that might indicate what was on his mind. And do it quickly. The clock is still running."

She looked at him strangely and he turned his eyes away from her, then listened to her leave the room. He placed his forehead in his hand and stared blindly at the desk top. The euphoria of his combat with Lessing was gone now, a momentary victory to break up the string of defeats. He had liked the little man, had learned to quickly, even though he had not wanted him or trusted him at first. The police had found his identification card and had notified them immediately. He had appeared to have been drinking, they had said, something the autopsy would deal with. Henry thought of the autopsies he had witnessed himself and of Kermit on a table now, a large "Y" shaped incision made from the base of the neck to the crotch, splaying him open like a gutted animal. The incision in the scalp, the skin pulled down over the face, the skull cap sawed through and removed.

He looked across at the chair where he had sat hours before, his eyes blazing, speaking of bully boys who followed people, threatened them, spied on them.

What the hell had happened. He hoped it was an accident, drunken or otherwise. Anything else meant problems. Slowly he grasped his own thoughts and felt disgust with them. What was it Knutsen had said? Something about his own need for victory in this final game. Was the game really all that much to him? Had the years made him so insensitive, even to life and death, that only results mattered?

The buzzer on the intercom brought him back and he glanced at his watch. It would be the television crews for his briefing. He straightened his necktie and reached for the notes on his desk. Damn it, he thought. He wished he could be more sure of what he was about to say.

Horton sat at his desk, the chair turned so he faced the wall of tinted glass windows behind him. The ebony cigarette holder protruded from the corner of his mouth, his teeth clamped around the mouthpiece so it was extended at a slight upward angle. There was no pleasure in his eyes and the lines on his face seemed to have deepened perceptibly. His mind replayed the unpleasant telephone conversation he had just finished, the excuses, the self-defensive arguments, the blatant unwillingness to accept responsibility for mistakes. And the end result had left him without the intelligence he had needed. Damn them, he thought. Now time would have to be expended to insure that contact with Knutsen could not be traced back to the Agency and that in itself would involve risk. And still he would not have achieved the advantage he had sought. Someone would pay for this, he told himself. And he would see that they paid dearly.

29

The news broadcast had left them stunned, silent, and Richard had noticed that El Tiburón had suddenly grown pale.

"We better get back," he had said, and they had hurried to the van and had started back toward the cabin, driving faster than they should.

They did not speak as El Tiburón drove the van through the main streets of the town, deserted now except for the occasional pickup truck or battered sedan, his eyes moving from side to side, watching for unwanted police cars. When they had passed the dull, yellow-brick high school, the van turned clumsily onto the narrow bridge that crossed the canal, then onto the dirt road that would take them down past the fishing camps and the small marina that occupied the southern tip of Lake Okeechobee. Both the camps and the marina were quiet as they moved past, and farther on they turned again into the even narrower dirt road that would take them down into the glades and the cabin.

"You're afraid he's going to do something, aren't you?" Richard said, his voice barely audible above the night noises of the surrounding marshes.

El Tiburón looked across at Richard. His face was a dull blur in the light of the dashboard.

"I mean Juan," Richard added.

El Tiburón nodded, then realized the gesture might not be seen in the darkness of the van. "I'm scared shitless he'll lose control," he said, leaning forward as he fought to see the road ahead.

"You couldn't really blame him," Richard said, "but it would really fuck everything up, especially after what that FBI prick said tonight."

El Tiburón nodded, more to himself this time. "We just have to think this thing out, make sure we know what we're doing," he said.

Richard turned in his seat to face him, leaning closer to overcome the noises outside. The gesture seemed ridiculous in face of the isolation that surrounded them. "Do you think *they* killed that kid?" he asked.

"I don't know what to think. None of it makes sense. I just know we have to do something positive or the whole damned thing is going to explode in our faces."

Richard fell silent again. At length he said, "Some of us were talking the other night, all of us except you and Juan, really. Everybody thinks the deadline has to be extended."

El Tiburón glanced at him, then back to the road. "That's not what worries me," he said. "But we have to do something else, too, and I'm not sure what. Besides, we still have to control Juan if we try to extend the thing." He paused. "If we still have anything to extend," he added.

He cut the van sharply to the left, avoiding a small animal which had darted from the marsh to his right, turned, then rushed back to safety. The left side of the van pressed against the rough marsh grass, causing a scratching sound that was magnified inside.

In his mind the news broadcast replayed itself, leaving him with the same stunned confusion he had felt at first. It had begun with the death of a member of Henry's staff, a supposed accident, followed by the report of a murder in Soho, a young boy, unidentified at first, found with liberation handbills in his pocket. The information had been presented as strange, unconnected events, but the hint of a connection had been there and the idea had terrified him, and still did, and he fought to conceal it.

The explanations, what few there were, came when the report switched to Henry. Even that had been different; there was a solemnity that had not existed before. He had been in his office, seated behind a desk, and the formality of it had been disconcerting in itself.

El Tiburón remembered how he had listened, conscious only of Henry's words and his own breathing. Yet it had begun as other press briefings had, with Henry reading their latest communiqué, followed again by his own clever, questioning analysis of the group's willingness to negotiate in good faith.

And then his even cleverer ploy, his hints that the time limitation might not only be due to a lack of interest in the demands themselves, but perhaps a need to insure the safety of the kidnappers. And, finally, the killing blow, the suggestion that the government would pursue the demands even if Norris were released. He struggled to remember the exact words; the calm, cold look on Henry's face.

"The government of the United States will take every step to make these demands a reality, whether former President Norris remains a captive or is freed in a gesture of good faith. The moment he is harmed, however, those efforts will cease."

Calculated, clever, and devastating, El Tiburón thought now. The words had a ring of truth about them. Not for him, but then they were not spoken for him. But for others, those who wanted the demands to be agreed upon, who needed them, and who would want to believe.

Henry had also explained away this Knutsen man's death as an accident and listening, he had told himself it did not matter if it had been or not. But it did matter. If it was connected to the boy's death, it meant something entirely different. But what? He doubted that even Henry knew, and that, if true, could be the most frightening fact of all.

He slowed the van for a rough spot in the road. Sito Miranda, he thought. Was he one of the children he had met, one of those, perhaps, who had come to the loft to deliver the explosives? He had always avoided those who helped, never wanting to know their names, or allow himself to be known in return. It had been for security reasons, he had always told himself.

No, it was because he couldn't face the results, the penalties others had to bear, and it was easier not to know who they were.

"Did you know that boy they found near the loft?" he asked.

"Christ, I've met so many kids named Sito," Richard said. "I'd haveta see a picture to know for sure. Did you?"

"Like you said, they all look alike." He hesitated, then glanced quickly at Richard. "You asked me before if I thought they killed him. Do you?"

"I think they're capable of it," Richard said. "But it wouldn't make any sense, not unless they were trying to provoke us into killing the old man."

In the distance El Tiburón could see a flicker of light where the cabin should be. The last part of the road was treacherous, overrun with ruts and bumps, and he slowed the van to negotiate them.

Henry had implied that it could be a Rican faction trying to force WAR's hand, or some extremist at the other end of the spectrum who had mistaken the boy for a member of the group because of the independence handbills or after overhearing something he had said. No, this had been deliberate, calculated, very much the style of Henry and his peers, in fact. But that did not make sense unless Henry had a reason to want Norris dead. The thought of FALN flashed into his mind. Pressure on WAR, forcing them to act or lose face. The only thing that had been said that made sense was that the boy would be alive if they hadn't taken Norris. The fortunes of war, he told himself, immediately feeling sickened by the truth of it.

He halted the van fifty feet from the cabin where the trip wire had been set and he and Richard jumped óut and hurried up the wooden stairs. Inside, the eyes of the others hit him immediately. Norma was at the window, near the door, and she seemed both concerned and relieved. As he stepped past her, Wally stared at him with a personal anger that seemed self-directed. Just below him, Juan was seated on the floor, a blood-soaked handkerchief against his mouth, his eyes wild and glazed.

"Where's Carol?" he heard Richard say.

As he did, she stepped into the doorway that led to the rear room. She looked frightened.

"What happened?" he said.

Wally jabbed a thumb toward Juan. "Fucko, heah, did one a his space cadet numbers," he snapped. "When ol' Henry tol' about the kid, he went past me like greased lightnin' an' had the ole man by the throat before I could get to 'em. A couple more seconds an he woulda done the job."

El Tiburón's mind flashed back to his own hand-to-hand training and the slowness of a throat kill. He knew Wally was exaggerating. "Is he all right?" he asked, watching Wally's expression return to self-indictment.

"I think so," Carol said behind him. "He's in pain and has trouble talking, but I can't tell if it's anything serious."

El Tiburón stepped toward the rear room. Juan shouted at him.

"He should be dead and you know it. But you don't want him dead."

His voice was hysterical and El Tiburón spun around, rage exploding within him.

"If," he shouted, then hesitated, allowing the volume of his voice to lower.

"If he dies . . . or is hurt so badly . . . that we fail . . . I will kill you, Juan . . . brother of my blood or not." He had spaced his words, emphasizing each phrase, the final one coming in a near whisper.

Behind him, Norma wrapped her arms about herself. Richard stepped forward, looking as if he too was ready to attack.

"You. You want him alive," Juan screamed.

Wally reached down and grabbed him by the shirt, slamming him back against the wall. For the first time, El Tiburón noticed the bloodstain on the sleeve of Wally's shirt.

"What happened to your arm?" he asked.

"He tried to cut me," Wally said, still holding Juan's shirtfront. "Jus' like the street punk he is."

El Tiburón stared down at Juan, his mind filled with a growing rage, everything he feared might happen now a reality. Juan glared back at him, defiant, his hate directed now, perhaps as it always had been, at everyone. El Tiburón turned and walked to the rear room, without speaking, moving past Carol who fell in behind him.

Norris lay flat on the floor, his hand up to his throat. His eyes were pained and moist. El Tiburón knelt beside him and removed his hand, then gently felt for any sign of serious damage.

"He'll be all right," he said.

"He tried to kill me," Norris whispered, the pain of speaking filling his face.

El Tiburón looked up at Carol. "We need some hot water for a compress for the muscles," he said. He looked back at Norris, as he listened to her footsteps retreat from the room. "He'll be gone from here tonight," he said. "You won't have to deal with him again."

Norris's eyes questioned him. "The boy," he rasped. "They can't hold me responsible."

"Someone was responsible." El Tiburón's eyes were hard and distant as he spoke. The boy was a solution. He looked back at Norris. "What will they do if we kill Henry?" he said.

Norris shook his head. "I can't tell," he said. His mind cleared and he reached out and took El Tiburón's arm. "Nothing. They couldn't do anything," he whispered. "And they won't."

"You recall our conversation the other day," El Tiburón said. "This will serve several purposes. And the deadline will be postponed." He added the last with a faint smile, then looked hard at Norris. "But doing it is going to require much from you. If my goal fails, so does yours."

"I'll help you," Norris said, his voice suddenly stronger, causing El Tiburón to wonder how much acting had gone into his demonstration of pain.

"We'll write a communiqué later. You will emphasize our commitment to the justice of the demands and our need for vengeance."

"You can't be specific about your plans," Norris said.

El Tiburón exhaled slowly. "How willing we both are to accept sacrifices," he said.

"I want to survive," Norris said. "It's a strong impulse."

"Like winning," El Tiburón said.

"Survival is winning," Norris answered. "Sometimes that's all winning is."

"Then, hopefully, we'll both win together," El Tiburón said.

When he returned to the front room a half hour later, Juan was seated at the table, his eyes still raging in a sullen face.

El Tiburón sat opposite him, Norma to his left, Wally to his right. Richard and Carol were at the windows. He concentrated on Juan, his mind filled with plans now made.

"You acted like a fool, Juan. You endangered everything we wanted to achieve," he said.

"What about Sito Miranda?" Juan snarled. "Or are you more concerned . . . " He stopped himself and looked away.

"You knew him?" El Tiburón asked.

"I didn't have to know him," he snapped. "He was a brother and they killed him."

"He'll be avenged," El Tiburón said softly. "But the right way, not your way."

The expression in Juan's eyes changed, now a mixture of confusion, doubt, and suspicion. "How?" he asked.

"That's up to all of us to decide." He looked Juan in the eyes. "*None* of us has the right to decide anything alone." He looked at each of them individually. The same expression of concern and confusion was present in every face. Only the suspicion was missing in the others. "There's no question that we can't overlook the boy's death. The way we do what has to be done is the important thing."

He looked at Juan. "You think Henry's people killed him, don't you?"

"I know they killed him," Juan snapped.

El Tiburón smiled at his stupidity. "How?" he asked softly.

"Who else would do it?"

"Anyone who wanted the old man dead," he said. There was a mocking sound in his voice now. Juan was a fool. They were all fools.

"Then you don't think it was them?" Norma asked.

"Maybe *they* want him dead. Maybe they want an excuse to avoid our demands. And maybe it *was* some madman, just as he said. Or, maybe," he paused. "Maybe it was FALN trying to force us to act stupidly and lose respect among the people. The important thing is that we react." He looked back at Juan. "And in a way no one expects."

A glimmer of understanding flashed in Richard's eyes. He left the window and moved to the table behind Juan. "We kill Henry," he said.

El Tiburón looked up at him surprised by his quickness. He had thought of Richard as the biggest fool of all. "I would support that," he said calmly.

"I kill him," Juan said.

El Tiburón looked at him. That's it, asshole, play into my hands, he thought. "How can we trust you, now?" he asked. "From the beginning you've challenged everything. Our mistake was including you at all. You've rejected all your training, acted like a madman."

Juan glared at him. "I could do this. You know it."

"I'm going to do it," El Tiburón snapped, jabbing his thumb into his chest. "At least I know *I'll* follow the will of the group."

"But you're needed here," Norma said. She hesitated, catching the look in his eyes. "But maybe you're right," she added.

Juan stared at her with hatred, then back to El Tiburón. He could see the hunger in his eyes. It was almost laughable and for a moment he wondered why he had never before acknowledged the baseness of the man.

"I'm a better shot," Wally said, causing Juan to turn angrily toward him.

"I can shoot as well as you can, cracker," Juan said.

El Tiburón waved his hand. "The first thing we have to do is lull them into a sense of confidence, make them feel we're weakening."

He ignored Juan, concentrating on the others. "I suggest we tell them we're postponing the deadline and then move against Henry."

He had seen Juan's reaction. He had jumped slightly in place, but he had kept silent. He wanted something more than Norris now, he thought.

"For how long, the postponement, I mean?" Wally asked.

"I don't think we should set a time. I think we should make it indefinite, with the clear understanding that the first sign of betrayal on their part will mean his death." He hurried on before anyone could object. "That way, we could create a reason, if it became necessary, and they would be on the defensive. They couldn't say *we* abandoned our own cause by killing him."

"That's good, it makes sense." Richard said. "But I think Wally's right. It should be him, not you. We need you here."

"We need Wally here," El Tiburón said. "And we need you here to handle the explosives in case of attack."

"What about Norma and me?" Carol said. "Are you excluding us because we're women?"

Stupid bitch, El Tiburón thought. "Henry will have to be followed before he's taken, just so the person can pick a safe place and have a chance to escape." He smiled at her. "A man might notice if an attractive woman kept showing up. Besides, they may have pictures of all of us by now. We have some phony beards we can use, but both of you would look silly in them."

Their laughter broke the tension and he noticed with pleasure that only Juan had not joined in.

"I'm still the best choice," Juan said. He sneered. "Besides, then your old man will be safe, won't he?"

"You'd fuck it up," Wally snapped. "You're just a sneaky little creep."

El Tiburón raised his hand again, before Juan could react. "What would you use?"

Juan pointed to his Stechkin.

"No," El Tiburón said. "You could get on a plane disguised, but never with a weapon."

"One could be brought from New York. One phone call and someone could be there by car five hours later," he said.

El Tiburón nodded, then cupped his chin in his hand. "I was going to send Juan ahead when the time came. I wanted him to meet our people near Ponce to check on the hiding places and escape routes. They know him and he knows the area." He looked across at Juan. "You'd go to Ponce immediately afterward and stay there, no matter what?"

"Yes." His eyes were blazing now.

"All right," he said, slapping both palms on the table. "This is what you do. You leave tonight for Washington. Wally will take you to a restaurant attached to a motel in Palm Beach. You eat. You call a cab. You'll be carrying only a small bag and you'll have the cab pick you up at the restaurant. When you get to Washington you use cabs, even when you follow Henry. After you know where you'll make the hit, you call New York. Not before. Like you said, it's a short trip by car. And until it arrives you have no gun. Agreed?"

Juan jerked his head down.

El Tiburón stared at him, then glanced at Wally. "Take him tonight," he said. "Juan. You'll need money. Will a thousand be enough?"

He nodded again, a slight smile on his lips now.

"Don't fail us Juan."

"He's a dead man," Juan said.

"What if he gets caught?" Norma said.

El Tiburón looked at Juan. "That's understood, isn't it?"

"I escape," he said. "One way or the other." He looked at Norma. "And if it's the other way, I'm gonna tell God how you do dirty things and don't like Jews."

"Get ready," El Tiburón said. "I'll get the money."

He walked into the rear room and stopped, looking down at Norris. He had no doubt that Juan would kill Henry. He was too good to fail, too well trained. And he had no doubt he would die doing it. Dealing with it had left him emotionally exhausted. He walked across the room and squatted next to Norris.

"How is your throat?" he asked.

"Better," Norris said.

El Tiburón looked at the floor for a moment, then back at Norris. "Tell me something, Edmund. Is it always this way when you try to accomplish something? Do you always end up feeling so damned demeaned?" He smiled at himself. "You must think that's an odd phrase for me to use. You certainly must feel demeaned yourself, being held here this way. But I feel it too. Being forced to act like a barbarian to accomplish what I want. Of having to deal with the banalities of fools, both among the opposition and among my own people. Being used by them." He shook his head.

Norris's eyes narrowed. "Everyone is used, Tiburón. You're using me right now to get what you feel you must have. There are dozens of men in Washington who are also using me, using my situation for their own interests. Even this man, Henry, is using me to escape his own problems." He pointed a finger. "And they're using you, too. All of them. And your own people are using you."

He rubbed his throat gently. The need to talk, to respond, had produced some pain.

El Tiburón noticed the discomfort. "Don't talk if it hurts you," he said.

"No, I'd like to." He raised his chin, stretching the neck muscles before continuing. "You see it's necessary for people to use those who lead them, to demean them, bring them down to their own level, at least in their own minds. They resent the fact that those who lead are superior to them. The fact frightens them. The fact that they need someone like that."

He smiled across at the younger man. "Your only mistake was that you didn't kill me when this all began. Now it's too late. Now you have other goals that are more important than me or what happens to me. Now you're *forced* to lead."

El Tiburón's eyes hardened. "You're telling me that if I continue to lead it will only get worse. More demeaning."

Norris smiled again. "Leadership—like yours was—is often born out of bitterness. And if it is or not, it almost always ends in it. Someday, Tiburón, if you continue to lead, you're going to look into the mirror one morning and you're going to see Edmund Norris staring back at you."

"But at least I'll have accomplished something for my people." The younger man drew a deep breath. "You make a very good case for killing you, you know." His voice was tired and held no threat in it.

"I certainly don't intend to," Norris said.

A small smile formed on El Tiburón's lips. "Why is it, when I ask you a question, you always tell me exactly what I don't want to hear?"

30

The waiting was unbearable. Nineteen hours had passed since the news broadcast and there was still no reaction, no word. Henry picked up the photograph of Rivera and stared at the smooth, clean features. He felt he knew this man, better perhaps than he had known most men in his life. And he knew the man should have reacted by now.

You're losing, he told himself. There won't be any word and later someone will find Norris's body. One and a half days left, that was all. They'll be quiet now and they'll get away, and then a message will come telling where the body is, if they even do that.

He felt helpless, physically weak and continued to stare at the photograph, knowing he would see that face for years. Already he dreamed about him, heard him speaking in those dreams, although he could not remember exactly what the voice had sounded like. There had also been a dream in which he had been surrounded by sharks. Kermit would have enjoyed that dream, he thought now. He placed the photograph on the desk and picked up the report he had received earlier that morning. Four martinis in less than an hour, enough to allow any man to accidentally walk in front of a truck. Or enough to get the courage to do so deliberately. He flipped the page. An old photograph album on the desk of his study. Pictures of Kermit as a student in Norway. Smiling, surrounded by university classmates. No notes. Nothing out of place. Nothing but some ashes in a fireplace that the lab said were photocopy papers too completely burned to decipher.

But there was also nothing about him drinking to excess, nothing from his neighbors or associates, nothing that indicated anything except an odd little man fully absorbed by his work. A completely different man from the one who had sat in the office the previous morning, distraught, pressured, wearing his nerves on his sleeve. Something had happened. He looked at the report again, the statement of the truck driver, claiming Knutsen had stepped from the curb at the last moment, looking directly at the truck. If that was to be believed, he had simply chosen to end his own life. But why, damn it? There was no reason for it, nothing that would even hint at a reason.

He looked at Rivera's photograph again. No reason for the boy in New York either. He had learned long ago to reject coincidences, to find a common thread. But the only thread was WAR and that seemed impossible.

The intercom buzzed and he grabbed for the receiver. Mary's voice floated across the line.

"It's noon, Pat. Can I order you something for lunch?"

"No. I'm not hungry." He replaced the receiver abruptly and was immediately sorry he had cut her short. You just can't stand losing, he thought. You never could.

~~~~~

Dalton Wilkerson faced a battery of reporters just inside the front gate of the Norris estate. His thin, angular face was drawn and there were deep circles beneath his eyes. It had taken more than an hour to convince his mother-in-law not to see the reporters, to remain inside with her daughter. She had been drinking and her presence would have proven a disaster. He reached into his pocket and withdrew a typewritten statement she had approved for release to the press. He glanced through it, noticing the slight tremor in his hands. He knew the statement also was a mistake.

"Gentlemen," he said, looking around, then adding, "Ladies. I will read the statement Mrs. Norris has prepared. I will not comment on it when I am finished, but copies will be available."

Murmurs of disappointment, annoyance, passed through the more than two dozen newspeople gathered in front of him, followed by angry snarls at television cameramen, banging people with their cameras as they jockeyed for position.

Wilkerson drew a deep breath, then wiped a shank of hair from his forehead.

"Mrs. Norris wishes. . . "

"Let us get a sound level, please," one member of a television crew shouted.

"Fuck you and your sound levels," another voice within the group shouted back.

"What do you need?" Wilkerson asked.

"Just say your name and then count," the first voice shot back.

Wilkerson obliged, feeling the sweat beginning to form along his body.

"That's good, that's good. All set," the voice shouted.

"Thank Christ," intoned another voice.

Wilkerson breathed deeply again, the lack of sensitivity of the group adding to his unease. He looked into their faces. Like starving men praying for a bone with meat on it, he told himself. He cleared his throat, feeling the dryness of his mouth.

"Mrs. Norris wishes to express her gratitude to all those who have sent messages of support and wants each of them to know that they have provided a great source of strength during these difficult times.

"It is, however, a matter of serious concern that the formal efforts to free the former President appear to have been tainted by political concerns. In a letter sent today to President Jordan, she has expressed those concerns and has urged that future dealings with President Norris's captors be conducted in the spirit of the humanitarian goals so frequently expressed by the administration.

"It is the belief of Mrs. Norris and members of the Norris family that the primary consideration during this difficult period must be the safety and speedy return of the former President, not the many political and economic problems involved in the demands.

"There is also concern that political differences and animosities between President Norris and those who opposed him in the past, are presently impeding the successful completion of negotiations with the group commonly known as WAR. The present administration is therefore urged to help set aside those differences and to alter the tone of negotiations from one of antagonism to one of conciliation.

"In that same spirit of conciliation, the former first lady wishes to point out that both she and President Norris have always had a deep concern for the welfare of the Puerto Rican people and their ultimate goal of rising beyond commonwealth status. It is clear that there is no reason why that status cannot be determined immediately, and Mrs. Norris wishes to assure the members of WAR that she and the entire Norris family will do everything in their power to support that objective.

"The Norris family urges the administration to do the same."

"That concludes the statement," Wilkerson said.

A barrage of questions erupted from the newspeople and the group surged forward like an attacking horde.

"Does this mean that the family is condemning the way the negotiations are being handled?" one woman shouted, pressing so close that Wilkerson took a step back.

"The statement speaks for itself," he said. "There is no further comment."

"Are you suggesting we give away Puerto Rico?" shouted another voice.

Wilkerson held up his hands and started to move away. "Copies of the statement will be available in a few moments," he said.

"Do you support this statement?"

He turned and moved quickly toward the house, as members of the Secret Service contingent stepped in to physically block the pursuing reporters.

It was like being thrown into a cage of wild animals, he thought, each one hoping you'd do something that would give them an excuse to eat you.

He hurried along the driveway, approaching the porticoes that led to the front door. Ahead, the door swung open and Pamela Norris began to emerge, her daughter grasping her arm from behind, restraining her. He broke into a run.

Damn it, he thought. She'll come out the door and fall on her face.

~~~~~

Cramer Lessing exploded when the news of the Norris press conference was relayed to his office. His normally colorless face turned scarlet and his soft, thick lips trembled with rage.

"Goddamned lying bastard of a sonofabitch," he shouted into the telephone. "He promised us he'd keep them under control."

"There's no indication the rabbi had anything to do with it," Josh Carling insisted.

Lessing growled back into the phone. "He promised us, damn it. He gave us assurances. He used us and suckered us into a goddamned press conference with him and now he's stabbed us in the back."

Carling breathed into the phone. "What do you want to do, Cramer?" he asked.

"You get down here. We gotta work up some kind of statement for the President, something that will shove it right back into their teeth. We already have the opposition in Congress and their damned national committee sharpening their knives. They're going to use this whole kidnapping thing as a political issue. We have to find a politically viable way out of this crap."

He slammed the receiver down and grabbed his head with both hands. "Bastards," he hissed. What was wrong with these people? Whose goddamned side were they on?

The buzzer on the intercom shattered his concentration and he snatched at the receiver as though grabbing for a weapon.

"Mr. Henry is on line three," his secretary's voice said.

He punched the button without answering her. "Henry," he snapped. "You heard? You heard what those goddamned fools have gone and done."

"Who did what, Cramer?" Henry's voice was light, almost joking, and the sound of it nearly lifted Lessing out of his chair with anger.

"The goddamned Norris family. They just held a press conference and attacked the administration." He paused only to gasp a deep breath of air. "We need something, Henry. Damn, we need something bad. We have to respond to this thing and fast."

"Calm down, Cramer. I have your response. We received a new communiqué from them twenty minutes ago."

"Oh, Jesus. What does it say?" Lessing felt like a man anticipating a kick in the groin.

"The deadline's been extended." Henry's voice was almost laughing.

"Extended. Jesus. For how long?"

"It's indefinite. But it's not all good news. There are some implied threats attached to it." He waited, listening to Lessing breathe.

"Well tell me, damn it," he said finally.

Henry's tone became more serious. "They state very clearly that the length of the extension will depend entirely on our efforts to satisfy the demands. They also warn that their patience has grown thin and that swift action is needed. If positive efforts aren't forthcoming, they say, appropriate action will be taken. In short," Henry added, "it's an hour-by-hour deal and at the first sign of a screwup on our part, they'll blow his brains out. They also say retaliatory steps will be taken over that kid's death in New York." He waited a moment. "There's also a part you're not going to like, Cramer. The communiqué includes a signed statement from Norris, saying very plainly that they are completely devoted to their demands and warning us not to believe otherwise."

Lessing rubbed his forehead. "Well we don't have to announce the bad news, just the extension," he said.

"No deal, Cramer. I've got to spell out the terms as far as the deadline is concerned, or they could regard that as a screwup. We just can't risk that. That includes the Norris statement. As far as the vengeance for the kid goes, I think we can slide over that with some delicate phrasing."

"What do you think they'll do? About the kid, I mean?" Lessing said.

"Well, if the past is any indication, probably some bombings. We're alerting all Bureau offices in major cities and all government installations as a precaution. But I would recommend added security for high-level personnel."

"Hell, I don't care if they blow up the Washington Monument, just so long as we get out from under this thing."

Henry paused. "I'm preparing a statement that can be issued either by me or the White House. But it has to be exactly as I write it as far as the communiqué is concerned. And remember, Cramer, I'll keep a copy."

"Just send it over and don't worry about it," Lessing purred. "We're not going to do anything to rock the damned boat at this point. Just having the extension is a winner. If anything the President will praise the decision of these rotten bastards as a display of decency, or some other bullshit thing."

He listened to Henry's subdued laughter. "Okay, Cramer. But we're still a long way from home. This just gives us the time we needed to work, nothing more."

"I don't care," Lessing said. "It saved our ass today. Let me know if anything else develops."

Lessing leaned back in his chair and grinned at the ceiling. The door to his office opened and he straightened up and watched Josh

Carling enter, his face weary, clouded, and beaten. He slumped in a chair and looked across at Lessing.

"What is it, Cramer?" he said, confused by the pleased look on Lessing's face. "Has your mind finally snapped?"

"Things are looking good, Josh," he said. "Like the boss says, the Lord is smiling down on us."

31

Light snow flurries swirled about them as they walked across Lafayette Square, the glow of the streetlights varying the intensity of the fall, slowing it in shadow, then raising it to an oncoming rush where the light was stronger. They had just finished a quiet dinner together at the Hay-Adams, the first public time they had spent together since the madness of the kidnapping had been thrust on them. Mary walked close against him, clutching his arm, the brim of her large, floppy hat brushing against his shoulder.

"Are we going back to the office?" she asked, her breath rushing ahead of her in a cloud.

"Not tonight," he said. "I told them to beep me if anything developed."

She pulled him to a halt and stared up at him. "You mean I'm getting a night off? I can't believe it."

"You make me sound like Simon Legree," he said, grinning at her. "And after I just bought you dinner."

"Thank you for the dinner," she said, bowing her head. "But working for you, sir, has not exactly been a vacation."

He started up again, pulling her along with him. "You liberated females are all alike. First you complain that all you do is file documents and answer telephones, and then, when you get some real work, you think you're being taken advantage of."

"Well, you know what we *females* are like. We're all governed by monthly cycles and the effects of the moon on gravity. Lord, it's no wonder you've been a bachelor so long." She marched along with him for a moment, then pulled him to a stop again. "By the way.

If we're not going back to work, may I ask where we're going?"

He began walking again, keeping her in tow. "I thought we'd stop for a brandy someplace in Georgetown, then go back to your place. That is, if I'm invited to go back," he added.

"Are we going to walk?" she asked, a slight note of concern in her voice.

"I thought we would. Do you mind?"

"All the way to Georgetown?" Her voice was a full level higher.

"You make it sound like we're going to Maryland," he said. "It's only a dozen or so blocks, then down M Street to Wisconsin Avenue. Besides, we've been cooped up for days now and I like walking in the snow. Do you really mind?"

"Oh, no, master. Not at all," she said. "If it makes you happy, I'll do the *female* thing and simply obey."

"Oh, shut up," he said. "And you still haven't said whether I'm invited to your place or not."

"I'll think about it," she said.

They turned into Pennsylvania Avenue, walking arm and arm past Blair House and on across Seventeenth Street. Henry's briefcase swung loosely at his side; his step was light and his chin slightly elevated, allowing the gentle snow to fall against his face.

Across the street, fifty yards to the rear, Juan Hernandez brushed at the snow that clung to his false beard. He had waited for them in the street until they had emerged from the Executive Office Building, then again until they had left the restaurant, and the cold had already sunk deep within him until his teeth chattered uncontrollably. Now they were walking like two crazy people, acting like it was summer.

He thrust his hands deep into his pockets, keeping his eyes on them as they sauntered along the opposite sidewalk, wishing they would take a cab or enter a building into which he could safely follow.

He hated the cold. It had always been the one thing about the North American mentality that escaped him. Living in the cold, when the sun was available. He had done so too, but only because he had been sent. He shuddered, thinking of the others, of the oppressive heat of the cabin, wishing now that he was there with them, suffering the insects and humidity. Even the snakes and the alligators seemed preferable. He should have let Carlos come, let *him* freeze.

No, the problem was the surveillance, the stupidity of it. If he were armed now he could end it. Quickly, here on the street, or earlier, as they walked in the park.

His mind raced with the idea. He had not seen the woman's face. The large hat she wore had hidden her features. Henry's wife, he thought. Or just his woman. But it didn't matter. He could have taken them both and been gone. But this one day of watching would be enough, he told himself. He would follow him for the rest of the night, then make his call to New York. And tomorrow he would do it. He smiled to himself. Tomorrow was the last day of the deadline, the day Henry had expected Norris to die. But it's going to be you, baby, he told himself.

He continued behind them, still shivering, his jacket too light for the weather, the two shirts he wore not enough against the cold. At Washington Circle he fell in behind them, increasing the distance as he did. When they crossed the Rock Creek Parkway and turned into M Street he closed the distance again. The number of pedestrians had increased, providing easy cover, and by the time they reached Wisconsin Avenue he was only a dozen yards behind.

A half block down they turned into a narrow alley. He stopped outside it. Ahead, a sign read *Blues Alley*, and he could hear the faint sounds of jazz drifting out toward the street. He would follow them inside now, away from the cold. And then he would follow them again when they left, hopefully to where Henry lived. Then it would be over and he could place the call. He opened the door and was engulfed in the dim light and cigarette smoke. He could not see them at first, but he knew he would. The music lifted his spirits. He only wished it was salsa.

~~~~

It was two o'clock when the beeper awakened him. He slipped quietly out of bed and went into the living room, to a telephone he could use without disturbing Mary's sleep. He was still groggy, still satiated with their lovemaking and he tied his robe and sat quietly on the sofa for a moment, gathering himself.

The agent who answered the phone was excited, his voice eager, almost shrill.

"We've had contact, sir. On one of the phone taps in New York," he said.

"Do we know who it was?" Henry said, feeling his heartbeat quicken.

"They think it was Hernandez, sir. He only identified himself as Juan, but the gist of the conversation indicated he was part of the group." The agent hesitated, then rushed on. "Sir, the call came from Washington, the trace confirmed it. A phone booth near Scott Circle."

"Washington. Christ. Did you send men out there?"

"Two units, sir. The area was deserted. There are a lot of hotels around there and we were wondering if we should send men out with a photograph?" the agent said.

"No, don't do anything," he snapped. "I'll be there in a few minutes. We want to follow him, not catch him."

The agent stuttered. "Well, sir, he . . . he made arrangements to meet the person he called in D.C. tomorrow. He was vague about the location. He only said they'd meet in the same place they met the last time they were there."

"That's all?" Henry asked.

"No, sir. He also told him to bring the package he had left with him. They were very careful about what they said."

"Who is this other guy?"

"His name is Luis Negron. There's a round-the-clock stakeout on his place now. Information on him is that he was involved in that takeover of the Statue of Liberty a few years back."

"Do we know how he's traveling?"

"Car, sir."

Henry drew a deep breath. "Okay, listen carefully. This is to be relayed to New York immediately. I want a transmitter placed on his car. Preferably before he leaves New York. If not, have them set up something at the toll booth entering the Jersey Turnpike, some routine check by a Jersey state cop, checking tires, license plates, lights, all that. While he's doing it, he can place a magnetic transmitter. Now I also want a three-car tail, all the way to Washington. Tell them to use a front tail as much as possible, with the other cars laying back in radio contact and changing every twenty minutes. And for Chrissake, tell him to notify the Jersey state police not to stop any of the cars even if they're speeding. In fact, tell them to cancel all stops for the day. That should send them up the wall. Now repeat everything back to me."

The agent rattled off the information flawlessly, then asked how it should be communicated to New York.

"Telephone, then teletype, with a confirmation," Henry said. "What time are they scheduled to meet in D.C.?"

"Four P.M., sir."

"All right. Get moving. I'll be right down."

He sat back, feeling the nervous energy raging in his stomach, the contrasting numbness in his arms and legs. Washington, he told himself. Scott Circle, only five blocks from his office. But why not? Hadn't Patty Hearst been hidden only a few blocks from FBI headquarters in San Francisco at one point. He considered the package that would soon be on its way. Explosives, he told himself. He thought of Lessing's comment about the Washington Monument. And that's exactly what you'll do. Let them plant anything they want and then follow them. The public could be kept away from any area for a dozen reasons. The city was always involved in some sort of extraordinary security. The important thing was to keep on them and follow them back to Norris. Damn, he thought. You could have passed him on the street last night.

Mary appeared in the bedroom doorway. "What is it, Pat? I woke up and you were gone."

He smiled at her, as the numbness in his body disappeared. "We've had contact in New York. I've got to get down to the office. I think we're finally going to get our shot."

"I'll get dressed," she said.

"You don't have to. Nothing will happen until four. I just have to stay on top of it," he said.

She stared at him. "You just try and stop me," she said.

32

The detailed map of Washington was spread out on a long table in the main office, Henry, Desverne, and five agents encircling it, their faces intense and brooding. Henry jabbed at the map.

"We lost visual contact with Negron's car here, after it left the Beltway on Route 240, and entered the city limits on Wisconsin Avenue. We're getting a fixed signal in Georgetown, somewhere near the Key Bridge but until we locate it, we can't be sure whether he's simply parked the car and moved on, or is actually making the meet."

"Last word was they expect to have the car pinpointed in ten to fifteen minutes," Desverne said.

Henry continued to stare at the map, as though divining information from it. "It's still too long," he said, "especially if they moved on. They could be using a two-car blind, which means they'd come back to Negron's car after they do whatever they're here to do." He jabbed at the map again. "All right. We know Hernandez left the Tabard Inn at seven this morning, a full two hours before we placed him there. He paid his bill, so he probably won't be back. That means he's moving, probably somewhere between the Inn, here at N and 18th, and Georgetown." Using Dupont Circle as a central point, he took a grease pencil and drew a wide arc, covering the north, south, and west.

He looked at each of the others. "I'm eliminating the western quadrant of the city as far as a meeting is concerned. It's a calculated risk, I know, but it has to be done. Even so, I still want prime locations, like the Hill, Union Station, and the Mall covered. But we should concentrate our main manpower within this arc."

"What about MacMillan Reservoir?" Desverne asked.

305

"I don't think so, Dez. They're well trained, so they'll pick some-place where there are crowds. That's why I'm including the Mall, be-cause of the museums. But I think they're going to want to stay reasonably close to the car." He shot his fingers along the map. "The farthest point north, then, is the zoo. To the west, Georgetown Uni-versity, Kennedy Center, Watergate, and then southwest to Arling-ton Cemetery. In the south, the whole area around the tidal basin, the monuments, every damned thing."

Desverne let out a low whistle. "That's a lot of area, and they could be in any one of a hundred small bars, or in somebody's apart-ment."

Henry licked his upper lip, still staring down at the map. "I know. But we have one advantage. We know the bastards are here, the car's wired, and sooner or later we'll have them. I just don't want them to plant any explosives without us knowing where." He looked up at the clock. It was three-thirty.

~~~~~

He had spent the morning on the move, staying among groups of tourists, visiting churches and museums; he had even watched a film in the National Air and Space Museum, then moved on to a por-nographic movie house, where the smell of dried semen had long ago replaced the odor of popcorn.

At three-forty-five he entered the Brickskeller in the Marfax Ho-tel, ordered a bottle of San Miguel beer and took an isolated table in the rear. Above, from the bar's second floor, he could hear the en-thusiastic cheers of people playing darts. He and Luis had been in the bar two years ago, selecting it because it served the Philippino beer so popular in Puerto Rico among the four hundred different brands it boasted. He sipped it now, thinking of home, satisfied with the plans he had made. He and Luis would take the car train to Flor-ida, then a flight from Orlando; he patted his jacket pocket, enjoying the pleasant feel of the tickets he had purchased that morning. An-other roar came from above and he smiled to himself, thinking how each of those voices would soon be discussing the assassination that was now only hours away.

At five after four Luis entered the bar, ordered a beer, chatted with the bartender to allow time for anyone following him, then walked slowly back to the table. He was short and stocky, in his late twenties, with the body of an athlete. He dropped into the seat next to Juan and stared at him with eternally somber eyes.

"Man you sure got the Yankis in an uproar. I never seen so many three-piece suits driving around the *barrio*," he said.

"You bring the piece?" Juan asked.

Luis reached inside his trenchcoat and withdrew an oblong package, wrapped in brown paper. "An' there's one more in the trunk of the car," he said, placing the package on Juan's lap.

"You never asked what I wanted it for?" He was grinning.

Luis shrugged. "I figured you wanted to go duck hunting."

Juan leaned forward. "We're gonna take this Henry guy." He spoke flatly, only his eyes showing emotion.

Luis stuck out his lower lip. "Heavy shit," he said. "When?"

"Last night he left his office around six to have dinner. Tonight I'm gonna be in the southeast corner of that little park across from the White House, feeding the pigeons. You're gonna be on the east side of the park on Madison Place. An' when you see me start out of the park, you come around the corner. If I can take him there, I take him as soon as you pull up. You'll know if you see the wrapping come off the package. If he gets in a car or, if there's too many people around, you just pick me up and we follow him."

"An' after?" Luis asked, his face still expressionless.

"We cut out. We lay low, switch the plates on the car, and tomorrow we're on the car train headed south, then to P.R. by plane." He patted his jacket pocket. "I got the tickets here."

"You comin' with me to get the car?"

Juan shook his head. "I'll be in the park at five-forty-five. You be there then too. Anybody bothers you, you jus' tell them you got car trouble an' you're waitin' for a tow truck. If things get too heavy you come around and get me and we'll wait for him to go to his apartment."

"Maybe the apartment's better," Luis said.

"I want the downtown traffic and the confusion," Juan said. "Later we hit one of those nice dark little streets near Georgetown University, switch plates, and get our asses into Virginia."

"It sounds rough to me."

Juan glared at him. "It's hit and run, right out in the open. Just like we were taught. Gunfire that close to the White House is gonna draw everybody there. They'll think somebody's tryin' to shoot their way in. And when they do that, they create a diversion for us, while we head away from it."

Luis nodded, smiling for the first time. "I better get the car," he said. "It'll take me about forty minutes to get there and back."

～～～～

Henry and Desverne sat at the communications desk, listening to the radio messages of four stakeout cars that now covered every possible escape route. Henry looked at his watch.

"The bastard's been sitting there in that car for half an hour," he said. "It's too damned open there. Nobody can get close to him. Where's our nearest car?"

"Alongside St. John's Church," Desverne said.

Henry stood and began pacing, then looked back at Desverne. "Let's go over there. I want to be closer. I want to see what's happening. He's too damned close to the White House."

"I know. Ever since we called it's been like an armed camp over there," Desverne said.

"That's what I'm afraid of. They're going to move in and take him and I think Hernandez just hasn't shown for a pickup. But you never know with these nuts." He hesitated, licking his lip again. "We'll use earphones so we can monitor what the hell is going on without having to expose the handsets. You and one other man follow me, five seconds behind. I want one of you to have a shotgun and the other a Thompson under your coats."

Mary came up beside him. "We're going to the unit at St. John's Church," he said.

"I heard. Let me go with you. It will look more natural, walking over there with me."

He smiled at her. "Is it just that you want to be in on it, or do you intend to play bodyguard?" he said.

She colored slightly, forcing his smile to widen. He glanced out of the corner of his eye. Desverne had left to get the equipment. "What are they supposed to think when they see us?" he said. "That we're two sinners off to church to do penance together?"

"Maybe they'll think we're making arrangements for a wedding," she said, spinning quickly and going for her coat.

He watched her, sensing the mixture of pleasure and nervousness he always felt when he did. More like a father taking his kid to confirmation lessons, he told himself.

～～～～

It was freezing in the car. The motor had been off for half an hour now and the cold had seeped in, leaving his fingers numb. The thin leather gloves he wore for shooting did not help, and he put his hands between his thighs and pressed them together. To his right, Juan was seated under a statue, feeding pigeons, just as he had said he would. He must be frozen, Luis thought. He shook his head. He did not like the plan, but then, he would not have liked the plan to kidnap Norris had he known of it. He still regretted he had not been part of that. It had set raging fires of pride among the militant parts of the Puerto Rican community in New York. An act of bold defiance, striking back for years of abuse.

He reached down and felt for the Stenckin under his seat. It was ready for use; only the safety had to be disengaged. This would be an act of defiance as well. It would be as bold as the earlier Puerto Rican attack on Blair House or the assault on the House of Representatives. He smiled to himself, wishing Carlos was there. Then he would know it had been a mistake to leave him behind.

～～～～

He sat, hidden in shadow, on the side of a statue depicting Rochambeau, facing east so he could see Luis and the car. Every few seconds he tossed pieces of bread to his right, where a horde of greedy pigeons had gathered, each time stealing a glance at the front entrance of the Executive Office Building.

His shoulders trembled from the cold. It would stop, he knew, when everything began, when the adrenalin started to move through his body, leaving him bathed in sweat. He tightened his jaw and the muscles in his upper body, struggling to control the shaking. His hand moved to the false beard. The cold had loosened the adhesive and he pressed his fingers against it. The previous evening he had taken the beard off too soon, not allowing his face to warm sufficiently, and small pieces of skin had pulled away. Even now the abrasions stung his face.

The brown paper package lay next to him on his left, like a small packet of shirts from a Chinese laundry. His hand dropped to it absentmindedly, feeling where the paper had been unwrapped so it would fall away easily when needed. He had used the men's room in the Brickskeller to assure himself the Stenckin was loaded and fully operative, and as he sat in one of the stalls, it had given him a sense of confidence just holding it in his hands.

More bread for pigeons. A few people moved through the front entrance and down the stone stairs. He squinted against the street lighting, sure he would be able to recognize Henry when he emerged. Slowly, he began to tear another piece of bread, pulling at it like someone yanking feathers from a bird. He looked to his right again and stiffened. The floppy hat, the man beside the woman. Both hands reached for the package, bringing it to his chest as he stood. After three steps, he looked to his left. The car was moving, ready to turn the corner into Pennsylvania Avenue. His eyes darted back across the street. They were moving down the stairs, no more than fifty yards away. He moved to the curb and stopped, waiting for the car. Already sweat was forming on his body.

～～～

Halfway down the stairs the message came through the earphones, the excitement in the voice unmistakable. He nudged Mary with his elbow.

"The car's moving," he said, without looking at her. "It's turning right into Pennsylvania Avenue. Just move easy and try not to stare at it. We'll stop at the corner as if we're waiting to cross."

At the bottom of the stairs he could hear movement behind him. Dez and the other agent, he thought. They, too, had heard and would move cautiously now. His right hand slipped into his topcoat pocket, feeling for the revolver he had placed there. His fingers wrapped around it loosely. Stepping into the sidewalk, they turned right, and ahead he could see the car moving slowly in the righthand lane. Only one person inside. He glanced toward the entrance of the White House. There was no one in sight, other than a single uniformed sentry in the small guardhouse.

Behind the car one of the Bureau's sedans moved up. Too close, he thought. Too damned close. They slowed as they reached the corner, his eyes seemingly averted from the car but still watching it. He's going to make a pickup, he thought. His eyes moved along the other sidewalk and as he saw the bearded man for the first time, he heard Mary scream and felt her shoulder slam into his.

"Watch out, Pat."

His left arm swung out, striking her, knocking her out of the line of fire, while he threw his own weight forward and to the right. There was a stinging pain in the upper part of his left arm, followed by a burst of gunfire ahead. His mind registered the fact automatically, senselessly. When you're hit you feel it before hearing the sound. He rolled to his right, pulling the snub-nosed revolver from his pocket. From behind came the roar of a shotgun, followed by the steady deafening burst of the Thompson. Metal on the car exploded, lifting sparks into the air, answered by the flashes of returning fire behind the car.

The pursuit car slammed into the rear of the other, sending it skidding forward, turning it slightly to the side. Henry pulled himself to his knees, hearing his own voice shout for Mary to stay down, then his legs propelling him forward, two shots from his revolver exploding in his hand.

To his left, Desverne ran ahead, the Thompson spitting out in short, regular bursts. Ahead, the agents in the pursuit car were out, firing shotgun blasts into the windows of Negron's car. Dez raced past the car, staring down into the street ahead of him, then spun and leveled the Thompson back toward the car. Henry ran to the car window, his gun out ahead of him. Negron's body was thrown forward against the steering wheel, the top of his head lifted off, the jagged fragment of skull hanging out over his forehead, gray brain tissue, mixed with blood, splattered against the remnants of the shattered windshield. On the seat next to him was a Stenckin, its barrel smokeless, unused.

"He's dead," Henry called to Desverne.

"So's this one."

In the distance, for the first time, Henry heard screams drifting back to him. He walked around the car, his entire body shaking, his nostrils filled with the smell of cordite. The man's body lay twisted in the street, one leg bent up behind the other, both hands still clutching his throat, where the forty-five caliber shells of the Thompson had all but severed his head from his body.

Desverne reached down and gently pulled away the already partially removed beard, then looked back at Henry, his face pale and frightened. "It's Hernandez," he said, hesitating, as if he didn't want to acknowledge his own thoughts. "Christ, Pat. It was a hit on you. We never thought of that."

Desverne stood and walked toward him, staggering slightly. His eyes were fixed on Henry's left arm and he pointed with his free hand. "You've been hit, Pat."

Henry could feel the blood now inside his shirt sleeve and he looked down at the flow inching along his hand. He flexed the arm cautiously, feeling for broken bone. "It's just a flesh wound," he said. Wearily, he leaned back against the car, gathering himself. Then his eyes darted among the others. "Where's Mary?" he said.

Back on the sidewalk a small crowd had gathered and he ran toward it, pushing people aside. She was face down on the sidewalk and beneath her body, a pool of blood moved steadily out, spilling over the curb and into the gutter. Gently he turned her, staring as her head fell back, the eyes gazing blindly up, the mouth open in a silent scream as blood ran across her cheek.

Somewhere from the rear he could hear Dez's voice screaming for an ambulance. His mouth began to move, but there was no sound and he could feel the blood on the sidewalk, her blood, seeping through the knees of his trousers.

Part Four

33

Five days had passed and still nothing of consequence had happened. The mood of the others was strained, matching his own. The death of Juan and Luis had sobered them, but even more unnerving was the endless waiting. Henry had been absent from the television newscasts, replaced by a subordinate, and it had caused them all to question whether he had moved his base from Washington, even though newspaper reports had indicated otherwise.

El Tiburón stood in the open doorway, feeling the rush of moist, hot air moving in off the marshes. The assassination attempt had been a disaster. The place chosen for it completely brazen and completely wrong. So typical of Juan, he told himself, struggling with his own guilt. It only matters how one dies, he said silently. But that also did not mean stupidly.

He turned back into the room, leaving the door slightly ajar. Wally was seated at the table. Even more than the others, he had grown increasingly bitter in recent days and his features now seemed black and sullen. El Tiburón sat next to him, his forearms on the table in front of him, his legs wrapped around the chair.

"What do you think?" he said.

"You know what I think," Wally answered, staring into his folded hands.

"We'll talk about it when the others get back," he said.

Wally's eyes darted up to him, impatient and annoyed. "There sure ain't a helluva lot to talk about," he said.

El Tiburón counted five breaths, pacing himself before answering. "Then you think it's time to call the game off," he said.

"Ol' buddy, I don' think we were ever in no game. Not as far as the damned demands were concerned. They're jus' jerkin' us aroun', buyin' time. An' the time's on their side, not ours. By now they've identified Juan and Luis. And through them they'll I.D. us, sure as shit. Then they jus' gotta start movin' pictures around. An' a lotta people in town have seen us."

He had spoken in a near-whisper, sensitive to the fact that Norris was in the rear room, El Tiburón thought. He nodded his head. "Then it's really only a question of what action to take," he said finally.

"I don' see where we got much choice," Wally said. "We lost ourselves two people, an' all we got in return was some fuckin' broad. If we let it lay that way now, we are gonna look like fools."

He nodded again slowly, unable to argue against the logic thrown at him. The others were due back soon and it could wait until then, but the outcome was already unnervingly obvious.

An abbreviated version of Henry's strike force was now housed in an abandoned mansion along Palm Beach's millionaire's row. The house was protected by a high wall, but from the upper levels there was a clear view of the ocean, creating a stark contrast to the mood within. They had moved there three days previous, after a hurried communications network had been established, linking the house to the main operation center in Washington.

The move had been forced by the autopsy performed on Hernandez. Faint traces of dirt found imbedded in his clothing and shoes had tied him to an area in central Florida. The soil, known to natives simply as *black muck*, became dry and windblown in summer, adhering to the skin and producing an itchy rash. In winter it was damp and gluey, sinking deep into any fabric it touched.

Hernandez had virtually become a topographical map of the area he had been in, but it was still too large and sprawling. Even so, Henry had moved. Small military units had been strategically placed throughout a one-hundred-mile arc, each heavily armed with automatic weapons and silencer-equipped sniper rifles. When the location was pinpointed, an assault team could be there in no less than one hour. But it was still very much a waiting game; a mistake on WAR's part was needed and Henry knew that any concentrated search too close to the group's hideout would produce quick action against Norris. That remained a problem.

Another problem was Henry himself. He had become withdrawn to the point that even Desverne could not penetrate his shell. He had refused to go to Mary's funeral, claiming he lacked the time, and he had driven the men with a simmering rage that had made them all nervous and prone to mistakes.

Looking over the latest WAR communiqué, Desverne wondered if that nervousness had somehow found its way there as well. There was a renewed hysteria, a return to revolutionary didactics, and it sounded an alarm in his head that Henry did not seem to hear. He had tried to discuss it with him that morning and had been curtly dismissed. The problem to Henry now was one of encirclement, of cutting off any possibility of escape and the frame of mind of the terrorists no longer appeared to concern him.

He picked up the communiqué and walked toward the small room Henry had selected as an office, determined to try again. The door to the room was open, but Henry was not inside. He crossed the room, stopping at the double French doors that opened on to a garden. Henry was seated on a stone bench, his forearms resting on his knees. He was staring straight ahead, looking at nothing, and the muscles in his jaw twitched with a steady pulsing beat.

He walked up to him and took a deep breath, expecting the worst.

"Pat, I've got to talk to you," he said.

Henry looked up at him, then back into the garden. "Sit down," he said, his voice soft and distant.

Desverne slid on to the bench and folded the communiqué in his hands. Henry continued to stare straight ahead.

"I'm still worried about the tone of their latest communiqué," he began. "I think we're running out of time."

"We have a day, maybe two," Henry said without emotion.

Desverne was startled. "Then don't you think we ought to do something, try to force the issue a bit, or at least give them some cock-and-bull story?"

Henry shook his head. "We've gone as far as we can. If they make a move with Norris, we'll be able to reach them. Or if they move alone. Getting Norris back alive was always a question of luck."

Desverne watched him, wishing he could force himself to push harder. He knew what was on Henry's mind, but he couldn't bring that up either. "What are you going to do when it's over, Pat?" he finally asked.

Over. Henry realized he hadn't thought in terms of it being over for days now. "Go to Vermont, I think. But I'm not really sure. I'd given some thought to it. Just about . . ." His words trailed off as he struggled against images that continued to move with a will of their own. There was no feeling for the images now, only a sense of emptiness. Bitterness and emptiness, they were really the same thing. He had never understood that before, perhaps because each had been a part of him for too long. It was odd how they had each had the same name, had been so much alike. He shook his head slightly and straightened up, then looked at Desverne.

"We have work to do," he said softly. "That's enough to keep us going right now. So let's get at it and do it right."

They walked back to the house. You're going to win this thing, Henry told himself. You're going to win it, and then you're going to walk away. He wished he could also tell himself he would forget.

~~~~~

"I just don't see the advantage of it," Richard said.

"There is none," El Tiburón answered. "Unfortunately there are too many disadvantages in doing anything else."

They were gathered on the front steps of the cabin, out of earshot of Norris. Wally had remained inside with him. His views were known, along with his willingness to follow whatever decision was reached.

Carol McGovern could feel a slight trembling in her hands. She looked at Norma, noting the set line of her jaw, the cold hardness of her eyes.

"He's right," Norma said. "If we don't follow through with the threat, no one will take us seriously in the future."

"But they said they'd go through with the demands if we let him go," Carol said, surprised by the timid sound of her own voice.

Norma's face showed disgust. "And then when they double-cross us, we look like a bunch of assholes," she snapped. "Where do we get off trusting them now, Carol. You're talking like a child."

Carol lowered her head, wishing she could reach out and slap

Norma's face. Jew bitch, she thought. El Tiburón watched her closely.

"There are only two choices," he said. "We continue as we are now, or we kill him, take as much victory as we can from it, and then attack again."

He was still watching Carol and he noticed her cringe slightly when he spoke of attacking again. She would not be with them then, he thought. She had been tested now and had been found wanting.

"Then I vote we kill him," Richard said. "I guess I just hoped we could win it completely."

"I do, too," Norma said.

Carol remained silent and El Tiburón decided to save her the need of speaking. "Since Wally feels that way too, we may as well consider it decided," he said.

Carol raised her head. "Who does it?" she asked.

Norris's words played back in his mind. Your only mistake was in not killing at the outset. Now it's too late. "I will," El Tiburón said.

34

He had brought two chairs into the room. Norris sat in one, facing him, his eyes glazed in disbelief, the lower lip trembling.

"You shouldn't do this," he said. "You know me. You know I'm not against you, against what you want. We've grown to understand each other."

El Tiburón was wearing a lightweight windbreaker, the Graz Burya automatic stuffed in the right-hand pocket, out of sight. He would reach into his pocket when the time came and shoot through the material. He would not force him to look into the barrel. The power of the weapon would knock him back. It would be sudden and unexpected and, in that sense at least, merciful.

"It's a question of options," he said softly. "I wish there were another alternative."

Norris's mind raced, obscure and faltering with fear. An hour before they had been talking about birds and the conversation had been friendly, earnest.

"There is an alternative," he said. "A good one."

El Tiburón stood, slipping both hands in his pockets as he did. He closed the few feet between them, trying to be casual. "I wish there really was," he said, feeling his hand wrap around the pistol.

"There's something you don't know," Norris said, his words running together in a hurried delivery. "And if you used it against them, against the government, it would force them to agree to what you want. They'd have to. The embarrassment of it all would force them to do something to ease the tension it would produce. And it would unite everyone who opposes them. All kinds of revolutionary groups, students, everyone who's swallowed the whole new moral image that's been projected. Believe me, Tiburón." Norris caught his breath, his mind clearing, thinking faster now out of desperation. "I've wanted to tell you about it all along. I've just been afraid. I was part of it, I helped start it all."

He looked down at Norris, sorry it all had degenerated into pleading, yet curious. "What are you talking about?"

"Sparrow Hawk. The Sparrow Hawk Project." Norris's lips trembled as he spoke. "It was started ten years ago and it's still in operation. The government financed selective terrorist groups through Third World operatives of the CIA. They provided the money and, to some degree, the expertise for bombings and other acts of terrorism. It involved all the major terrorist groups who showed any inclination toward violence."

Norris was breathing hard, as though he had run up several flights of stairs. El Tiburón stared at him, his eyes wide and disbelieving. "Why would they do that?" he asked.

The trembling had moved to Norris's hands and he clasped them together to control it. "The public didn't take radical groups seriously. They didn't consider them a danger. Because of that, we were limited in the kind of actions we could take against them. The public just didn't understand the danger. That's why it was called Sparrow Hawk. Because that small falcon lives in just about every town and city and farm area, but they go unnoticed because of their size. People just don't think of them as birds of prey. It was the same with leftist groups. So we financed actions that would draw attention to them, cause fear of what they might do next. Then we could move, not only against them, but against other groups as well, and the more the groups did, the more acceptance government actions against them would receive."

El Tiburón's face had paled. He withdrew the automatic from his pocket and leveled it at Norris's face.

"You're lying to me." His voice was low, shaking with rage.

Norris raised his hands in front of his face, as though it might ward off the weapon.

"You can prove it to yourself," he said. "And then I'll give you a signed statement admitting it all. And you can use that against the government. Expose all of them, past and present."

"You're telling me that we, that others, have been supported, financed, used by the CIA? We've been their tools?"

"Yes." Norris's entire body was trembling now. His eyes were fixed on the gun, unable to look away.

"I don't believe you," El Tiburón said. "You're trying to buy your life, and you're lying to do it."

"I told you. You can prove it. Just test it and then I'll give you the statement. But then you'll have to free me. That's all. Just let me live."

"And how do I prove it? You have documents tucked away somewhere?" His voice was sarcastic, filled with ridicule and contempt.

"There were no documents. Everything was verbal for obvious reasons. I doubt the present administration even knows about it. It's like so many covert projects. Once they begin, they just continue, and those who weren't involved at the beginning seldom hear about them."

El Tiburón's face was twisted, brutal. "Then how do I prove it?" he snapped.

"Just call your contact, the person you've been getting your funds from, and arrange a meeting. The place will be surrounded by CIA people. They want me back, or they want me dead. They don't want me to talk about this. Just prove it to yourself. Then I'll sign a statement for you."

"And the governments these people, these traitors, worked for never knew?"

Norris shook his head. "Never. They were providing minimal training and indoctrination. But never the vast sums of money that went into this across the country."

The gun dropped to El Tiburón's side and his head snapped around. He shouted for the others. When they entered the room he turned back to Norris. "Tell them what you just told me," he ordered.

Norris repeated his words, watching the shock, disbelief, and anger grow in their faces.

"You're a fucking liar," Norma snapped. "All of it's a lie." She reached for El Tiburón's hand. "Give me the gun," she screamed. "I'll blow his goddamned head off."

He pushed her away, then looked at each of them individually.

"You don't believe this, do you?" Richard said, his voice almost begging a negative answer.

"I believe it," Wally said.

The others looked at him, then back at El Tiburón.

"We better find out," El Tiburón said. He stared at Norris, then reached out and slapped him hard across the face, knocking him from the chair. "Tie him up and put him back in that fucking closet," he said. "If he's lying to us he'll die so slowly he'll wish he'd never been born."

Wally stared at him. "You gonna set up that meetin'?"

El Tiburón nodded. "We'll drive into Palm Beach and call one of our people in New York, have him contact the mission and arrange a meeting in Palm Beach tomorrow. What would be a good place? Somewhere you could spot any surveillance?"

"Right on Worth Avenue," Wally said. "The feds would stick out like whores in church."

"And what if he's telling the truth?" Carol said. "What do we do then?"

"Then maybe he lives, providing he tells the world about it in writing."

35

They met in Central Park's Conservatory Gardens, just two men chancing on each other and stopping to talk. The heavyset man was dressed in a cashmere polo coat with matching scarf wrapped high on his neck. He was smiling, but his lips seeemed to be trembling from the cold. The younger man glanced about as he spoke, his eyes constantly moving. He seemed unconcerned by the cold, the heavy sweater he wore beneath a light denim jacket appearing to provide adequate warmth.

Across Fifth Avenue, in the rear of a van painted with psychedelic colors, two agents watched in silence—one through the lens of a sixteen-millimeter camera, the second over the barrel of a rifle-design directional microphone. It was ten-thirty in the morning and traffic along the upper portion of Fifth Avenue was light, causing only minimal breaks in their surveillance. A block north, on the third floor of an abandoned Board of Education building, a second team of agents monitored the meeting with identical equipment. Two blocks to the north and one to the south, pursuit cars waited with motors running.

They had all been in place since six o'clock, concerned that the time set for the meeting might involve a code that would change the rendezvous by several hours. But it had occurred exactly as stated.

The telephone call from Palm Beach had been monitored, as had the subsequent call to the mission. Throughout the night, members of the strike force had prepared surveillance of two meetings, the one now underway and a second that was being arranged at that moment. The following day, at noon, Palm Beach's exclusive Worth Avenue would be inundated with federal agents and the net spread so carefully for WAR would finally be drawn tight.

The young man turned abruptly and started south through the park. A block below an agent left the southerly pursuit car and began strolling along a bisecting path. The heavyset man walked slowly back toward Fifth Avenue. He stopped on the sidewalk, looking up and down the street, then moved quickly across to an open public telephone on the corner of 107th Street.

Inside the van, the directional microphone followed his movements and the agent's face broke into a broad grin as the melodious beeps of the touch-tone dialing played back through his earphones and into a tape recorder.

〜〜〜〜

"You're sure," Henry said. He was staring at Desverne, his face glowering.

"No question at all," Desverne said. The call went to an unlisted line at their headquarters at Langley. He made arrangements to meet with their people tonight. It was even a collect call, for chrissake."

Henry picked up the report and stared at the telephone number. "Those bastards," he said, reaching for the telephone and dialing the number.

The phone rang three times before being answered by a male voice that simply repeated the number.

"This is John Walter Henry," Henry said. "An hour and a half ago a telephone call was received at this number from a certain diplomatic official in New York. We have a recording of that conversation which will be delivered to the President in one hour. You tell that sonofabitch Horton to call me at my Palm Beach office before then, if he wants to avoid that."

"I'm not sure I can reach the director by then," the voice answered.

"Then I'd say you people have a very serious problem," Henry snapped, hanging up the phone.

"How deep do you think they're in this?" Desverne said.

"Too deep," Henry said. "And there's a trail of bodies I want answers about."

"You think they were involved with Kermit and Mary?"

"I'm not sure. But they're going to answer some questions about it, as well as about that kid in Soho."

Eighteen minutes later, the call from Horton came in. Henry

cringed as he listened to the soft, airy voice drift across the line.

"It would seem that some of my people have been working at cross purposes with yours," Horton said. "There have been good reasons for it and perhaps they should have been made clear at the outset."

"Go on," Henry snapped, imagining Horton sitting with his ebony cigarette holder jutting from his mouth.

"One of my people will leave Langley in twenty minutes and should be in your office in a matter of hours. He is authorized to make a full disclosure of our concerns. But only to you. I think when you hear him out, you, perhaps better than anyone, will understand why we have to work covertly in this matter."

"Your man will have *all* the answers?" Henry asked. "Including answers about some recent deaths?"

"He will. There's only one condition I have to insist on. My man is to work with you, following your orders, until this matter is resolved. You'll understand when he explains the security implications. We have to be certain there's an appropriate solution."

"And what about the meeting with your friend from the mission?"

"The meeting will take place any way you choose," Horton said.

"You fuck with me one more time, Horton, and I'll hang you out to dry," Henry said.

"You've made that all too clear. You hold the cards. Our only concern now is that the government is protected."

"The government, or the Agency?" Henry said.

"They're the same, like it or not," Horton said. "A government *is* what is best about it and what is worst." There was a hint of laughter in his voice.

36

Wally drove the van slowly along Worth Avenue, moving with the light, unhurried traffic, as if searching for a parking space. Rolls Royces, Lincolns, and Cadillacs littered the curbs, mingling there with lesser vehicles with a touch of disdain that seemed to have been built into them. Along the sidewalks, stopping occasionally before shop windows, older women moved alone or in pairs, taking part in their winter ritual. He had worked with his father in the gardens of these people. Houses used only three months of the year, the gardens always tended, yet hidden behind walls and hedges, awaiting annual viewings. His father had told him that he, too, could have that life one day. The recollection made him smile, wondering what his father would think if he saw him now. He would not be pleased, he decided. But, then, he was not very pleased himself at the moment.

In front of the Taboo Restaurant, two men stood talking beneath its garishly painted sign. They were dressed casually, and their conversation seemed unconcerned. Only their shoes set them apart. Sturdy business shoes that contrasted with their clothing. Up ahead a shadow moved on the roof of the Bonwit Teller Building, then disappeared. He slowed the van at the corner of Hibiscus Avenue, glancing across the street at the heavyset Hispanic who stood in front of the Gucci window.

Checkin' out the shoes, he told himself, pulling the van into a right turn into Hibiscus Avenue, noting the delivery truck parked near the corner. There had been two other delivery trucks on Worth Avenue and a large van with a florist's decal on the side. Ten after twelve, an odd time for so many deliveries.

He drove on, looking casually into the passing side streets. Two blocks down a dark sedan was parked with four men seated inside. Another block, another sedan. He smiled to himself and circled slowly, moving with the crawl of traffic, then up Worth Avenue again.

The men in the business shoes had crossed the street, still standing and talking, passing the time without concern. The delivery trucks and the florist's van were parked where they had been, seemingly empty and unattended. Up the street the Hispanic remained in place, patient and waiting, his eyes on the passing traffic now, his interest in shoes gone.

Wally drove past him, moving to the end of Worth Avenue, then right into Cocoanut Row, past the yacht basin and its massive white crafts and yet another sedan parked quietly with men inside.

He drew a deep breath as he turned left onto the Royal Park Bridge. He would drive back slowly, taking his time, keeping his eye on the road behind. He had planned the return route earlier. North on Route 95, then west to the Florida Turnpike, and finally south again, a slow, easy circle before plunging into the back roads that would eventually take him to Belle Glade. It was a route that could not be easily followed, and it would also take him through places he would not see again for many months, perhaps years.

He began whistling through his teeth, trying to ignore the gnawing in his stomach. The others would not be happy when he told them, even though they expected it. He had known from the beginning that it would end this way, and it still bothered him, the stupid expectations of the others even more so.

"You don't win against these fuckers," he said aloud. "You play to a draw, if you can, an' hope time picks a winner." Those stupid spics just couldn't see that, he told himself.

~~~~~

Norris sat huddled in a corner of the storage room, listening to the subdued sounds of conversation that pushed through the curtain, indistinguishable. He had been in the small, cramped room a full day now, leaving only to use the battered portable toilet tucked away in a putrid closet. They had not spoken to him even then and the change had been frightening. It was their own form of torture, a way of making him count the hours. He rubbed his leg. The pain throbbed, coursing up into his body. But what if the Agency wasn't trying to locate him. He could simply be sacrificed under the assumption that Sparrow Hawk would never be mentioned. Then they would kill him; they would never believe the truth, not without proof. Or if they were waiting they might simply capture Wally, find out. But Wally might never tell them where he was. No, he must return. And the surveillance had to have been there. The Agency would never gamble on exposure. Like all creations of government its instincts for survival were ever-present. But these people, these so-called revolutionaries, they could still kill him, even after they knew. Out of hatred. Out of anger. And if they didn't, there would be hatred and anger then too. Another scandal. One more disgrace.

He wiped the sweat from his face. But you can deny it. Say it was simply a ploy, something to gain time. Who can deny you the right to stay alive. It was a question of winning, of beating them. And the administration will deny it, too. They'll have to. It continued under them as well, whether they knew or not. But perhaps they did. There was no way to be certain.

He could hear footsteps in the outer room, someone pacing back and forth, then stopping and beginning again. Tiburón, he thought. Pacing, nervous, not wanting to know that he had been used, outwitted. And is he really any better, are any of them? He touched his cheek where Tiburón had struck him. It was still sore, tender. He should not have done that. He had no right.

He folded his arms across his chest and began rocking his body. How many more hours? Wally had left several hours ago. He must have. How long could it take? But when he does come back, then you must deal with them, make them agree to let you live. Give them nothing until they do. But how will you ever know if they lie to you? Lie to you, promise to let you live, but never meaning to. So you convince them that they must. You convince them.

~~~~~

Henry stood inside the Bonwit Teller display room, well back from the window where he could not be seen easily from the street. The CIA agent stood next to him, cleaning his glasses, his eyes still fixed on the man across the street. Henry looked at his watch. It was one o'clock.

"They're not coming," the agent said.

"No, they're not. Or more probably, they've already been here and have seen what they wanted to."

"That would mean he told them," the agent said. His face was expressionless and he was still looking out through the window.

Henry glanced at him, disgusted by the calm, uncaring image that met his eyes. "Wouldn't you, if it was the last chip you had to play?" he said.

"No, I wouldn't." The agent glanced at him briefly, then looked away again.

"That's right. I keep forgetting what super patriots you people are." Sparrow Hawk, he thought. Another insanity and one that had produced his own problems, as well, created them, because the Bureau had never been told.

The agent replaced his glasses. "What do you plan to do now?" he asked.

"First, I'm going to leave your man standing there until hell freezes over, with one surveillance team watching him. Then I'm going to see what we've picked up so far and try to make something out of it."

"We should have been tailing people all along, just as a precaution."

Henry turned to face him. "You still don't understand, do you? We intend to get him back alive, if possible. Your concern about covering the Agency's ass gets taken care of after that. And if you do one thing to interfere, I'll put a bullet right between your eyes. You understand *that*?"

The agent blinked twice from behind his glasses. "Bullets can go both ways, you know."

Henry grinned at him. "But my people still hold trump, don't they?" He turned and walked toward the window, pulling a radio unit from his pocket. He snapped out orders to the units outside. It was all they had now. Photographs and motor vehicle checks. But at least it was something. Something new, current. More than they had had up to now. And if the autopsy reports on Hernandez had been right, they weren't far away. And that meant somebody would come into the area, somebody who might be identified or at least give them a vehicle to look for. Blind luck, the one thing it always boiled down to.

Desverne came through the door without enthusiasm.

"What does it look like so far?" Henry asked.

"Most of the photos I've seen don't match with anything we have. But I've got men double-checking right now. Several people came through the street more than once, but there could be a dozen reasons for that. No stolen cars, but a number of rentals. But considering the area, that's understandable too."

Henry tightened his jaw. "I want all the photos sent to each local and county police agency within fifty miles. We'll expand that later, if necessary. And start with the ones of younger people, twenties and thirties. Tell them I want every one of their people to see them fast. I know they're going to bitch and moan, but tell them what we have here and get those photographs on the wires as quickly as possible."

Desverne winced at the futility of the order.

"I know," Henry said. "But what the hell else can we do."

37

" You're sure?" El Tiburón asked.

Wally nodded, fighting to hide his own disgust. "The place was crawlin' with wing-tipped shoes."

"Did you see any of them talking to him, or doing anything that would make you think he knew they were there?"

Wally shook his head, avoiding El Tiburón's eyes. "But they were all around him," he said. "He'd have to be a fool not to know."

"They could have followed him from New York," Richard said. "They could have followed our man there and then picked up on him, couldn't they?"

El Tiburón studied the pleading that filled Richard's face. "They could have. But I don't think so."

"Why not?" Norma demanded.

"You mean it was just a lucky guess on Norris's part? That the person we contacted would be picked up and followed?" He shook his head slowly. "No. He knew. He knew the person we were getting money from was a plant and would tip off the people he worked for. It's the only thing that makes sense."

He watched the logic of his words register; produce pain in the eyes of the others. They were still proud of what they had done, believed in the importance of it. And now they had to accept the truth of being used and of being led into that position by someone they had trusted, *him*.

"I think we all have to accept what's happened. And I have to accept it more than any of us." He smiled weakly. "I *was* the one who brought the financial relationship to the group from my days in FALN."

"And it doesn't bother you?" There was no anger in Carol's voice. There was just a sense of pain, for him, he thought.

"It bothers me badly," he said. "Stupidity always bothers me. But I don't think it's all as black as we're making it."

Norma glared at him. "Really. Are we supposed to enjoy being used like a bunch of fools?"

He reached across for her hand, but she withdrew it. He kept the hand extended. "I'm not your enemy," he said softly.

She drew a deep breath, then reached out and took his hand, squeezing it.

He looked easily at the others. His face was haggard, like a man who had not slept in days, and he had not shaved that morning and it added to the look of someone battered. "We've taken certain actions in recent years that *we* decided on, that *we* carried out," he said softly. "We believed in those actions, believed they could accomplish certain ends. No one else decided what those actions would be and I, for one, still believe in them."

He had their attention now, their faces glued on his, wanting to believe in his words.

"We felt violence was necessary to produce change, to call attention to the need for change. At the same time, the government of this country felt violence on our part would serve its purpose by frightening the majority of its citizens and forcing them to accept repressive acts against people who opposed government policies. We always knew violence was a double-edged sword, that it could work against us as well as for us."

He smiled at each of them individually. "We gambled with our lives and our freedom, and the government gambled with its money."

Carol began to speak, but he raised his hand in a pleading gesture, stopping her. "Then we did something they did not expect. We took Norris. And they know now that we can expose them. *We* can explain the reasons for our past actions, but I doubt they can explain the reasons for financing them."

Richard's face had brightened. "And the people will even wonder if they really didn't finance Norris's kidnapping because they were afraid he'd talk."

"And they'll also wonder if they refused to meet the demands we made because they wanted us to kill him," El Tiburón answered.

Wally folded his arms across his chest. Unlike the others, he did not seem pleased. "There's still the question of the price as far as he's concerned." He motioned toward the storage room with his head.

"That's right," Norma said.

"What price do you want?" El Tiburón asked.

"A blood price," Wally said, his voice close to a whisper.

El Tiburón leaned forward, answering quietly. "We can do that and I think it will be accepted as a just payment. Or we can turn him loose for his own people to deal with and state that in our final message. That might also force their hand on the demands."

"The hand's forced anyway, ol' buddy. I jus' don't happen to think mercy is part of this game," Wally hissed.

El Tiburón looked at the others. Richard seemed confused and Carol simply looked away. But there was no question of Norma's view; her eyes blazed with it. He nodded slowly.

"Let's prepare the final communiqué. We should leave here before dark. They know we're close by after what happened today, so I don't think we can afford to wait."

"How do you figure we'll go?" Wally asked.

"I think we should keep to the original plan and have you take everyone through the glades. That's still possible, isn't it?"

Wally nodded his head. His face was emotionless, his arms still folded across his chest. "You'll be coming with us?" he said.

"No," El Tiburón said. "You'll take a written copy of Norris's statement with you and I'll take a tape recording of Norris reading it and deliver it to a newspaper or radio station. Then I'll meet you at some point you predesignate, where you'll come out of the glades."

"That will be dangerous for you," Carol said.

"And for you," he answered. "If I'm caught, you'll have to make it to our friends in P.R. by yourselves. But there's no choice."

Wally continued to stare at him. "And the old man?" he asked. There was distrust in his eyes.

"I'll take care of that too," he said.

~~~~~

He had eased himself along the rough wood floor and up against the curtain so he could hear them. It was much like the quiet debate that had taken place when other communiqués were being prepared, except this time there seemed to be a finality to it. Perhaps it was the tone of their voices, or that they slipped in and out of whispers, he could not be sure, but it was there all the same. They plan to trick you, he told himself. It's instinctive. You know it. You can tell. But others had tried that in the past. This time the trickery would involve his life. In past times it had been things that involved success or failure and those were more important, more difficult to think clearly about. Both in writing and on tape. Yes, they are clever. They'll have both, just in case the government denies the validity of one or the other. Tiburón is not a fool, just an innocent. And to get what he wants he'll have to make one mistake. He'll have to let you live, or make himself appear as corrupt as the people he attacks. And his ego will not allow that. His tragic flaw is that he needs to be heroic. It was like the slogan he repeated so often, about it mattering *how* one died. For him it also mattered how one won, the one great flaw in his ability to lead.

The sound of a chair pushed back, grating against the floor. Footsteps. He slid back along the floor to the far wall, his body hunched and tense, waiting. The curtain pulled away, exposing light behind. He squinted against it, trying to identify the person standing above him. El Tiburón's voice made the identification before his eyes could.

"Come out now. We have some work to do." His voice was a strange mixture of command and request.

Norris struggled to his feet, grimacing at the pain in his leg. He moved slowly past the curtain, shielding his eyes from the light. The women were at the table, Norma looking fierce, Carol simply grim. The men were at the windows. He walked unsteadily to the table and sat.

"From what I heard I gather a new communiqué is to be sent."

He had spoken the words dully, but with a sense of authority that surprised El Tiburón. He looked at him closely now, taking in the sharpness in his eyes, the firm set of the jaw. The old fool thinks he's here to do business, he thought.

He pushed the communiqué toward him. "I want you to read this over, then copy it in your own hand. After that you'll read it into a tape."

He sat across from him as Norris glanced around the table at each of them, then picked up the communiqué and began reading. He held the paper almost at arms length to compensate for his missing glasses and El Tiburón suppressed a smile at the hard cast his eyes took on. When he had finished he placed the paper in front of him, smoothed it with his hands, and looked at each of them again. El Tiburón took several fresh pieces of paper and a pen and slid it across to him. He watched, amused, as Norris remained motionless.

"Well?" he said.

"We haven't discussed what happens to me, once this is finished," he said.

"And we're not going to. Copy the statement and sign it or I'll blow your head off."

"There's a surprising calm in your voice when you say that, Tiburón. But if you intend to kill me anyway, what difference does it make?" He picked up the communiqué again, holding it to one side, then pointed to the center of the page. "Here," he said. "When I copy it, I intend to insert the fact that I am making this truthful admission under the promise that you will spare my life. I'll also read that into the tape."

El Tiburón's eyes widened. "What do you think you are, some fucking lawyer negotiating a lease? You'll do what you're told."

Norris pushed himself up from the table as the others stared in disbelief. "I'll go back to the storeroom and you can shoot me there," he said.

El Tiburón leaped from his seat, grabbing him by the shirtfront and pushing him roughly back into the chair. "Damn your ass," he hissed.

Norris looked up into his face. "Or you can shoot me here," he said.

El Tiburón took a step back and looked into his eyes. He shook his head slowly. "You always surprise me," he said. "Always."

"You do it, you old bastard." Norma's words seethed with anger.

"Shut up," Carol snapped. "What difference does it make what he adds to it."

Norris looked at her, his eyes firm but calm. "The difference is for me," he said. "If you kill me after I sign it and tape it, you become as evil as the people you're exposing."

El Tiburón smiled at him. "And what if we just cross that part out later? And erase that portion of the tape? What happens to your protection then?"

"It would just create doubts about the authenticity of the document and I'm sure you wouldn't want that. I'll gamble on that. The result will be the same anyway, won't it?"

There was a slight smile in Norris's eyes and everything within

El Tiburón screamed for him to call the old fool's bluff. "I don't have time for your fucking games," he snapped. "Do it. Then I'll drive you home to your foolish wife and fat-faced little daughter." He looked down at him contemptuously. "Or maybe I'll just put a bullet in your brain. We'll have to see, won't we?"

Uneasiness passed through Norris's face and he looked away, back to the communiqué, then picked up the pen and began to copy it.

El Tiburón's eyes met Wally's and he winked at the hulking, still distrusting figure. Norris wrote slowly, taking his time, very much like a lawyer trying to avoid a mistake.

The others watched him, their shock at his boldness showing in their faces.

He signed the communiqué with a flourish, then passed it across to El Tiburón. "Now the tape?" he said.

El Tiburón read the communiqué, then looked across at Norris. "You have a very large pair, Edmund. But this will do just fine." He stood and walked to a leather satchel, withdrew the tape recorder and returned to the table, adjusting it to record as he did. He placed it in front of Norris. "Here you are, Mr. President," he said.

He turned to the others. "We better get our things together. We can start moving as soon as this is finished."

"I want to get the explosives," Richard said. "I can rig most of it like hand grenades, just in case we need them."

"Good. Wally, if you can load up the boat, and if Carol and Norma can start getting our stuff together in here, I'll take care of the lawyer."

Norris glanced up at him and smiled weakly, then picked up the microphone of the tape recorder and began reading the communiqué.

Richard slid through the trap door in the cabin floor and disconnected the trip wires attached to the tin-can alarm system, then moved beneath the cabin, stepping out at its rear.

He walked slowly toward the explosives, hidden in the marshes to his left, watching the shallow water for the vermin he had come to expect. It seemed cooler now, almost pleasant really, for the first time since they arrived. Even the insects seemed to have disappeared and it was quiet, the only sound the light movement of the marsh grass. He smiled to himself. It was the first time he had enjoyed it here, he thought, reaching up to retrieve the plastic explosives lodged in a low-hanging bough.

The bullet struck the back of his head and slammed his face against the trunk of the tree, splattering it with bone and brain fragments and blood. The only sound had been his head hitting the tree, the silenced spit of the rifle no more than another movement of the marsh grass. His body hung against the tree as though pinned there, then slid slowly down, his legs crumbling beneath him, his eyes bulging as his face slipped into the warm, putrid water.

Wally came down the steps of the cabin, shielding his eyes against the setting sun. He walked to the corner of the cabin, reaching beneath it for a rope tied to a stilt. Hand over hand he retrieved the rope, watching as the square bow of the flat boat slowly emerged. He grabbed the bow, pulling the boat half on to the dry land. Inside, toward the rear, a small cottonmouth lay coiled. He picked up an oar and lifted it, struggling like a juggler against its twisting body, then dropped it into the water.

"We ain't takin' no passengers," he said aloud, pushing the swimming snake again with the oar, defeating its attempt to reach land and strike out at its attacker. He dropped the oar back in the boat and turned back to the stairs. His body jolted and both hands flew to his throat, blood flowing past his fingers where the bullet had ripped through his windpipe. He staggered, fighting to scream out a warning, feeling the blood that poured into his lungs. He staggered again, his hand reaching for the stairs, the words he wanted to scream, warning them, repeating over and over in his mind. The second bullet struck his temple, cartwheeling his body to the ground, driving his head under the cabin. The snake swam back and struck, its fangs sinking deep into his lifeless cheek.

El Tiburón pointed to the rear room. Norris looked at him hesitantly, fear coming to his eyes. He stood uneasily and walked into the room, his muscles tense, anticipating pain, the sound of the exploding gun. He turned when he reached the window. El Tiburón was standing in the doorway, the automatic in his hand, hanging loosely at his side. Behind him, Norris could see the women moving in and out of view, stuffing clothing into canvas bags.

"You're not going to keep your word, are you?" He heard the trembling in his own voice, a gasping, almost choking vibration.

"I never gave you my word, Edmund." His eyes were hard and expressionless, the blue seeming to intensify. "I suppose it always had to end this way. I just preferred not to admit it. As you said, Edmund, it was my one mistake. I won't make it again."

"Don't kill me. It doesn't serve any purpose. I won't change my story. I'll tell them it's all true, that I wanted everyone to know. I swear to you." He could hear the begging in his voice, but he didn't care. The gun began to rise and he heard his voice rush on, unable to understand his own words, just hearing the sounds, the wheezing, pleading sounds.

The door opened behind him and he heard Norma's scream, the fast movement as she lunged for a weapon. He began to turn, her voice still in his ears, then cut short in mid-scream with the burst of automatic weapon fire. Figures in the doorway. Carol's form coming into view to his left, then flying back to the floor in another spit of gunfire. The word, *no*, screamed in his ears, his own voice, and he spun back to Norris, leveling the Graz Burya. Norris turned and moved down and away, running, hiding. He swung the barrel toward him as the pain exploded in his hip, spinning him sideways, the sound of the shot behind him, then the burst of his own weapon banging against his ears. He leveled the pistol again, sighting along the barrel, lowering it from where the first shot had entered the wall above Norris's head. His shoulder exploded in pain, throwing him forward, turning him. He hit the floor, flat on his back, the weapon falling from his hand, skidding across the floor. He strained his body, rising and reaching, his fingers inching toward the barrel. A heavy shoe pressed down on his wrist and he fell back exhausted, staring up into the face. The Blue Jay. His mind began to cloud, the view of the face, Henry's face, coming now through a haze.

"I didn't expect to meet you this way, Blue Jay," he whispered. His voice trailed off into a groan, the pain in his hip and shoulder filling his body. So this is how it feels to be shot, he thought. The Blue Jay above him, the face cold and hard. Eyes filled with hate. You shouldn't hate me, he thought. It's all just a game. Just ask Edmund. He'll tell you. Just a game, Blue Jay. A game. His eyelids fluttered and the haze became deeper. Birds, thousands of birds seemed to hover in the air. Everyone a blue jay. All of them. Then the face of a man, wearing glasses, the sound of his voice, distant and quiet.

"Did he buy it?"

Henry looked into the agent's face, the hard gray eyes behind the absurd horn-rimmed glasses. He was still wearing a tweed jacket, even in the middle of a swamp.

"No, he just passed out from the pain," he said.

"Too bad," the agent said.

"He was going to kill me. Just as you came in." Norris's voice came from the corner, where he was still huddled, shaking uncontrollably.

"Are you all right, sir?" Henry asked, realizing now how little he really cared.

"Yes. Thank God you came when you did," Norris said.

Henry walked to him and squatted down next to him. "Just take it easy. We'll get you out of here right away."

"How did you find me?"

Henry's face remained impassive. "Just luck," he said. "We took photographs of everyone passing through an area in Palm Beach where they were supposed to meet a contact. Then we showed them to local police agencies. There was a deputy in the county sheriff's office who recognized this Wally character and told us about a cabin he had here. We just moved in, taking a chance. It was just luck, nothing spectacular." It never is, he added to himself.

The agent walked up beside them and held out a sheet of paper.

"You find what you wanted?" Henry said, watching a smile, the first he had ever seen from the man, form on his lips.

"There's a tape, too," Norris said. "He has it." He pointed at El Tiburón.

The agent walked back to the body sprawled on the floor and yanked the cassette from the pocket of his shirt. Henry watched in silence as he pulled the tape from the spool, struck a match and methodically burned it.

He helped Norris to his feet. "We can get you back to your home, now," he said.

"No. Not right away," Norris said. "I want to go somewhere where I can clean myself up a little. And I want the media notified, so they can be there when I arrive."

Henry stared into his face. What difference does it make, he thought. What difference does any of it make.

They started for the doorway. El Tiburón's head moved and his eyelids fluttered again. He raised his head slightly and tried to speak, his head falling back, his mouth forming a weak smile. Henry stared down at him for a moment, then took Norris's arm and moved him through the door, past the other bodies and down the front stairs.

Outside, a dozen soldiers, dressed in green berets and camouflage fatigues mingled with a handful of his own men wearing flak jackets. Henry slipped his own flak jacket off and let it drop to the ground, then took Norris's arm again and helped him along the long, dusty road. Norris's body stiffened at the sharp eruption of sound behind him. Then he stepped out again, favoring his leg.

It was over, he thought. He had survived it. He had actually won. A small smile came to his lips. He looked at Henry and wondered why he looked so foolishly grim.

T hey sat in the private study on the third floor of the White House, the television set's flickering screen filling the darkened room with shafts of color. Lessing looked at Jordan's face, the muscles along his jaw drawn tight. His fingers were drumming the arm of the chair.

What did the man want? Lessing asked himself. It was over and they had survived it. Won, actually.

He looked back at the television screen, the news replay of Norris's return home. He was flanked by his wife and daughter, his son-in-law behind them. The familiar smile flashed across his face, and he raised both hands above his head in a waving salute to the dozens of reporters gathered before him.

Jordan stood as Norris began to speak into the array of microphones in front of him. He walked to the television set and snapped it off, then turned on a lamp on a nearby table and dropped into a chair beside it.

"I can't stand to listen to that sonofabitch again," he said, drumming his fingers on the arm of the chair. He looked across at Lessing. "Well, he's back among us again. But I suppose that had to be expected. Do you have the reports of the rescue? We'll have to issue a statement of praise for everyone involved."

Lessing picked up a manila folder on the table next to him and walked over to Jordan, handing it to him.

The President opened it and read through the reports. "And Henry just handed his resignation to this Desverne guy and said he'd be leaving in the morning? Crusty character, isn't he?" He turned the final pages of the report over and stared down at the attached wire-copy photographs. The bodies were lined up in front of the cabin in a final grisly portrait. "Which one was the leader? The one who called himself El Tiburón?"

Lessing came to the side of the chair and pointed down.

"They shot him right in the center of the forehead," Jordan said, shaking his head. "It's a helluva way to end up. Too bad one of them didn't survive, though. We might of learned something from them." He shook his head again and closed the folder on his lap.

~~~~

The Florida Turnpike stretched ahead in an endless boring line, a ribbon drawn tight by a surveyor, unimpeded by any obstacle. Henry held the wheel in both hands, his eyes straight ahead on the road, his mind days away from the moment. She smiled at him, brushing away the silky strand of hair that had fallen along her cheek, as her face faded away. Stay, Pat. There's no point in packing it in now. We're back on top again. Dez's eyes so incredulous. Still a believer. It would take three days. Three, slow, unhurried days to Vermont. But there was no reason to hurry, no rush for anything. There would be snow, hopefully, snow and kids laughing and walking with skis over their shoulders. Fireplaces and brandy and time, too much time, always too much. She could have been a good skier if she had had time. The photograph in his wallet, yellow with age now, showed her sitting with skis resting against the wall behind her. Pennsylvania Avenue, there in his arms. Mary, both Marys. Odd how they had the same name, looked so much alike, but really didn't. Rows of palm trees ahead, the branches swaying like large, clumsy fans. Soon pine trees, the branches moving up and down under the weight of new snow. There should be snow. Snow and time.

Off to his left, high above, dark shadows moved in ever-widening arcs. Henry watched the shadows. Moving, always looking. The vultures circled, searching the ground below for something dead. He looked back at the long, straight, unending road and drove on.